"Think a young Katharine Hepburn—beautiful, smart and beyond capable. Winslow is an example of the kind of woman who emerged after the war, a confident female who had worked in factories building tanks and guns, a woman who hadn't yet been suffocated by the 1950s—perfect housewife ideal." —*Vancouver Sun*

"I absolutely love the modern sensibility of these novels, of their feminism, sense of justice, their anti-racism, their progressiveness, which somehow never seems out of place in a tiny BC hamlet in 1948." —Kerry Clare, author of *Waiting for a Star to Fall* and editor of 49th Shelf

"An intriguing mix of character, plot, time, and place. Highly recommended." —Ian Hamilton, author of the Ava Lee novels

"Fantastic . . . readers will stand up and cheer." —Anna Lee Huber, author of the Lady Darby Mysteries and the Verity Kent Mysteries

"Richly conjured . . . deftly plotted . . . this series just keeps getting better!" —Catriona McPherson, award-winning author of the Dandy Gilver series

"Complex, suspenseful, and deeply felt, this is a smart series for the ages." —Francine Mathews, author of the Nantucket Mysteries

FRAMED IN FIRE

THE LANE WINSLOW MYSTERY SERIES

———————

IONA WHISHAW

FRAMED IN FIRE

A LANE WINSLOW MYSTERY

TOUCHWOOD

TouchWood Editions
touchwoodeditions.com

This book is a work of fiction. Names, characters, places, and incidents are either
products of the author's imagination or used fictitiously. Any resemblance to
actual events or locales or persons, living or dead, is entirely coincidental.

Edited by Claire Philipson
Cover illustration by Margaret Hanson

CATALOGUING DATA AVAILABLE FROM LIBRARY AND ARCHIVES CANADA
ISBN 9781771513807 (softcover)
ISBN 9781771513814 (electronic)
ISBN 9781771513845 (audiobook)

TouchWood Editions acknowledges that the land on which we live and work is
within the traditional territories of the Lkwungen (Esquimalt and Songhees),
Malahat, Pacheedaht, Scia'new, T'Sou-ke and W̱SÁNEĆ (Pauquachin, Tsartlip,
Tsawout, Tseycum) peoples.

We acknowledge the financial support of the Government of Canada through
the Canada Book Fund and the Canada Council for the Arts, and of the Province
of British Columbia through the British Columbia Arts Council and the Book
Publishing Tax Credit.

PRINTED IN CANADA AT FRIESENS

26 25 24 23 22   1 2 3 4 5

For Kappa,
my prodigious aunt

PROLOGUE

THE MAN STOPPED THE CAR. He got out and, standing for a moment, gazed along the edge of the forest. The evening was almost golden, the way the clouds filtered the setting sun. Even the air, with the March chill closing in, felt fresh, just as he loved it. There was another car nearby, its hood shining in the sun. Someone fishing, no doubt.

He could hear the creek cascading over the rocks toward the lake. He went along the path he knew so well.

Approaching the cottage, he didn't think about what he would say. He pushed open the small gate and walked up the two steps to the door. A crow called out from somewhere in the forest, its voice rising over the sound of water. He listened to that call—gravelly and dark, the way crows are—and smiled. He did not think it a warning. He turned and rested his hand on the doorknob. There was a male voice, and the door was thrown open. A tall man filled the doorway.

"What do you want?" The voice low and furious, the

"you" emphasized, as if the man had warned him off before. And then the man in the doorway turned his head slightly without removing his eyes from the man on the step and called out, "Get me that rifle."

The surprised man put up his hands, chest high, palms outward. A gesture of calm. He wanted to say, "Take it easy," but the rifle was pointed now. What the hell was this?

He stepped backward down the steps, his hands still up, in an attempt to calm. "No need for that," he managed. He heard a scream, and a shot exploded into the silence. The crows flew up out of the tender trees that grew in a circle near the cottage and raised their voices in anger and fear.

CHAPTER ONE

March 1948

LANE WAS JOLTED AWAKE IN terror, her body seized by the certainty of death. She found herself sitting up, gasping in great draughts of air, her heart pounding in the dark. Her eyes focused on the faint drift of the curtains, lifted by a gust of cold air coming in through the open window. It was an ordinary movement. She was not dying. But she still felt herself taking in air as if she had somehow stopped breathing in her sleep. Darling was, amazingly, still asleep beside her, lying on his side so that his back was to her. How had he not heard the commotion of her gasping? She was grateful he hadn't.

She swung her legs off the bed and reached for her dressing gown, slipping it on as she crept out of the room. Once in the hallway, she could see the cold stretches of light from the full moon coming in through the sitting room window and reaching along the floor, as if feeling for some unquiet sleeper to wake. She leaned against the wall and put her hand to her heart, relieved to be out of the bedroom, certain of what would come next.

Perhaps she could forestall it. Before she had married, she had been able to sit up in bed, turn on the bedside lamp, read, go fetch a glass of hot milk, or just wait it out. She made her way to the kitchen and gently shut the door so that light and noise would not wake Darling, and then sat for a moment looking at her hands lying palms down on her lap. She could feel the shaking beginning somewhere inside her.

This hadn't happened since she'd been married. She knew that she had secretly hoped the closeness to another creature she loved would banish these episodes. She stood up and ran water into the kettle and put it on the burner and then realized the hot water bottle was in the bathroom cupboard and she would have to tiptoe down the hallway to fetch it. God, she thought, looking at the clock on the wall. It's two thirty.

Instead, she stood uncertain and immobile, feeling more alone than when she'd actually been alone.

"RASHERS OF BACON on a weekday. How far have we sunk into dissipation?" Darling asked, appearing in the kitchen smelling of soap and resolve, as he did every morning when he was preparing to make the long drive from King's Cove to Nelson, where he was in charge of the police station.

"I thought we could use cheering up," Lane said, cutting slices of bread.

Darling looked at her, and then went to where she stood over the breadboard and said gently, "Why don't I handle the toast?" He put his arms around her and held her for a moment. "Do we need cheering up? It's the middle of March at last, the month when spring comes."

She relinquished the bread and the toaster. "You pretend you're being helpful, but you are motivated entirely by not wanting burned toast."

"You must admit, you do sometimes like it darker than is absolutely necessary. How did you sleep?" Darling opened the wings of the toaster and positioned the bread.

"Fine. I mean, I had a nightmare." Lane realized the truth of this as soon as she said it. She had forgotten there'd been a nightmare. What had it been about? She busied herself with dropping eggs into the frying pan. She felt a tension in her throat. Why could she not just tell him she'd been up what felt like most of the night and only crawled back to bed at five thirty? After all, she had warned him before they were married that she had these episodes. It would not surprise him.

Darling abandoned the toast to its fate, pulled Lane away from the stove, and made her sit opposite him. "Darling, are you all right?"

"Of course I am. I was just a little rattled. It's ridiculous, I don't even know what it was about." His solicitousness somehow made her feel worse, as if she were feeble. "There, that's done it. You've incinerated the toast!" She got up and went back to the stove, her mind a turmoil. It occurred to her that what she was feeling was shame. Shame about her own weakness. She had never felt this embarrassment before about these episodes; they were simply what they were, but there'd never been anyone else to see them or

5

need them explained. They were infrequent enough that they hardly made a dent in her life, and she knew she was luckier than many. Look at poor Robin Harris, her grouchy apple-growing neighbour, thirty-five years after the Great War, still haunted by guilt, his whole being transformed into a kind of permanent surliness. God knows what his nights must be like, she thought.

She flipped the eggs quickly and slid them onto plates along with the bacon. Darling was at the garbage bin, scraping the toast.

"This, according to Angela, is what Americans call *over easy*. See what you think," said Lane.

"This, I'm afraid, is what is universally called *burned toast*."

"Nothing a little butter and jam won't fix. Now then, what have you got on today?"

"The usual mayhem, I expect. Petty crime, drunken fights. Ames is following a robbery from the bookstore the night before last."

"The bookstore! Cash?" Lane asked.

"No, funnily enough, books. The owner is going to give us an inventory today of what is missing. The thief broke a pane of glass quite carefully and managed to unlock the door from the inside. Minimum of mess."

Lane felt herself relaxing. Stealing books was an interesting crime. "How fascinating. Ames will soon sort it. Is he well read?"

Darling shrugged. "Well enough, I suppose. I imagine he mostly reads paperback thrillers, but for all I know he reads himself to sleep with Spinoza every night like Jeeves. Why?"

"I was just thinking, if there was some pattern to what was taken, he might be able to develop a profile of the thief."

"I shall pass that on. No doubt he will gush his appreciation as he always does where you're concerned. What are you up to today?"

Until that moment, Lane had had no idea beyond trying to gain back her equilibrium, but she said, "You know, I think I'll drive up to New Denver and see Peter Barisoff. I haven't seen him in ages, so perhaps he'd welcome a visit. I have a box of chocolate biscuits I could take with me." In fact, she hadn't seen him since the horrible business of his friend being killed at the hot springs the previous winter.

When Darling's car had been swallowed into the rising mist hanging over King's Cove, Lane stood at the door, looking at the yard through the window. It may have been March, but the brown, trodden-down grass and the layers of flattened and greying autumn leaves still covered the ground, and the sky had been an ever-changing moody grey for the last few days.

She turned back. They had bought a wireless, and she thought of turning it on to hear the news—and, more importantly, the weather—but she could not imagine shattering this quiet.

She washed the breakfast dishes thoughtfully. She knew her reluctance to speak about these intermittent nighttime fears could affect her ability to talk honestly with Darling, and it worried her. If she could not tell him, could not come to understand why it was that she suddenly felt shame, she would slowly and inexorably retreat into the solitariness that could begin to fill her marriage with shadows.

She made a cup of tea and sat on the window seat looking out at the lake. The longer she waited to say anything, the harder it would become. What was the nature of her reluctance? She didn't want him feeling sorry for her. She imagined herself resisting his embrace, saying, "Just leave it. It's all right." Imagined him being hurt by these rejected attempts to comfort her.

Then she remembered when she had learned that her father had died, and how Darling had responded then. They hadn't even really had a relationship then, but he had brought her a cup of strong, sweet tea and then taken her to lunch, only talking about it if she seemed willing. He had reacted by being practical and by listening. In fact, respectful solicitude had always been his way. Why would he not do the same thing now? She was creating a problem that did not exist; she could see that. She knew that her instinct to close herself off had begun in the depths of her own childhood, when her father had called her a coward. Perhaps somewhere inside she confused emotion with cowardice.

She got up with determination. Seeing Peter Barisoff, who had coped with more in his long life than she ever had, would give her some perspective. As a Doukhobor, he and his people had been forced to flee Russia to protect their mode of worship and their pacifism. At first, they had been welcomed with land that they farmed communally. But over the years, internal strife, government suspicion of their religion, their clinging to the Russian language, and their insistence on educating their children on their own had led to the collectives being broken up. Now Barisoff lived on his own in a rented cottage.

Anyway, she thought, what happened to her the night before was no different from what had happened to her in the past. The only difference now was that she was in a relationship that provided friendship, love, and companionship that she had never dreamed would be hers, and this quintessentially lonely struggle was suddenly thrown into sharp relief by contrast. She would use the drive to and from New Denver to try to understand this. One thing she knew: she could not lie to Darling.

"GOOD MORNING, SIR. Nice ride in?" Sergeant O'Brien greeted Darling from his stool at the front desk.

"Very nice, thank you. Ferry was on the right side for a change. Anything?" Darling paused with his coat over his arm and his hat in hand before going upstairs to his office.

"As a matter of fact, someone tried to burn down a house up on Ward Street. Householder's apparently a light sleeper and got onto it before much damage was done. Put it out with his garden hose. Two thirty or so in the morning."

"We've already determined it's arson? How do we know it wasn't a faulty furnace?"

"That, sir, is because the householder found a gas can right at the back where the fire started."

"Hmm. Well, get Terrell onto it. If Ames has a break in his stolen bookcase, he can go with him."

"Sir."

UPSTAIRS, DARLING HUNG up his coat and hat and surveyed his desk with that little thrill of satisfaction he always got seeing it aligned and tidy, inbox squared with the corner, writing pad centred, chair pushed in. He could begin his day with his mind clear. But in the next instant he knew his mind was not entirely clear. He turned to look out over Elephant Mountain, his usual locus for thought. It was shrouded in mist from the rains the night before. Lane had looked tired. He suspected she'd had a bad night but was determined to paper it over. He had tried to ask her, and she had . . . not rejected him, exactly, but moved away almost imperceptibly. He'd woken briefly when she'd come back to bed early in the morning, felt her trying not to disturb him. He had too much respect for her to get involved where he wasn't wanted, but he wished she could feel able to share her pain. Was he hurt by it? He wasn't sure, but he knew he was a bit worried. Could her pulling away begin to eat into the sense of intimacy he'd come to love? He'd never imagined in all his life he would love someone as he loved her or be close to someone in quite this way. His own father had been distant as he was growing up, and Lane had been a miracle. Perhaps pain, even when not inflicted by a partner, naturally caused people to try to pull away. He felt for a moment a kind of powerlessness about how the drift might even be stopped.

He got up and stood, still looking out the window at Elephant Mountain, solid, always there when he needed it for his contemplation. His love for her, he thought, was like that. Perhaps that was all he could do. Just be there. He turned back to his desk. There was always work to distract him in the meantime.

"**THE LIST OF** books is pretty unrevealing," Ames reported to Darling later. "A row of Penguin papers, authors ranging from F to J, and one large coffee table sort of book called *The Grand Opera* that was displayed on a nearby shelf. It looks like they just swooped an armload into a box or something and fled. There were three copies of a biography, several novels, a couple of mysteries."

"Hmm. Your Miss Winslow thinks you might be able to learn something about the thief by the books that were taken. Who was the biography about?"

Ames scanned his list. "It had just come in. *Samuel Turner, A Life*, by . . . hmm, Samuel Turner. Never heard of him. There were a couple of copies of a book called *Turn on the Heat* by Erle Stanley Gardner. It's all here." Ames handed over the list. "I wonder if she's right, that we could learn something about the thief from seeing what he took." He bit his upper lip in a meditative manner. "It's a pretty mixed bag."

"You can ruminate on that later. Go with Terrell and find out what you can about the arson attempt on Ward Street. Is Mrs. Treadwell at the bookstore all right, by the way?"

"A bit shaken up, as you can imagine. She's pretty well on her own there. Her granddaughter used to work with her at the shop, but she's gone off to the coast to university. I suggested that she hire someone to help her, at least part-time. She said she'd be okay till her granddaughter gets back in May. She got the glass repaired, so that's something."

Darling shook his head. "I think there's a fat chance of that granddaughter coming back here in the long run."

Young people who got an education tended to go elsewhere to put it to use.

THE SLOW APPEARANCE of the sun through the clouds lifted Lane's heart no end. She had driven with her usual trepidation along the narrow single-lane Adderly Road, with its precipitous drop-off to the inky lake far below, and was relieved to meet no other driver coming the other way, which would have necessitated an awkward standoff. She was especially relieved when she saw that a large truck was just leaving Adderly and would soon be on that bit of road. Pity anyone coming north who met that on the narrow curve!

In the uplift of the moment, Lane began to see her problem in a new light. Of course she could tell Darling what was weighing on her, she told herself briskly. To love him and marry him, she had had to overcome all kinds of natural inclinations to be private and not risk her heart; this was just one more. And if he was overly sympathetic, it was just a sign of his kindness.

By the time she reached New Denver and was crawling along the appallingly rutted road that led to Barisoff's farm, she was in a much more cheerful frame of mind and looking forward to speaking Russian again. She parked the car by the path that led toward the house.

The modest wooden cottage with its greying clapboard looked peaceful nestled among the evergreens. Too peaceful, she realized. There was no smoke issuing from the chimney. But it was turning out to be a beautiful morning, and it was dispelling the listless feeling of exhaustion she had been carrying around after a bad night. Perhaps Mr. Barisoff was at the back in the garden or visiting his adult son, who, she remembered, was supposed to have taken over the second house on the property.

She took the tin of chocolate biscuits and went to knock on the door, but there was no answer. Disappointed, she made her way around to the back, where Barisoff, with what she suspected was his usual industry, had begun work on his large garden. Some rows of dirt had been turned over, and a shovel stood against a small tool shed, but there was no sign of the man himself. Beginning to fear that the whole expedition would be in vain, she walked along the path to the second house, but not only was there no one there, it had the air of a place that was not being lived in at all.

She was just going to turn back, her mind on why his son had not returned as he had been so insistent on doing the year before, when she saw that there was a path that led through the woods.

She had always been unable to resist the lure of a path and she walked along this one. Grey-yellow fronds of dead grass encroaching from the sides of the otherwise well-worn path deposited dew onto the bottoms of her trouser legs, but the intermittent slashes of sun through the trees transported her to a solitary sense of golden peace. The path curved and began to head slightly downhill until it opened onto a down-sloping meadow, with a gaspingly beautiful view of Slocan Lake.

The morning sunlight, establishing itself more firmly against the dark clouds that had covered it, now sparkled off the lake. The silence was blissful. Lane scouted about until she found a little outcrop of rock where she could sit and be warmed.

She saw him before she heard him. He was emerging from the woods at the edge of the meadow, and for a moment Lane thought she was hallucinating both man and horse. He moved a few yards into the clearing, and then stopped and gazed at Lane, his horse nodding against the reins.

CHAPTER TWO

"SIR, YOU'RE NOT GOING TO like this."

Darling wondered with a touch of irritation how the men must see him, because it was not the first time a bit of news had been introduced like this, as if the whole station was held in thrall by what he might like or not like. "Yes, Ames, it's likely I won't. What is it?"

"The householder with the fire? It's Mr. Lorenzo Vitali." Ames had sent Terrell on ahead to take pictures of the damage, and to see if the gas can could be traced to any of the local gas stations. He had had a call from Mrs. Treadwell at the bookstore asking if he could come down to check her security arrangements. He'd promised her he'd be right along. "I met him just now as I was leaving to help Mrs. Treadwell. He's come in to make a statement."

"Mr. Vitali? Send him up." Darling was on his feet, his face set in a worried frown. He was very fond of Lorenzo Vitali, the owner of the lovely local Italian restaurant. He went into the hall to meet him at the top of the stairs.

"Lorenzo, I am sorry. Tell me what's happened." He led him into the office and sat opposite him, paper and pencil at the ready. "Signora Vitali is all right?"

"Yes, yes, thank you, Inspector. Is fine. Lucky only back stairway burned," Lorenzo said. "I get hose and put it out quick. Only this morning I saw gas can, and then I know, someone try to do this on purpose." He shook his head, turning his hat in his hands. "On purpose. I don't know why."

Anxiety registered starkly on his face, and Darling saw it with concern. He could think of at least one reason someone might do this, but he had been hopeful that, with time, its power would diminish. Anti-Italian sentiment left over from the war. Lorenzo's Italian restaurant, on the slope down toward the train station, had slowly been growing in popularity, as people began to put the war behind them and return to the patterns of daily life. Europe dropped away again into the faraway, where it had always been before—somewhere people came from, not somewhere they went to fight wars.

And if it wasn't lingering anti-Italianism, it could be the strong dose of general anti-foreigner sentiment that was still rooted in some quarters. Lorenzo had worked hard, provided wonderful food, and been nothing but charming in his interactions with his neighbours, despite the coldness of some. This was a blow.

"We will investigate, see if we can sort out what happened. Do you mind if I ask you some questions? It might help us discover a direction to focus our search."

Lorenzo leaned forward and looked at the paper Darling

had at the ready. "No, please, ask, ask. I will tell you whatever I can think of."

"Your immediate neighbours on Ward Street—has there been any dispute or argument over something?"

"No, not at all. There is on one side the Smith family, and on the other, the Ratchet family. Both quiet families, both with small children. On Dominion Day, we always have picnic together in our yard. I make something, they bring bottles of beer and soda. No, is always good. Mr. Smith, he come out this morning to look at damage, and he very kind, he says is terrible what happen. He says I should put light for nighttime on porch. Guy across street is not so nice. He never says hello. His wife always pushes the kids inside house after school if I am outside. Usually, of course, I am at restaurant. So is my wife. But I don't think they would try to burn my house down."

"Has anyone threatened you about the restaurant?"

"Well, you know. At the beginning other restaurants maybe not so happy. What you can do? But customers come, they like food. Everything is going okay." He shrugged. It wasn't going entirely okay. "I try two times to join Chamber of Commerce, but both times nothing."

"It's a bit drastic for someone to set fire to your house over a Chamber of Commerce application. Can you think of anything at all that might have caused someone to pick your house?" The other thing, Darling thought, is that perhaps it wasn't targeted. It was simply delinquents making trouble. After all, whoever it was had not done a very good job of it. "I'm wondering if it was more random, perhaps some kids?"

Lorenzo looked down at his hat, turned it a few more times. "Okay. Maybe you are right. Just kids. I hope so." He stood up. "Thank you, *Ispettore*. I must go to the restaurant now. I hope everything is okay there. You tell me if you find anything." He shrugged again, as if he had little hope that anything would be found. "Please give my best to your *signora*."

SIMPSON COULD SEE the clearing up ahead and made for it, figuring he must be close to where they used to come. He thought he could see the corner of a cabin through the trees in the distance. He cleared the edge of the forest and then stopped, uncertain. There was a woman in a turquoise sweater sitting very still in the middle of the meadow he would have to cross. If he could turn quickly and go back into the woods, he could avoid a confrontation. He imagined her being afraid, maybe hurrying away or demanding to know what right he had to be there. He watched her for a moment longer and was about to turn back when she stood up and began to wave. His heart sank. He'd have to go on and deal with whatever was about to happen. He waited to try to gauge her intentions. He did not want to appear to be a threat to her.

To his surprise she called out, "Hello," waving again.

LANE WATCHED THE horseman, intrigued. He seemed to be appraising her, or perhaps he just didn't want to be bothered socializing with a stranger. She had some sympathy with this view. But then he dismounted. She put her hand over her eyes to block out the sun to see him better. He seemed to be equipped as her neighbour the prospector was when he went out on horseback to explore. Saddlebags, bedroll, rifle. He walked up the hill toward her slowly, and she saw that he had a waterproof coat folded and placed behind the saddle.

"Hello," Lane called again when he was near enough.

He took off his cowboy hat and nodded. He had thick, dark hair, combed straight back, and a long, narrow brown face and dark eyes. She guessed he was a little over thirty. He looked at her and nodded. "Ma'am." He dropped his horse's reins, patting the side of the animal's neck in a reassuring manner. He turned back to Lane and settled his weight onto one foot, as if waiting to see if more conversation was required.

"Have you come far?" Lane asked, smiling in a way she hoped would put him at ease. She could sense he didn't particularly want to stop and talk.

He turned and nodded in the direction he had come from. "From over the border."

"Oh!" Lane said, looking in the same direction. "I didn't know one could just ride over like that. My name is Lane Winslow, by the way." She put out her hand.

He nodded, took a few steps forward, and took her hand and shook it briefly, not pressing, as if hand shaking was not his chosen way of greeting. "Tom Simpson." There was a long pause, and looking past her, he asked, "Do you live here?"

"Oh, no. I live miles away by Kootenay Lake. I came to visit a friend, but he's not there, so I thought I'd walk a bit before I make the long drive back. Good job I did—it's a

19

beautiful place." She looked past him at the horse, which had wandered farther into the meadow and was now pulling up hunks of grass with a sideways motion of his head. "What a beautiful creature."

Simpson nodded and offered a slight smile, his face relaxing fractionally. "That's Rocky. He waited a long time for me to come home. Now he pretends he doesn't even know me."

Lane smiled. "I remember some rather aloof horses my sister had when we were young. I see you have the badge of the US 104th. Did you serve with them?"

Simpson put his hand up to his collar. "Yes, ma'am. Europe." He was surprised she recognized it. He wasn't completely sure why he still wore it. Perhaps it was just a continuation of that adjustment from warrior to civilian. "Most people wouldn't have recognized it."

Lane was a little sorry she'd opened the subject, as she was not entitled to speak about her own war. "I worked in an office in London. I remember seeing the insignia and admiring that it looked like a lone wolf."

He gave a little smile. "I guess that's why I like it too."

"Are you visiting someone?" Lane asked.

He shook his head and then hesitated, as if considering whether he should explain. "I came up here in the summer when I was a kid. Our people used to live around here." He looked across at his horse.

"I'm not sure how far the border is from here, but I expect you've been riding for some time. I have a box of chocolate biscuits I brought for my friend. We might as well eat them." She sat down and patted the stone next to her.

Simpson put his hat back on and hesitated a moment, looking toward the settlement. He couldn't remember a time when a stranger, a white woman, had asked him to sit down and eat cookies. He had a sudden thought that his grandmother would greet this unusual social situation by saying, "Sit down and eat the damn cookies," and it made him smile momentarily. In truth, he would have liked to continue on, so he remained standing for another moment. Finally, he gave in to his curiosity—after all, she did have cookies. He settled onto the ground a few feet from her and stretched his legs out, moving them up and down to work out the kinks from his long ride.

Lane wondered if he did not feel comfortable sitting next to her. She had been about to stand up and offer up the biscuits to be eaten on foot when he settled himself on the ground near her.

"Long ride today?" she asked.

"Pretty long. Maybe ten hours."

"How absolutely exhausting. You definitely need some biscuits!" She opened the box and leaned over to offer it to him.

He nodded his thanks. "You sound English."

"I am, yes. Are you American?"

"Not exactly American. I was born on this side, so they would say I'm Canadian. My people don't have these borders." Simpson drew an invisible line in the air. "I live on the other side now. I lived in Washington most of my life. Kind of makes me American, I guess." He shrugged.

She was certain that this was the first time in the nearly two years she had been here that she had met anyone indigenous to North America. "It's hard to believe in that whole war now, sitting here in this place of so much beauty and peace."

Simpson bit into his biscuit. "I think it is why I wanted to come back up here. All that machinery of destruction over there. I used to tell myself when I was over there, I'd come back here first chance I got, just me and my horse. I want to remember the quiet like it was."

Lane tried to imagine the ride, the solitude and silence after the din of war. "I came here for the same reason, I think. I settled in a tiny little hamlet with a few other families. I didn't even have a wireless for the first year and a half. I just wanted silence. I liked the idea of an empty land." She held the box out to Simpson, who took another biscuit.

"I have a weakness for cookies," he warned. "This place wasn't that empty," he added. "Not that long ago, all my people lived around here. Years ago, my mother and my uncle used to drive up in a Model T every summer with my grandmother. They were coming back to visit, too. After I was born, I came a few times as well." Another pause.

"Your family?"

"Our family, and everybody, yes; this is where my people came from."

"Oh. How is it that I didn't know that?"

Simpson popped the remainder of his biscuit into his mouth, looking out at the lake. "In my grandfather's day everybody had to leave, to move away. There was no way to carry on their way of life. Some moved west to the Okanagan and joined up with the Okanagan tribes, and some moved north, but my family, they moved south to the lower reaches of our territory. Every now and then people come back and look at the old place. When I was a boy, we still used to come right around here pretty regularly in the summer."

He waved his arm at the meadow and the forest leading back up toward Barisoff's cabin. He turned back to look out at the lake, thinking to draw the conversation to a close. She wouldn't likely be that interested in the comings and goings of his relatives. She surprised him again by continuing the conversation.

"Ah. Under those circumstances it must be poignant to come back to a place of your childhood. I often long to go back to the places of my childhood, but it is out of reach." Lane thought of the house in Bilderlingshof, with its long, shaded veranda where they took tea in the summer, and the forest past their lawns, and the outbuildings where she loved to play. It seemed now to be just a story she'd heard once in her childhood.

"You don't go?"

"I can't, really. It was a lifetime and a war ago. Latvia, where I lived, was in the thick of things, and our house was taken over by the Soviets. My grandmother and grandfather had to live in one room, and finally had to leave and travel to Scotland, a place they scarcely knew. It was hard on my grandmother, I know. She had to leave her mother's grave. So, I just remember that place, and am grateful to be here, a place I could choose."

"Well, then," Simpson said. He shook his head. "We had to go all the way across the ocean to France and Belgium to stop some people in Europe taking away the land of some other people in Europe. They said we were defending our country, as if we were stopping people from coming here to take it. But all these people that live around here now? They didn't think too much of the fact that people already lived here. After being in the war, I see it's kind of the European way." He shook his head, but his voice carried no bitterness.

Lane frowned. She thought of Barisoff, already a kind of refugee himself, and the empty rows of barracks in New Denver where, she had learned, the Canadian Japanese had spent the war. "So, this was your grandfather's land?"

Simpson was silent and very still for a long moment. "Not the way you think of it. It's the other way around. The land doesn't belong to us. It's more like we belong to it. When I come here, I feel it welcome me back, as if I was someone who has been away from home." He glanced at her. "I guess if you went back to that place you come from, you might feel the same thing."

"You know, you are absolutely right. No matter who lives in that house now, I would feel I belonged there. What made your people leave?"

"Now that's a very long story, ma'am." He picked up a twig and tossed it away, as if that was all he was prepared to say.

Lane took another biscuit and looked out across the lake and fold after fold of mountains going into the distance, green to dark green to blue, finally, at the edge of the sky. She had thought of it as empty, new, pristine, uninhabited. Isn't that how the posters she'd seen in England portrayed it? Land to be given away to farmers and growers and miners. But of course the miners and loggers had made their depredations long before she got there. She was intrigued by the idea of belonging to the land rather than the other way around.

"I must say, even after being in the war, it's still hard to imagine how people can just take a place when there is someone already living there."

Simpson almost chuckled. "I don't guess you've been here that long."

"No. Only a couple of years. I don't know why I'm surprised. I guess I just didn't expect it would be happening here as well."

"Then maybe you're not used to the way things are done here. Those people who want silver or timber or farmland, they do whatever they want. They want to build a dam, so they mess up the fish runs and drown our villages, and we can't travel along the rivers like we used to. That way when we have to move somewhere else, they say, 'Oh, look, no Indians here. I guess they don't exist.' They are all for 'progress.'"

"But you do exist, obviously."

"Yes, ma'am. Me and my horse here too, for that matter. All the other people. They still exist."

"I guess when people came here from Europe their idea about land was completely different. Land is something you own. If the Crown says it's empty, you can buy it. Heavens, I bought a piece of land myself, and feel I own it. But you are describing something very different. The opposite, in fact."

Simpson nodded. "That's about right."

"So, no one is left in the old territory?"

He lifted his chin in the direction he had ridden from. "I bet there's still some people here. They made a reserve for us over by the Columbia River. I know there's a few people there."

"And you remember being just here, as a child? Did you stay around New Denver?"

"More like we camped here when I was a kid. We had temporary shelters in the summer, but in the old days, when people still lived around here permanently, they also had these pit houses dug into the ground for the colder times. You can still see where they were." After a period of silence, Simpson got up. "Thank you for the cookies, ma'am. They were very good."

Lane stood up as well. "Oh, are you off, then?"

"I thought I would take a look around, see what's left."

"Oh, right. Yes. May I walk with you? I'll see if the man I was going to visit has come back."

He nodded several times but said nothing and took up the reins of his mount. They walked together through the meadow and then into the forest along the narrow path, Lane leading the way.

When they got to edge of the area Peter Barisoff had framed for his garden, Lane heard Simpson stop, and she turned to look at him. There was a pile of large rocks that looked as though they had been cleared to create more garden space just near him, right at the edge of the clearing. He had dropped the reins and stood with his hands in his pockets, looking closely along the length of the garden.

A few weary wintered-over cabbages leaned intermittently along this back edge of the plot. Weeds and grasses that had grown over in the fall and died over the winter lent the garden a desolate air. Barisoff's cabin was just beyond the garden.

Lane looked to where Simpson had turned his gaze, but she could see nothing besides the tumbled rocky edge of the garden where Barisoff had begun his work of clearing a new bed.

"What is it?" asked Lane, approaching him.

"This is sort of like a place I remember. They used to say our ancestors were buried around here. I haven't been here since I was a little kid, so this might not be it. I remember a little house like this, and some land behind it." He shook his head. "I guess most of the houses of the settlers look like this."

CHAPTER THREE

TERRELL STOOD IN THE SMALL backyard surveying the damage. The support for the back stairs, which comprised a small, covered landing outside the door he assumed would be the kitchen entrance, and six steps down into the yard were quite badly burned. The arsonist had lit the fire, it appeared, in the space underneath the stairs, perhaps splashing gas onto the four-by-four supports and then the stairs themselves. The dry grass under the stairs was scorched away, and several items that had been stored there had burned badly. As well, there were signs that the fire had lapped a good way onto the porch.

He stepped back and surveyed the house. There was an open window on the south side of the stairs. Perhaps a bedroom? The smoke would have poured in there, alerting Mr. Vitali. He was lucky, Terrell thought; these wood-framed houses could go up like tinder.

"Hey, what are you doing? I know the people who live there!"

Terrell looked across at a woman standing on the back porch of Lorenzo's neighbour on the north side. She was holding her door open as if she might want to flee back into the house if Terrell became threatening.

Surprised she hadn't noticed his uniform, he reached into the inside breast pocket of his jacket to get his identification. The woman flinched. "It's all right, ma'am, I am the police. Here's my warrant card." He crossed the yard slowly, holding up the card. "Constable Terrell. I'm here to look into the fire."

The woman eyed him and then said, "Oh." Her tone could not have been more doubtful, as though she suspected he was impersonating a policeman.

Boy, he thought, they really are not used to coloured people in this town. "Did you happen to see anything early this morning, Mrs. . . . ?"

"Smith," she said reluctantly. "We only woke up when we heard Mr. Vitali putting the garden hose on the fire."

"Do you remember what time that would have been?"

"I don't know. It was the middle of the night. Maybe quarter to three? My husband went out to help him, but Mr. Vitali had pretty well got it under control then. Maybe if you lot got out and dealt with all the delinquents, we wouldn't have this sort of thing going on!"

"Thank you, ma'am. You've been very helpful. I'm going to take some photos now. If you think of anything else, you could call the Nelson Police Station."

The woman grunted something, watched Terrell for another moment, and disappeared into her house.

Terrell rolled his eyes and, pulling the camera case off

his shoulder, turned back to photograph the damage. He noted the location of the gas can and wondered if Mr. Vitali had touched it. It was on its side, about three feet from the bottom step. He snapped a picture of the whole scene, and then one of the can in relation to the porch, where it appeared to have been tossed hastily. He looked around, imagining the arsonist sloshing the gas around on the back of the structure first and then around to the steps, then dropping the can and throwing a match. Probably safer than leaning in with a lighter, though if it was a delinquent, as Mrs. Smith suggested, he might be just dim enough to do that, and perhaps come up with singed eyebrows or hair. If a lighter had been hastily dropped it might have survived the conflagration, but the owner would undoubtedly want it back. He leaned forward to look more closely at the space under the steps. There was a pile of broken and charred glass, and the skeletal remains of some sort of basket that would, he assumed, have been used for gathering vegetables from the garden. He did not see a lighter, but he was reluctant to sift around in the debris until someone with more expertise could have a look. He would contact the fire chief. He would want to be involved.

Then the arsonist would have run. The most likely place was through the little gate into the alley. Terrell walked across the garden, wood-framed beds already turned over by the hard-working Mr. Vitali in preparation for some early spring planting. He was about to go to the gate when he was gratified to see a good-sized boot mark in the turned-over earth. He rolled the film forward and took a picture. The heel was deeper than the rest of the print.

Terrell imagined the miscreant running toward the gate with long strides, landing with his left foot in the garden. How much would he have weighed? Aside from the heel, the print wasn't that deep. He noted that the soil was damp from the rain the night before. A kid with big feet? Going to a different enclosed bed, Terrell stepped into the dirt in an imitation of the imagined flight of the firebug. Fishing in his jacket pocket, he pulled out his tape measure, measured the length and depth of his mark, and made a note in his book, and then measured the first one. This confirmed that the perpetrator was much lighter than he was. He was of pretty average height and weight for a full-grown man. So, more likely a teen. Possibly whoever it was lit the fire and then got spooked.

He turned to the gate. It had an easy flip-up latch. Interestingly, it was closed and latched now. But Mr. Vitali would have closed it, perhaps, when he'd found the gate open.

Taking out his handkerchief, he used it to lift the latch, and then he surveyed the immediate vicinity, the fence, and the ground. Alas, he thought with chagrin, no fragment of cloth conveniently caught on a nail. In fact, no partially exposed nails at all. Vitali kept his property in pretty good repair. Feeling it safe to step onto the compacted dirt alley without disturbing any evidence, Terrell looked up and then down, wondering which way the arsonist might flee. He chose down as the easiest and most likely escape, but the alley, all the way to the next cross street, was free of any obvious clues. As he turned back to the yard, he saw the curtain twitch in Mrs. Smith's house. He sighed and, with a massive effort of will, stopped himself from wagging his finger disapprovingly at her and winking, and instead went about preparing to dust the gate latch for fingerprints.

BARISOFF, LIKE THE other small farmers in the area, took what produce he did not store and preserve to the general store and sold it or traded it for other goods. This just looked to Lane like a typical garden at this time of year, though it came to her that Tom Simpson might be seeing it differently. It was clear Barisoff had already started the process of turning over the soil for spring planting closer to the cabin. Perhaps he was planning to expand the garden and had been clearing rocks into a pile.

"I wish I could remember exactly," Simpson said, walking a few steps away from the garden, back toward the stand of trees through which they had come. He moved slowly, looking at the ground. Stopping, he stooped down and cleared an area with a few brushes of his hand. Then he turned and walked back and stopped at the edge of the garden where the dirt had been disturbed.

"Do you think a burial place might be here, specifically?" Lane asked, curious.

"I was so young. I'm not sure. If this had been a grave, there would probably only be four stones, not as many as this. We used to walk all around gathering berries and stuff from where we usually camped near the lake." He shook his head. "I could be wrong. It must have been closer to our camp. It's the rocks that made me think it was here, I guess. But as I said, that's too many anyway."

Simpson started to where there was a little clearing beyond the garden. "There was a pit house nearby, I remember that. I think I noticed the remains of one near here, just by the path we came up."

Lane followed him. He stopped and pointed. Lane looked into the woods and could see nothing at first, then she saw what he was showing her.

Just where he indicated, she could see a round indentation in the ground, not very deep but nearly fifteen feet across. Shrubs and several trees had colonized the space, but it was, nevertheless, very distinct. It looked like a giant had trowelled out a perfectly round crater.

"I wouldn't have been able to tell at all," she said in amazement. "It just looks like the surrounding forest if you don't look closely."

"It looks pretty old. It's probably from well before even my great-grandparents' time. Usually there were several, where some families lived near each other. They're all over here, along the river, the creek, near the lakes. Some of them are hundreds, maybe thousands of years old."

Lane looked with wonder across at the woods and field behind Barisoff's cabin. Perhaps the place was alive with Tom Simpson's ancestors, and Barisoff might not even know. She was about to ask more about the structure of such a house when they heard a shout.

"Hello, Miss Winslow!"

Lane and Simpson turned to where Peter Barisoff was visible through the trees, waving at them from the little back stairs of the cabin.

"Oh, good, my friend is here after all. He is very nice.

You can meet him. Perhaps he can help." She walked back and began to make her way around the garden to meet Barisoff.

"I saw your car. I'm happy I didn't miss you!" He spoke in Russian to her. "You have a friend with you?"

Tom had not followed Lane, but stood at the edge of the clearing, holding his horse loosely and watching.

"Yes, come and meet him. He is here to visit a place he came to as a child. He rode all this way across the border."

Barisoff lifted his hand as they drew near. "Hello, my friend. You come on a horse. That is something. You are welcome."

Tom Simpson took Barisoff's offered hand and nodded once but did not speak. Lane would have described his expression as wary.

"I see you've been expanding your garden," Lane said.

Barisoff nodded and went to stand by the disturbed soil and sighed. "I move rocks, now animals are digging," he said. Then he looked with interest at Simpson.

"So, he came as a child? I heard that there were once a people who lived up and down all these waterways," he said to Lane in Russian.

Lane said in English, "Mr. Barisoff is interested that you came as a child. He said he'd heard there were people here once."

Simpson nodded. He watched Barisoff. He did not speak; his wariness was still evident.

Barisoff also fell silent, but after a long moment he smiled and said, "You are most welcome here."

Lane opted for a change of focus. There was an irony

that Simpson was being made welcome in a place that had possibly once been his. She pointed at where the rocks had been piled and asked, "How far will you expand the garden?"

"I was going to make it bigger," Barisoff said in Russian. "I moved this pile of big rocks away from here a few weeks ago, but I didn't dig yet. I was going to maybe get started today. As you see, some creature has tried to help me." Barisoff knelt and began to replace the dirt, which was damp and crumbling. "Why would an animal come and dig here?"

Abruptly he let out a strangled cry, stood up, and began to say a prayer in Russian. He pointed. "Blessed be His name," he croaked. What he had exposed was a skeletal foot, with barely discernible scraps of something that might once have been a sock.

Tom Simpson stepped back suddenly, causing his horse to pad anxiously "I was hoping to find my ancestors, but this is surely not one of them! Not buried so close to the surface like this."

"We mustn't touch anything," Lane said, though two men less likely to want to meddle with this gruesome scene would be impossible to imagine. "You do not have a telephone?" she said in Russian to Barisoff.

He shook his head and said in English, "No telephone. In store."

"Right," said Lane, in English again. "I'll go down to the store and call the police. Mr. Barisoff, why don't you put some coffee on? I'm sure we could all use some."

Not waiting for a response, Lane dashed around the side of the cottage and down to where she had parked the car.

It was only then that she groaned inwardly about having to telephone Darling to tell him they had found a body. He already had a dim view of her penchant for finding this sort of trouble.

She parked her car so as not to be in the way of the old cylindrical gas pump and hurried inside. The man seated behind the dark expanse of wooden counter was smoking and leafing through a much-thumbed magazine. Lane struggled to remember his name. Berenson? She had met him in the winter a year before. He was a grizzled, bearded specimen with unkempt hair, who looked as if neither he nor his clothes had frequent experience with a good washing. He had the look of a man who had a jaundiced view of most things.

"Ma'am," said the man, getting up and parking his cigarette in a miniature Goodyear Tire ashtray. "What can I do you for?"

"May I use your telephone?" She was going to add, in case he was reluctant, that it was a matter of extreme urgency, but of course whoever it was had been dead a good long while.

The man pulled a battered black telephone out from a shelf under the counter and plunked it down. Taped onto the base of the phone was a tired and grimy piece of paper that read "5 CENTS."

"Weren't you up here sometime about a year ago? I never forget a pretty face."

Lane gave the faintest pinch of a smile as she dialled for the operator and waited. "I was visiting Mr. Barisoff," she said.

Finally, she heard a voice: "Where can I direct your call, please?"

Looking sideways at the man, who'd resumed his position behind the counter and now sat watching her with avid interest, Lane said, "Can you put me through to the Nelson Police Station, please?"

She could hear the man behind her shift. She ardently wished she could have found a way to ask him to leave for a moment, but it was his store and his phone. And, she told herself, this wartime instinct for secrecy was hardly necessary here.

"Hello, Sergeant O'Brien. May I speak with Inspector Darling, please?" A further wait.

DARLING PICKED UP the receiver. He hoped it was not another report of arson. A skilled arsonist could keep everyone on the hunt for ages. "Darling."

"This is Lane Winslow. I'm calling from New Denver to report something."

"And sounding very official. Presumably you are being overheard."

"Yes, that's right. I've been visiting Mr. Peter Barisoff, just outside the village, and he has discovered . . ." Here she hesitated. "Something that suggests a . . . an informal burial, and I wonder if you could send someone around."

Darling waited a beat and then said incredulously, "'Informal burial'? Please tell me you have not found a dead person. You're really getting to be too much. In fact, you were too much five bodies ago."

"That's right," Lane continued doggedly. She could feel

the shopkeeper's eyes boring into her back. "I should have said years, possibly decades?"

"Decades?" Darling asked in surprise. "I'll come with Ames. He'll be delighted. He's making no headway with the books. See you in an hour and forty minutes or so. Can you stay put?"

Lane nodded. "Yes, of course, Inspector. Do you need directions?"

"No. Goodbye, darling," the inspector said. "Ames!" he shouted into the hall, as he stood up and took his hat. At least it's not raining, he thought. He'd best get the van up there as well. He was sure Barisoff would love to be rid of whoever it was. Unless he'd put the corpse there himself.

"You don't want to go getting too excited about some skeleton, ma'am. Them Indians buried people all over the place around here. You can't plant a turnip without finding a skeleton. They're a real nuisance, if you want to know." The shopkeeper had gotten up and was leaning on both fists on the counter, looking at Lane and shaking his head.

Lane fished in her pocket and pulled out a handful of coins. Putting her nickel onto the counter, she smiled brightly and said, "Thank you—Mr. Berenson, is it?"

"That's right." He pushed the coin back across the wooden counter. "Listen, you don't hafta—" But Lane was out the door.

"Hey, I don't remember your name!" the man called to the shutting door. As tempted as he was to put a Closed sign on the door and follow her up to old man Barisoff's, he reckoned he'd find out what was what soon enough. He sat down and lit another cigarette, coughing on his first inhale. He stood up and went around the counter to watch her as she turned her car and headed back onto the road.

"YOU MIGHT PREFER me not to say anything, sir," said Ames, who had contented himself with a facial expression of gratified surprise at the news that Miss Winslow had found the skeletal remains of someone. They were just pulling off the ferry on the north side of the lake out of Nelson. They had a good hour and a half ahead of them, and Darling would rather not spend it listening to Ames giving voice to his adoration of Lane.

"Yes, I would prefer it, Ames, and you can stow the impertinence. What have you heard from Terrell?"

"He's taken some shots and had a discussion with a neighbour who threatened to call the police, even though he was in uniform, and he dusted what he could for prints. Only one blurry set. What he doesn't know is if the arsonist dropped the gas can right where he found it on its side. He'll have to ask Vitali if he picked it up at some point, maybe this morning. If so, he'll have to get Vitali's prints to compare. He said he's also going to go to the fire station to see what the fire chief makes of it in his investigation."

Darling grunted an acknowledgement. "So, no theories yet whether it's targeted or just delinquents?"

"No, sir, except he found about a size nine-and-a-half boot mark in a section of turned-over earth. He figured out that the guy probably weighed a lot less than he does by making a similar footprint and measuring them. He thinks it might be a kid."

"Does he, by Jove? Anything else?"

"He suspects the arsonist tossed a match as opposed to using a lighter, though he allows it's possible a lighter might be found. He'll know more after talking to the fire chief."

Darling nodded speculatively and settled back in the passenger seat. "It's unusual that we should have these two property-type crimes at once: the bookstore theft and the fire."

Ames glanced at his boss. "You can't think they're related." He swerved to catch a turn in the road.

"You couldn't just pay attention to the road, could you? I'd like us to arrive in one piece," Darling said. "I don't think they are related. I think it's unusual because we don't usually have that many property crimes here all at once. Usually, we are dealing with drinking or careless driving. Arson and careful bookstore thefts are out of the norm."

"Sir," Ames said cheerfully. "I've been thinking about the books, sir. At first I thought it was random—that whoever it was had just scooped up whatever they could take. But Miss Winslow might be on to something."

Here we go, thought Darling glumly. "Yes, what?"

"I'm just wondering if the person was after some particular books, and just took the others as cover, so to speak."

"A desperate opera lover?"

"That was strange, sir, because the opera book was sitting nearby and not on the shelf with the other books. That might just have been what you call a crime of opportunity. I was thinking more of the biography. I stopped by the library to ask about this fellow, Samuel Turner. He was a local settler in the 1890s, started up a logging operation that ran great guns and then got into the railway business, building lines to transport ore. Something of a pioneer, made a lot of money. The book was apparently privately published; in fact, he wrote it himself in the early teens. I haven't had a chance to go back and talk to Mrs. Treadwell, the bookstore owner, to find out how she came by the books."

"Does the library have a copy of the book?" Darling asked.

"Ha! Good thinking, sir, but I'm ahead of you. It has one copy, which has not as yet been checked out. Well, I mean, I checked it out to see what was in it. They apparently accepted it as a donation. It arrived one day in an envelope with a typewritten note explaining that as Turner was a local personage of importance, the library ought to stock the autobiography. The librarian doesn't recall when it was, or if they kept the note. She said she will look for it, though she has an idea it was an anonymous donation."

"Well, good for you. Initiative. I like to see that in my sergeants. I hope you will not be disappointed when you discover the thief was after the Erle Stanley Gardner. I'm glad you took out the book. It will do you good to bone up on some local history."

"I'd rather read the Erle Stanley," remarked Ames.

"The vicissitudes of a policeman's life, Ames. You have to take the rough with the smooth."

CHAPTER FOUR

WHILE SIMPSON WAS TETHERING HIS horse to the fence, Peter Barisoff was talking quietly to Lane in Russian as he went about preparing the coffee. "I feel sorry for this man. In Brilliant, down near where my son's wife's people are, there's been trouble. The Indians used to fish and live there, and they want to tend their graves sometimes. One of our people threatened an Indian who'd tried to take the fence away from the yard because he said someone was buried there. They told him it was private property, and he would get a good beating if he didn't leave. It was like that Russian forgot where he himself came from."

"I had no idea, but of course there must be conflict under those circumstances."

"I'm ashamed. We were refugees here; we were given land and a chance. Only it wasn't really the government's to give. My people don't even believe in this idea of private property anyway."

A quiet knock indicated Simpson was about to join

them. Barisoff welcomed him and urged him to sit down, with what Lane could see was an added dose of hospitality. She thought of the way different people reacted to hardship. In Barisoff's case, when the same Crown that had given his people, the Doukhobors, land to settle on and own communally had then taken it back and forced them to live on private plots of land like "everybody else," he'd ended up here. His response was kindness. He had given over the second, very small, cabin on his property to a homeless Russian some years before. Now she could see that he wanted, through any small action, to make amends to Simpson for a loss so monumental it could never be remedied.

They were sitting at his wooden table, which occupied the midway position between his kitchen area and the sitting area. The afternoon had chilled considerably, and he had lit the stove to warm the place up. The kettle sat on the small cast-iron stove, water keeping warm in case the police who were coming would want something hot to drink as well.

"That person—he could not be one of your people?" Barisoff asked Simpson.

"I am reasonably sure."

Lane wanted to ask about this *reasonably*, but Barisoff continued. "That is very edge of where I put garden. We maybe not even see, if some animal not dig up."

"A dog?" Lane suggested. "Or coyotes."

"That would be like coyotes," Simpson said. "They're pretty nosy."

At long last, they heard the police car pull up on the road outside the cottage.

Barisoff opened the door at their knock. "Please come in. There is coffee. Is getting cold outside."

Ames and Darling had removed their hats. "Thank you, all the same. I think we'd better get right out to the site, Mr. Barisoff."

"Hello, Miss Winslow," said Ames, displaying a smile too sunny for the sombre work at hand.

"Sergeant Ames, Inspector Darling, this is Mr. Simpson. He arrived earlier because he is visiting a place he came to as a child. He was looking for where his people's ancestors might be buried nearby, when we found this other, er, burial," Lane said.

Darling offered his hand. "Mr. Simpson. Where have you come from?"

"From across the line in Colville. About four days' ride."

Darling evinced something of the surprise Lane had felt. "Ride? Did you come on horseback?"

"Yes," Simpson said, offering nothing else.

Darling nodded, as if he might take up the question later. "Well, we'd better make tracks. Can someone show us the way?"

"Why don't I stay here and tidy up?" Lane offered. "You fellows can go and have a look. Is the van coming?" she asked Darling.

"Yup. Should be along any minute."

"Right then, I'll wait for them and show them where to go."

Lane made this offer with a little disappointment. She would have loved to be at the graveside, as it were, listening to the discussion, but she worried that Darling might already feel she was too involved.

"No, you better come along. You may have some observation that we will not be able to proceed without. I'll send Ames to get the van boys when we hear it arrive," Darling said, almost with resignation.

"Leave everything. I will clean up later," Peter Barisoff said to her in Russian. "Better you come with inspector," he finished in English.

Simpson's horse was in a small clearing at the side of the property, chewing his way through the long yellow grasses that drooped tiredly along the ground.

"He looks a fine beast," Darling said as they made their way along the edge of the dug-up garden, following Barisoff to where they had found the skeleton in its shallow burial place. He wondered about keeping a couple of horses. He'd spent a brief period when he was a young constable in Vancouver as part of the mounted unit. He'd quite enjoyed it.

Surveying the scene, Darling now wished he had asked Ashford Gillingham, the coroner, to have a look. Photos would have to do.

"Ames, can you fetch your camera?"

"Sir," replied Ames, and started toward the car.

"You found this foot partially exposed like this?"

Lane responded, "No. In fact, Mr. Simpson noticed the recently disturbed earth. Mr. Barisoff said he hadn't yet begun to turn the earth over to expand his garden. He'd only moved the rocks to one side. He wondered if an animal had been at it and began to brush a little of the soil aside, and there it was."

Darling nodded. He turned to Mr. Simpson. "You

came here on your ride up from Washington. Is this place significant in some way?"

"I came up here to revisit places I was taken as a child, by my mother and grandmother. I was hoping I could find the burial place of my great-grandfather. We used to come in the summer to hunt and pick berries. My great-grandfather died some years before that, and he was buried east of an old pit house. I was going to ride around until I found a place that was really familiar. I think it might have been near a creek, but as I said, I was only a boy, so my memory of it is a bit foggy."

Darling nodded. "I can see it might be difficult in this wooded area to know exactly. There seems to be nothing that distinguishes this place from any other. Was this house here when you were a boy?" He pointed at Barisoff's cottage.

"I'm not actually sure, now that I think of it. I wondered about the grave being here because of that pit house nearby." Simpson walked toward where he had shown Lane the crater and pointed. "It might not be this one; there must be others around here. By the time I was here as a child, my people had mostly moved away. Some went west or north, but my family moved south to the US."

"So, before that you were able to hunt and so on, on Crown land?" Darling pursued.

"It was the land where our people always lived. It didn't use to belong to the Crown." He shrugged. "'Crown'" is a way to say the land is empty, so they can give it away to miners."

Darling looked down at the grim find. "Could this be your great-grandfather or any other relation?"

"I don't think so, sir. Not buried like that. A traditional grave would be round, there would be four stones aligned on it. It would have been carried out with respect. There is nothing respectful about what is out there."

The driver of the van announced his arrival with his signature grinding of the gears.

"Ames, go fetch the van boys, and then I want you to take photos of the area. It will be up to Gilly to speculate about how long he's been there."

They stood in silence for some moments. Darling was thinking about how to proceed. He would have to take statements from Simpson, Barisoff, and Lane after the body had been moved.

"Mr. Barisoff, when did you acquire this land?" Darling asked. Lane repeated the question in Russian.

"I did not acquire it. It is not mine. I am allowed to live here, to rent. I came in 1940, when the communes were broken up." He shrugged. "I hope one day I can buy it."

Darling nodded at Lane's translation. "So, when you came in 1940, your house was already here?"

"Yes," Barisoff said in English. "Already here. Also, second house, you remember, poor Mr. Strelieff lived there. I don't know who live here before."

"And your garden? Did you push it out to these boundaries, or was it already like that?"

Barisoff walked along the width of the garden toward the house and looked around as though he was estimating. "I think maybe was here when I move." He indicated an imaginary border five or six feet closer to the cottage than the current border of his garden. "I make bigger."

"And so you moved these rocks recently to expand it further?"

Barisoff nodded. "I think to move to edge of trees." He resumed in Russian, turning to Lane. "I started when it stopped snowing, maybe three weeks ago. I began by moving a big pile of rocks from there. I thought I could clear along that edge and grow a few more carrots, but I admit, I'm getting old. It was hard work. Now that I moved the rocks, I don't think I really need a bigger garden. My son moved away to Brilliant to his wife's family. And my back hurt. How many carrots do I need to grow? So, I moved the rocks and then gave up on it."

At Lane's translation, Darling murmured, "Hmm. And he did not see any evidence of this skeleton at the time?"

Barisoff shook his head vigorously and said in English, "I see only dirt. Only bones we find now, after maybe animal dig here."

The van boys had arrived with shovels and a stretcher and stood by awaiting orders.

Darling obliged, directing the diggers to remove the skeleton carefully and leave it as intact as possible; fragments of clothing, footwear, and any artifacts should have their exact locations noted and be carefully bagged. As an afterthought, he added that any possible graves below the body should not be disturbed. Ames was instructed to carefully record the exhumation with his camera.

Tom Simpson stood by his horse, watching the proceedings and waiting.

"Mr. Simpson. Thank you for your patience. I will want to talk with Mr. Barisoff for a few more minutes, and then you, if you have the time. Where are you staying while you're here?"

Simpson waved his hand back down the path he and Lane had walked on. "I'll just be camping on the meadow, sir."

Barisoff looked up at the sky. The band of dark clouds was still parked ominously along the mountains. "Mr. Simpson. It might rain. There is nice house with no one in. I keep it good in case son come. Please. You must use. You stay as long as you want, to find great-grandparent. I know how important. My grandparent buried far away. I know what this means."

Simpson rubbed the back of his neck as he considered this offer, as if contemplating the relative merits of sleeping on a bed with a pillow against using his saddle as a headrest.

"Thank you. That's kindly. I'll only be here a week, maybe."

"Very good. You will eat with me too."

"Well," Darling said. "That's helpful. We may need to come back and ask more questions as we go." He turned to Lane. "I've got Ames tied up here, and I'll need your help with any Russian translation. Would you mind taking a few notes for me while I talk to these gentlemen?"

Lane, who had been watching the exhumation process, her mind turning over all the possibilities of how a body came to be buried just there, nodded. "Certainly. Anything I can do." Did she see her husband mouth the words "I bet!" as she passed him on the way back to the cabin?

Darling, Barisoff, and Lane settled at the small wooden table where Barisoff took his solitary meals. Their host found a partially used scribbler that had once belonged to one of the students who had been taught by the Russian, Strelieff, when he had been living in the other cabin on the property before he was murdered the year before. After sharpening a pencil with a penknife and sweeping the shavings into his hand to toss outside, he gave both items to Lane. Even through the closed windows they could hear the rocky scrape of shovels burrowing into the ground under the corpse.

With Lane translating and taking notes, they proceeded.

"Mr. Barisoff, you have lived here since around 1940, correct?"

Barisoff nodded. "After our communal land was taken, we were given land to rent, or buy if there was the money, from the 'Crown,' as Mr. Simpson said. So here we are, all with our little plots of vegetables."

"And you never met or knew the people who lived here before?"

Barisoff shook his head. "No. The houses were empty. This one was built around 1929, maybe for prospectors, when everyone was looking for gold and silver, I don't know."

Darling nodded and Lane wrote. "It would be useful to know what New Denver was all about," Darling mused. "Supporting local mining activity, or the Japanese encampment."

Barisoff shook his head again. "Japanese not come till 1942," he said in English. "Before, nothing. Some loggers, a store. Not even too many miners anymore. Same store." He lifted his chin in the direction of the gas station and store where Lane had borrowed the phone.

"That's a thought," Lane said. "How long has Berenson been here? He's the shopkeeper," she explained to Darling.

"Yes, that's right!" Barisoff interjected in Russian. "He was here a long time, he told me. He said he came when he was young, and they start mining. He was a soldier in the war, and he came here right after, maybe 1919. He tried mining, but he told me he was already too late, and then took over the little store from a woman who ran it. I don't know. Sometimes I don't believe everything he says. He told me he'd been a soldier, but then another time he told me he was happy he managed to avoid signing up. I think there are lots of people here who aren't honest about where they come from."

"I'll put him on the list. So, Mr. Barisoff, you wanted to expand your garden; you took all the stones and rocks off along that edge, but you stopped."

"I did. I didn't see anything unusual, except maybe the big pile of rocks. I didn't even notice the pile until I thought of expanding the garden. Someone who lived here before must have collected them from down by the lake and thought of using them and then didn't, so they just left them."

"How long ago did you do this, again?"

"I can't say exactly, but maybe ten days? I started clearing about three weeks ago, but then it got really cold again, so I stopped."

This caused Lane to glance around quickly. There was no calendar, and no clock on any visible wall space. Perhaps he had something in his little bedroom? Otherwise, he lived, she thought, in a natural rhythm of time almost inconceivable to her. Her time during the war had been marked out by the precision of the twenty-four-hour clock, which accounted for and marked every hour, each one dictating her every activity. It must, she thought, be a little like what we remember of childhood, when there was nothing but time suspended in place, marked by meals or birthdays or the coming of snow. She had tried to get back to that when she moved to King's Cove, but the tyranny of the clock developed during the war was hard to break.

Darling sat back, thinking. Everything would depend on what Ashford Gillingham, the local doctor who served as the pathologist, said. He found it difficult to imagine the gentle Mr. Barisoff would kill and bury someone in his garden, but he would have to keep an open mind. If that body had been there less than eight years, then he would have to consider even the unlikeliest possibilities.

"Thank you, Mr. Barisoff. I may have questions for you as we go."

Lane spoke in Russian just as Barisoff was pushing himself stiffly onto his feet.

"What did the rocks look like? I mean, were they in a row as you might place them if you are putting a border around the garden?"

Barisoff sat again with an "Oof." "No," he said. "They were piled up haphazardly. Do you think that is important?"

Darling looked inquiringly at Lane, who translated.

"And they have always been there since you moved into the cabin?"

Barisoff shrugged. "I guess so."

52

"Thank you. Could you ask Mr. Simpson to come in?" Darling asked.

"Sure, Inspector. I go fix house for Mr. Simpson; you talk to him."

When Barisoff had gone out the door, Darling sighed. "Your interest in the stones is?"

"I don't know, really. I was thinking of cairns. In Scotland they can be anything from trail markers to grave markers. I mean, if Mr. Simpson's people travelled here, perhaps they indicated either a trail or where good hunting is, for example."

"Or a grave marker," Darling mused. "It certainly had someone dead under it. That someone could be anyone, from a claim jumper from the nineties to someone from Barisoff's dark past who turned up to threaten him. I'll have to go through the missing persons lists and unsolved cases of yesteryear."

Lane smiled. "Don't you usually assign poor Ames to that sort of drudgery?" She paused. "I think . . ."

"Here we go," said Darling, smiling. "You think what?"

"Well, it's just that I think it is singular that a body is so close to where Simpson thinks he has ancestors buried. There's the entire expanse of the Selkirk Mountains available, but a body is plunked just there. Though, it could have been buried before this cabin was here," she added, musing.

"I'll give you 'singular,' and throw in 'coincidental' even, but depending on when Mr. Simpson's ancestors were buried, it's possible that whoever put our corpse there would be unlikely to have known there were burial grounds anywhere nearby. If it was buried before 1929, it will make it difficult to identify the remains."

"Something in your missing persons files? Unless the stones were a marker on the grave. Though he said there wouldn't be this many on a traditional grave of his people, so that does suggest it is not an Indigenous burial."

"I," said Darling emphasizing the word, "will ask Mr. Simpson. Come in," he said, standing at the sound of the gentle knock.

Tom Simpson ducked through the door and removed his hat, pushing his hair back with his free hand. "Sir, ma'am."

"Have a seat," Darling offered. "Miss Winslow will take notes, if that is all right?"

Simpson nodded and sat in the offered chair. He sat with his hands on his hat in his lap. Though he was tall, he seemed, Lane thought, like someone who was reluctant to take up a lot of space. Most men would have put the hat on the table in front of them.

"Mr. Simpson, what is your full name?" Darling asked.

"Thomas Simpson. Everyone calls me Tom."

"And you are American by birth, from Washington State?"

"I was born on this side, during the summer, but my family had already moved south. I guess I think of myself as American. I served in Europe with the US Army, 104th, private-specialist in communications. I signed up at Fort Lewis, in Washington."

"But you vacationed around here when you were a child? What is your age?"

"I'm thirty-one. My grandparents and great-grandparents lived here in the summer. Even after the move, my mother and grandmother still came in a canoe to fish in the lake before I was born."

"Your family had a home here?" Darling was struggling to grasp the arrangements that Simpson was describing.

Simpson smiled suddenly. "I see you're thinking of a house, with a chimney and a front door. I live in one of those down south. I was telling Miss Winslow, in the old times, people sometimes lived in houses dug into the ground, to protect them from the cold and snow. Like the one I showed her outside there."

"And when was the last time you yourself were here?"

"When I was a kid. Maybe I was five or six years old when we left the last time."

"So, around 1921, '22. And why did you come back just now?" Darling asked.

"I just had a yen to see it again, I guess. My grandmother always talked about how beautiful it was when she was young, how full of game and fish, lots of different roots and berries. How quiet it was, except for the conversations of animals. She said in the old days our ancestors could understand them. I don't know about that, but I just felt a need to come here after getting out of the army. I was happy here as a kid."

"I understand the impulse. I flew a bomber out of England. I can't say I miss it much."

Simpson smiled. "Nope, me either, but I got training as a radio operator. That's something, I suppose."

Darling moved on. "Do you have a tribal name?" he asked.

"We're called the Lakes People."

"Lake People," Darling said.

"Lakes," Simpson corrected. "We call ourselves Sinixt."

"It's been a bit of a nostalgia trip for you, then?"

Simpson nodded. "Yeah, something like that. I know other people live here now, but it still feels like a place I belong to. We think of ourselves as still being from here. Just because we're not here anymore does not make it any less the place of the Lakes People. That's why my parents used to come up with us. Of course, there are lakes and fish in Washington, but by coming back we are keeping our home alive. Our buried ancestors look after it for us."

Darling nodded. "You mentioned stones to mark burials."

"They did that in the old days. They might make a little arrangement of four stones to show a burial, or a mound with a little token of that person's life. A hat, boots, a favourite object, that sort of thing. I don't think they'd use a big pile of stones like that."

"So, nothing of this burial looks like any tradition in your tribe?"

Simpson shook his head. "I don't see how that shallow burial could be part of anyone's tradition."

CHAPTER FIVE

——————

THE CALL TO THE POLICE station came a little after ten. Lorenzo was hoping to speak with Inspector Darling, but when he learned Constable Terrell was assigned to the fire at his house, he asked to speak with him.

"Hello, Mr. Vitali. I'm just waiting for the pictures I took at your house this morning to be developed. I'm going to talk to the fire chief and show him what I found. We may want to go back to your house. Do you have new information?"

"Before you go back, can you come here? Is problem here."

"Not another fire, I hope."

"No. Not fire, no. But problem."

Terrell walked down the hill to where Lorenzo's restaurant sat, just above the train station on Baker Street. It was sandwiched between a tobacco store and a lodging house, and it had a crisp, welcoming feel. Vitali had painted the exterior of his restaurant a creamy white with a bright red door and had hung a new "Lorenzo's Italian Kitchen" sign just two years before. When Terrell arrived, he saw that the Closed card that hung inside the window of the door was still up.

Lorenzo opened the door before Terrell had a chance to touch the doorknob. "Come in, come in, Constable. I am Lorenzo; this is Signora Vitali."

"How do you do." Terrell removed his hat. "Signora Vitali," he said, nodding. "You say there is a problem?"

"Yes. We find this pushed under back door, here." Vitali walked through to the tiny kitchen and pointed at the door. Terrell took out his handkerchief to receive the envelope he was handed.

Using the handkerchief, Terrell turned it over, but nothing was written on either side of it. He pulled open the envelope where Mr. Vitali had slit it with a knife and unfolded one small piece of ordinary cheap foolscap. Printed on it in pencil were the words "You're not welcome here. Be careful. A friend."

"It's not very helpful, is it?" he remarked.

For the first time, Mr. Vitali managed a slight smile. "You are right. Not so helpful. Be careful of what?" Serious again, he added, "But with fire . . ."

"Exactly. Do you recognize this printing by any chance?"

Both Vitalis shook their heads. Mrs. Vitali shrugged. "We work hard, we try to fit in. We try to join Chamber of Commerce. They don't want us, but it is okay. We still smile, make food. People come. They don't care."

"You have tried to join the Chamber?" Terrell inquired. He had slid the envelope carefully into his pocket.

Lorenzo Vitali nodded. "Before, when we come, nobody

want Italian anybody because of war. I understand. I just leave it."

"But you haven't tried since?" This increased the possibility that his "outsider" status could be a factor in the fire and the note.

Vitali shook his head. "One time, this year. I think maybe now war is really over, and everything get normal." He shrugged. "Maybe is better this way. My English is getting better, but still not good. I don't know. Meetings, I don't think they are for me."

"Can you let me know right away if anything else strange happens? Notes, phone calls, any more attempts to damage your property? And I'd like you to get a good, strong porch light to leave on at night for the next little while. It might discourage any further trouble. In the meantime, we are collecting what we can."

"I know, thank you, Constable . . . sorry, forgot your name."

"Terrell."

"Yes, Constable Terrell. Maybe you know how it feel a little bit."

Terrell smiled ruefully and nodded, thinking of Vitali's neighbour Mrs. Smith. "Maybe I do, at that," he said.

LANE STOOD BY the police car next to Darling. The van had left with the remains, and Ames was finishing up with some photographs of the site. "What will you do now?"

"We'd better stop and have a word with that shopkeeper. What about you?" Darling asked.

Lane looked back at Barisoff's cottage. Smoke was

curling out of the chimney. Simpson's horse was visible through the trees, grazing. "I had been hoping for a nice chinwag with Mr. Barisoff. His son married, apparently, so it would have been nice to catch up, but I think I'll leave them to it and head back home. I can see from his industry that it's time to begin preparing our own garden." She was sure her neighbours must be at it already. Perhaps she would pop up and see Gladys Hughes, the doyenne of the most magnificent gardens in King's Cove. She and her elderly daughters worked tirelessly in the gardens and orchards, and still managed magnificent baking and root cellars full of preserved food. She smiled. "I was thinking of going up to see Gladys to see what she was up to with her garden, so as you can see, I've already found a way to get out of the work of getting started. Besides, it's baking day at their house. I might come home with a nice brown loaf."

Darling smiled and took her hand briefly. "Thank you for taking notes."

"You know me, I always like to help the police with their inquiries. It is interesting. The burial, if you can even call it that, of that poor man is so in contrast to the reverence with which Mr. Simpson views the burial of his ancestors, or indeed, with all the well-tended church cemeteries we fill with our dearly departed. I'm sure Gilly will find a wrongful death in this one."

"And if he does, you'll be the first to know." He leaned over and kissed her lightly and then turned to where he could see Ames just coming around the house. "Come on, Ames. Step on it, will you?" he said impatiently, giving her the slightest suggestion of a wink, and then got into the car.

INSIDE THE COTTAGE Barisoff and Simpson watched out the window. "He married to her," Barisoff explained.

Simpson nodded, his hands in his pockets. "Lucky him. She's a good person. A little sad, but good."

"HOW DO," SAID Berenson as Darling and Ames came into the store. He had stood up when he had seen through the small murky window that two men were getting out of the car. "What can I do for you fellows?"

In the barely adequate light, Darling sized up Berenson. He looked like an almost perfect satire of the rough mountain dweller Western adventure stories liked to portray. Overlong, unkempt hair, greasy beard, grimy red tartan wool shirt and all. His mouth was on the move with, he assumed, a gob of chewing tobacco, which was confirmed when Berenson spat into a receptacle behind the counter. The shop carried essentials, by the look of it, and Darling could hear a whirring coming from a back room, perhaps from a refrigerator. There were some wooden boxes on the counter with potatoes and some dispirited-looking apples, probably the last thing to winter over before the vegetable season began in earnest. He knew from Barisoff that local growers brought their excess produce to Berenson for sale here. The ancient gas pump outside clearly made up the bulk of his enterprise.

Darling pulled out his warrant card. "I'm Inspector Darling from the Nelson Police, and this is Sergeant Ames."

"Yeah. I remember you fellows from last year when that Russki fellow died. That good-looking woman was around using the phone earlier. She was involved last year too, if I remember rightly. Something up?"

Darling ignored this attempt at rustic bonhomie. "Yes, something is up. We're trying to get a sense of how long everyone living nearby has been established here. How long have you been running your general store and gas pump?"

"Well now, let's see." Berenson scratched his beard and looked up. "I come back to Canada after the war in '19 looking to get in on the silver mining. Staked a few claims, but I never had the luck, and it was all winding down by then anyway. Hacked around till about 1935 and then bought this little outfit. Took over from a lady who ran it for a spell."

"So, you've been around here since '35. Do you recall who lived in the cabin Mr. Barisoff occupies right now?"

Berenson tipped back his head and made a show of thinking. "Now then. Nope. Can't recall. Coulda been anyone. Coulda been empty. I don't recall. There were miners and prospectors living all over here, but I couldn't swear to that place. Rough-and-tumble bunch, though. More'n one fight at the saloon. Oh, there was a small saloon up in the middle of town, if you can even call it that. It's someone's house now. It got took over for the people keeping an eye on the Japs here during the war. Not that they needed it. They was better organized than anyone around here. Had schools and baseball teams up and running before you could say Jack Robinson."

Darling nodded. Until Gilly had a go with the remains, he really didn't have much sense of how long the body had been buried at the bottom of Barisoff's garden and what period they should be concerned about.

Ames stepped in. "Who are the other people who were here during that time?"

"You must think I'm some sort of telephone directory. You mean before the Japs and Russkis? I know Mrs. Gently up on the main road. She's been there since the early teens. Used to run a boarding house with her husband. He died with his heart a couple years ago. There was that Chinaman who ran a little eatery for the prospectors and the like. He married a white girl, not that nobody cared about that sorta thing up here. He retired and moved in with one of his kids when his wife died. They got a small farm just outside of town. After mining died down, we got some farmers moving in. Decent English stock. Settled the place down a bit, I hear. That's about it, except Wakada; he has a place a little out of town. Stayed on. I think you met him. Oh, and Stella Bisset. She lives back down the road by the lake. She's been here since Adam and Eve were playmates." He put his finger to his head and twisted it. "Not all there, if you know what I mean. She's the one I took the store over from. She was getting mighty forgetful, even then."

Ames turned to look out the window in the direction that would take them back down toward Kaslo. "She owned the store?"

"She did. Now I do. I take stuff down to her from time to time. Try to help."

"And the name of the Chinese man?" Ames had his pencil poised.

"Ken Chan."

"Anyone else? Were there Indians living here?" Ames asked.

Berenson snorted but didn't speak for a moment. "I ain't never seen one. This is no place for them."

"Oh, why is that?" Darling asked. Ames wondered if Berenson could see that slight narrowing of the eyes that was Darling's hallmark sign of distaste.

"Look around. It's white man's country. You can't stop progress. Anyway, they was never here. Nothing here in the old days. Just God's own country, waiting for us."

BACK IN THE car, Ames waited to start up the engine. "Where to now, sir?" But he received only silence as an answer.

Darling was thinking about Berenson and God's own country. Simpson, he thought, must feel the loneliest man on earth sometimes.

"I can't decide if we should question the old-timers or wait to see what Gilly says. If it's more than twenty or so years, we're going to have to come back; if it is less, we may have to interview some of the newer people," Darling said. "There's no hurry, I suppose."

Ames felt like this was heading in the direction of a drive back to town to await the post-mortem, so he made a move to turn on the car. "I gather you don't really like the Russian fellow for it?"

"I don't really have an opinion yet, and you shouldn't either." But Darling didn't think for a minute that Barisoff had done it. Apart from the gentle nature of the man himself, the remains looked to Darling's albeit untrained eye to have been placed there long before 1940, when Barisoff had taken possession of the property. "Home," he said abruptly. "We might as well wait for Gilly, his wonders to perform, so we know what we're dealing with." Watching the unchanging view of the tight forest they were passing, Darling thought about that old saying "You can't see the forest for the trees." Take the fire at the Vitalis', something that was front of mind for him because of the hurt it so evidently caused his friend. The problem was, he reflected, that you needed to understand the trees in order to understand the forest. What did an individual act of vandalism add up to on its own? With a surge of anxiety, the question came to him: What more might happen that he could not prevent?

"HMM," SAID MCAVITY, the fire chief, sucking on his teeth and looking at one of the four photos Terrell had brought him. They were standing before the open door of the fire hall, taking advantage of a momentary burst of sun, which had caused the front of the city fire truck to gleam in the obscurity inside. "You from down east?" he asked suddenly, looking up from the pictures.

"Nova Scotia, yes," Terrell answered, surprised. "Yourself?"

"I thought I heard an accent. We Maritimers gotta stick together. New Brunswick, myself. Came out after the Great War. It felt just too sad back there then." He smiled suddenly. "My great-granduncle started an outfit that makes fire hydrants. Doesn't that beat all?" He went back to the photos. "Well, from this here," he pointed, "I'd say the locus of the fire was right here, on the siding under this little porch—you see how it has a centre and a sort of tail on it? From this I'd say it was done on purpose, without a doubt. If you want, I can go up and have a look-see. These snaps are pretty good, but it might not hurt."

"I'd appreciate that, sir, just to be really sure of

65

everything. I saw where the guy ran off after setting it, out the back gate and into the alley. The dabs on the handle of the gas can were very blurry. Nothing to be learned from them. I suppose the person would have worn gloves, though I'm inclined to think it's a kid. There was a footprint in the garden, biggish boot, but not too deep. I figured a skinny kid with big feet."

McAvity nodded. "Whose house is this again?"

"Lorenzo Vitali. He and his wife run a restaurant near the station. I've heard the boss talk about how much he likes it."

Frowning, the fire chief shook his head and looked again at the pictures, one after another, as if an explanation would jump out on this second perusal. "Now why would anyone want to burn out Lorenzo Vitali? Runs the only decent restaurant in town. You want to eat there, trust me. Took my daughter there the other day for her birthday. It also would have been my anniversary. It would have been thirty-five years in harness, but the wife died a few years ago. Anyway, Lorenzo even . . ." McAvity hesitated and glanced at Terrell. "Well, it was a nice dinner, anyway." No need to tell a policeman that Lorenzo had given them a discreet but completely illegal little glass of bubbly.

"I'm sorry about your wife, sir. That's a great loss. I can't imagine being married five years, let alone thirty-five."

"One for the ladies, are you?" McAvity winked at Terrell, his head tilted.

"No, sir." Terrell felt a bit embarrassed by the suggestion. "I mean with the war and my work, there's not been much opportunity. So, you can't think of why someone would want to go after Mr. Vitali?"

"I don't want to be naive. I've seen some pretty sorry excuses for committing arson. Not everyone here is playing with a full deck of cards, if I'm honest. Too much time at the Legion, too much time in the mines, one blow on the head too many in a fight at the mill. I never understand why someone thinks setting something alight is the answer to a problem. But I don't see why anyone would want to hurt them—unless they don't like Italians. Plenty of that going around as well. Here, you got time to go up there with me just now and have a look?"

"Sure thing. Let me hop down to the restaurant. It won't take a moment. They found a note shoved through the restaurant door this morning—a warning note saying they weren't welcome and telling them to be very careful."

CHAPTER SIX

APRIL MCAVITY STARED OUT THE window of the café, her mind in a wander. It was a rare moment when there were no customers, somewhere between the last lunch seating and the few old ladies who made their weekly outing to shop and then stop by for their cup of tea and some pie. She mostly enjoyed it when they came in. They were loudly chatty and gossipy and patted her arm affectionately and called her "lovey" and "pet," and seemed delighted to have a plate of pie placed before them. The only thing she didn't like was when they got horrible about someone. Still, she'd love to reach a stage of life that was so simple that a piece of apple pie would be the greatest delight on offer. Maybe she would not make it to that age. Her mother hadn't. She took the comb out of her near-blond hair and regathered it, scooping it into an attractive wave above her right eye, anchoring it on her head with a businesslike shove. It wasn't dissatisfaction she was feeling, exactly, but a kind of wanderlust. A new place, or a new job, or even a new way to see what she already had. She wondered if she should have gone to university. Her father had told her he would pay her way, but he'd been unable to hide his relief when she had decided to stay. University wasn't going to give her quite what she wanted. She had once joked with Ames that she would like to join the police. They wouldn't be much interested, she thought, but she looked down the street toward the station and wondered rebelliously why she shouldn't. It certainly might go some way to explain why she had ever dated Ames. Nice guy. It had surprised her when her father had shaken his head, his pipe poised and pumping out a heady tobacco smell on the porch of their house by the lake on a summer evening. "He's a lightweight. I can't see much in this for you," he'd said. He was too kind to give much more of an opinion on the matter of her beaux, but she had seen very quickly that he was right. Ames was three years older than she was, but she was ten years more mature. The business with Violet Hardy had been almost a relief, not that it stopped her from never letting him forget it. And now look, Violet had dropped him. Violet, April decided, was too much of a heavyweight for him. And then, to her amazement, he had picked up with Tina Van Eyck. It was like the three bears: third time lucky. Tina was never going to be easy to deal with, but April knew she was the right woman for Sergeant Ames. He'd grow with her.

She was just going to check the pies were cut and ready to go when she saw Constable Terrell making his way up the street from the direction of the train station. Flushing, she turned and busied herself with wiping down the tables again. She knew the cook, Al, was sitting out on the back step, smoking a cigarette and reading the paper, and would stay there until he heard her calling an order. She was relieved. He'd begun to make the odd crack about Terrell.

She could no longer disguise from herself that she quite liked Terrell. Her good-natured banter with him covered up some churning feeling, the strength of which had surprised her. What had surprised her even more was that when she thought of him, among the increasingly romantic, imagined accidental meetings with him, she saw herself standing beside him, notebook in hand, attending a burglary. Nah. They probably wouldn't let married people work at the same station.

"Cripes, now I've married him," she muttered. Wouldn't that be a howdy-do with her father! Wouldn't it, she reflected sadly, be a howdy-do with nearly everyone in town, judging by some of the opinions she heard uttered by her old ladies. It was then that she resolved never to give in to her feelings, so that he might be saved the embarrassment of the town's disapproval.

WHEN LANE BUMPED up the King's Cove road and pulled open her big metal gate to drive the car onto the grass beside the barn, it was early enough to hope for a cup of restorative afternoon tea from the Armstrongs at the post office, just through the little stand of birch trees that separated her property from theirs. She parked the car and looked up at the skeletal trees. In another month they would be covered with a lacy veil of that fresh, vibrant green that was the spring's harbinger of the summer to come. The lake in the distance below the hamlet sparkled in the late afternoon sun.

She sighed with utter contentment that this little corner should be hers—well, theirs; she hurriedly included Darling. And in the next instant she wondered if it really was, and if it had all belonged to a people who had vanished, leaving nothing but spirit behind. She imagined people hunting in the forests behind her and up in the mountain that loomed above King's Cove. Fishing where there was now a busy wharf. Was the meadow that she loved so much on the way to Angela and Dave Bertolli's magnificent cabin full of edible and medicinal plants and roots that she knew nothing about?

She crossed the little wooden bridge over the gully, a couple of planks really, put there by Lady Armstrong, the previous owner of her beloved house. She was Kenny's long-deceased mother and had developed a reputation for flinging open the windows in the attic. Smiling, Lane realized that with the weather warming up, that ghostly lady would soon be back on the job. No amount of fiddling with the latches on the windows seemed to prevent her activities. Not that Lane minded, being a lover of fresh air herself, and she did not begrudge Lady Armstrong staying on in her beautiful house in her spectral form.

HYSTERICAL BARKING AND wiggling greeted Lane when she arrived at the post office. Alexandra, the resident Westie terrier, was helping Kenny move something in the wheelbarrow toward the garden. It looked like dirt.

"Compost," he said by way of greeting. He took seriously

his self-assigned role of helping Lane become a better gardener. "Good time to shift it onto the beds. Give it a turn."

"Ah," said Lane. Perhaps tomorrow. She followed Kenny through the high latticed fence into the garden, to dutifully watch the procedure. While he pitchforked the dark clumps of compost onto the garden, Alexandra sniffed Lane's boots.

"What have you been up to today? Heard your car leaving before noon," Kenny asked.

"Well," said Lane, drawing the word out a bit.

This caused Kenny to stop and look at her, his eyes slightly narrowed. He had a nose for intrigue, and Lane had provided plenty of it since she'd moved to King's Cove. Clearly Lane had something to tell them.

"I believe the kettle is on," he said, turning back to his task. He scooped out the final clump, tossing it a couple of times to break it up, and threw it across the garden. Lane smiled after him. She bet the kettle was always on in their snug little kitchen.

They went into the house through the veranda and then into the tiny hallway that passed the bedroom and the formality that was the little-used parlour and presented themselves in the kitchen. The kettle not only was on, but had boiled, and the water was now steeping tea in the brown teapot. Three cups were on the table, complete with saucers, a little civilized gesture Eleanor adopted when someone stopped by. On a plate was a satisfyingly generous pile of oatmeal lemon cookies.

"I saw you come across," Eleanor said with her enormous smile. "I assume Kenny has been boring you with compost. Come, take the weight off."

Lane settled into her usual chair with a sigh. It was a rattan chair with a high back and an undetermined number of pillows that had been squished down with time by the Armstrongs and their guests. The fire, which always seemed to be burning in the wood stove, warmed the tiny kitchen. A long window along the sink framed the forest just past their root cellar and small orchard. A little blue corner of the lake was just visible.

"She's got something," Kenny said, indicating Lane with a lift of his chin as he took off his thick sweater and hung it on the nail by the door.

Lane slipped out of her own wool jacket, poured milk into her cup, and spooned in a couple of generous teaspoons of sugar. "This is just what I was hoping for," she said. "When will you teach me to make these lovely biscuits?"

"When you stop gallivanting around," said Eleanor, the tea strainer and pot poised over Lane's cup. "So?"

"You remember old Mr. Barisoff, up in New Denver? I told you about him."

"The poor old Doukhobor fellow who lost his friend in that dreadful murder at the hot springs last year? Nothing's happened to him?" Eleanor asked, pausing her pouring.

"Thank you. No. Not to him. I went up to visit him because I haven't seen him since last winter. He wasn't there when I arrived, so I followed a path out to a meadow where I met the most extraordinary man. He'd come up on horseback from across the border. He said he was there to check on his ancestors."

"An Indian fellow?"

"Yes. He said he was from the Lakes People. I had no

idea the whole area had once had a local Indigenous population. I've never seen any such people since I've been here. It makes me see everything with new eyes. Those posters I looked at in England before I decided to come here never showed any original people, except for in some parts of Canada—quite clichéd, now I think about it. Pictures of people in feathers. You would be forgiven for thinking it was just countryside as far as the eye could see just waiting for us to come and develop it."

Kenny nodded. "When I was a lad, you used to see them come sometimes in their canoes, fishing. Quite intriguing, really. Now there was a name for those boats. A fish name. Barracuda? No. Wait. Sturgeon, that was it! Sturgeon-nose canoes. Goodness, I haven't thought about that in ages. They were even seen a couple of times after the Great War, in the twenties. I never knew where they came from, exactly, because you didn't see many around here, but I always wondered if they sorta belonged here."

"You know, I had such a sense of all this just being 'ours.' Our orchards, our houses, our lake, our towns, even. The man, he's called Tom Simpson, told me that the original people were, effectively, chased off."

"That must be true," Eleanor said thoughtfully. "I didn't come till after the Great War, of course, but there were mines and railroads and farms and lord knows what all. Not much room for people who make a living hunting."

"It made me think of our housemate, your dear mama, Lady Armstrong. She has not left the place she loved. All those people who were here before—perhaps they too have not really left."

"Yes, I rather hoped Mother would leave you alone, but she's very persistent," Kenny remarked, sloshing more tea into his cup.

"What interests me is that her presence there says, as nothing else can, 'This was mine,' or even, 'This is still mine, even though I'm gone.' It's a reminder that we oughtn't forget. If she is here in spirit, perhaps people just never really leave. Where they were is always a little bit theirs."

"Well then, thank heaven whatever other spirits are around aren't all as much of a nuisance as Mother with her window opening."

"Mr. Simpson's ancestors' burial places could well be under someone's garden now."

Kenny nodded and handed a bit of oatmeal biscuit down to Alexandra, who'd been waiting with increasing impatience. "Why not? There was a time there were no gardens, and in the scheme of things, not too long ago."

"Exactly. For example, Mr. Barisoff told my husband he'd only been there since '40, and there was a much smaller garden there, put in by the previous owner."

Eleanor eyed her with a slight frown. "Told Inspector Darling? Now, why would he be telling him that? What was the inspector doing talking to your Mr. Barisoff? Is there something you're not saying?"

Lane squirmed slightly. This was always the critical moment. She shouldn't really talk about her husband's work, but on the other hand she was constitutionally unable to keep anything from the Armstrongs, and anyway, she'd been there with Simpson and Barisoff when the skeleton appeared. A skeleton of someone who had been long dead.

Kenny and Eleanor leaned imperceptibly forward, and even Alexandra cocked her head slightly and was looking closely at Lane, her ears up.

She described the finding of the skeletal foot where there had been a pile of rocks that Barisoff had moved to expand the garden. "It looked as though an animal had dug about, and so when Mr. Barisoff went to clear a bit of the soil, there it was. It gave us all quite a turn, I can tell you."

"Well, I'll be!" Eleanor exclaimed. She frowned. "But might that not be the relative your Mr. Simpson was looking for?"

"He said not. Proper burials are much more formal. It looks like this person was just put in a relatively shallow grave and had stones piled on him."

"'Shallow grave.' If that is not synonymous with 'murder,' I don't know what is," declared Kenny with satisfaction.

"We don't absolutely know that," cautioned Lane. "There's the post-mortem to be done."

"Oh, please!" scoffed Kenny. "The question really is, how are you going to be involved?"

"Not at all," Lane said firmly. "Nothing to do with me. I shall provide nourishing meals for the inspector, and he will sort it out."

"Ha!" Kenny said. He leaned back in his chair and put his feet up on the fender of the stove and ate a speculative oatmeal cookie. "You know, there was a murder over a claim out there at the Bluebell mine in Riondel. I wouldn't be at all surprised if it was something like that. There was a lot of hope that there might be gold around there in the

Slocan Valley, and the place was flooded with prospectors and charlatans and mining companies. Lots of silver, not as much gold. I expect bumping off the competition was all in a day's work."

"I imagine poor Sergeant Ames is even now going through the dusty archives of unsolved cases for the area," Lane said.

AT HOME, LANE stood in the waning light, looking over her garden, but she was not thinking of tossing compost or turning it over. She was thinking about her day, which seemed now to have been centuries long. It had taken her to some distant past before all the European settlers, when a whole history was unfolding among the original people who had been here for eons, people about whom she knew nothing. The anxieties that had beset her, not only about her bad night but about her sudden reluctance to expose herself to Darling's sympathy, had been completely obliterated by the events at Mr. Barisoff's and her new unfolding view of her world.

It reminded her, as nothing else could, that being distracted by something important prevented one from dwelling on things. They'd said that about London during the bombing, she remembered. That during the worst of it, people's mental well-being got better because they were so focused on survival and helping one another.

She went to her little writing desk, pulled out her notepad, and turned her mind to Tom Simpson, very much alive, and began to write.

No darkness like the present darkness
Night sweeps a cloak over history
But the spirits stay on

Ghost fishermen on spirit waters
Shadow hunters' quiet whispers
They've said they are all but gone

But right here, sons and daughters
Alive as you or me, the People linger
Keeping an eye on the dawn

Should she repeat "darkness" twice in one line? She read it over and decided that for now it could stay. It might reveal itself as a mistake later. She hovered over "linger." "History" and "whispers" had some sibilant way of relating, if not actually rhyming, but "linger" wasn't even making an effort. Is it "linger" she wanted? Or something about returning? Still no "s." Deciding that at least she was happy about the third lines in each stanza, she pushed the paper into the drawer where it could mingle with her other ham-handed poems. Perhaps they would exchange ideas and solve the problem for her if she ignored them in her usual manner.

Darling would be home soon. She got up and stretched. She wouldn't, she resolved, bother Darling with her episodes at all. He had enough on his plate. As if her thoughts had called him, she heard his car coming down the road. She had left the gate open so that he could pull in behind her, and she went up the slight hill by the barn to welcome him back.

He got out of his car and removed his hat, smiling. "Hello, you," he said, pulling her into an embrace. It was, she thought, nestling in, smelling his skin, the closest thing to home she could imagine.

CHAPTER SEVEN

"I WAS HOPING YOU WERE PLANNING for leftover meat-loaf," Darling said, standing in the kitchen rubbing his hands together. "It is what I have been dreaming of all the way home."

"How well you already know my failings," Lane said. She pulled open the fridge and took out the remains of the previous day's meatloaf. "Here, cut this into suitable chunks. Will we have toast? We had some this morning. Is that too much of a good thing?"

"Is there ever an occasion that is not improved by toast? Do you want to trust me with it? I made a bit of a hash of it this morning."

She put down the jar of beans she had acquired from Mrs. Hughes's root cellar and looked at him. "That was my fault, I'm afraid. I . . . I could see you were a little worried about me."

He pushed the meatloaf aside and said, "Come, sit down. There's something I want to say." He took her hands. "I know you have bad nights sometimes. I knew that before. I'm surprised, considering what you went through in the war, that you don't have more of them. You are the most courageous person I know. You may tell me about them, or not tell me. They are your bad nights. Equally, you may wake me up at three in the morning and ask me to play gin rummy. Or drink rum. Or gin. The one thing you must not do is add concern about what I might think to what you must already bear."

"I think I'm worried that you will be overly sympathetic, and I don't feel I could bear that, but I don't know why, really. I'm ashamed of being such a ninny, perhaps. Being unhappy was not well tolerated in my household."

"More fool your household," he said. "Were you ashamed of it before you married me?"

"No. I don't think so. I thought it was just the wages of what I'd done during the war. I thought it would eventually go away. In fact, I thought it had, as I've been free of it since the wedding. I suppose I must feel that it is churlish of me to have unhappy things happen when I am so happy now."

"I am, of course, the most perfect husband, but I don't think you can expect that sort of thing to go away just because you've married someone. These *are* the wages of war. I've seen it in others. I get quite bad nightmares myself sometimes, about the crash." Darling's Lancaster bomber had been shot down in the spring of 1943 in occupied France. He didn't know the full extent of her war work, though she'd confided during their honeymoon that she felt herself responsible for the death of a French contact.

"What strikes me as so interesting is that I was feeling

a little oppressed about the whole thing in the morning, but from the minute I got out of myself and was sitting in that beautiful meadow, and then meeting Mr. Simpson, it is as though nothing could ever bother me."

"You are passing lightly over the fact that you found another body," he said, his eyebrows raised. "Which poor Gilly has to interpret for us. It is interesting to me that you had to go digging about in Barisoff's garden to find it. Don't you think that is taking the whole thing too far? I'm sure poor Mr. Barisoff must find you an absolute menace. The only times you ever see him, people have died."

Lane cut slices of bread and handed them to Darling to toast, and then pried the lid off the jar of beans. "I hardly think it's fair to say that man died because I visited Barisoff with a box of chocolate biscuits. He's been dead for years. How many years, by the way? Shall I put a little oil and vinegar on these and we can eat them as a salad?"

"You're shocking, you know that, trying to pry into a case by hiding your probing under a question about a bean salad. Yes, to the salad. As it happens, Gilly is going to spend more time with our dead friend tomorrow. Apparently, it's not that easy to ascertain how old a corpse might be once it's skeletal, unless he or she happens to have tucked a page of the calendar for July 12, 1918, into his or her pocket."

"Kenny says he wouldn't be surprised to learn someone had been shot over a claim. Apparently, there was a murder over a claim in the early years over in Riondel."

Darling buttered the toast. "I'm delighted. You've involved the Armstrongs, and they already have some theories. I should be able to let some of my men go. Terrell perhaps, because he's the latest in, or, no, better Ames. He's a sergeant and he's costing us more money."

AMES HAD INDEED been assigned to go through unsolved cold cases, but in order to put off the moment when he'd have to go into the dusty basement file room, he turned instead to Gilly's little morgue, and was standing in the doorway with his hands in his pockets watching the pathologist at work.

"Well, what do you think?" he asked by way of greeting.

Gilly, who was painstakingly lifting frayed shards of cloth and piling them into a white enamelled metal dish, did not look up. "Why are you people always in such a hurry? I can tell you certainly that he is dead and has been dead a long time. If you've nothing else?"

"Oh. Yes. Right. I have to go see if he makes an appearance in any missing persons files. I was just wondering how far back I should go."

Gilly straightened up and gazed at his prize. "Fair question. I'd start before the Great War, see what's there. It may not be that old. But best to be safe. Maybe even end of the last century."

Ames turned on the light in the basement file room, relieved that it was not as dusty as the last time he'd been in, also looking into a skeletal cold case, as it happened. Credit where credit was due, he thought, O'Brien had made a thorough job of cleaning the place and making sure the files were in order, including, he was pleased to see, a separate drawer of unsolved cases. The light, an overhead bulb with a metal shade over it, did a scant job of lighting the cold-case section, which was in the last cabinet in the lowest drawer. He pulled it open and was surprised to see only a handful of files. Curious, he counted and found there were eleven, going back, he assumed, to the pioneering days of Nelson.

He pulled out the first file, dated 1889, and found it was indeed a suspected homicide. A young man of twenty-four had been found dead in a burned-out cabin southwest of town. Harry Browning, from Sudbury, Ontario. Profession: prospector. The brief report indicated that the doctor who looked at the remains suspected that the victim had been hit on the head and then left in the cabin when it was set alight. An added note a year later indicated that no next of kin had been reached.

"Poor guy," muttered Ames. "Lived alone, died alone." He pulled out the rest of the files and moved to the small wooden table that was more directly under the light, pulled up the chair provided for the purpose, and started going through them. It was a discouraging exercise. By file nine, he'd found three unsolved cases of missing children, two unsolved murders, and various unresolved burglaries. He opened the tenth file and was rewarded by the unsolved disappearance of a man. "April 1921. Forty-one-year-old Samuel Turner reported missing by his wife Edith Ann Turner when he did not return from a business trip." The signature of the officer who attended initially was unreadable. It took him a moment. He was still reading about the details of the later searches that were undertaken, the people interviewed before the man was given up for lost, when his eyes swung back up to the top of the page, where they remained, riveted. He recognized that name.

"Hot dog!" he said aloud. He put the Turner file to one side, quickly glanced at the last file, the theft of pay packets from a local construction company, and scooped the files into a pile and replaced them, leaving out only his prize to be taken upstairs.

"Sir," he said excitedly, standing in Darling's doorway. He was holding the file aloft.

Darling, who'd been waiting to hear from Gilly about the skeleton and was completing his written report, was startled by this sudden burst of enthusiasm from his subordinate.

"Do you have to do your puppy impersonation right outside my door? What is it?"

Needing no other invitation, Ames swept in and, taking the unoffered seat in front of Darling, plunked the file onto the desk. "Remember that book that got swiped from the bookstore, that one about pioneering life? Well, its author, one Samuel Turner, aged forty-one, was reported missing in May of 1921 and was never found. What do you think of that? I bet that's our man!"

"Evidently I don't have to think," Darling said with cool reserve. "You seem to have done all the thinking for me." He reached over and took the file and read through the two pieces of paper therein.

Darling shrugged and gave a grudging nod. "The report is very unforthcoming. It doesn't say where he was going on business."

"Exactly, sir!" said Ames enthusiastically. "*Ergo* he might indeed have gone up to New Denver. Plenty of business to be done there for a railway baron, what with all the mining and so on."

"*Ergo*, Ames, is applied to circumstances where there is a solid conclusion to be made. There is nothing solid or logical to suggest that is where he went when the whole of British Columbia—indeed, the whole continent—was at his disposal. And besides, by '21 the mining boom was pretty well dying out."

"I know, sir, but I mean, we have a whole dead skeleton and a missing person's file. We don't get that much crime around here. Let's say this Turner goes up to the New Denver area to . . . I don't know . . . start something new, a gold mine, say, and . . . and he meets someone, an old enemy, and they have an argument and Turner gets killed. He's buried in a shallow grave and that's that. Miss Winslow finds him twenty-seven years later."

Darling frowned at the file. "It doesn't have to be an old enemy. It could be a brand new one. Someone who thought he was jumping a claim, as you say, or with whom he had an argument."

Satisfied that Darling wasn't dismissing his theory out of hand, Ames pressed on. "Let's say that fellow downstairs is Turner—*was* Turner. According to his biography in the introduction to that book, he's a mover and shaker. He has interests in all the local industries. He's been involved in moving ore with his railways, but maybe he was looking into new land acquisition for logging, or even to get in on the mining boom himself. What do these mogul types look into?"

"Is there a photograph of the man in the book?"

"Good point, sir." Ames jumped up and went next door to his own office. He'd thrown the Turner book on his desk, secretly hoping he wouldn't have to really read it at all. He could not, he thought, think of anything more boring than a local history of mining development or whatever it turned out to be. Now he was revising his thinking.

Leafing through the book, he walked back to Darling's door and triumphantly held the book open. A photograph of a very young Samuel A. Turner shaking hands with someone in front of a bunting-covered timber railway station taken in 1909. Behind the two principals, rows of moustached miners in battered hats were crowding in, grinning, and leaning on shovels and picks. A locomotive engine puffed behind them all, like a dragon that had gathered them together for that moment, with a view to consuming them when the photographer was finished. Behind them, the splintered edges of the forests that had been sliced through to put this behemoth to work looked like an open wound. The steepness of the mountains around them was testament to the work, skill, and ingenuity it must have taken to accomplish this bit of "progress."

"How the West was won, eh, sir?"

Darling gazed at the picture. "Have you read this book?"

"Well, no. I . . ."

"Hop to it, then. See if you can figure out who his enemies were. He looks like the sort of man who wouldn't spare the horses if he thought someone stood in his way. And get down to the bookstore to find out how Mrs. Treadwell came into possession of this man's biography."

Darling sat musing for a few minutes after Ames had

left. It was the ragged edge of the forest in the photograph that occupied his thoughts. Those early days of local development. He was born and brought up in Vancouver and had little experience of these elemental industries that had gone into making up the province. The photograph seemed to capture the sheer destruction that was required to accommodate these early endeavours. Even Nelson, mellowed no doubt from its early beginnings, must have started out like this, with a kind of determined brute force, the sure conviction that the wilderness would submit to the will of pioneering men. Wouldn't leave much room for anyone who was already here.

He thought about the missing Turner. It was a good place to make people disappear, this part of the world. Steep mountains, a myriad of waterways, dense forests. Whoever killed that man in his shallow grave was, he decided, essentially lazy. He could have put the body in any bit of nearby forest—it would have been unlikely to ever be discovered—or put him in a sack with some rocks and thrown him into any lake. Instead, he buries him in the back garden. Or, if that wasn't the killer's house, buries him in someone else's back garden. Unless the killing took place before 1929, when Barisoff's cabin was supposedly built. Then it might just have been a bit of nearby forest. Still, the property was close enough to the community that the killer risked discovery. Did this indicate the killer was in a hurry to get rid of the body? Darling harrumphed. Of course, it had not been discovered, so the killer had been perfectly safe. He had no doubt that this killer, like all the grasping, desperate miners and railway magnates of the earliest part of the century, had disappeared into the mists of history. But he wasn't the only one. Disappearance seemed a way of life. What about all the people who must have lived here long before any Europeans came to mine the nascent riches of the ancient mountains?

There was Tom Simpson, quietly making his way up the valleys from across the border on a horse. Where were all his people if it was the case that they once called this territory their own? For the first time since he had come to Nelson, this new knowledge of an apparently once-thriving people struck him with a kind of hollow sadness.

Colville, Washington, four days earlier

"YOU'VE ONLY BEEN back a few months, and now you want to go off again?" She shook her head angrily. "We can't seem to keep a man in this house. What about your grandma and brother and sister?" His mother had remarried just before the war but had had the misfortune to lose her second husband to complications of diabetes. "What with the war and all, there hasn't been a grown man around here since George died." Mary Simpson sat at the wooden table opposite her oldest son, nursing a cup of coffee in her hands.

Tom Simpson struggled to find an answer. After he'd demobilized in '46, he'd travelled slowly around the country, staying finally with his army buddy Jeff Sanders in Spokane, rather than face coming home. She was right. He didn't really know why, except that he sensed he would have trouble leaving the war behind, and he hadn't wanted to bring it into the house with his little brother and sister. He wasn't sure he was ready even now. Instead, he spoke to what he thought might be worrying her. "I just got my army pension. There's more than enough there till I get back in a couple of weeks. And I've got that job lined up in Colville at the radio station."

His mother looked out at the yellowing field. "Your grandmother probably put this idea in your head, I know, but I don't want you to go. Now Angie even wants to go with you. She thinks it will be her time to find her spirit."

He smiled. "Nice try. Tell her she has to be alone for that. Anyway, I won't even be a couple of weeks. I just want to see. Gran wants to send me, and Rocky wants to go." He gestured with his chin toward the outside where his brown gelding stood snoozing in the burst of early springtime sun.

"This is why I didn't want you signing up. Now you've got the wandering bug worse than ever. You'll never settle down. You could never keep still as a child. Always wondering what is over the next hill."

Simpson looked down and thought that she was right. The idea of being alone in the mountains, moving through the solitude, filled him with longing.

"I don't think you can blame the US armed forces for that. How many times did we go back and forth when I was little?"

His mother sniffed and drank some coffee. "I never believed in that. Your grandparents were full of dreams, always living in the past. We have enough to keep us busy here at home. If I hadn't gone with them that time, you would have been born right here, and you wouldn't be full of these crazy ideas."

"Grandma says—"

"I know what your grandmother says. And I know she's probably right, before you say anything. But I was born here. I belong here."

"But that's the point, Ma. Here is there. It is all part of the land our people lived in. She says it doesn't matter about the dam, or the farmers, or the border. The land that holds us is still there. Its heart doesn't change, and it is happy when we go back. I just feel like this is important."

"Oh my God! Listen to yourself. Well, fine then. When are you and that head full of stars leaving? I'll pack some food for you." Mary Simpson finished the last of her coffee and pushed her chair back. The sound of the legs scraping on the floor seemed like the only real thing in that moment. She wanted to believe as her son did. It reminded her of what she felt about going to Mass. She'd look around the church on Sunday, at the priest lifting the Eucharist, listen to the sound of his Latin that, in her mind, always turned to strange English words, and think, They all believe. What must it be like to believe, to let everything go and trust that God is watching out for us? She saw little sign of it. Since she had been made to go away to school, her life had been a long lesson in "We just gotta look out for ourselves."

Her son patted her shoulder. "Thanks, Ma. I'll leave first thing, so I'll pack tonight." He glanced again at Rocky, who lifted his head in an abrupt motion as if he had heard his master's thoughts. In his room, Tom imagined himself riding north before first light, and he could scarcely contain his desire to be on the way. He felt guilty about leaving them, about how badly he wanted to go, but the need he felt was almost overwhelming. If he was superstitious, he'd almost think there was some fate waiting there for him.

He thought about his mother. She treated him differently, somehow, since he'd been back from the war. As if she recognized that she didn't have such a hold on him, as if she knew the war had changed him into someone just out of her reach. He had tried to reassure her, when she asked, that he was fine, no harm done. And in large measure, it was true. His friend Sanders had been wounded and, though he never said it in so many words, the few times he'd visited him, Simpson could tell his friend was a mess. He was thin, with hollow circles under his eyes, had lost that ready laughter, and no longer greeted him in the old way, "Hey, Indian, what's up?" He suspected Sanders was drinking too much. He'd say, "Hey, Irish, what's up?" when he saw him next, but he knew already nothing would be up. Sanders had had a wife at the start of the war, but she was long gone. But Sanders always seemed happy to see Tom. "At least you got people on that reservation you live on. Look around. If you didn't come by, I'd be invisible."

It wasn't this sort of battle fatigue, as he'd heard it called—though to him those words were too mild for what he saw in Sanders—that he himself had. The strain of fighting had taken the form of a longing for silence and solitude. Would he always be like this? He suddenly imagined taking his siblings, seven-year-old Angie and five-year-old Bobby, north with him, the way his grandparents had taken him. It was ridiculous, he knew. He hoped he would not always be plagued with this restlessness. But that night, as he closed his eyes, he thought about his mother saying he had a head full of stars. He didn't tell her he sometimes had a head full of gunfire. He thought about being in a meadow, the stars whirling in the sky on a moonless night, and he decided it was just about the most beautiful thing he could have in his head.

CHAPTER EIGHT

TERRELL STOOD WITH HIS HANDS behind his back watching McAvity investigating the burned area behind Vitali's house.

"He's damn lucky he woke up," the fire chief commented. "These houses go up like fireworks once they get going."

"I know. There were some pretty awful fires in the community where I grew up. Sometimes wood stoves, sometimes arson." He didn't tell McAvity why there was arson.

Turning to look at him, the fire chief nodded several times and chewed his bottom lip for a moment. "Well. It was arson, and I guess it will be up to you guys to find out who did it and why. I don't have much patience with people who do this sort of thing. You see graffiti, sometimes, and there was a fire in '41 aimed at a Chinese fellow. The world is changing. People just gotta accept that." He took out a handkerchief to wipe his hands.

"You're suggesting someone set fire to his house because he's Italian?" Terrell asked. They had started to walk to the back gate with a view to making their way back down the hill.

"It certainly seems possible. Lots of folks are still upset about the way the town is changing. Or they wonder why they fought against them in the war and now they're here dishing up spaghetti."

"So, it could be a vet, or maybe the teenaged son of a vet whose father didn't fare so well and resents the erstwhile enemy being successful?" Terrell mused. "If I'm honest, I can't see a vet setting someone's house on fire."

"Not in their right mind maybe, but if things have gone badly and they've been drinking all night? Out of control and filled with bitterness and envy. In fact, I wouldn't doubt that whoever did it had been drinking, because they did such a poor job of it."

"Here's the thing, though. Mr. Vitali and his wife came here before the war. That's a long time. Why now, suddenly?"

"Because whoever it is has tried to make a go of it, has failed abysmally, and looks around and sees an Italian making good. It wouldn't matter to him how long that Italian had been here. He's Italian, that's all that matters. People don't make sense, believe me. I see it every day in my job."

"I know just what you mean," Terrell said.

They'd arrived on Baker Street, and McAvity nodded toward the café. "Got time for a cup of coffee and a slice of whatever they have there today? My daughter April can dish something up for us. You know her?"

"Yes, sir. I didn't realize she was your daughter. We visit the café quite a bit. In fact, I think she knows all our orders by heart now." Terrell looked at the door to the police station, already thinking of how he'd do up his notes, and then shrugged. "Sure. I can take a few minutes."

April looked up to see her father and Constable Terrell coming into the café and her heart sank. What on earth could have brought her father and Terrell together? Then she gave herself a sharp mental rap on the knuckles. Neither the constable nor her father could tell from just looking at her how she felt.

"Good afternoon, April," said Terrell, waiting politely for the chief to pick which side of the booth he wanted.

McAvity dropped into the booth with an "Oof." "Hi there, Pumpkin. This young fellow and I were just looking at a fire up the road. We could use some of that coffee and a piece of pie right about now."

"Hi, Daddy. Do you expect me not to tell Grandma that you're eating pie? That could cost you something. Good morning, Constable. I do have apple pie today."

"Very nice. See this, Constable? I got a blackmailer for a daughter. Any man comes looking for her, I'm going to warn him. Apple will be fine for me too, honey." He smiled at his daughter's retreating back. "I know you were busy with the war, but did you leave a sweetheart back home?" he asked affably.

Terrell shook his head. "Nope. After university and the war, I joined the police and then came out here. Not much time."

"University, eh? Some sorta genius. Whatever I know I learned in the army in the Great War. Served me pretty good in my current job. Been fire chief here for twenty years."

"Yes, sir. That's great, sir. I learned a great deal in the army myself."

"You're a policeman now. Were you an MP?"

"Yes, sir. One of the things I learned is that in a strange sort of way, people can't help the stupid things they sometimes do. They're desperate and they can't think of another way to get what they want or need. And you're right. Drink can play a big role. When I look at this fire, I ask myself, what did this man want that he couldn't think of any other way to get, other than attacking Mr. Vitali?"

"I guess that's what university learning will do, eh? Thank you, Pumpkin." He moved from where he'd been leaning on the table with both arms to make room for the pie and coffee. "That looks great. And you can tell your grandmother. I'm not afraid of her!"

April laughed. "I am!"

Terrell watched April putting the forks on the table for them, as he had watched on other days when he and Ames had come in for lunch or breakfast. She was smart and attentive in a way she kept under wraps sometimes, hiding it under her banter. He would bet she knew everything going on in town and would have some shrewd observations. He wondered if she was happy dishing up pie in the café or had other dreams. He was, he thought with an inward sigh, unlikely to ever find out. He turned back to her father.

McAvity furrowed his brow. "That note they got. I don't like it, all this sneaking around with notes and midnight fires. Used to be it was a simple sort of town. You had a bone to pick with someone, you had it to their face. It led to a few broken noses, but you knew where you stood."

Terrell, not sure about the improvements suggested by broken noses, shook his head. "I'm wondering about that 'You're not welcome here.' Who would send a note like that? People who are angry or hurt, or envious even. I think, deep down, they are ashamed at the same time. Of their own failures or vulnerability, or the surreptitious action they are contemplating. I think that's why it's done in secret."

"There's some newfangled nonsense for you," McAvity said, lifting his coffee cup toward Terrell in a kind of toast. "Personally, I think they are cowards, plain and simple. Forget all this psychological claptrap."

April arrived with the coffee pot to offer top-ups and leaned on the seat back. "So, what have you two learned about that fire, anyway?"

"This young fellow is using a lot of big words he learned at university. But I'm keeping up. We differ slightly on what it takes to commit arson."

"Oh. What sort of arson? I mean, was anyone hurt?"

McAvity glanced at Terrell, who shrugged.

"It's still under investigation, but luckily no one hurt."

"Mum's the word then, I guess," April said, touching the side of her nose with her index finger. She caught Terrell's eye and then looked away hastily at what she saw there. "I'll leave you to it, then. As long as no one is burning down the café, I should be all right." She turned to go, and then added, "Anyone I know?"

Terrell shook his head. "I probably shouldn't say, just now."

"Don't you worry, Pumpkin, it'll be all over town by lunchtime," her father said. "In fact, you'll probably be telling us what's what by the end of your shift today." April's father smiled at her and gave her a wink. But somewhere deep inside him, not yet fully apparent to a man who dismissed psychological claptrap, was the beginning of a disquiet he'd best ignore just now.

THE AFTERNOON WORE on, and April felt more tired than usual when she went out the back of the café and sat on the steps in the alley for her break. It was just ahead of the afternoon swell of ladies taking tea, and there was only one weary-looking old man at the counter nursing a cup of coffee, exchanging a few words with Al, the cook, who was leaning in the kitchen doorway smoking a cigarette.

She pulled her cardigan around her and held her face up to the afternoon sun and closed her eyes. The stilling of her body seemed to unleash the turmoil she was feeling inside, and she shifted restlessly, watching a truck ineptly trying to use the entrance to the alley to turn around. She winced at the sudden sound of the gears grinding. She saw that it was Caleb Archer driving. Not surprising. He'd been in the same grade in school, only he was two years older. As dim as they come, but good-natured, and a little in love with her in Grade 12. That had ended with no harm done. He was married now and working for his father's construction company.

What was happening to her now would not end so well. She wished she could stop this steady slide, but every day that she saw Terrell it was worse. She played over and over in her head that one glance they'd exchanged. Had she seen the same thing in him, or was it wishful thinking?

And why would she be wishing for that, anyway? It could only end in tears. Indeed, could never begin at all. Had her father seen that exchange?

"Oh, God," she muttered just as Al called her in. She jumped up with relief and gave a wave to Caleb, who was still struggling with the turn but had just seen her and was smiling broadly and waving.

A group of five regulars had come in and squeezed into the booth her father and Terrell had vacated. Throwing on her warmest smile, she approached the table. "Afternoon, ladies. Lovely day. Tea or coffee today?"

The ladies chattered all at once like birds in a tree. Then Mrs. Conrad, often the voice of the gathering, said, "Looks like tea today, pet. Did you hear? Someone tried to burn down that Eyetie's house!"

Here it was then. "You mean Mr. Vitali, the one with the restaurant?"

"Is that what he's called? I never can sort out these foreign names. But that's the one. I don't hold with it, mind, but you have to ask yourself what he did to make someone that mad."

Stifling a desire to say, "Do you?" April said instead, "I'll get that tea started. We have apple pie today; can I get you all some?"

"Do you have ice cream?" Mrs. Heatley, a plump, shy woman, asked.

"Yes, we do," April said. "Very nice with this pie!"

"Really, Ann, should you be having that?" Mrs. Tilbury said.

Deflated, and blushing slightly, Mrs. Heatley shook her head.

"It's true. You do wonder why they're here," Mrs. Tilbury continued, the little artificial blue forget-me-not bouquet of flowers on her dark hat shaking its disapproval. "They're nothing but trouble. My husband said he tried to get into the Chamber of Commerce. Can you believe that?" April could hear the incredulous question all the way over at the counter where she was preparing two large teapots. Typically, Mrs. Renfrew was the source of outrage and indignation.

"I'm sorry he tried. He must have known he wouldn't be welcome. I must say, though, I don't see why he shouldn't be there. He runs a business here, after all. He's my neighbour. They've always been very quiet and nice," Mrs. Smith said.

"You're so naive, Freya. They run a business all right. One that's up to no good, mark my words. A business that drives good, honest Christians out! Look at poor Hilary. Her husband had that nice little diner just down near the station and they had to close down. They don't care. Cutthroat, that's what they are. And I heard they serve alcohol on the sly," Mrs. Tilbury said.

"You can hardly say they aren't Christian," Mrs. Smith said, ignoring the insult. "Italians tend to be Roman Catholic."

"There you are, you see? Poor Hilary. They're really in a bad way. He hasn't found any work since they shut down."

"I'm not sure you can blame the Vit . . . whatever it is, for that. Hilary's Bob came back a bit of a mess, and he never was much for holding down a job before the war, as I recall. She ran that place on her own most days," said Mrs. Renfrew.

The ladies all shifted their elbows to make room for the tea and cups. "Pie coming right up," April said. She hated to interrupt the flow of conversation. As distasteful as she was finding it, her father had been right. She was going to hear all about it before her shift was over.

"I . . . I don't think I'll have any pie," the hapless Mrs. Heatley said quietly.

April threw a quick, poisonous glance at Mrs. Tilbury and then said, "How about a nice dish of canned peaches instead?"

"Oh. Oh, yes. That would be very nice."

"And that woman, so brazen, going around looking like that. That's unchristian all by itself!" This sudden, almost shrill outburst caused everyone at the table to stare at Mrs. Tilbury, who jutted her chin out defiantly. April, putting the plates of pie onto her tray, realized that remark was about Mrs. Vitali. Going around looking like what? She always looked beautiful, April thought. Nice but not expensive dresses, hair pulled back neatly, a nice little touch of lipstick that highlighted her natural beauty. Was that what made her "brazen"? If so, she thought rebelliously, slamming the last plate of pie onto the tray, she'd get out her red lipstick and wear it all the time.

What Mrs. Tilbury couldn't tell them, tell anyone, ever, was that she had found a silk head scarf jammed into her husband's trouser pocket when she was preparing to take his suit to the cleaners. And she'd seen how he got it.

By the time the pie and peaches were distributed, the conversation had moved on to the new hairdressing salon that was opening at the north end of Baker, by the gas station. April watched them afterward still chattering on the sidewalk outside the window as she cleared the dishes onto her tray.

She'd been listening to this sort of talk every time they came in, but today she suddenly felt she saw it for what it was: pure, undiluted, small-town prejudice. What "big words" had Terrell been using with her father? More than anything, April longed to be somewhere where big words were a matter of course.

"I CAN TELL you for certain he was a he, and he was shot," Gilly was saying to Darling, who was peering at where Gilly indicated with a pencil. "I'd say it was at close range, judging by the impact and damage here on the rib cage."

"How close?"

"Not more than a couple of feet."

"Can we say how long ago it was?"

Gilly shook his head. "He wasn't buried very deep, am I right? Clothes are pretty decomposed but looks like—I know this is a bit fantastical—more rancher than miner. No footwear, so maybe boots were stolen. No point in wasting a good pair of boots, our killer must have thought. If it's less than twenty-five years ago I'd be surprised, but I should caution that there is no way of knowing. Just an educated guess."

"That would put it at 1921, '22, then?"

"Or maybe earlier. Or later."

"Ames has a candidate who disappeared in 1921. A local railway or mining magnate of some sort. Guy named Turner," Darling said.

Gilly gazed at his skeleton with interest. "The date certainly works—though again, I caution, it's very difficult to determine this sort of thing. When I think of a captain of industry, I don't think of blue jeans, though; I think of a serge suit."

"I suppose even captains of industry must climb out of their suits sometime."

Gilly nodded. "If it was Turner, he could have been camping or hunting."

"Anything stand out?"

"He had pretty good teeth, all in all, though there is a molar missing on the upper right side. I would say it was pulled out. You could try the dentist, Philipson."

Darling shuddered slightly. "He's a bit young to have pulled out a tooth in the twenties." He himself had had a cavity attended to by Philipson and had found him remarkably lacking in what he would have called bedside manner. Philipson hadn't said anything to Darling, exactly, during the drilling, but he'd shown very clearly with an impatient sigh that he disapproved of his patients complaining with even a wince about the pain. Darling had a momentary vision of the dentist attacking Turner, if this was he, with a pair of pliers.

"Yes, but presumably he bought the business from someone. There must be records."

Darling nodded, peering more closely at the skull. "I'll send Ames to have a look."

"Afraid to go to the dentist?" Gilly asked.

"Certainly not!" retorted Darling. "As it happens, Ames has been reading up on Turner. The bookstore was robbed, and all the copies of Turner's autobiography were swiped."

"You don't say? Nelson seems to be in the grip of a crime spree. I shall mind how I go. I've put all these bits of cloth and whatnot in here if you or one of your minions would like to go through them for clues."

CHAPTER NINE

TOM SIMPSON LAY BACK ON the narrow bed in the cottage provided him by Mr. Barisoff. He almost felt at home. It had the feel of an army cot. The kerosene lamp his host had given him glowed and hummed beside him on the table. The cabin had a musty smell he suspected came of damp being allowed to act unimpeded because the stove had not been lit all winter. Barisoff had said that the last time his son had been there was the previous summer. Before that it had been the home of a man who had taught the children of the Doukhobors in Russian.

This had interested him. Nobody who came to this part of the world seemed to want to let go of their past or their language. Now everyone—including, he thought wryly, himself—spoke English, because when the English first came, they weren't about to give up on their own language or ways. And yet they weren't too keen on the people already here keeping their languages. It was amazing the English-speaking government even let these Russians study Russian, he thought. But perhaps they hadn't known or had tried to forbid it. He'd heard that the Russians seemed to be in trouble all the time over something.

Who was better off, he wondered, people who were trying to pursue their own ways under the beady eyes of the government, or people like him, who the government appeared to believe didn't exist? He thought of how he rode here, high above the valleys, skirting farmers and miners who wouldn't welcome him, and across the border, almost like a formless shadow, with no one to stop him.

Wanting to ride away was something he came by honestly. He'd had an uncle, his mother's brother, who had simply left one day. Gone off in his car with a suitcase. According to his grandmother he'd married someone from New Mexico and lived in some city, but no one knew where. His uncle Pete. He wondered now why his uncle had done his own riding away. He had fond memories of him. When Pete had been an older teenager, maybe seventeen, Tom had been just a small boy. He remembered his uncle had put him on a horse when he was barely three. He couldn't remember so many details of it—what his uncle said to him, whether he'd been afraid at first. But he remembered the physical feel of the saddle, his small hands gripping the pommel, the smell of the horse. If he was to trace his love of horses, he supposed it must have begun there, with Uncle Pete. How old was he when Pete left? Not much more than four, he was sure.

He turned onto his side and pulled his book from under the pillow. *A Ship of the Line*. His friend Sanders had given it to him before he'd left Spokane. He remembered wondering why Sanders would imagine he'd be interested in a story set in the navy during the Napoleonic Wars, but he'd said, "Just read it, and think of us on that damn ship to England." His own taste tended to stories involving horses, but out of deference to Sanders he'd started the Hornblower story at home and found he was enjoying it. He felt sleepiness coming on, and the satisfying weariness of a long day in the saddle, so he turned off the lamp and settled into the silent, velvet darkness. As he drifted off, it was the rolling sea he felt.

"I WONDER WHEN that policeman is coming back," Simpson said. He was sitting opposite Barisoff, who had made some oatmeal and had served it into two chipped white bowls. "I also wonder who that fellow was."

Barisoff shook his head. He'd been rattled by the discovery of the skeleton. "I wonder all night, who is he. He maybe belong to someone once, now is all alone, like he was thrown away. You sure not yours?"

Tom shook his head. "My great-grandparents are here somewhere. I remember seeing where when I was a boy, but I wonder now if it was closer to the water. That was how my people used to be buried." He pulled a drink of coffee, encountering some grits. "This is good, like camp coffee. I brought some with me, so we should make sure to use mine. I don't want to eat you out of house and home."

"Eat out of house?" Barisoff asked.

"You know, eat all your food. I won't be here today or tonight, though. I am going to follow the Slocan railway line to a place my grandmother told me about. Maybe I'll camp there overnight. I could shoot something for the pot on the way home."

"Shoot something? No, I see, you mean animal. Is no need. I, my people, no eat meat. Is mean kill something. If you want, of course, do for you."

Tom nodded. "If you don't kill animals, does that mean you are pacifist? No war either?"

Barisoff shook his head. "No war. God does not like killing."

"Maybe God has a point. I was in Europe for the war. There was an awful lot of killing. I decided it was no good for the people getting killed, and not much good for the people doing the killing."

Looking at him, Barisoff nodded. "You okay now?"

Simpson sighed and looked around the cottage. It was simple, clean, quiet. He wondered what Barisoff did all day. He was too old to go out to a job. He didn't see any books. Maybe he had a bible somewhere. "I'm okay. I like being out by myself. Maybe that's how I stay okay."

"You go. I have bread and cheese for you. I have garden to work in. I hope I not find any more dead people! If policeman come, I tell him you come back tomorrow."

"Thank you," Simpson said, getting up. "I'm going to a place called Lemon Creek. If he's in a big hurry, he can find me there tonight."

DARLING WASN'T IN a big hurry, because he wasn't sure what he ought to be in a hurry about. He'd learned that the man had been shot at close range, had had a broken wrist during his youth, had had an upper right molar pulled,

109

and was between twenty and forty years of age when he died, and very little else. If it was Turner, they ought to try to track down a relation. Perhaps his wife was still alive. Or maybe that anonymous book donor knew something. Or the book thief. Or maybe they would, in due course, find they'd nothing to go on, and he'd be buried properly, nameless, an unsolved crime of yesteryear. Yesteryear or not, an unsolved crime irked him.

He realized he'd told Tom Simpson that he might wish to interview him further. Now, he wondered, about what? The man was, he assumed, just visiting, and he couldn't keep him here indefinitely. He was too young to have committed the crime himself. The only remote connection was that he was visiting the graves of some relatives, great-grandparents. He couldn't be sure, but he assumed they must have been older than this man when they died. But of course, not necessarily. Perhaps he ought to send word through that beastly shopkeeper that Simpson was free to leave, provided he gave his address in the US. No. He'd go himself. He couldn't send any message through the store. It would satisfy that shopkeeper's nosy instincts. In any case, Simpson said he was staying for a week, so he had a few days to mull it over. Perhaps Lane would like to go back. Would that be like deputizing her in any way? He most certainly could not do that. But if her visit had been shortened by the finding of the dead man, she might like to have a proper visit with her Russian friend.

Much more immediate was the problem of the fire at Lorenzo Vitali's house, and that repugnant note. He bellowed for Terrell, who was just at that moment coming into the station after his coffee and pie with the fire chief.

"Well?" Darling asked, when he'd given the constable leave to sit.

"I was just with Mr. McAvity, the fire chief, sir. We went to have a look together. He confirmed an accelerant was used, and likely a match was put to it. I'm a bit worried. Mr. McAvity said it was a near thing that the house didn't go up. What if it wasn't kids? What if someone meant to kill the Vitalis?"

That, Darling realized, must be the thought buried in the back of his own head that was causing him disquiet. He hadn't wanted to dredge it into the light. If someone genuinely wanted to kill Vitali, it was going to be a ghastly cat-and-mouse game of trying to discover who it might be before the person struck again. "Yes. Well. You're right. Looking at it that way alters things considerably. How are you on security arrangements?"

"Sir?"

"Go have a look at the restaurant's locks, et cetera, and then the house. I don't want to frighten them more than they already are, but until we know the full intentions of the arsonist, we shouldn't take any chances. And we should keep an eye on it on our rounds."

AMES HAD SPENT a nervous half-hour with Dr. Philipson, simply because he disliked dental offices even more than hospitals. While he waited where he'd been instructed to sit by the ferocious receptionist, he could hear moans through a closed door. The sound of someone with their mouth full of pain-inducing equipment. He wondered if the receptionist had once been a cheerful, welcoming person and had turned into this gorgon after a steady diet of listening to people in agony.

Ames could hear the swish of water running and then convulsive spitting, as if the patient wanted to spit away all memory of the experience. He could picture the round bowl in which blood whirled away down the drain. Finally, a slightly bedraggled-looking man in his forties emerged and, slipping on his jacket, he wiped his mouth with his handkerchief. He made for the door and avoided looking at Ames, as though he was ashamed of his part in the whole thing.

"Dr. Philipson will see you now," the receptionist said after another five minutes, which the dentist used, Ames imagined, to wipe the blood off everything before admitting a new victim. He was not shown into the treatment room, but into an office with a nice oak desk and a framed diploma on the wall proving that Philipson was what he said he was. A glass case held some books, piles of periodicals, and a small trophy.

Wondering what the trophy was for, Ames held up his warrant card and said, with a nervous laugh, "Not here for my teeth, just need some information. I see you have a trophy. For some sort of dental race?"

Dr. Philipson, a man in his fifties, frowned slightly and looked behind him at the case. "Ah, no. My son's, actually. A skiing competition. How can I help?"

Ames explained about the corpse and hoped-for dental records for Samuel Turner.

"Pre-1922? I can't think who would have had the practice

then. I took over from Timmons, who retired in '34. I moved here from Vancouver because our son was a competitive skier. After . . . after he signed up, we just stayed on. I grew up here, so it was coming home, really."

There was a sadness in Philipson's eyes that suggested to Ames that perhaps his son never returned after the war. He nodded and said, "I'd be happy to do the searching if you want."

"That's all right, Sergeant. Harriet can do it. It's just a question of finding records for this Samuel Turner, is it not? I'll get her on to it and telephone you at the station if we have something. If we do, I'll be happy to come along and have a look at the fellow."

"That's a point, actually, Dr. Philipson. I wonder if you could come have a look anyway and tell us what's what. You might not have any dental records for Turner, and he might not even be Turner, so we may have to look farther afield to find a match."

"Yes, of course. I'll get Harriet to clear my schedule for tomorrow morning. Is that soon enough? By then she will have found, or not found, some records as well."

The sun was providing a pale March presence when Ames was back on the sidewalk. He took in a massive gasp of air to clear the dental office out of his system, but then almost immediately chided himself, and thought of Dr. Philipson's son. It was an unimaginable loss, and like so many others he'd met in the same situation, Dr. Philipson likely would never talk about it. He contemplated a stop at the café for a quick coffee, and then thought about his sugar intake. Dentistry, he thought glumly, is like death and taxes; it eventually comes to us all. He turned instead back to the police station.

BARISOFF WATCHED SIMPSON ride off toward the road. He would ride south for twenty-five miles, he'd said. It would take him most of the day. He shook his head slightly and wondered at how different people were. He wanted nothing more than to stay right where he was, grow his garden, and feel himself anchored to this little part of the world; a man like Simpson, he could sense, always wanted to be on his way somewhere.

In the cottage, he contemplated finishing off the pot of coffee that was on the stove, but he knew it would be bitter. He would reward himself for a solid morning's work with a nice new coffee. He'd drink it sitting on the back step in the sun. With this resolve, he finished cleaning up after his cheese-sandwich making, wrapped the cheese in oiled cloth, and put the bread into the metal breadbox he'd been given by his son, and muttered a brief prayer at the thought of that son. They were not estranged, exactly, but Andrei had made it clear he had his own life, and had moved to Brilliant, far enough away that visits would not be frequent. He imagined what his son's life was now, inventing a nice house for him to be in, his wife baking, perhaps, cutting beets for soup. He knew that he was unlikely to ever go there.

The sunlight had begun to produce something almost like warmth as he stood contemplating the garden with his hands on his hips. Why had he ever thought to make it bigger? It already seemed vast, with its demand to be turned over, the compost to be spread and worked in. If he'd left well enough alone . . . no, that restless soul, whoever he was, would still be there, waiting, waiting to be discovered. For a start, he decided, he'd put the rocks back where they'd been, along the back border of the garden.

He got his shovel and the wheelbarrow and skirted the outside of the garden to where he had tossed the rocks. He loaded them up and parked the wheelbarrow by the edge of the garden and contemplated the space that had been left when that poor man had been taken out. It suddenly seemed almost sacrosanct, this space. A man had lain here for how many years? Had it been imbued with his spirit? Had his spirit longed for justice? He knelt and, rocking slightly, said a prayer for the soul of the dead man, then he put his gloved hand to the ground to begin the increasingly painful process of getting back on his feet. He might have missed it, but for his prayers: a small stone, the size of a quarter. Still on his knees, he picked it up and brushed the dirt away and felt almost startled when two eyes appeared to be looking back at him.

IT WAS DUSK when Simpson found what he was looking for, a faint path toward the rail tracks. He dismounted and followed the path down to the tracks, leading his horse. A little farther down the hill, he sloshed across a narrow creek, the horse's hooves splashing and clattering on the rocks. The way continued, slanting toward the river, twigs and underbrush crackling underfoot. At last, he could see the water through the trees. This is where she said it was.

He stopped, as if he might feel the importance of this place of ancestors if he just stood still and listened. Then he began to see the indentations. This had been a whole village. The round hollows were all around, filled now with brush and slender trees. "Would you look at that!" he said to Rocky. He stood, shifting his weight onto his left leg, to take it all in. "This whole place used to be full of our people. What do you think?"

After some time, he took in a deep breath. "You must be thirsty. Let's go down and have a look at that water." Winding carefully among the remains of the pit houses, he led Rocky to the edge of the river and patted him on the flank. "There you go." He stood, his hands on his hips, looking out at the quiet scene before him. The surface of the water rippled slightly, reflecting the grey and blue of the sky above it, and he imagined himself like the water: quiet on the surface, but something moving inside him, a dark current of uncertainty. His grandmother had told him that Frog Peak would not be visible from here, but that it was to the southwest, watching over everything; watching over him. She had told him the Sinixt name as well, but he couldn't quite remember it. His mother must have used the old language once, but now she spoke only English, and it was what he had learned. He imagined waking up every morning by this quiet water with the peak nearby, guarding him, reminding him of the centre of his belonging.

He bedded down near the river, listening to the water lapping in the dark. He imagined movement all around him, a ghostly stirring of the ancients going about their daily lives, returning from the hunt, setting out to fish, children like Bobby, still a little boy, playing among the houses and by the water with the other village children, and Angie, old enough now to learn to prepare fish for drying and how to go into the bush looking for food. When he finally slept, the village fell silent, the ghosts spiralled into stars, and the feeling that had propelled him to this moment became an understanding that he was here for a reason. Perhaps in the morning, when sunlight flooded through the trees like a river across the ancient village, he would know what it was.

CHAPTER TEN

THE NOISE AND SMOKE IN the hall were climbing steadily
as the men clustered with drinks and cigarettes in their
hands, the meeting over, nothing new adopted, everything
safe and as it should be. This post-meeting drinking time
was really what attracted most of them to the meetings.
Despite the uncomfortable folding wooden chairs and
the chairman banging his gavel, dragging them painfully
through each item of business with that ponderous self-
important manner he had, there would be drinks after and
that delicious freedom that came from being away from
women for a short time.

The tray of salmon paste and ham sandwiches on the
sideboard would be gone by the end of the evening as the
drink took effect, though most of the men had had a good
supper before they left home. Smith, discouraged by the
intransigence of his fellow merchants and the task he'd set
himself, had just secured another drink. He was girding up
his loins, figuratively, for a conversation he knew he'd better

have. He saw the man he wanted, Gilbert Tilbury, with a couple of men from the building trades. He dashed back his rye as part of the girding process, put down his glass with a clunk on a windowsill, and made his way toward the group.

"Hello, Gilbert, Ben, Chuck. Keeping well?"

"You bet," Ben from the lumber store said. "Where's your drink? Here, let me get you one." He put his cigarette between his lips and started toward the ersatz bar. They weren't, strictly speaking, licensed to serve booze here.

"No, thanks!" Smith called after him. Did Ben have the look of a man who had just been waiting to be rescued from this conversation with Tilbury?

"You can get me one!" Tilbury said, holding up his empty glass and waggling it, his voice just a bit too loud. He looked as though he'd already had plenty to drink. He inclined to sloppiness.

Chuck had turned and was talking to someone else. It was now or never.

"I say, listen, old fellow. There's something I've been meaning to mention. Can we just step over here?" He pulled the puzzled but unprotesting Tilbury away from the milling crowd to a couple of chairs against the wall, but neither sat.

"What is it?" Tilbury asked, but he was looking at where Ben might be with his drink. Out of the light, the shadows gave both men the look of conspirators.

"Listen, not my business and all that, but that Italian woman, Mrs. Vitali . . ."

Tilbury turned, his face suddenly red and blotchy, his eyes narrow. "What about her?"

"I mean, it's rather obvious—you pursuing her all over town sort of business. It's not like some of your other times. You aren't very subtle with this one. It's only a matter of time till it gets back to your wife. I'm sure you mean nothing by it, but it's not fair on the lady, either, what? Brings the organization into disrepute."

Tilbury worked his mouth, and then said in a loud hiss, "As you said, none of your bloody business!" He looked out again in the direction of the bar. "Where's my bloody drink?" When he turned back to Smith, his expression had transformed into a smirk. "Lady? Is that what you call her? A whore, more like. We knew what to do with women like her over there, eh?"

Smith's stomach clenched at this. He could well imagine Tilbury had, or wished he had, comported himself in the worst possible manner overseas. It was hopeless, talking to him. He was too drunk, for starters. He saw no percentage in pursuing this conversation any further. What had he imagined? That Tilbury would be a better man? Would see the error of his ways? Until this moment, he had not truly understood what sort of man Tilbury actually was.

"Listen, old fellow, I think you ought to get along home now. Let me give you a lift." Smith began to propel Tilbury by the arm toward the door. He was winding up to protest, but Smith could see some of the others looking relieved and giving him a nod of approval, and it gave him the impetus he needed to get Tilbury out the door. With very ill grace, Tilbury sat in the passenger seat, scowling into the night.

"Where are we going?" he mumbled. "I don't want to go home." He turned to Smith, who was easing the car into the street. "You have no idea. My wife's a lunatic, you know that? Crazy as a coot." He slumped against the window and stared into the darkness. "I just want a little happiness. Is that too much to ask?"

Smith glanced at him. "You won't get any happiness chasing a married woman."

Tilbury snorted but said nothing. Smith felt he should have known not to talk to a man this drunk. He tried to imagine working up the courage to approach him again on the subject.

When he'd dropped Tilbury off at home, he drove up the street toward his own house and parked. He could see the Vitalis' lights were on and he shook his head. It was really too bad. Vitali had once again been turned down at the Chamber, in spite of his best defence, and now poor Mrs. Vitali was having to withstand the ghastly attentions of Tilbury. And poor Mrs. Tilbury, for that matter, he thought, getting out of the car. She hadn't looked happy for quite a long time.

"I HAVEN'T ACCUMULATED as much compost as you because I was very neglectful last autumn about raking up the leaves. I shall do better this year. But what I have is distributed and turned under. I feel very virtuous." Lane was standing at the edge of Kenny Armstrong's garden watching him work, or rather watching him stop work and remove his hat and push back his thick white hair.

His hat back in place, he said, "I'm ready for a sit-down myself. I put the chairs back out on the porch. It's almost warm enough to be June today. I suppose I'll just have to drag them back in when we get one of our March snow-falls! Come."

Lane closed her eyes and turned her face to feel the full warmth of the sun. On a little wooden side table between them were two cups of tea. The Armstrongs alone must be enough to keep the whole Ceylonese tea trade alive, she thought.

"Any news of your friend buried up in New Denver?"

She shook her head. "Nothing yet. I've been thinking about him a good deal. He was buried face down as if the person who put him there wanted to make sure he was dead, would never be able to draw another breath, nor yet catch a glimpse of heaven. Or the killer was afraid to look him in the face." She took a draught of tea and felt the incongruity of the lovely warmth and flavour of the tea when that man had had every simple pleasure taken away from him. "The truth is, it is a sordid, cowardly murder, done for reasons we will likely never know. And poor Mr. Barisoff. He is such a sweet old man. They are pacifists and vegetarians, you know, his people. He was horrified to his core, I'm sure, to find a body in the garden. The epithet 'wouldn't hurt a fly' must apply to him as to few others."

Kenny frowned. "They don't suspect him, do they, the police?" He didn't want to say "your husband."

"No, I don't think so. He only moved there in 1940, I think. I don't even know if his little house was there when that man was buried, or, if it was, who lived in it. Maybe no one lived there, and that's why the killer felt free to put the body where he did. I feel a bit bad. I'd meant to go and have a nice visit with Mr. Barisoff and the whole thing went up in smoke."

"What's happened to that Indian fellow?" Kenny asked.

"He said he was staying for a week. I told you he came up from the United States on a horse?"

"You did. It's how we all got about, not that long ago. And the apples from King's Cove are still carted down to the wharf with that horse of mine and the wagon. Maggie doesn't carry the mail, but she's still got work to do." He nodded toward the field where his mare was passing a contented semi-retirement. "That and boats of one kind or another. That road you take to Kaslo wasn't even built till '22, long after we settled here. I think I heard those people of his used to live all up and down the lakes. But when 'progress' types cut down every lick of forest and built dams and railways all over the place, it didn't leave much for them. They depended on things the way they were for their living. Price of progress, I guess."

Lane looked around at the rivers of forest that ran between all the houses in King's Cove. Some of the growth was newer because there'd been a fire in '19, but it nevertheless had a feel of undisturbed nature. "Progress for some people, I guess. I can see why no one wants a sawmill here. I can't see there'd be much left for us either if someone came and cut it all down. I wonder if I ought to go back. I'm rather interested in Mr. Simpson. We'd be a right League of Nations: a Brit, a Russian, and Mr. Simpson, who'd have every reason to dislike us."

"I bet you could broker a peace between the Russians and the West with your kind manner," Kenny said, smiling at her.

"That's as may be, but I think there are sorrows inflicted on people that are hard to get past. You know, Simpson said something interesting. He said when he went to Europe to fight, he saw a bunch of Europeans trying to take away the land of other Europeans, and that's when he came to understand at last that that was the European way. It gave some ghastly historical perspective to what his people endured."

Kenny shook his head. "Not much comfort. And he's not wrong. I don't suppose we like to think of ourselves like that, but it's true nonetheless."

"Still," Lane said, "I'll take another tin of chocolate biscuits and hope for the best for my little visit. I'd best be off to contemplate the contents of the larder." Lane stood up and took up her cup to shoot down the last dregs of the now cool tea. "Thank you for the tea. Why hasn't poor hard-working Eleanor come out to join us?"

"Some sort of baking project. I don't like to get in her way."

"I bet you don't!"

"Actually, I think a tin of her homemade biscuits would do wonders for your League of Nations. Let me see what I can do."

MR. AND MRS. Vitali sat on the two high stools that were normally pushed under the work counter in the narrow kitchen of the restaurant. The recent threats had had no effect on the custom that day. But now they sat in rigid silence. A second envelope lay between them on the table; the note inside said, "I warned you. No one wants you here!"

The usual labourers and men from the trainyard had come in for lunch, and the evening trade, while not bustling, was respectable for a weeknight. They had finished the cleanup and readied the restaurant for the next day. Lorenzo had made himself a cup of espresso in the little pot he'd brought from Italy all those years ago, and he sat before it now, distractedly using his spoon to crush the lump of sugar he'd dropped into it, his face a landscape of worry.

"I don't think you should be drinking coffee now, my dear. It will keep you awake. You need sleep." Mrs. Vitali lifted her hand and touched his face briefly. "Your face is full of new wrinkles from worry."

Lorenzo shook his head. He could have been disagreeing, or sadly agreeing, with that motion. "It is probably a good idea if I don't sleep. What if they try again tonight?" He pointed at the envelope. "That policeman, the black one, came with the inspector, and they said we should get some more lights at the front and back of the house, just for now. Here too. I don't see when I will go. We are here all the time."

"We should do it quickly. Whoever dropped this off came in the night. Maybe they wouldn't dare if there was a bright light. I'll get the lights at the hardware store when I shop, and you can ask Mr. Smith next door to put them up. He is an electrician. It's his job." She did not tell Lorenzo how it pained her to go into the hardware store. That's where it had started. Tilbury making ever ruder passes at her. She had only been once, to buy a canning pot for the restaurant, but it had been enough. Now Tilbury would not leave her alone. He knew her necessary routine for shopping and ordering for the restaurant and seemed always to be in wait for her somewhere, as if he did not have a business of his own to run. Only recently he had waylaid her when she'd been coming out of the Rexall and was heading down the hill toward the new cheese shop on Vernon Street. He popped out at her from a recessed doorway, pulling at her arm, wanting her to stand close to him in the shadow. "Come on, love," he'd said, attempting allurement, but sounding threatening instead. "Just meet me like I said. No one is gonna know. I can see you feel the same as me." His breath had been tinged with nicotine and drink, hot against her cheek. He'd pushed her scarf off her head.

She'd yanked her arm away. "Leave me alone, or I talk to police!"

He'd thrown his head back with a laugh. "Ha! Who's going to believe a DP like you?" Then he'd returned to wheedling. "Come on, pretty please?" He'd leaned close to her, pulling her near, pouring hot breath into her ear. "I'll put a good word in for your husband."

Sickened, Olivia had raised her voice, not caring who heard. "You have wife! You a disgrace!" She'd yanked her arm free and walked hurriedly away, feeling for her scarf, but it was gone. She had not stopped at the cheese shop but had gone down Vernon and around near the station and back up the slope on Baker to the restaurant. She'd leaned against the outside wall by the back door, her shopping bag on the ground, her heart pounding. It was only when she'd had a glass of water and put the groceries away that she wondered what he had meant. Put a good word in for Lorenzo for what?

Now, in the quiet of the restaurant, she wondered if she should tell Darling. She thought he might understand, not make too big a thing of it. But with Lorenzo opposite her now, his face creased with worry, she knew she could not. And anyway, if she talked to Darling, he would go and talk to Tilbury, and who knew what he might do then. She had been happy in Nelson, though she missed her family at home, but she still did not feel she understood the people. It had been clear that many had not been fond of Italians for the same reason that the people in her little Calabrian village didn't like outsiders. That, at least, she almost understood, but she didn't feel she could read people. Canadians were more . . . internal, perhaps, than people in her village. You couldn't tell what they were really thinking. And with that dreadful man, you couldn't tell how far he would go.

She had felt so safe here, but now, with the fire, the notes, and Tilbury, and not telling Lorenzo, she felt very alone and very unsafe. Still, she had said she would be going for lights, so she would go and face that vile man down if she had to.

Imagining a day when new people might come from Italy and she wouldn't be so lonely, she buttoned her coat right up to the collar and put her hat on firmly, and then pulled on her gloves and picked up her handbag. "Come. Let's go home. I will go first thing, before I prepare for lunch tomorrow, and I will buy the lights. In the meantime, you could go to Mr. Smith tonight, ask him to put them up. Okay?" She adopted a smiling businesslike manner that suggested it was best not to sit around mulling anxiously about what could happen.

"All right. Yes. Let's go. You can make us that big Canadian remedy, hot cocoa, and I will go to Mr. Smith."

LORENZO STOOD IN the dark on Smith's front porch, the wind that whipped up the valley feeling almost as icy as a winter wind. He'd heard someone stir inside at his knock. Finally, the porch light came on and the door was opened. Mrs. Smith was looking at him with surprise. It surely was the first time he had come to their front door in all the years she'd known them. She often spoke with his wife or him over the fence, and on Dominion Day she'd come out the basement door and into the alley to come through the gate of the Vitalis' yard for their big picnic.

"Mr. Vitali, come in. Goodness me, it's cold. Dear, it's Mr. Vitali!" Lorenzo stepped into the covered porch and then through the second door into the living room and stood stolidly by the door, turning his hat in his hand. "I can speak to Mr. Smith?"

"Yes, of course. Come sit down. He'll be right out."

Lorenzo shook his head. "No, is okay. I wait."

"I saw that coloured fellow that calls himself a policeman snooping around in your garden. I hope he isn't making any trouble! I kept an eye on him, just in case."

"Oh. Thank you. Is very nice. Constable Terrell, he is very okay. But you keep eye for neighbour. Is good. Ah, Mr. Smith."

Smith had come through and could not make out why Lorenzo was hovering just inside the threshold. "Come in, old fellow. What can I do for you?"

"No, is okay. Police say I should buy special lights to put on porch and outside restaurant. Tomorrow Olivia buy them, but you can put them up? I pay you, of course."

"Nonsense! I'd be happy to do it. Can't have people going around setting us all alight, can we? Just let me know when you've got 'em, and I'll come around to do them. Getting them at Tilbury's, is she?"

Mrs. Smith, who had been standing beside him, glanced up at him and then looked down, shifting uncomfortably. Now why was that? Lorenzo asked himself, turning back to Mr. Smith.

"Yes, I think is only place you can buy them."

Smith moved a hand unconsciously along the side of his face and nodded. "Yes, of course. Bit of a monopoly, what?" He tried to laugh, but he wasn't sure Lorenzo understood him. "Listen, old fellow. I'm sorry about the Chamber of Commerce. I've tried every time. Some of the others . . . well, I just think they have to get used to the idea, that's all. It'll come."

Lorenzo shrugged. He was surprised about the shift in the conversation, and then he wondered if perhaps Tilbury was one of those needing to get used to the idea. You never got any notice about who'd rejected your application. For all he knew, even Smith could have. But no. The Smiths had always been very nice to him, and he didn't doubt that Mrs. Smith believed herself to be helping him when she was watching Constable Terrell at work.

"That's okay. You right. Maybe one day. Thank you so much for help with lights. Thank you." Lorenzo put on his hat and stepped the one step down to the covered porch.

He put his hand on the door and then called back, "Good night, Mrs. Smith."

Smith followed him out and stood at the outside door. He looked momentarily undecided. "Listen, I say," he walked down the three steps and joined Lorenzo where he was on the sidewalk, pushing his hands into his pockets because of the cold. "I'm just telling you this, you know, I'm not supposed to, but it's not fair you don't know. It's the wine."

Lorenzo stopped and frowned, puzzled. "Wine?"

"You know. In the restaurant. Word is out you sometimes serve wine, even though it's against the law. One of them said someone saw you giving it to that inspector. They think . . . well, I mean, they think . . . that you might be bribing him."

"Bribing?" Lorenzo asked. He was not familiar with the word.

"You know, giving him money and things to look the other way. The other restaurant owners think you are getting a big advantage. I'm just telling you, old chap, so you know the lie of the land, you see?"

Lorenzo shook his head. He thought he did see. "I never give inspector money. Wine as gift, yes, for special occasion. Money, never. That is what they think?"

Smith nodded ruefully. "I don't doubt you for a minute, Vitali. Not for a minute. But I thought you should know what's being bandied about. The law being what it is, you maybe shouldn't even give away a glass of wine. People will use any excuse to come down on a fellow."

Vitali lifted his hand and said good night, and then

turned toward the gate. Profound weariness came over him as he climbed up to his own covered porch entrance and slipped off his shoes. Inside the house he sat down in a heap without taking off his coat. The forces lined against him had seemed manageable and predictable in the early years. A natural resistance to a "foreign" presence among the restaurants, a slow start as people became used to them, then the war. A bad time, yes, but understandable. Now, in the almost three years since the war had ended, it had seemed they were finally seeing daylight. His friendship with the inspector and his wife, he was sure, signalled the real turn in his fortunes. If the inspector could accept them, it would show the way for everyone.

Now, suddenly, the ground seemed to have become quicksand. First the fire, and now this suggestion that he was bribing the police. The idea that Inspector Darling could be bribed was shocking. And how could a wicked rumour like this be disproved? If he tried to respond in any way to it, it would just bring it into the light, cast even more doubt on himself, and, in many ways worse, the inspector. He had been planning to show the second note to the inspector, but now . . .

His wife had made hot cocoa and prepared the tray to carry into the sitting room the moment she heard the door close. She stood now, holding the tray, looking at him slumped in his easy chair with his coat still on. She put the tray on the table and went quickly to kneel beside his chair. "Caro, what has happened?"

CHAPTER ELEVEN

"**You know, I think I** would like to go back to have a proper visit with Mr. Barisoff. There's nothing like a skeleton to put a damper on a cup of coffee and some chocolate biscuits." Lane and Darling were sitting in front of the Franklin, the open cover of which displayed a cheerful fire that cut into the chill of the March night. Looking over at Darling's profile, Lane's heart warmed sympathetically at the pall of worry that animated his face in the flickering light. They had been persuaded by a few nice days that they no longer needed the furnace going, and now they were paying for it by having to wear woollen socks and thick sweaters. "Would you mind? I mean you wouldn't think it was me interfering with the case?"

"It's funny you should mention it. I was just wondering if I could ask you to go there without you thinking I'd deputized you in any way. The thing is, I don't think we need to detain Mr. Simpson. I would have telephoned him through the bearded grocer, but I just couldn't bear to give Berenson any role at all. He is the most repellent individual."

"So that's when you thought of me?"

"There's hardly a moment I don't think of you, though I will deny it if ever asked. But yes. If you were going up anyway, perhaps you could let Mr. Simpson know he doesn't need to stay around on our account."

"All right, then. And I promise to only do what I am asked, and nothing else. You're right about Berenson. He is repellent. He's a bit like a spider, sitting in that shop. All things must come to him because he's the only store in town. I have this feeling he collects and hoards all gossip for some later nefarious use." Lane looked at the skeptical face Darling made. "Well, of course that is completely unfair. He may be a perfectly civic-minded individual who just doesn't have very good bathing facilities."

"I've been very lucky in you. You have a sort of self-correcting personality that I don't have at all. Once I have a bad impression of someone, I find it very difficult to shake."

"I shall endeavour to stay on your good side, then. You are like Mr. Darcy. But I don't blame you. You see the worst in people every day. I, by contrast, spend my days here drinking tea and eating cake among the blameless citizens of King's Cove."

"I'M SORRY TO say we didn't find any dental records for your Mr. Turner. It's plain he didn't come here for dental services. I know his daughter. Perhaps I could ask her." He shuddered inwardly. He really hoped this skeleton was not Turner, for his daughter's sake.

Dr. Philipson was standing at the top of the stairs into

the basement morgue with Ames, who felt a bit crestfallen at this news. He'd hoped for a quick resolution. "Well, that's too bad. But I just read that Turner was originally from Kingston in Ontario. We have an autobiography he wrote."

"Kingston? I had no idea. I met someone from there at a dental conference in '45. We still keep in touch. Do you want me to see if he can track anything down? I don't know how many practices there are in Kingston, but there can't have been that many before the war."

"Can you?" said Ames. "Yes, if you don't mind. I'd be very grateful." They had made their way down the stairs, and Ames had opened the door and turned on the light in the little makeshift morgue. "All right then, have at it." He pointed to where the skeleton was laid out and lifted the sheet to reveal the skull. "Do you need anything else? If not, I'll leave you to it. Give me a shout when you're done," Ames said, and then retreated quickly up the stairs to the warmth.

He proceeded up to Darling's office and poked his head in the door. "Sir? No dental records here for Turner, so I have the dentist perusing the teeth of our fellow downstairs. He can match it against anyone else he has on file. I'm a bit disappointed. I thought we might have found our man and solved an old mystery. He's offered to check with a colleague in Kingston, where, you will be pleased to know, I learned from that damn book that Turner came from."

"Nothing to say he's not Turner, though, is there? It simply means he never had to see a dentist here. Good for you on the book. Anything else of interest?"

"Not yet. It's extremely boring. Full of details of land

purchases, hiring, railway building. His constant theme is that you can't get good help, and the continual obstruction by government officials, and what a grand fellow he is. He gets a sympathetic ear finally and is granted land for his railway to support the mining, but there's lots of competition from other outfits. He imports cheap labour from China because he doesn't like the local Indians. He describes them as 'indolent.'"

"Charming. Does it happen by any chance to record his disappearance? That would actually be useful. Make a note of his business partners in the day. If that's him downstairs, perhaps he's been murdered by one of them. Or the competition."

"Hmm. I see what you mean. I should read with a little more focus."

"Attaboy," Darling said. "Keep at it. I'm going to see how Mr. Vitali is getting on with putting up some security lights."

The weather had descended into a fine icy drizzle, and Darling, umbrella in hand and his collar turned up, arrived at Lorenzo's restaurant a few minutes later. He was surprised to see it dark, and a peek in the windows showed no activity. A surge of wind whistling down the hill made a parry at his umbrella, but he shifted its angle downward and went down the street and back up the alley. There he found a truck blocking the road and a man up a ladder securing a light with a metal hood onto the frame below the roof. He could see that it would shine directly onto the space outside the kitchen door. Lorenzo was standing with his hands in his coat pockets, watching the procedure.

"Good morning, Lorenzo," Darling called. "I'm pleased to see you were able to act quickly on the security lights."

Lorenzo glanced at him, making no move to come forward to greet him. He looked up at the man on the ladder, and then, looking almost past Darling, said, "Yes. Mr. Smith, he help me. I hope so it helps."

Puzzled by Lorenzo's coolness, Darling continued, "And up at your house?"

"Yes. All done. Thank you, Inspector. I must go in, help prepare for lunch." He turned to go in. He stopped when Darling addressed him again.

"If anything happens, be sure to give me a call."

Barely turning to the inspector, Lorenzo said, "Everything okay now. If something happen, I will call Constable Terrell. Thank you."

Darling watched him retreat into the restaurant and frowned. The man on the ladder seemed satisfied with his work and came down and began to fold his ladder. "That should do it," he said. Darling waited while the man went up the stairs and into the kitchen. In a moment the light blazed on, creating an artificial sunniness for a moment. Then it went off. Darling heard the man saying goodbye to the Vitalis and then watched him come down and begin to load the ladder back into his truck.

He was uncertain what to do. Perhaps Lorenzo didn't want to talk in front of this man. Ought he to wait until the truck had left and then go and have a word? But Lorenzo had assured him that nothing more had happened and had said he needed to get ready for the lunch crowd. He was about to turn and head back to the station when the kitchen door opened and Mrs. Vitali came out, wiping her hands on a dishtowel. In a hurried whisper, she called him. "Ispettore!" She reached into the pocket of her apron and pulled out an envelope and held it over the railing at the top of the landing.

Darling reached for it and was about to say something, but Mrs. Vitali had slipped back into the kitchen and closed the door. Darling went to the top of the alley, and once on the street and out of sight of the restaurant, he opened it and pulled out the paper with its ugly message. He turned it over and looked at the back, where there was nothing, and folded it and put it back into the envelope. He wished he hadn't opened it. He'd thought it was a note from her or her husband that might explain Lorenzo's peculiar behaviour. Now if there were any prints, they'd be smudged.

He was nearly back at the station and becoming increasingly worried. The campaign against the Vitalis seemed to be escalating. He felt a headache coming on, so he crossed the street to the drugstore and waited patiently while an older woman with a number of shopping bags fished around in her handbag for money. He held the door for her when she had finally finished her transaction and turned back to the chemist.

"Good morning, Mr. Clear. Just a tin of Aspirin, please."

The chemist gave a brief nod and reached onto a shelf behind him, saying, "That'll be eight cents. It's cheaper by the bottle."

"That's all right. I have a bottle at home." Darling reached into his pocket for change, brought it out, and selected a dime. "Typical March weather, eh? Warm and sunny one minute and then it wallops you with winter the next."

Mr. Clear gave another brief nod. "As you say. Will there be anything else?"

There was no mistaking a dismissive tone from the usually friendly Mr. Clear. Darling held up the tin of Aspirin and shook his head. "No. Thanks very much." He tried to infuse warmth into this but received no answer at all.

An anxiety that was still somewhat formless after his interaction with Lorenzo began to crystallize. Perhaps the fire and the warning notes had simply made Lorenzo more anxious and cautious, but that didn't account for the lack of the garrulousness and friendliness Mr. Clear usually displayed.

BERENSON PUT THE nozzle back on the pump and leaned in toward the driver. "A dollar and fifty-five cents, please." He took the two-dollar bill and went into the store to get change, his mind preoccupied. Something was going on. When the truck pulled away, he stayed outside, leaning on the gas pump, looking out over the tops of the trees, trying to imagine what it was. He shrugged and went back into the store and began to roll a cigarette.

He looked up at the sound of the bell and was surprised to see an Indian. He couldn't recall the last time he'd seen his kind around the area.

"You need something?" he asked. He stood up and moved close so that he stood over the man, with the counter between them. He set his mouth in a firm line and waited.

"I heard you got a phone here. I need to make a call," Tom Simpson said.

"It'll cost you five cents," Berenson said, leaning down to pull the instrument off the shelf. He plunked it down gracelessly but did not loosen his hold on it.

"I think I can manage that," Simpson said. He put his hand in his pocket and pulled out some change and sorted through it to get the nickel, which he pressed onto the counter and pushed toward Berenson.

"You're not from here," Berenson said, finally relinquishing the phone. He picked up the nickel and dropped it into the cash drawer.

"I guess you'd say that." He was waiting, his ear to the receiver.

Berenson eyed him narrowly. This man was being a bit forward, he thought. He didn't budge from where he was standing, forcing Simpson to move a few steps along the counter, still holding the receiver. He turned away from Berenson and spoke quietly when the operator answered.

"Why you calling the police?" Berenson asked, when the short call was completed.

"Not really any of your business," Simpson replied, pushing open the door. "But thanks for the use of the phone."

"You come in here, you show me some respect!" Berenson shouted after him. He leaned over to put the phone back and nearly jumped at the sound of the door opening again.

Simpson was standing in the door, looking at him as if he was trying to control an impulse to say something angry. "That's a two-way street," he said finally, and disappeared up the road.

DARLING HAD JUST hung his hat on the hat stand in his office when the phone rang. "Yes?"

"Phone call for you, sir. I'll put it through," O'Brien said.

"Hello. Is this Inspector Darling?"

Darling said it was, trying to place the voice. Vaguely familiar, but not enough to give it a name.

"This is Tom Simpson. Listen. Would it be possible for me to come up to see you?"

"Certainly," Darling said, realizing that Simpson must be telephoning from Berenson's general store, and noting that even a perfect stranger seemed to know to be guarded around Berenson. "In fact, my wife is heading up that way. She could give you a lift into town. Unless you're planning to ride?"

Simpson laughed. "No, sir. We had a good ride yesterday. Mr. Barisoff said my horse could help himself to the grass around his cabin while I'm gone. He said he'd lend me his car, but if your wife is agreeable to bringing me into town, I'd prefer a lift. I can hitchhike back. I appreciate it."

"Splendid. I'll see you when you get here."

When Darling had replaced the receiver, he bit his lower lip. He realized he was condemning Lane to a long day of driving because he knew she would never be comfortable letting Simpson try to hitchhike when she could drive him. He hoped she wouldn't mind too much, and then reassured himself that her natural nosiness might be satisfied by a long drive with an interesting man. He turned his thoughts back to the phone call. A man as self-contained as Simpson would not be coming up on a whim. He wished he could have got a clue about why he needed to come all that way to see him. In the absence of this knowledge, he sat in his chair and swivelled the seat to face the now misty top of Elephant Mountain. Usually helpful to his thinking, the mountain offered little in the face of the morning's baffling coolness from people who were normally extremely friendly. Nor was it assuaging the very real worry that Lorenzo might be facing more danger from his persecutor.

Sandon, July 1915

"HOW DID I live without you?" The man rolled onto his side to look at the woman beside him, propping his head up on his hand and running a feather escaped from the pillow across her cheek. The warm sheets had bunched up over her breast and he pulled at them so he could see her.

She only sighed and looked at him with calculating eyes. Finally, she moved as if to get up. "Don't. There's no point. You always do this. It's tiresome." She waved her hand to indicate the cluttered room, full of her clothes and a dresser with a small bottle of scent, a jar of cream, and a wooden box. "I have to clean up. I have an appointment." The room was at the back of the rooming house and the window faced the ravaged mountain directly behind them. The sash was pushed all the way up, and the fragrance of the summer dispelled some of the fusty air that had built up in the room over the course of the afternoon. The mountain blocked out the sun at this time of day, which was a relief, but in the winter it rendered all these back rooms too dark all day long and bitterly cold, in spite of the little wood stove.

"I'm serious. I'll set you up. I'll buy this place and you can run it like a proper hotel."

"That would make me very popular with the miners." The woman rubbed her eyes and stretched out her back. "God almighty! Go back to your wife. I have work to do, as if you didn't know this. I came from France to work, to be independent. I don't need—don't want—to become your protégé." At thirty-two she was long past any hope of protection by a man. She had learned over the years to bury the hope that she could do any of the things she had imagined: buy a small farm or even a little dry goods store here or in one of the other bustling mining towns. Her course was set, and her work would close every door to her. Still, she always felt the warmth of the money she was saving. She told no one, not even this infatuated young man.

"Please, Estelle. Let me do this."

"Please, Sam," she said, in imitation of his tone. "Don't make promises you can't keep. You think I haven't heard it all before?"

"I can keep this promise."

Estelle was up buttoning her skirt, pulling it around so it sat right on her hips. "Well, I don't want this hotel. I want a little cottage with a garden. There, I have disappointed you. I am a farmer at heart. I came from a farm. It is something I know. Not glamorous."

He sat on the bed, watched her pinning up her hair, thought of her on a pretty little farm, keeping a room always for him. "Why did you ever come all the way out here?"

"My father was a widower, and I was a mouth to feed he could not afford. I heard there was gold here. I always wanted to travel." The real story was colder and more brutal than that. She thought of the house she had fled as a fourteen-year-old. She closed her eyes for a moment and then turned to him, her reddish-blond hair tidy again, pinned away from her narrow face. "Now, leave. You can bring me that farm next time you visit."

She watched him from her window. He always went around the back so that he could wave. She smiled and lifted her hand and then took a deep breath. She suspected that it was true, that he was in love with her. She remembered what it was like to be a girl, dreaming of being in love.

She missed the simplicity of her girlhood dreams. They had sustained her through poverty and her mother's death at the hands of her father. She had said yes to the first offer. There was no ever after. It wasn't until years later that she learned she had likely been malnourished her whole childhood and that was why she had lost the baby. She never forgot the voice of the doctor telling her husband she would never be able to have children. She had been fifteen. Her happily ever after was his daily rage that he had married her and was now shackled to a useless—no, worse than useless—woman.

CHAPTER TWELVE

O**N THE WAY TO MR.** Barisoff's, Lane thought about the man in his garden. Darling had said he had indeed died by misadventure. The misadventure of being shot at close range. They were working on the theory now that the man might be the railway mogul Sam Turner, if building these little local railways made one a mogul; Lane wasn't sure what the local criteria were.

The door to the cabin was swung open before she'd even mounted the stairs. She held out the tin of biscuits given her by Eleanor. "I bring gifts," she said.

"Come in, come in," Barisoff said. "We have something new," he added in Russian.

Simpson had risen from the table where he'd been sitting. "Ma'am," he said by way of greeting.

"Hello, Mr. Simpson. Lovely to see you again. You must think I live on nothing but biscuits, or should I say 'cookies.'"

He smiled. "I don't make any judgments. I personally like cookies."

"You'll really like these, then. They are made by my lovely neighbour, Mrs. Armstrong."

When they had sat with fresh coffee and the cookies arrayed on a plate, Lane asked, "So, there is something new? I assume you mean about . . ." She motioned toward the back of the house.

"Yes, so interesting. You tell, Mr. Simpson," Barisoff said.

"We found something," said Simpson.

AMES WAS BACK at the library. He'd often been sent on this sort of errand in the past. He remembered his first few times. He'd been annoyed by the assignment. It was boring and felt like school all over again. But he was surprised now to find himself enjoying the research more each time. Old dusty newspapers provided by the library were sometimes treasure troves, direct links to the solving of a crime.

"You again, Sergeant Ames. I shall have to set up a special carrel just for you. What can I get for you this time?" Mrs. Killeen asked.

"I'll need all the papers for . . . hmm . . . let's say January through June of 1921."

"You'll be busy. Perhaps I should arrange for provisions to be sent to you. Any particular story?"

"Yes, the disappearance of that Samuel Turner character whose book you got. April 1921, he disappeared, apparently, and was never seen again."

Mrs. Killeen nodded. "Goodness, yes, now you mention it. I think I remember something about that. I was only a girl, but it made quite the splash at the time. Now isn't it odd that I didn't make the connection when that book came in?"

"Have you had any new thoughts about how the library got the book?"

Mrs. Killeen shook her head. "No. Afraid not. All I can say is that it was on the counter here with a note in it. No one can remember seeing anyone leave it. I didn't keep the note, unfortunately."

Settling Ames at a quiet table, she produced a pile of yellowing newsprint and said, "How's your mother?"

"She's great, thanks." He looked at the pile. "Well, here goes. Wish me luck!"

Ames started with the April papers. It would have been front-page news, so he concentrated on headlines and put the papers to one side as he rejected them. And then, there it was: "WHERE IS HE? Disappearance of railway man Samuel Turner puzzles police." The newspaper was dated Friday, April 8, 1921. The article said Mrs. Turner reported that her husband had not returned from a business trip as expected on March 26, and, further, that she had waited five days before reporting his absence and had wished to avoid publicity. The article detailed the efforts of the police and RCMP to locate Mr. Turner.

Taking up the next few papers, which all noted a lack of progress on the case, Ames looked for added information. Turner had only one business partner, a James Rolland, who was as puzzled as everyone else. As he read through April and then May, he wasn't surprised by how the police investigation seemed to dry up. There was little enough in the file—had they hit brick walls, or had they been keeping details under wraps for some reason? Then, in late May, he found something in one small paragraph on the second page. "Well, well, well," said Ames under his breath. He got up and stretched his long back, piled the papers back in order, and returned them to Mrs. Killeen.

"Find anything?"

"I think I might have," he said.

LORENZO AND HIS wife had fallen more and more into silences. All day at the restaurant conversation was limited to what was required to get orders out; in the evening, when they finally made their way home, Lorenzo shook his head at the usual offer of cocoa and said he was off to bed.

Olivia Vitali thought about making a cup for herself, but instead sat at the dining room table and looked out the window. The town, cascading down the steep hill, was settling for the night, with only a few lights still twinkling below her. Their new backyard security light created an artificial brightness that, while she knew it might dissuade any arsonist, destroyed her calming view of the darkling town. She felt a kind of shame about the light—as if there were something wrong with them that required this embarrassing thing singling them out among their neighbours. She longed for a cigarette, which surprised her. She hadn't smoked since she left Italy. Lorenzo had told her it destroyed the taste of food. She'd realized he was right, and that she'd only taken it up because her best friend had started smoking in secret as a rebellion against her parents. She saw herself on the sunny hill behind the village with Ana, the two of them smoking cigarettes under the olive tree, laughing. We laughed freely because we had nothing but our poverty and ourselves, she thought. She closed her eyes and recalled the sun on her face, the smell of dry grass and wild oregano, the sound of crickets. Now they had everything, but Lorenzo was worried, and she too was assailed by anxiety. The fact that they weren't talking about their troubles made her think that he was hiding yet another worry. So was she, for that matter, but at least that horrible lecher Tilbury hadn't been around when she'd gone to buy the lights. Mrs. Tilbury had been there and, if anything, had been effusively friendly. She was nice, Olivia thought. How could she be married to such a man? Did she even know how he behaved?

She would try in the morning to talk to her husband. She turned away from the unquiet light illuminating their now dishevelled garden and went to bed.

THINGS FELT BECALMED at the police station. Terrell had looked at the note Darling handed him and confirmed that it looked like the same handwriting as the first one. There had been no fingerprints on the first one besides Vitali's, and Terrell suspected there'd be none on the second. But he, like Darling, was worried.

On his way up to his office, Darling had nodded to O'Brien.

Where was Ames? It was unlike him to be late, Darling thought in irritation. As if in answer to his mental query, the phone rang. It was Ames.

"Hello, sir, sorry, sir. My mother had a fall and sprained her wrist. I told her not to go up that stepladder in her

148

bedroom slippers! Anyway, I'm just up at the hospital with her while she gets patched up. I'll be in as soon as I can."

"No, no. Take your time. I'm sorry to hear it. Give Mrs. Ames my best." When he'd hung up, he felt a slight and, he knew, unbecoming amusement at the thought of Ames having to do all the cooking at home for the next little while. Wondering whether Ames was capable of cooking anything at all, Darling's mind turned to a fresh cup of coffee. Feeling restive, he put his hat and coat back on and made his way down the stairs.

O'Brien appeared to be shuffling papers, and he could see Terrell on the phone at his desk in the back corner of the room. "I'm going for a fresh cup of coffee; after that I'll be stopping by the barber for a trim. If there's any crime while I'm gone, shuffle it over to Terrell. Ames is helping his mother," Darling said, his hand on the doorknob. He knew he didn't have to elaborate because O'Brien would have listened in to hear why Ames was late.

"Bad luck, that," O'Brien said.

ONCE ON THE street, Darling decided that the coffee would be a reward for surviving the barber, so he turned instead in the opposite direction to where the barber pole turned in a stately manner on the next block.

"Morning, Eric," Darling said to the barber.

The shop was empty, and the barber was laying out some instruments on the bench in front of his chair. He looked up and seemed to struggle for a moment with what to say. "Er . . . good morning, sir," he finally managed. "I'm . . . did we . . ."

Darling looked around the empty shop, somewhat flummoxed by this response. "I should have called, of course. I was hoping I could catch you for a quick trim this morning. The usual."

"Of course, Inspector. Please, sit."

This was more like it. Darling removed his coat and hung it on the hook by the door and plunked his hat on top of it.

In silence, the usually garrulous barber draped the cloth around Darling and took up comb and scissors. Puzzled by this silence, Darling essayed a remark about the weather.

"March, eh?" was the only answer he got.

Then he remembered that Eric Strong had been, and might still be, the chair of the Chamber of Commerce. Didn't they usually have a meeting at this time in the month? Perhaps he could tell him what might be circulating about Lorenzo Vitali. He vaguely remembered that Lorenzo had tried a couple of times to join but had been turned away. Was this rejection the same thing that was animating these attacks against him?

"You know, maybe you can help me, Eric. Lorenzo Vitali, the fellow who owns that Italian restaurant down the hill there, has had a couple of, I think you could call them 'attacks' against him. Someone tried to burn his house down, and he's found a couple of notes of warning shoved through the back door of his restaurant."

"Oh, yes?" Strong said noncommittally. He lifted a strand of Darling's hair with his fine-toothed black comb and snipped at a row of dark fronds.

"Well, I was wondering . . . I mean, you have your ear to the ground among the Nelson merchants; has there been anything said about him? I mean, is there a reason he keeps getting the bum's rush?"

"I'm sure I don't know," the barber said stolidly.

At this Darling turned right around to look at him. "I can't believe that. You're the most respected merchant in this town. Everyone turns to you. I thought you were the chairman. You must know something."

Strong had removed comb and scissors from the vicinity of Darling's head because of his sudden movement, and now stood, undecided, with his hands down, his work suspended. He thought for a long moment as Darling turned back to face the mirror. "I'm afraid the discussions at the Chamber are confidential." Comb, snip. "In any case, I'm sure there is nothing to worry about."

"But there is. Someone tried to burn down the Vitalis' house," Darling said, watching Strong in the mirror and feeling the beginnings of some unfamiliar anxiety.

"I certainly hope you are not implying that any of our businessmen were out throwing gas and lighting matches in the middle of the night," Strong said coolly.

Wanting to say, "What the devil is the matter with you? You're not usually like this," Darling instead said, "So you do know about it."

"It's all over town. You might ask yourself what Vitali might have done to deserve it. And I'm sure you will come up with an answer." The barber took the cape off Darling's shoulders and brushed the hair off his suit. "That will be thirty cents, please."

Looking scarcely any different in the hair department, Darling went out the door before he even put on his hat. He was feeling a kind of rising anger that came, he knew, of this new worry. This was now the third person to give him the freezer treatment. Pushing his hat onto his head, he made for the café. At least a cup of coffee was a good honest thing and wouldn't give him any backchat. But he wasn't, now, at all sure about April.

It was with relief that Darling heard nothing but the usual friendly tones in April's voice when he sat down at the counter.

"Inspector, good to see you. I have a fresh pot of coffee, as it happens. In fact, you look as if you could use one." She turned to pull the coffee off the burner and filled him a mug and followed it by pushing the cream jug and the sugar bowl in his direction. The inspector didn't usually take sugar, she knew, but the way he looked this morning, he might.

Darling nursed his cup of coffee between his palms after pouring a dollop of cream into it and watching it swirl.

"Is everything all right, Inspector?" April asked, looking at him with concern.

Darling turned and gazed around the café. It was empty.

"You know, I'm not sure what the heck is going on in this town," he conceded. He toyed with whether he could say anything else. He couldn't talk directly about the case, and he wasn't sure if what was happening to him was related to the case.

"You mean about poor Mr. Vitali and the fire," April said with a nod, thinking she understood. "I have to agree with you there—about something going on, I mean. Yesterday my usual group of ladies was in, and they were talking about Mr. Vitali, and they weren't being all that nice. Apparently, he's been trying to get into the Chamber of Commerce, and they are all shocked by that. Mind you, I will say at least one of the women allowed that as he runs a local business, after all, why shouldn't he be allowed in? Though she was shut down in a hurry. You know what people are like in a group. They said he'd driven a café owner out of business, and that he was suffering now, and it was all Vitali's fault. One of the women was especially sharp, that Mrs. Tilbury, from the hardware store. Then they started in on his missus. Can you imagine, that beautiful woman? And she's always nice to everyone! It's disgusting. I nearly threw the pie right in their faces."

"Now, that's interesting. Do you remember the name of the fellow with the eatery? I think I remember there was a place there when I first came to Nelson. I don't think I ever ate there. It was gone by the time I got back from overseas."

"I went in a few times with my dad when I was a girl. You didn't miss much. It was sort of depressing. The food was okay—I mean, how much can you do to a hamburger? But I remember at least one time when there was an argument in the kitchen loud enough for us to hear out in the booth. In fact, there was a bit of language used that caused my dad to hustle me out of there in a hurry. Now that I think about it, I don't think the Vitalis had even come here yet. They didn't come till the thirties sometime."

These details were, of course, interesting, so Darling nodded and set his mouth in a thoughtful line, and then prodded gently, "Name?"

"Oh, yes, sorry. Now let me see. Hilary, that was the wife's name, and Bob! That's it. Hilary and Bob."

"No surname?"

"Drat. No. The ladies will be back in today, no doubt; do you want me to try to find out?"

"No, absolutely not. I can't have you spying for the constabulary."

April appeared undaunted by this repressive answer. "You know, I kind of want to be a policeman . . . woman. In fact," and here she rested both hands on the counter and looked at him in a way that made him wish he'd taken his coffee to go. "I was going to ask you about it. I mean, what would be my chances of becoming a police officer?"

"On the face of it, it is possible. We don't need anyone right now, of course. But there are some women police officers in Vancouver. It's dangerous work. I'm not sure your father would approve."

"He does dangerous work, so he's hardly in a position to object," she retorted. "Damn," she added, as a couple of men came in and took a booth by the window.

"But he's a man," Darling said to her retreating back, and then immediately felt aghast at himself. He put a coin on the counter and started back to the station, nodding at April as he left. It was a sign, he thought, of how discombobulated he was by getting the cold shoulder that he could have blurted out something so insensitive. Something that he categorically did not believe. Or did he?

CHAPTER THIRTEEN

―――――――

"**W**HAT DO YOU THINK IT is?" asked Lane, picking up the object that Tom Simpson had put before her. It was no bigger than a pebble, but quite definitely had little bulbous eyes. She thought it might have been a carving of a frog or a toad, but the back half was broken off. "It looks a bit like a frog."

"That's what it is," he said. "You're right, these cookies are good. You should thank that lady who sent them."

Lane smiled. "I will. So, what do you make of this? He's almost endearing with these bulgy eyes. And you found him near where we found the skeleton?"

"Near enough. Mr. Barisoff found him. It might just be an artifact from people here before. Probably not from one of the Lakes People, though; we don't make little fellows like this one. Anyway, I called the inspector this morning and asked if I could come in. I didn't tell him why because that store guy was breathing down my neck. But, and I'm sorry here, ma'am, if this isn't convenient, he did say you might drive me into town."

Without a moment's thought about making the long drive two more times, Lane said, "Of course! I'd be happy to." She looked an apology at Barisoff. "Do you mind? We ought to be leaving now."

"No, no. You go. I would drive Mr. Simpson, but my friend Hiro Wakada coming today. Too late to change."

"And give him my best. Make sure he has some of Mrs. Armstrong's cookies." Wakada had been at the Japanese internment camp and had decided to stay on after the war.

HAVING DRUMMED UP her courage to once again use Berenson's phone to let the police station know she was coming in with Simpson without actually revealing anything to that Nosy Parker Berenson, they set off toward Nelson. An awkward silence descended on Lane and Simpson. All she could think of were questions she would like to ask, but she didn't want to be intrusive. They did have the war in common, though. Finally, she tried, "You did communications with the 104th?"

"That's right. It was a pretty good school for me. I got great training, and now I've got a job handling the equipment at the radio station."

"You must have been right in the thick of it, and critical to every success!"

"It was pretty thick all right. What about you?"

"Oh." Lane hesitated. "I just worked in an office."

He turned to look at her. "That's important too. I have a feeling there were thousands of people in offices making

156

sure we had everything we needed out in the field." He paused and glanced at her with a slight frown. "You seem like the kind of person who would have been closer to the action."

Lane tried a sheepish smile. "Oh, you know. They like to keep women away from the messy stuff."

He shook his head and looked out the window past her, toward the lake. "I heard there were women in Europe doing all kinds of dangerous things. Flying planes, parachuting into enemy territory, weapons training."

He was uncanny, she thought. "Alas, no such adventures for me. Just a dull uniform and a dull office job. But I suppose you're right, it probably was important to the war effort on the ground. I know women did do those things, but probably not in very big numbers. You know, the brass generally hadn't got much use for women right on the battlefield."

"Among my people it's women who are in charge. That's what made me think you might have had a combat job. You remind me a little of my grandmother, who is kind of the head of my family. You have that same way of being in charge of things, and you cover it up the same way she does, too. She can make you think something is your own idea, but you know she's holding all the marbles."

Lane felt a tumble of confusion at this observation. She did not feel herself in charge of anything, but, if she thought about it, she'd never much put up with a man being in charge of her when she had left her father's house. There was Angus, who had controlled her like a puppet all through the war. When she discovered nearly two years ago that

Angus had not been killed in combat but had manipulated her and lied to her to cover up his role in recruiting her into intelligence, she had not slid into her old worshipful role, as he had assumed she would. Instead, she'd shed him like the anachronism he was in her life. She became, if not brave, at least strong, self-reliant—and yes, commanding even, at times.

Now here was Simpson talking about a family where a woman was genuinely in charge. "What about your father?"

"I didn't really know him. He was gone pretty early. But to hear my mother tell it, if she said, 'Jump,' he said, 'How high?' And she was pretty young when she had me. Maybe that's why he left; I don't know. It's not like that in all the families all the time now, but it is in ours. I don't think girls have it very good. The work is hard, but when a woman is older, even the chief has to listen to her."

"So, if there's property, say, it descends through the female line?"

"Something like that. Only we aren't too big on property in the way you think of it."

"Well, that certainly could not be more different from the settlers who came here and took over, I guess."

They travelled in silence for some time. Then Lane said, "What are you going to be looking for, exactly?"

"I'm not sure. I'll know it when I see it, though."

"You seemed pretty sure that he could not have been your relative."

"Maybe not in the way you think of relative, but like I said, I'm wondering now if he could be a Native person."

"Because of the frog."

"Hmm," he agreed. "Of course, there's a chance it might not have been his, but something that was there from before."

"Of course. From when your people lived here. How long might they have been living in this area?"

"Thousands of years. There's a place my grandmother told me about on the Slocan River that was a whole big village. I rode out there and spent the night and came back yesterday. I didn't find any little figures like this, but as I said, those little carvings are not typical for us."

"I just can't get over being here for almost two years and knowing nothing at all about a place thousands of years old! I would love to see it."

"I'm willing to bet people have lived here their whole lives, ma'am, and don't know either. Don't feel bad."

Simpson hesitated after this for so long that Lane thought they might make the remainder of the drive in silence. He was gazing away from her out the passenger window. She was just settling into her own thoughts when he spoke again, as if he had made a decision.

"I was planning on trying to catch a ride to get back, but if you were in the mood for more driving, we could go back to New Denver by the other route. If you didn't mind a little walk, I could show you."

"Are you sure? I'd absolutely love it."

ALMOST RELIEVED WHEN the phone rang, Darling barked his name into the receiver.

"It's his nibs on the line, sir."

"Whose nibs? For God's sake, O'Brien, speak English!"

"Dalton, sir."

"The mayor?"

"Yes, sir." O'Brien sounded as if he was covering the receiver so as not to be overheard. Why was he being so cagey?

"Well, don't keep him waiting. Put him through."

"Darling?" The mayor's deep resonant voice bounced down the line at him, sounding irritated.

"Mayor Dalton. Good morning. Oops, almost afternoon. What can I do for you?"

"Listen, Darling." He stopped. Darling listened. "You couldn't come along and see me?"

"I could, certainly. When?"

"The sooner the better, I think. Are you free now?"

He would have liked to imply he was right in the middle of something critical, but he wasn't, with all the cases on hold for lack of information and progress. "Now is fine. See you shortly."

He looked outside and was pleased to see the sun making a bit of an effort, so he left his coat and took up his hat and bounded down the stairs. Maybe now he'd learn why everyone was behaving so strangely.

"Off to see the mayor, O'Brien. I'm expecting my wife to arrive shortly with a man named Simpson. Can you get Terrell on to it in case I'm not back?"

O'Brien pointed out the window. "There they are now, sir, just parking out front."

Darling looked through the glass in the door and pushed it open. Lane and Simpson were just alighting from Lane's little Morris. He'd better fund her a tank of gas, as she was on station business, he thought.

"Mr. Simpson, Lane. I just have to run up to City Hall. I shouldn't be too long, but one of the men will get you started."

"Righty-ho," said Lane. "Mr. Simpson just wants to look at the remains, if that's all right. I'll tell you about it when you're back."

Darling nodded. "By all means. Terrell can help with that. Back in a jiff." With a light step, anticipating that he would soon find out what the heck was going on, Darling made his way up to the mayor's office and announced himself to the clerk in the foyer. The mayor's secretary opened the door to the mayor's inner office with a nod.

There was something in the nod that unnerved him. He found the mayor standing at the window, his hands clasped behind his back. Perhaps he also found that gazing up at Elephant Mountain helped him think. He whirled around at the sound of Darling coming into the room.

"Ah. Inspector. Thank you for coming so quickly. Sit down, sit down." He approached his desk and then paused to point at a decanter with amber liquid at the ready "Drink?"

Darling stood in front of the visitor chair with his hat in his hand, waiting for the mayor to sit. "No, sir. Thanks." He was going to add that it was at least seven hours too early for him but realized that the mayor might take a drink and didn't want to offend him.

In the event, the mayor didn't take a drink, but sat down and planted his tightly clasped hands in front of him on the desk. "Look here, Darling." Another pause.

The mayor fidgeted with his hands, moved some paper, re-clasped them.

"Sir?" Darling's hopeful anticipation dissolved into stomach-churning anxiety. The mayor was behaving like someone who had something very unpleasant to say.

"Look, there's a story going around that you, er, well, I mean, aren't completely on the up and up." Having finally spit this out, the mayor looked up at Darling, scrutinizing him, as if an answer was to be found in his face. Seeing Darling about to speak, he put up his hand to stop him. "The word, Inspector, not to put too fine a point on it, is that you are taking bribes."

Darling was so staggered by this that he was rendered speechless. He could feel the blood draining from his face, as the probable consequences of such a rumour tumbled about in his mind. The sheer difficulty of shoving such a rumour back in the box, the destruction of the trust he'd built up, the loss of his ability to do his job effectively, and then, conscious of where he now sat, dismissal even.

"Nothing to say?"

"I'm sorry, sir. I'm flabbergasted. But let me assure you at once, I certainly am not on the take. From whom am I meant to be taking bribes?"

The mayor shifted uncomfortably again. "I'm not sure I can tell you."

"Because you don't know, or can't say?" This was a nightmare.

"It was just passed along to me by a citizen, a concerned citizen, and if I may say, a completely trustworthy citizen.

Naturally I need to follow it up. We can't have our police department under suspicion."

"Can you tell me who the concerned citizen thinks I was taking bribes from?"

Dalton got up and returned to his position looking out the window with his hands behind his back.

"Sir?" said Darling after a very long moment.

Wheeling around finally, the mayor said, "Look here, Darling. I've never had any reason to doubt you. You've been exemplary. The force had some difficulty with a crooked cop in the thirties, and I think all my predecessors worked to clean the place up. Now, I didn't hire you, I inherited you, if you will. Is there something from your background that you kept from the hiring committee?"

Darling knew that crooked cop. He'd been Darling's direct supervisor. He'd ended up being a crooked cop somewhere else. It horrified him to think anyone could think of them in the same way. He shook his head. "When I was hired, I provided a complete list of positive reviews from the Vancouver Police Department, where I trained. The idea of taking bribes, being influenced even, in any way, is abhorrent to me."

Dalton set his mouth in a grim line and nodded. "Well, I believe you, as I said. But you understand, I will have to investigate this. We need to nip this sort of thing in the bud, you do see that. If there's nothing in it, why, then we go back to status quo, what?"

"If there's nothing in it"? Darling thought. That hardly sounded like unconditional endorsement. "Yes, of course, sir."

"I'll leave you on the job, of course, pending the outcome. Innocent till proven, all that stuff."

Wondering how effective he would be at his job with this hanging over him, he nodded. "Sir, if I may add, Sergeants Ames and O'Brien and Constable Terrell are above reproach. They are excellent police officers to a man. I should not like anything to impugn them."

"Terrell, he's that coloured fellow, isn't he? What do we know about him?"

Swallowing the bolt of anger he felt building up, Darling said, "He has the best references I have ever received for an officer. He is from Nova Scotia."

"He's a long way from home. How can you be sure he's not running away from something? I mean, he doesn't really, you know . . ."

"Doesn't really what, sir?"

"Damn it, Darling, don't make me say it. You know, fit in."

"I am at a loss to understand why not, sir. I have spoken to his superiors in Halifax, and they were extremely sorry to lose him, and assured me I was getting a police officer of integrity and talent. So far, he has been fitting in very well."

With a slight nod, Dalton shrugged. "That's as may be. Well, you know your business best. Your loyalty to your men is certainly commendable. It says something."

But not enough, Darling thought glumly. He rose. "If that will be all, sir?"

"Yes, yes. Oh, and let me reassure you, Inspector, the man I've put in charge of the investigation is of unimpeachable character."

Darling got out onto the street and felt the cool air on

his hot face. He was absolutely unequal to returning to the station just yet and turned down the hill to the waterfront park. The weather, which had been sunny when he'd gone into City Hall, so full of patently foolish optimism, had begun to cloud over, suiting his mood in every way.

LANE EXCUSED HERSELF from the proceedings involving Simpson and went out onto the street. There was something she was hoping to find at the hardware store. Her mind was full of what Simpson had told her, and she looked at everything with new eyes. She mentally removed the whole town of Nelson from the landscape so instead it was just the forest cascading down these steep hills toward the water as it must have done at one time.

With a thud she was back, having bumped into a passing shopper. Uttering an embarrassed apology, she saw she was just about in front of Tilbury's Hardware. She pushed the door open, and the bell alerted the proprietor, who was putting boxes on a shelf.

He immediately stopped what he was doing and gave her a broad smile. "Well, hello. How can I help you?"

"Good afternoon. I was wondering if you had any toasters." She looked along the shelves as she spoke, and then back at him. To her consternation he was coming uncomfortably close to her and was smiling into her eyes, and in the next instant had taken her elbow.

"Just over here, miss." He steered her to a section of shelf near the counter that ran across the back of the shop. He stood a short step behind her and pointed. "I've got the traditional model, but these new ones might be of interest."

To her horror he pointed to a toaster with one hand, but with his other hand he touched her bottom and lingered there. She turned sharply to escape his paddling fingers and was about to give him a piece of her mind, when she heard a sound from the doorway behind the counter. A woman was standing watching them, half hidden in the darkness of the storeroom.

"On second thought," Lane said, "thank you very much." She walked swiftly to the door, wondering if Tilbury—she assumed it was he—had seen the woman, perhaps his wife, watching them. She could hear him calling after her to "come in again sometime." Not bloody likely. If that was the man's wife in the back room, she was glad she'd said nothing. What a frightful thing, to have to hear a woman upbraiding one's husband for that sort of lechery!

CHAPTER FOURTEEN

December 1947

VIOLA TILBURY SAT ON AN empty wooden crate in the basement, wishing she could light the furnace, but it wouldn't be worth it for this short visit. Before her was a box of identical books, one of which she held in her hand, open to a page with a photograph of her father, so young and handsome, in 1911. He was standing with other men on a just-completed section of railway, a locomotive steaming behind them, as if it were anxious to see the track completed so it could get on its way.

Why had her mother never told her about her father's book? They had lived since she was a child as if they were in a permanent state of grieving. Her mother had gone into mourning when her father disappeared, and the shock of being broke had been the final straw. They had moved back to her grandfather's house in Ontario. She put her finger gently on the face of the man she knew to be her father. She could almost remember him like that. She'd been twelve when he'd disappeared, and the terrible longing and anxiety had coloured her whole adolescence. She remembered her mother withdrawing into herself, having to coax her mother to eat, to drink, to survive, having to look after her, though she herself was struggling. Even after they moved, her mother could not seem to find the ground under her feet and had become reclusive and constantly angry. Viola struggled now with the memory of her own anger at having to leave and go to Kingston, a place she had never known; she remembered her loneliness and the void inside for her missing father that never seemed to heal.

When he'd gone, he'd taken the sunshine away. He'd been a font of energy, had loved her, had taken her for walks and for sodas, and had been full of laughter. And now, these! The miracle of books written by her father, about his brilliantly successful life and all he'd accomplished. She stood up and picked up the box of books and carried it upstairs. In the kitchen, she set the box on the table and then looked around. She felt overwhelmed by the task she had reluctantly set herself to do. She would not leave such piles of stuff to be gone through by her husband's nieces. Finally, she sat down, feeling weariness overcome her. As soon as her mother had died, Viola had taken the money from her grandfather's dwindling estate and moved back to Nelson. She had been living in her father's house for only three months when she met Gilbert Tilbury. He'd said he remembered her from school and had always thought she was cute.

The day she married Gilbert Tilbury, she felt as though she'd moved from a permanent twilight into the brightness of a sunny day. She'd shut up her father's house again, feeling as if she could put the past behind her at last. Gilbert had inherited his father's dry goods business and was making a modern hardware store, and she was happy to work right alongside him.

Now she sat wearily in the kitchen of her father's house. Even though Gilbert had said they should get rid of it, she had been feeling an increasing reluctance. If she lost this house, she lost every connection to her father. In the childless and increasingly fraught years that followed her marriage, she had begun to wonder if she might need the house after all. And she was beginning to think the rumours she'd heard about Gilbert were true. But now there were these books, these wonderful books. She pulled them out of the box. She saw a few papers and an old housekeeping journal at the bottom but left them and held the books close to her.

LANE HAD RETURNED swiftly to the police station, trying to regain her equilibrium. O'Brien nodded and asked if she wanted to pop downstairs and have a look at the skeleton with Terrell and Simpson. Lane smiled, relieved at the distraction, and grateful to the sergeant. It was a fine thing that O'Brien recognized it was the sort of thing she'd enjoy.

"Yes, actually. Do you think they'd mind?"

"You can but ask," O'Brien said.

She found them in the cold little room used as morgue and post-mortem room. Terrell had removed the sheet from the remains and Simpson was looking carefully through an enamelled tray of cloth fragments. Lane asked if anyone minded her being there.

"That's okay, ma'am," Terrell said. "I don't think it's all that pretty, though."

"What is it that you are looking for?" she asked Simpson.

"I'm not sure, really. But I don't want to leave without seeing anything I can," Simpson said.

"We certainly are having trouble putting a name to the man. If you can find anything useful it might help," Terrell said.

"We found a little stone figure where this man was buried. It makes me wonder if he may have been someone of Indian origin. I guess I'm hoping to find something that might tell me that, at least."

"How are you finding things here?" Lane asked Terrell, as they watched Simpson going through the scraps, carefully inspecting each one.

"I couldn't be happier. I like a small town. I grew up in one, but it's different enough that it's still interesting. Very good station, too. I miss my mother and grandmother, of course, but I'm glad I made the move." He put the basin on the table and got a second one to put the scraps into.

"I'm glad. The inspector not being too hard on you?" She smiled.

Terrell returned the smile. "Just hard enough, ma'am."

After a few minutes of watching Simpson pick up and turn each scrap of fabric, Lane, now consumed with the fascination of this activity, had very nearly got over her fury at what had happened at the hardware store. She spoke to Simpson. "Anything catch your eye?"

"So far it looks like he was dressed like any rancher or cowboy."

Wondering if the missing Turner would have dressed like a cowboy, Lane turned her mind to Darling as he'd hurried off to City Hall. He'd looked almost upbeat; perhaps a visit to the boss would bring good news—an infusion of new funds to update equipment or hire new staff, she speculated.

"Ah," said Simpson, "here's something."

Lane turned to see what he'd found. It was no more than an inch by about two inches and brown, though she couldn't tell if it was the original colour or dirtied.

"It's handwoven," Simpson said. "I think it's a kind of weaving done by Indians. It looks like it used to be . . . maybe blue? And another colour." Simpson seemed subdued.

Lane peered at it under the light. "Was it part of a belt, do you think, or the handle of a bag?"

"It's pretty small. I'm thinking this man wore this around his neck. A little bag that had something in it that was important to him. I'm thinking about the little frog we found." Simpson reached into his pocket and took out the little figure, and placed it next to the scrap of cloth, as if to see if they belonged together.

"I wonder if my husband is back yet. This is very important, don't you think?

"Yeah, I think it is," Simpson said. He turned his gaze back to the figure and shook his head. "Poor guy."

Lane hurried back upstairs and found O'Brien, just hanging up the receiver on his desk phone. "Is the inspector back yet?"

"He just went up to his office."

"Do you think he'd mind if I went up to see him?"

O'Brien shook his head. It was hard to know what he'd

mind. The inspector had looked, he thought, like death warmed over.

Lane found his office door closed, so she knocked and waited. There was a pause, the scraping of a chair, and then Darling opened the door.

"Ah. Have you found anything of interest?"

Lane hesitated. There was something in his face that she couldn't put her finger on, a disquieting expression she hadn't seen before. "Yes, I think so." She told him about the finding of the little figure. "Mr. Simpson has identified something among the bits of cloth that Dr. Gillingham collected."

In spite of his mood, Darling was interested. "You don't say? Show me."

Downstairs, they found Terrell putting the scrap tray back on the shelf. The skeleton was again under its sheet.

"I understand you've found something," Darling said.

Simpson explained to Darling about the weaving, and what he thought it might mean. "I didn't like to ask, sir, because I didn't think it was any of my business, but may I ask now how he died?"

"According to our pathologist, Dr. Gillingham, he was shot at close range in the chest. You can see where the ribs were damaged by the bullet, or bullets." Darling approached the skeleton and pulled back the sheet. "I don't know if I can show it to you with the clarity the pathologist did. Yes, here, you see?" Darling pointed at the left side of the collapsing rib cage. Simpson leaned over and looked.

"It might account for the frog. If he was wearing the little stone frog on his chest in a woven bag, it might have damaged it. Knocked the back off it."

Darling took up the piece of weaving and looked at it under the light. "I tell you what, I'll get Gilly, Dr. Gillingham, to have a closer look at this. If what you say is the case, it possibly puts paid to our working theory. It has been a practice over the years for your relations to come back to where your ancestors lived?"

Simpson nodded. "It has been off and on." He looked again at the skeleton. "But we don't carry these little figures."

Lane looked at her watch. "I wonder if we ought to think of the return trip. Mr. Simpson has promised to show me the remains of a village by the Slocan River. Mr. Simpson, do you think you have everything you need?" she asked.

Simpson nodded. "I think I've learned what I can. It occurs to me," he added, "that if he is an Indian, maybe he came up here to prospect. My grandmother knows a lot about different tribes. He might even have come up here around the same time as my grandparents. They might have known him, or someone on the reservation would have known him. That little piece of weaving would help. It could be that someone might recognize it."

"It would be very helpful if you could make inquiries," Darling said. "I certainly can have a good photograph taken of it and give you one to take back. If it looks like he's from across the border, I might have to involve authorities there as well, but I'm guessing you'll have better luck finding out anything that is there to be found." He looked at his watch. "Sergeant O'Brien is a dab hand with a camera. I can get him to do it and have a photo ready tomorrow. Would you be able to come back?"

"I'm sure Mr. Barisoff would be willing to drive me. This good lady has gone to a lot of trouble already!"

Lane stayed behind with Darling for a moment while Simpson made his way upstairs. "Are you all right?"

"Never better," Darling said in a way that suggested he didn't want to discuss it.

"Only, the mayor, I wondered—"

"Nope. He's fine too. You'd best be off, or it will be the middle of the night before you get back, and I can imagine how much you'll love driving that road in the dark."

"If you're sure. There's stew left in the fridge if I get back too late."

"Don't get back too late, how's that for a plan?"

She kissed him lightly on the cheek. "Righty-ho." But she could not shake a sense of unease.

It was as they drove out of town that she realized Darling hadn't fussed about her driving home at night.

Simpson leaned back and crossed his arms. "You know, whoever that guy is he should have a proper burial. And someone somewhere is missing a family member. It's a real shame."

THEY HAD DRIVEN for about thirty minutes when Simpson said, "Slow down. It's along here. There." He pointed at a break in the bush at the edge of the road that proved to be nothing more than a cart track. "Can you drive along there for a bit?"

Lane turned the car onto the narrow track and bumped

along for a few hundred yards until they reached a dead end. "We'll have to stop here. How far are we going?"

"I don't reckon it's more than a quarter mile. We have to cross here, and then get to the railway and cross that."

There were breaks in the billows of grey clouds collecting against the mountains behind them, and Lane was hoping they were a sign that the rain would hold off. They followed the path Simpson had followed before down an embankment, to the railway, and across the shallow creek. She wished she'd worn her Wellingtons, as she had missed her step crossing the rocks in the creek and now had one wet shoe, and her trousers were damp up to the knees from the high grass.

They scrambled down a steep hill until she could just see water through the trees.

"I'm a bit turned around, I think. This is the Slocan River?" she asked.

"That's right."

They walked through a forest of evergreen and stands of leafless birch and larch, the river glinting grey and deep green just through the trees.

"There," Simpson said, coming to a stop.

At first Lane felt she was simply standing in an ordinary bit of forest and looked around quizzically, but then she saw them. It was as if they emerged and built themselves before her eyes. A series of great depressions all around her.

"I think this big one here is where they would have had gatherings," Simpson said, pointing at a circle some twenty feet across and perhaps four or five feet deep at its centre.

"There was a structure of some sort?" Lane asked.

"Yup. Walls, a roof with a smoke escape, a door. I imagine they were very cozy in the winter."

"The only images I've ever seen of Indian homes, and this was back in Britain, were tipis. This is amazing."

"We had something like those. Not exactly tipis, but originally it was a mat woven out of tule and placed on a tripod sort of stand. I still remember that. It's funny, I remember the smell—a sort of nice grassy smell." He stopped and looked around. "The thing is, this is one of the few villages that was not drowned by a dam. And in that direction, out of sight, is Frog Peak. He looks out over everything."

Lane looked where he pointed. "I can just imagine what it must have been like. This village full of people, fishing, going about their lives, being looked out for by Frog Peak there." And then it was over, she thought. She looked through the trees at the quiet river. Progress at the expense of a people made invisible.

Simpson turned reluctantly away. It was remarkable; that was how he imagined it as well. It made him sad to think that he, an exile really, would never feel that absolute security of knowing he was where he belonged. "We'd best get on, ma'am, if you don't want to find yourself driving home in the dark." He began to retrace his steps through the wood toward the car.

In the car, Lane turned to him. "Mr. Simpson, thank you. I feel like I've looked right into history." Simpson gave her a brief smile. "Yup. That's us. A relic of the past."

That night, on his cot, he found he was restless. The Hornblower book was not doing its usual job of making him sleepy. He lay flat on his back, his arm over his forehead, looking up at the dark ceiling. The idea that he had been propelled by some inner drive to come to this place still had a hold. But going to the decaying village had only made him melancholy and did not seem to quiet that sense of urgency he felt. He had surprised himself with talking to Miss Winslow, and even showing her the village. She was easy to talk to, and she seemed genuinely interested. Had that been a mistake? One thing he knew for sure: it wasn't going to change anything. Not for him, not for his people.

He turned over onto his side. It wouldn't matter. He would be leaving soon, taking with him nothing but a couple of photos. He imagined himself in his new job, settled at home, the war finally behind him, but he couldn't imagine this feeling of disquiet away.

CHAPTER FIFTEEN

***

BERENSON DIDN'T BOTHER KNOCKING. HE hoisted the bag he'd been carrying onto his hip and turned the doorknob to open the door. "Brought you some grub," he said.

He found Stella in the kitchen, seated at the table with what appeared to be the remnants of her apron on the table in front of her. She looked up at him with tears in her eyes. He put the bag by the sink and shook his head.

"Now what's up?"

"I have to sew this," was all she said, but there was a hint of desperation that made Berenson's heart sink. She could be winding up for one of her spells.

Sitting down next to her, he took the apron and examined it. She released it passively and looked at him, wide-eyed. "It's not so bad," he said. "Why don't you wait and do that in the morning, when it's lighter?"

"He'll be angry," she said, snatching the apron back.

Berenson looked around the kitchen. It was worse than he'd ever seen it. What dishes had been used were left sitting on the counter and on the table in front of her, most of the food uneaten and crusting onto the plates. It was clear the stove hadn't been lit in some time. And now she was thinking "he" was here somewhere.

"There's nobody here gonna get mad. He's gone. In fact, he was never here. You understand? I'll light this stove, and you try to pull yourself together and make us something to eat. It's freezing in here." Indeed, he'd not taken off his woollen jacket, and she was in her frayed and grimy pink padded bathrobe, which she no doubt hadn't been out of for days. She didn't smell too good, either.

The wood he'd chopped for her nearly a month before and stored in the listing garage behind the house was almost untouched. Shaking his head, he collected an armful and went back into the cottage. He was relieved to see she'd gotten up and was looking into the bag.

"Fill that damn kettle. I'll have a fire here in no time." With some effort he bent over to open the stove to lay a fire and pushed some wood into it. He wasn't getting any younger. "Why don't you use your stove?"

It was pointless, he knew. And hopeless. What happened to someone like her? They must have places, but that was out of the question. He sure as hell wasn't going to have her at his place. He watched her taking the food out of the bag. A loaf of bread, a carton of eggs, some cans of soup, a bottle of milk. She was as thin as a stick, he thought, looking at her back. He could almost not remember what she had looked like when he first met her. No use thinking about that. She was bad now, but if she went into a home where she wouldn't have to do anything for herself, she'd be finished. How was he going to get her to understand?

LANE LOOKED OVER at Darling, his profile lit only by the fire in the Franklin. He'd hardly spoken since they'd sat down for their evening drink. When she thought back to dinner, she realized she had dominated the conversation talking about her trip to the site of the ancient village.

"You have been quiet. Something at work?"

He looked up at her as if he had been miles away. "Yes. You know how it is. In fact, I am rather tired. I think I'll turn in. You stay on and enjoy the fire."

Lane watched him disappear down the hallway and then turned back to look at the flames, feeling a roil of anxiety. Perhaps it was just something at work, but she felt he was . . . she tried to put a name to it . . . pinched, closed, something more than just unforthcoming. He'd been unforthcoming many times over cases, but this was different. It was almost as if he were keeping whatever it was even from himself.

She got up and stretched and went to stand in the dark in front of the window to look out at the lake. There was a half moon that had managed to elbow its way through the clouds and was reflected in pale yellow on the water's shimmering black surface. Illumination that only intensified the darkness. What had happened that afternoon while she was with Simpson? She'd come back quite late, and he'd come in even later. Late as it was, neither had eaten, so they'd warmed up the stew and she'd blathered on about her trip. Why had he been so late?

Perhaps something had come up at the last minute, or maybe the mayor said there would be cutbacks. Had Darling stayed at his desk long after the night shift had come on, going over the budget, trying to figure out how to tell people there would be changes? But he would have said. He would have been voluble and angry. He would have been upset and worried about his men. There wouldn't have been this rigid silence. She could feel her own anxiety climbing, and she turned abruptly and told herself it wouldn't do anyone any good at all if she became a nervous wreck. When Darling was ready to tell her, he would. With this resolve she closed the door of the stove, put the whisky glasses on the kitchen counter, and padded off to bed. Only then she remembered that ass, Tilbury, pawing her behind. There was something, she thought, Darling definitely didn't need to be burdened with.

DARLING FELT HER come to bed carefully so as not to wake him, and he waited in the dark until he heard her steady breathing, hoping that its soothing sound would lull him into sleep as well, but he lay awake for what felt like an interminable time, his guts a knot. What had he done that would make someone think he was on the take? He tried to recall any interactions that would have caused a "trusted citizen" to believe he had accepted anything remotely like a bribe. And who would be investigating him? Investigating *him*! The idea created a wave of apprehension that in the dark felt like guilt. His thoughts became steadily less organized, and he finally fell into a restless sleep after one in the morning.

DAVID BERTOLLI STOOD indecisively in front of the fridge in the new supermarket, on his way out of town after school. Had Angela asked him to bring home a bottle of milk? Or had she said she had milk but needed something else? Deciding that with their brood of three boys a bottle of milk would never go amiss, he took one out of the fridge and then looked down the bread shelf. Unlike the other energetic ladies of King's Cove, his wife did not fill her days with baking. Still with only the vaguest notions of what might be on hand at home, he approached the counter with his milk and a loaf of Wonder Bread, the chosen favourite of the boys.

"I know I'll get home and be in trouble because I've forgotten something important," he commented to the man by the cash register.

"Oh, don't I know it! I work here and I always forget what Marge wanted at the store. Always wanting something. Will this be all?"

David looked around again. The store was mostly empty. "Let me just run up and down the shelves and see if anything comes to mind," he said.

"Take your time."

Crackers, sugar, cans of soup and beans. At the side near the refrigerator were some open wooden bins with potatoes and carrots and a few desultory and tired apples. He picked one up and felt it. A Red Delicious, any crunch it might have had long gone. Thank heaven the one thing they had was plenty of apples. It's what King's Cove was famous for, after all. He made his way back to the front.

"I guess that's all. I'm sure I'll remember something

else the second the ferry has dropped me on the other side. You hear about that fire?"

The cashier rang up the bread and milk. "Thirty-five cents, please. I did hear about it. Glad it wasn't my house. You can bet your bottom dollar the police won't do anything about it."

Fishing the coins out of his pocket, David frowned. "What do you mean?"

"I had a kid run off with some chocolate bars the other week, and I went into the station with a perfect description of him and I've yet to hear. I expect he was the son of one of our civic leaders." He almost snorted his contempt. "But what do you expect? When the top guy is crooked, you know the rot's gone all the way through. Need a bag?"

David nodded. "I don't understand—are you saying the mayor is crooked?"

"Not the mayor, that inspector who runs the station. I confess, I was shocked to hear it as he's a vet and all. But that's the modern world, I guess. Everyone out for himself."

"But wait a minute, Inspector Darling? There's never been a more honest man. You must have gotten the wrong end of the stick."

"I wish I had. Chamber of Commerce meeting last night. Impeccable source." He leaned on the counter and said in a stage whisper, "Had it from the mayor himself. Investigation underway."

"I don't believe it!" David said, taking up his bag.

The cashier shrugged. "Suit yourself. I know what I know. You mark my words, when it comes out it will be the biggest scandal in this town since the thirties."

The drive home, already made uneasy by a sudden squall of rain that forced him to drive no faster than thirty, was filled with misgivings. Frederick Darling could not be "crooked," whatever that was supposed to mean. He'd yet to meet a more honest and upright man or one more serious about his job. By the time he'd got to the turnoff at King's Cove, the rain had lessened, leaving streaming muddy trails in its wake, and David was furious. The man had suggested the police failed to catch the juvenile chocolate thief because he was the son of someone important. Was he implying the police in general, and Darling in particular, were in league with the powers that be? But then why would the mayor, certainly a power that was, confide to someone at the Chamber of Commerce that there was an investigation going forward?

His mind still reeling, David hurried up the steps and plunked the groceries on the kitchen table. Angela looked into the paper bag and said, "No cereal."

"Sorry, I completely forgot what you asked for. You'll never believe what happened."

"I believe you forgot the cereal. You almost never remember what I ask for. You artistic types! I should pin a note to your overcoat. The kids can eat toast tomorrow morning. It will serve them right for sneaking cornflakes in the afternoon." Angela put the milk in the fridge and plopped the bread into the breadbox, and then turned at the sound of her husband collapsing onto a kitchen chair. "Good grief! What's the matter? No cereal is not the end of the world."

"Something's happened that I just can't believe, and I have no idea what to do about it."

THE SUN CAUSED the drops on the dishevelled shrubbery and overlong grass in the yard to sparkle. Lane loved the morning above all else, but this morning, in the silence left in the wake of Darling's departure, she was filled with a continued gnawing unease. He'd said he was going to drive up to New Denver in the afternoon to give Simpson the photo of the cloth and stone figure. When Lane had offered, he'd shaken his head in a distracted manner and gone off with hardly another word. She'd been unable to get anything from him with bright inquiries about the progress of the arson case. Looking back, she felt she'd been exaggeratedly chatty to try to counteract his near silence. It must, she thought disconsolately, have been very annoying when he was clearly struggling with something.

Her reflections were interrupted by the ringing of the telephone in the hall. Two longs and a short. Hers. With a sigh she went into the dark hallway and picked up the earpiece on her old-fashioned wall phone. "KC 431, Lane Winslow speaking," she said into the trumpet.

"Lane, darling," Angela said, and then hesitated.

"Hello, Angela. Is everything all right?" Now Angela was behaving peculiarly.

"I'm just going down to the mail. Would you have some coffee on hand if I stopped by?"

"Certainly. Is everything all right?" She realized she'd already asked that. "I'll put a new pot on. When are you coming?"

"I'll just leave now. Dave dropped the boys off at the school. It's a lovely morning. It'll be a nice walk."

Wanting to say, "Your forced jollity is fooling no one,"

Lane instead said, "The coffee will be ready," and rang off.

Beginning to feel that everyone had gone slightly mad, Lane emptied the grounds and coffee from breakfast onto the flower bed just below the porch, refilled the basket from the coffee tin, and then stood by the stove, listening to the electric element click as it heated up. With a breath of resolve, she cleared the breakfast plates into the sink and began to wash them. She had just dried the last fork and pushed it into the drawer when she heard Angela come in.

"Helloo?"

"In here. Coffee's nearly ready."

Angela came in in a flurry of woollen jacket and energy. "Thank heavens. I barely get a swallow in the mornings, getting that mob out of the house." She took off her jacket and dropped into the chair Darling had been brooding in an hour before.

Lane poured the coffee and put out the bottle of milk and the sugar bowl. She watched Angela spoon sugar into the coffee and stir it with great concentration. She was about to speak when Angela said, "I've really only come to make sure you're all right."

"Of course I am. Why shouldn't I be? You're being very mysterious."

"Oh," Angela said and sat back, momentarily flummoxed. "Has Frederick not said anything?"

"No, Frederick has not said anything. He has, in fact, said less than nothing. What's going on?"

Angela stirred her coffee again. "Oh, dear, I didn't mean to be the one to tell you. You see, David stopped off at that new supermarket on the way home yesterday, and of course forgot what I asked him to bring. Honestly! I don't think he's ever remembered anything I've asked for in the nine years we've been married."

"Angela . . ." Lane said, beginning to feel real panic.

"Yes, yes, okay. It's just that the guy who runs the store told David—I don't know how to even say this—that Frederick is under investigation. He implied he was 'crooked' in some way. David told him it was absolute garbage, of course!"

CHAPTER SIXTEEN

***

DARLING ARRIVED AT THE STATION to find Terrell front and centre.

"There's been a second fire, sir. Not directed at any residence, but it's peculiar. A big empty oil drum behind the train station was set alight. The call came to the fire hall at 3:20 in the morning. It was contained, but the blaze was big enough that it alarmed a householder a short way up the hill. The fire chief just called me a few minutes ago to let me know. I'm on my way out to have a look, sir."

"And good morning to you," Darling said, feeling a dreadful combination of exhaustion and wired anxiety. He was going to have to meet with the men and try to tell them what was up, but he had not, in spite of hours of wakefulness, come up with a way to broach the subject. Well, he thought, this gave him some breathing space.

"Run along then. I want to meet with everyone at, say, 9:30. That give you enough time?"

"Sir," said Terrell slipping on his coat.

When he'd gone, O'Brien, who'd been waiting in the background, said, "'Morning, sir."

"O'Brien."

"You look a bit under-rested, if I may say so."

"You may not. I will want to see everyone at 9:30, interview room. Can you manage that?" Darling knew the sarcasm was a direct result of his exhaustion and worry and felt marginally sorry.

"Me as well? Only, the phones—"

"You can slap a Closed sign on the door and leave the phones unanswered for ten minutes. And let's hope no one dies or gets themselves robbed in the interim."

Darling trudged up the stairs and shut himself into the office. He pulled his foolscap pad toward him and took up a pencil, which he examined closely for sharpness, and then printed in caps at the top "BRIBERY INVESTIGATION."

Underneath he wrote, "Who?" and followed it up with "Chamber of Commerce." And then he put his pencil down and turned to Elephant Mountain.

LANE STOOD IN front of her window, watching the thin mist of cloud moving across the forget-me-not blue sky above the lake. Angela's apologetic goodbyes still echoed in the hallway. Lane was angry in a way she could not remember having been before. The worst of it was that she could not talk about it with the people she trusted the most, the Armstrongs. Angela had readily agreed to keep mum about it, but Darling would never want something like this to be the subject of idle speculation among his neighbours.

She thought about telephoning him, just to . . . what?

See if he was coping? Let him know she knew? He would be up to his neck in trying to deal with it. He wouldn't need her fussing about him. And then it came to her: what was really bothering her was that he had not confided in her in the first place. What did that mean?

What did it mean, her own just thoughts reminded her, that she had not confided in him when she'd had a bad night? Or had had to deal with that appalling man? She had been ashamed about her bad night, that was one reason, and she hadn't wanted to worry him. The other was so trivial as to be ludicrous in light of what else was happening. Well, not wanting to worry him was her excuse, wasn't it? Was Darling feeling shame as well, or was it as simple as not wanting to worry her? Or was he afraid that she might believe the rumours? No. He must know in his very bones she could not doubt him.

TERRELL STOOD OVER the oil barrel, peering inside and smelling what was rapidly becoming a disagreeable stench: ashes doused in water. "It would have just burned down if you hadn't been called out," he commented.

"Likely," agreed McAvity. "The caller said the flames were shooting up. When she stepped outside, she could hear the 'whoop' all the way from over there." He turned and pointed to a few houses along the curve of the road out of the town. "It suggests a lot of gas was used. It burned up most of what was in here. Here, I saved this part till you got here." He took the barrel and knocked it on its side and then turned it over to empty whatever was left from the conflagration.

They both leaned over to stare at the black mess on the ground. McAvity found a stick and poked at the ash. "There's still some remnant of something. What do you make of that?" He isolated a blackened but still somewhat solid piece of detritus and moved it away from the pile.

"Something cardboard-like, maybe? So dense it didn't quite burn through." Terrell toed it gently over. "A book cover? Someone came all the way here with an armful of books to burn?"

"You're probably right," McAvity said, registering a little disappointment. "Someone just burning their personal garbage. Didn't want to stink up their own backyard. Still, I'll fish out whatever solid matter I find and use some of my idle time waiting for a real fire to see if I can figure anything else out. It's certainly against city bylaws to burn household garbage like this. People in the country do this sort of thing all the time, but even there they are limited as to season—though that doesn't stop a lot of them. Then I have to run out to God knows where to put out the house fire, or shed fire, praying the whole time they don't start a forest fire."

TERRELL WALKED BACK to the station, his mind turning over why someone would cart their books to an out-of-the-way place to burn them. When he walked in, O'Brien was at the door.

"Just in time. I was about to lock up. Meeting down in the interview room."

The men didn't sit because Darling didn't; they leaned

with their backs against the wall, arms crossed or hands in pockets.

"The mayor called me in yesterday," Darling began. "I won't beat about the bush. He said he had heard that I am on the take, that someone has been bribing me. To what end I cannot imagine."

This elicited a gasp. "What absolute garbage, sir!" Ames exclaimed indignantly. "Where in God's name is that coming from?"

"I have no idea. But it's apparently going around the town. There is to be an investigation, though His Mayorness has not told me whom he has tasked with the assignment." I must keep my bitterness in check, Darling thought. "I don't know what form the investigation will take, but I imagine our books, our finances, our procedures, the resolution of our cases, unsolved cases, and so on will be gone through. I imagine you will be interviewed individually. I want to be absolutely clear here: you are to be completely truthful. Do not be afraid of offending me; in any case, I am unlikely to ever see the contents of your interviews. I have done nothing myself; the idea is repugnant to me, and I am confident, indeed I reassured the mayor, that you yourselves are the most upright police officers I've ever worked with. Nothing but absolute candour will get us through this. Is that clear?"

A collective response of "Yes, sir," and nods all around.

"It'll be one of the RCMP, I expect," O'Brien said. "Oh, goody."

"I suppose you're right. I was not told. Now, while I have you all here, let's quickly run over what we're working on and then get back to work.

"One is we have John Doe. Very cold case indeed; it may be connected to the disappearance of Turner back in 1921. We are waiting for dental records. What we know about Turner is what, Ames? You've been reading up on him."

"Yes, sir. Born 1880 in Kingston, Ontario, came out here for the silver and gold rush up in Sandon, made a packet building some of the railway lines used to ship ore out of the area. Lived in town, had a wife and daughter, left one day in late March of 1921 on either a business trip or maybe a camping trip, and never returned. Wife waited five days from when he was supposed to be back to report it. Searches at the time found no trace of him. Wife and child returned to Ontario, apparently, leaving the house vacant. I've sent to Ontario to try to track the wife down to see what she can tell us, especially as regards to his wardrobe. One important thing I've just learned is that he was dead broke at the time of his disappearance."

"You don't say," Darling said. "Well, since you applied yourself so assiduously to this, we have new information. Mr. Simpson, who was present at the discovery of the body, has found a small stone carving near where the body was. He is going to take the photo of a fragment of cloth found with the body and the stone back to his community on the off chance someone recognizes it. Terrell, the fire?"

"Sir. As you know, Mr. Vitali's house suffered some fire damage the other night. A clear case of arson. Gas can nearby, footprint of fleeing arsonist. As well, a couple of warning notes delivered to the restaurant saying the Vitalis aren't wanted here. It seems there is some sort of campaign against him, but for what reason is unclear. I believe the

Vitalis could be in danger. And I should add, sir, that I just came back from going over that fire in the oil drum with McAvity. It was an illegal garbage fire, but what made it stand out was that clearly a large amount of gas was used, and in the refuse we found what could be fragments of book covers that were not wholly incinerated. The chief has taken these scraps to go through more carefully and will contact me with his results."

"Books?" exclaimed Ames, standing up straight. "I wonder if they might be the books stolen from the book-store. I mean, it could be just a coincidence."

Darling nodded. "Look into that, Ames. O'Brien, let's go over the files to make sure they are at least in order for the investigator."

"Sir." O'Brien frowned in an effort to recollect something he was supposed to pass on, but no business resulted. Something about the Turner case.

"And let's not lose our focus. Back to the Vitali fire. Ames and O'Brien, you're both local boys. Do you remember an eatery run by people called Hilary and Bob? Apparently, it closed in the thirties, before the war, anyway, and about the time the Vitalis set up shop."

O'Brien nodded. "I remember the place, sir. Pretty indifferent food. Definitely what you'd call a greasy spoon. I used to get the odd lunch there when I was starting out."

"And do you remember the surname of Bob and Hilary?" Darling asked with slightly exaggerated patience.

O'Brien looked at the ceiling and twisted his mouth as an aide-mémoire. "Oh, wait! I think I know! The wife was a friend of my mother, sort of. Mother used to breathe a sigh of relief when she left after a visit because she was such a gloomy guts. Mrs. . . . Mrs. . . . damn! Mrs. . . . Stamp. That was it! It's funny, now I think of it, Mother hasn't mentioned her for years."

"Terrell, something for you to follow up on. Everybody clear? Business as usual." Darling turned and made for the door. The men stood for a couple of moments listening to his footsteps recede up the stairs.

"Well, let's get at it," O'Brien said, making a shooing motion with his hands. "Crime waits for no man."

Ames was last out of the interview room, and as he turned out the light, he realized he felt a slight letdown that Darling had no sarcastic response to his burning book theory, as he might normally have had. It showed, he thought, what a lot of strain the boss was under, and he was heartily sorry. One thing this fire possibly did, though, was bring the book robbery and the Vitali fire under one roof.

TERRELL'S ANXIETY ABOUT the investigation into his boss was kept steady by a sense of duty. He had been given orders to look into the Stamps as a possible source of grievance against the Vitalis, and he focused on this now. Underlying the immediate worry engendered by Darling's revelation was an absolute certainty that it would come out right in the end. He was not often wrong about people, and he knew he was not wrong about Darling; a straighter or more intelligent man was hard to find.

He pulled out the phone directory and ran his finger down the entries under S until he found "Stamp, R.," next to which was a phone number and an address on Sixth

Street. He jotted down the information and then picked up the phone. After five rings he was about to hang up when someone picked up the receiver.

"Hello?" The voice was female, a combination of tentative and challenging.

"Is this Mrs. Hilary Stamp?"

"Yes. Who is this?"

"This is Constable Terrell of the Nelson Police. I wonder if I could come by and have a word. Do you still live on Sixth?"

There was a longish silence and then, "Why do you need to talk to me?"

"We're just following up on a matter. It wouldn't take long. Is your husband at home?"

"I suppose so. When are you coming?"

Not sure if Mrs. Stamp meant that she supposed her husband was at home, or she supposed it would be all right for him to stop by, Terrell said, "I can be there shortly. I'll leave now."

Mrs. Stamp hung up with no further answer.

Terrell held the paper with the address on it for O'Brien to see.

"That's up the hill, east of here. That number should be at the end of the street near the school," the sergeant said, reaching up for the car keys and handing them over. He watched Terrell go out the door and shook his head, wondering what sort of reception he'd get.

CHAPTER SEVENTEEN

UNAWARE THAT THE BOTTOM HAD fallen out at the police station, April replenished the pie under the glass dome and wiped down the counters from the morning rush, thinking it odd that none of the fellows from the station had come in for their morning coffee. Ames always ate his breakfast at the café and lately had brought along Terrell, who had fallen in with the habit himself. Perhaps they were busy.

Her father had told her that he'd had to go out on a call about a fire in an oil drum near the station, and that he was going to call that young officer, Terrell, to look at it with him. April had pretended to leaf through the morning paper to cover up the slight leap of her heart. What would her father think? she wondered now. He obviously liked Terrell. Well, that wasn't actually clear. He'd adopted him. He'd said at dinner once that the kid was new in town and needed to feel welcome. After he'd gone to the Vitalis' house with him he'd said with undisguised admiration that he was a "smart guy." Was that the same as liking him? Accepting him?

Reminding herself sternly that it didn't matter, because nothing was going to come of it, she emptied out the two pots of coffee that had been used for the breakfast rush and prepared two more for mid-morning and lunch. Then, drawn by a hurried movement on the sidewalk in front of the café, she looked up and saw Mrs. Tilbury from the hardware store walking swiftly in the opposite direction from her business, wiping tears from her eyes. Without thought, April hurried out onto the sidewalk and caught up with her.

"Are you all right, Mrs. Tilbury? Has anything happened?"

Viola Tilbury looked up, startled to find herself accosted, and shook her head violently. "No, no. I'm all right. Leave me alone!"

April watched her make her way down the street and turn up the hill at the corner. Feeling she shouldn't have impulsively gone out to help, she returned sheepishly to her wiping. Al, the cook, a cigarette hanging out of the corner of his mouth, watched her through the service window, and then lifted his chin in inquiry. "What's going on?" he asked.

"I don't know. One of the ladies from the afternoon group crying about something. I don't guess she'll be coming in this afternoon, but maybe some of her chums will gossip about it. They can't help themselves."

"What'd you think you were gonna do about it?"

"I don't know. I felt sorry for her, okay?"

"You wanna watch that soft-heartedness of yours. It'll get you in trouble one of these days." But he said this without much conviction. He took the cigarette out of his mouth between his thumb and forefinger and flicked the ash into the ashtray he kept under the counter.

Tempted to ask, "What is that supposed to mean?" but afraid to hear the answer, she said instead, "So will those smokes of yours. They make you cough."

"Ha. They're good for you, so that's how much you know. I heard they help you breathe better. Don't them policemen usually come in by now?"

"Busy, I guess," April said noncommittally. She looked up, surprised to see a tall man in an RCMP uniform pushing open the café door. He didn't sit at the counter the way people on their own tended to, but took a seat at a window table, settling in and putting his cap on the seat beside him.

"Just a coffee, miss," the officer said, when April approached.

"Sure thing, Officer. I know it's early, but the pie's pretty good today."

"Well, let's have a piece of that as well. Got apple?"

"We do. Don't you fellows usually eat at the little place near the water there?"

He smiled. "I guess the boys from the police station come here."

Getting no further comment from the officer, April went to start the coffee and prepare the pie. She watched him take a small notebook out of his inside pocket and write something at the top of the page, underlining it twice.

He was in his fifties, she speculated, and though she didn't know all the badges, she assumed he was high up. She was trying to decide what sort of face he had. She settled on *trustworthy*. He looked confident and in charge, handsome, almost, in that jowly way older men sometimes were. Maybe a little full of himself. Maybe that and his age were what made her think he was high up.

"Sorry it took so long. I had to brew up a new pot. Hope you like the pie," she said when she'd set his food on the table. "So, what are you doing up this end of town?"

He laughed slightly. "Why? You the one who keeps an eye on things around here?"

She flushed at this. "Sorry, sir. Naturally nosy. It is pretty central here, and a lot of people come in, so I do get a sense of things."

"Those boys at the station talk to you about things?" He had a genial manner and accompanied it by pressing his fork energetically into the pointy end of his piece of pie.

"If you mean about the cases they're working on, certainly not. I never know what's going on till the rest of the town does, from the papers." It was an odd question, she thought, and then was aware of a slight prickling of caution.

"I bet you do hear a lot from the customers. Pie like this would make anyone want to stay and chat." He held up his fork and smiled.

"There's only so much about shopping and the latest spats between people you can listen to before it gets boring," she said, smiling in her turn. "Here, I'll get the pot and top you up."

When she came back with the coffee he asked, "They ever talk about them?" He inclined his head toward the police station.

She shook her head, more alert than ever. "Not so you'd

notice. But the police are pretty popular here."

He let that sit for a moment and then smiled again. "I bet you're sweet on one of 'em, eh?"

April felt a rush of anger. Partially because he was fishing and partially because he was being a patronizing bastard, treating her like some sort of lightweight.

"Actually, I'm thinking of joining the police," she responded, "if you must know."

The officer put up his hands in a peace offering. "I meant no offence, miss. That's a great ambition. There's always work a girl can do around a station." Finishing his pie, he fished in his pocket and put some money on the table. "So, let's see what's what at the Nelson Police Station, shall we?" He put on his cap, touched its brim in a salute, and left.

April watched him cross the street and make for the police station. Her innards were churning. Something was up.

WHEN THE PHONE rang, Lane almost didn't hear it, so preoccupied was she with her jumbled thoughts about the idea that her husband was taking bribes. Not quite certain that it was for her, she picked up the receiver and waited for a moment to hear if anyone else answered on the King's Cove party line. The Armstrongs and Hugheses and possibly Robin Harris were all on her line, and she wasn't sure who else. Hearing nothing, she said, "KC 431, Lane Winslow speaking."

"Oh," said the woman on the other end of the line, as if she was surprised to hear anyone answer.

"Yes, hello. Who is calling, please?" Lane said.

"I so sorry, miss. Is Mrs. Vitali, you know, from Lorenzo?"

"Oh, yes, of course! How are you, Mrs. Vitali?" Intrigued but pleased, Lane wondered why on earth Lorenzo's wife would be calling her. She glanced at her watch; Mrs. Vitali surely should be up to her elbows in lemon risotto or some sort of tagliatelle by now, shouldn't she?

"I must speak with you. When, where can we talk? Nobody can know. Nobody."

"Would you like me to come there? When do you close the restaurant?"

"Restaurant close today. My husband is sick. I so sorry, can you come? We talk at restaurant. I know is long way. I not usually ask such a thing . . ."

Hearing distress in her voice, Lane said immediately, "Of course. I will leave now. I'll be there in an hour."

"Thank you, miss. I do not have anyone else to talk to. I don't know what to do." Mrs. Vitali seemed on the verge of tears.

"I'm leaving right now!"

"Come to back, in lane, you know?"

"I'll find it."

Mrs. Vitali had seemed to her to be the most contained and self-possessed of women. Even in her apron and immured among the pots and pans in the kitchen, she had an exotic glamour that Lane envied because it was anchored in a kind of confident stillness. What had happened to push her to make such a desperate call?

Of course, because Lane wanted to make good time, she got behind a logging truck at the most winding part of the road. She felt more than the usual impatience. It was a kind of purgatory, watching the pile of logs strapped to the vehicle in front of her. She began to imagine the ropes breaking, a log sliding off the truck and into her windshield, and had to snap herself back to attention. Her gratitude when the driver in front of her pulled over into a lay-by was very nearly expressed by blowing him a kiss, but she contented herself with a quick wave, and she sped the rest of the way to the ferry. By a turn of fortune, it was just loading up on her side of the lake.

April 1921

IT HAD BEEN almost a week. He should be back. Mrs. Turner sat rigid in the parlour, looking at the darkness of the empty fireplace. He had never been gone this long. Home by Saturday, he'd said, unless business held him up. She turned to direct a look of accusation at the telephone, which had not rung in all that time. A hard lump of fear had embedded itself in her chest, like a rock: unmoving, silent, painful.

She had sent her daughter to her friend's, telling her that she would be in Vancouver, the only lie she could think of to get the girl out of the house, away from her growing panic. With Viola staying with her school friend at their big house along the lake, she felt freer to think about what to do. The police. She must get the police.

Should she telephone them? Or go in? If she was seen, people would know something was amiss.

The door to the parlour opened and the maid looked in. "Madam, could I bring you a cup of tea? You didn't eat much this morning."

Mrs. Turner waved her off with an angry gesture. "Do not come in here unless I call, is that clear?"

With trepidation, Mrs. Turner approached the phone and asked to be put through to the police.

The young officer who came to see her, Constable O'Brien, was nice, she thought—calm, reassuring. For one blissful moment she felt the hardness in her chest melt. They'd get to the bottom of it, he said, but each question he asked, each note he took, rebuilt the edifice of her fear.

"So, usually he calls you if he has to stay away?"

"Yes."

"And you said he was going up to Sandon?"

"Yes, I assume so. He still has an office there."

"Have you ever been there yourself, ma'am? Do you know who his associates are?"

She shook her head miserably. "No. He doesn't like me involved in his business in any way. Besides, I have responsibilities here—the household, my daughter."

The officer looked quickly around the room. "Daughter?"

"She's twelve. She is staying with friends up the lake. I . . . I thought it best."

He nodded. "I see. I wonder, ma'am, if I may: Why did you not call earlier?"

Looking down at her hands, which she opened out flat as if she was stretching them, Mrs. Turner did not answer at once. Finally, she said, "I thought he would come home. He would be upset if I made a fuss."

"So, have you telephoned his associates or his office?"

She nodded, still not meeting O'Brien's eyes. "I did

finally, this morning. They said he had never been there at all."

O'Brien watched her. She looked embarrassed. Why? He made a note: "Never arrived at office."

She finally looked up at him, her eyes tearing. "He must have had an accident on the way there. It's the only explanation."

He nodded. "We can check the route. What was he driving?"

"His blue Chrysler. He was very cautious. He hated what those roads did to it."

AMES HAD LEFT the Turner file on the counter, and O'Brien, who was going to put a new label on it, suddenly slammed his own forehead with the heel of his hand. It was no wonder Ames hadn't noticed. His signature was appalling. He'd forget his own name next. Now he stood at Darling's office door.

Surprised to see that O'Brien had made what was, for him, the considerable trip up the stairs in person, Darling said, "Yes?"

"Yes, sir. I have the Turner file here, sir." He held it up. "I don't know how it slipped my mind, but I was the one who initially went out to see his wife back in '21, when she reported him missing."

"Sit." Darling held out his hand for the file. "And?"

"I didn't do the investigation, so that's probably why it slipped my mind. What I remember is that she waited nearly a week to call us, which I remember now I thought was strange because she said she'd phoned his colleagues up in Sandon, where he had an office, the same day she called us, and they told her he'd never arrived. She concluded he must have had a road accident."

"I see what you mean. If he had had an accident, and she'd acted more promptly, his life might have been saved."

"That's correct. They scoured the road—nothing. In those days it was just the one road, up around Slocan. That Kaslo road wasn't built yet. He apparently was driving a brand new Chrysler, and they never found that either. The thing that really comes to mind, sir, is that I remember being surprised that she'd waited that long, and that she was sort of embarrassed. I don't mean about waiting, I mean about him disappearing. Looking back, I sort of wonder now if she knew something that she never told us. I mean, I even wonder if she knew where he was."

"But was nevertheless willing, apparently, to put the police to a lot of trouble to search for him. Well, when we catch up with her, maybe we'll find out." Darling stood up. "Right, I'm off up to New Denver with this photo. If anyone comes around, have the files in order, and tell them I'll be in first thing."

LANE, NOT KNOWING she'd crossed paths with Darling, pulled to a stop on the street at the bottom of the alley leading to the restaurant's back door. The afternoon was clouding over, and she pulled her thick cardigan closer around her. Worried about which door would be the one to the restaurant, Lane wished she'd counted how many doors from the bottom of the block to Lorenzo's. To her relief, a door at the top of a set of stairs opened and Mrs.

Vitali stepped out with an unlit cigarette. Seeing Lane, she hastily pushed the cigarette and matchbox into her apron pocket and waved, hurrying down the stairs.

"Miss Winslow, thank you so much. Sorry to make you drive such long way! Please, come in." She shook Lane's hand and then preceded her up the stairs. "I will make coffee. You like Italian coffee?"

"I love Italian coffee, thank you. Don't worry about the drive here. It's beautiful. I never mind making it."

Mrs. Vitali busied herself with Lorenzo's little espresso pot while Lane sat and watched her. She looked, Lane thought, as self-contained as ever.

Finally, small cups before them, Mrs. Vitali sat down and took a deep breath. "Something is wrong. Since the other day Lorenzo is being very strange. He won't talk to me. Two nights ago, he went to visit the neighbour to get help with lights." She pointed toward the back door. "Neighbour is electrician, and when he come back, he go right to bed and not say anything. Then yesterday the inspector is here, when lights was put up, and he barely say anything to him. Usually he is very friendly, now very rude. And now Lorenzo stays in bed—but I don't think he is sick."

Lane frowned over her coffee and conducted an internal debate. On the whole, she decided, more information on the table was better than less. "I'm having the same trouble. The inspector is behaving very strangely at home as well. And then my neighbour told me that there is a rumour, more than a rumour, that my husband is taking bribes—you know, when people give him money to look the other way, but—"

Mrs. Vitali slammed her hand on the table. "I know 'bribe.' Where I come from it is everyday thing. It is not true—not true for Ispettore! Now someone thinks Lorenzo is involved. No! I can't believe he think Ispettore Darling take any bribe. How come your neighbour hear this?"

Lane, uplifted by Mrs. Vitali's resounding vote of confidence for Darling, said, "Apparently her husband heard it from the man at that new supermarket. That man said he heard it at the Chamber of Commerce meeting. The mayor told him directly that there was going to be an investigation."

"Ha! Chamber of Commerce! You see? Is bad place. I tell Lorenzo we don't need it, but he keep trying to get in. For what? We have plenty of customers."

That was interesting. Lorenzo trying several times to get into the Chamber of Commerce. And now Lorenzo was refusing to talk to Darling. What had he heard? "Have you talked to your neighbour, what's his name?"

"Mr. Smith. No. But maybe I go. Good idea."

"Would you like me to come with you?"

"Oh, please, yes."

Mr. Smith occupied a long narrow shop on Stanley that was crowded with radios, light fixtures, phonograph players, and various kitchen gadgets like kettles and, Lane was intrigued to see, shiny new automatic toasters. At the end of the narrow corridor was a long counter, and behind it was Mr. Smith, apparently in the act of unwrapping a new delivery of electrical cords. A young man could be seen through the door to the back, stacking boxes.

"Mrs. Vitali, ma'am," Smith said when the women

approached him. "How are those lights working?"

"They work very good, thank you for putting up."

"It's a crying shame when things come to this," he said, shaking his head. "How can I help?"

Lane spoke. "Mr. Smith, my name is Lane Winslow. I said I'd come along to help. Mr. Vitali seems to have been very disturbed by something you might have told him the other evening when he came to you about the lights. Unfortunately, he hasn't told Mrs. Vitali. Would you be able to help?"

Smith looked at them and shook his head, then turned to call into the storage area, "Matt, can you come and cover the front for a few minutes? I need my office."

CHAPTER EIGHTEEN

"**B**EEN EXPECTING YOU, SIR," SAID O'Brien when the front door was opened and the tall RCMP officer came through. "Sergeant O'Brien, sir. I'm to give you every help and access to anything you require."

"I appreciate that. Inspector Guilfoil. How do you do?" He offered his hand. "Is there a place I can set up?"

"I can give you a desk here, if you like. It's central to everything. Or I have Sergeant Ames's office upstairs. You'll be able to interview there and whatnot. He can move down here for the time being. In fact, he's the only one in just now. Inspector is up the lake on a matter, and Constable Terrell is down at the train station picking something up. He should be along momentarily."

Guilfoil considered for a moment. "I think I'd better opt for the office, if it's not too much trouble."

"I'll just give the sergeant a call to let him know you'll be up." O'Brien reached for the phone, but Guilfoil shook his head.

"That's all right. I'll just pop up and introduce myself."

"As you like, sir."

O'Brien watched Guilfoil start up the stairs. "Charmer," he muttered under his breath. We should all mind our Ps and Qs, he thought—but still, there's nothing to hide, like the boss said. He tried to suppress a small glow of satisfaction that Ames would be slightly discommoded by the temporary necessity of mucking in with the hoi polloi downstairs.

Ames was on the phone, making notes on a pad of foolscap, and consequently did not immediately see the imposing figure of the inspector filling his doorway.

"I see. Right. Thank you for calling me back." He smiled. "I don't know that it will help exactly, but it's good to have the information." Ames hung up the receiver and then gave a small gasp. He jumped up. "Good heavens, sir, you startled me. Come in. Sergeant Ames."

Guilfoil introduced himself and looked around the office with a friendly smile. "Sergeant O'Brien downstairs suggested I might be able to use your office for a short time."

"Absolutely, sir." Ames lifted a cardboard box from the floor beside his seat. "I anticipated this. I've put everything I'll need in here, so it's all yours. I've left paper, pencils, and so on in this top drawer, and you'll find files in this drawer. I'm embarrassed to say I'm still completing some of the paperwork on a few of the cases."

Guilfoil laughed pleasantly. "You and me both, Sergeant. The bane of police work, eh? Don't worry about it. And I'm sorry about the office; I'll be out of your hair as soon as possible."

Ames moved to an empty desk on the main floor at the back of the room, adjacent to Terrell's desk, and plunked his box down. "Well, that's that, then. Does this telephone work?"

"Course it does." O'Brien indicated the upstairs with a movement of his head. "Waste of bloody time, if you want my opinion," he said quietly.

Ames glanced at O'Brien's desk and saw only a small but virtuous collection of files and some new labels he was apparently affixing to them. "Carry on, Sarge. I'll set up camp here."

"You seem to be in a good mood in spite of the invasion of the barbarians," O'Brien said, giving the lie to his desire to carry on with the labels. "Nothing to do with that lady mechanic?"

"Nothing to do with you, O'Brien," Ames corrected, pulling his supplies out of the box. As a matter of fact, it had everything to do with her. She was due, he checked his watch, in three hours' time, and they were going for a nice Chinese supper and then a film.

He and Miss Van Eyck had taken up a steady dating schedule, and he found himself more and more in the grip of feelings he'd never had before. She was, to be sure, a commanding sort of woman, but unlike some of his earlier flames, she seemed uninterested in how much sugar he ate, how he dressed, or any of the myriad other things that women seemed to want to correct about him. They both liked the pictures, and they talked endlessly about the films when Ames drove her the many miles home, analyzing what they might have done differently in telling the story, or what kind of film they'd make. What he knew was that he was happy when they were together, and he thought about her constantly when they were not.

If there was a fly in the ointment for Ames, it was that he wasn't quite sure where it was going. He had, he'd realized on the long drive home the previous Saturday, the same problem Darling had had when he first met **Miss Winslow**: the lady lived far away, and he suspected Miss Van Eyck would no sooner leave her house, and, more importantly, her job, than Miss Winslow had wanted to desert her beautiful house in King's Cove. Unlike Darling, Ames could not see himself quitting town.

He mustn't get ahead of himself, as his mother always said. Ames was about to get his notes in order from his recent phone call with a constable in Ontario when he was distracted by the arrival of a large, noisy motorcycle pulling up directly in front of the station.

"Would you just look at that," O'Brien said.

The two of them stood in front of the window watching as Constable Terrell put the kickstand down, pulled off his goggles and leather helmet, and dismounted.

"That's what you got at the train station?" asked Ames, joining Terrell on the street.

"It is. It's come all the way from home. Before that it travelled from Saskatchewan to Nova Scotia by train. It's almost as well travelled as I am."

"Shouldn't you have some sort of leather jacket?"

"In my closet. Say, I thought I saw Miss Winslow just now, heading up the street with someone."

Ames frowned and looked up and down the street as if

he might see her. "What sort of someone?"

"It looked like Mrs. Vitali, the wife of my arson victim. Nice-looking."

"Ah. Now that's interesting. You watch. Miss Winslow will solve that fire business before you can blink," Ames said, putting his hands into his pockets and giving the motorcycle another long look. "She's been involved in most of our big cases."

"Keeping it in the family, I guess. Well, I wouldn't be sorry if she did get to the bottom of it. It's got an ugly sort of harassing feel to it, like someone is trying to push him out."

This brought Ames back. He took his hands out of his pockets and looked at the door of the station, as if reluctant to go back in. "Speaking of pushing out, an RCMP inspector has taken over my office and probably plans to find us all deficient before he's through."

"As Sergeant O'Brien said so eloquently, 'Oh, goody.' How are you getting on, by the way?"

"Progress, but not helpful progress. I found out that Turner's wife died a few years back, and her daughter moved back here and married. I'll have to track down who she hitched up with. Problem is, she would have been a child when her father disappeared, so I can't see what good she'd do us. I almost think we should wait and not bother talking to her till the inspector hears back from that Indian fellow. If our skeletal remains turn out not to be Turner, there's no point in bothering her about it at all. He can just go back to being an unsolved missing person."

Inside, Ames asked Terrell how he'd got on before he took his seat at his new temporary desk.

"I went to see that couple, the Stamps, whose restaurant closed before the war. They look a lot older than I think they are. Mrs. Stamp works part-time at a fishing supply outfit down along the water, and I don't see he does much of anything. I bet what little she brings in, along with maybe a war pension, is all they have. It felt a little unrealistic to be investigating them in a campaign of harassment against the Vitalis. That sort of thing takes energy. These two were so apathetic that they looked like they'd given up on life altogether. Needless to say, they weren't excited to be asked where they were on the night of the fire. At home asleep, thank you very much. They wondered what business of mine it was that they ran a restaurant before the war, and she asked me to produce my identification again because how did she know I wasn't someone trying to gain access to rob them. I didn't like to say that I wouldn't have bothered."

Ames smiled. "Wait till she sees you in a leather jacket roaring around on that bike. She'll tell her friends they barely got away with their lives."

"I don't expect she has many friends, actually. Anyway, I don't think they're our arsonists. I should ask April to tell me again what was said."

"Any excuse in a storm," Ames said, and winked.

AT THE CAFÉ, the usual gathering of women was beginning to form, and because there were an unusual number of people in for an afternoon break, April found herself rushed and unable to pay attention to what they were gabbing about. When she finally got away from the customers at the counter and made her way to the ladies' group with her order pad, she was very surprised to see Mrs. Tilbury, who had seemed so distraught in the morning. But here she was, and, if April wasn't mistaken, giving her the very slightest warning look.

April took the orders and noted that as she turned back to the kitchen, they all leaned in and one of them began to talk in a low voice. April paused by the nearest table to collect some plates and give it a quick wipe.

"They're being investigated, you know. My John heard it last night. Butter wouldn't melt with that inspector but turns out he's crooked. Well, no surprise there. That's the police, isn't it? You read about it all the time." She turned to Viola Tilbury. "You're the one that should take credit; you told us about how that Eyetie was bribing the inspector."

"I know, I told my husband all about it when he got home that night. I let Mrs. Dalton, the mayor's wife, know as well. He can't have that going on right under his nose. It goes to show you can't trust anyone."

April felt herself almost congeal. She forced herself to finish the journey to the kitchen and place the order on the clip.

"Here, this is ready for table five," Al said.

Her mind racing, April took the food to table five, barely acknowledged the thanks, and moved closer to the ladies.

"I like that inspector," Mrs. Smith was saying. "He's very gentleman-like."

"That's just good cover, isn't it? You know what men are like. Show you one face, deceive with another," said Mrs. Tilbury bitterly.

This checked the conversation momentarily, as if

everyone was slightly embarrassed. Finally, someone said, "Has anyone seen the new picture at the Civic theatre?" The conversation picked up from there, and April was left with her thoughts as she cleared dishes and wiped up the counter and recently vacated tables.

So, the inspector was under investigation over a rotten piece of gossip. Is that what that smooth RCMP fellow was doing, having his coffee and trying to get information from her?

DARLING PULLED UP on the rough road that constituted the driveway of Barisoff's little cabin. The long drive, with the ever-changing bands of sun and cloud along the lake, had served to soothe his spirits somewhat, and had helped him gain some perspective. He realized that what had caused the most distress was the fact that he had not told Lane what was happening. The investigation itself was a nuisance, and would certainly reveal nothing, but he knew he could not hope to keep it from Lane. He was beginning a mental gathering of courage by the time he arrived in New Denver.

Mr. Simpson was sitting on the front steps and rose to greet Darling. "Inspector."

"Good afternoon, Mr. Simpson. I've brought the photos of the weaving for you. And of the little figure for good measure." He held up the manila envelope. "I don't think there's any screaming hurry to get back to us, but how long do you think it might be? I've written the station phone number and so on on the envelope."

"Come on inside. Mr. Barisoff has made some coffee

because we've been working all day in his garden. It's been good for me, and I've learned a lot. I might start a little garden at home. My little brother and sister might enjoy it."

"How old are they?" Darling asked, following Simpson into the cottage.

"The boy's only five, but my sister, Angie, is seven, and pretty eager about most things. She wanted to come with me here."

"Ah, Inspector. Is very nice to see you again. Please, sit down," said Barisoff, coffee pot in hand.

Darling removed his hat and sat down. "I can't stay too long, but I appreciate a little break. I hear you've been gardening."

"Yes, Mr. Simpson is big help in digging. Maybe he save me four days' work. Without interruptions, maybe five days."

"Interruptions?" Darling wondered what possible interruptions could take place in this sleepy village.

Simpson shook his head. "That guy from the store has been over twice, wanting to see where the body was. We'd piled the rocks along the edge, and he came and kicked them around. Wasn't too nice to me when I asked him to stop. Wanted to know if it was any of my business.

"Second time he come I told him go away, we busy. He not happy Mr. Simpson staying here, so I get to say not his business either." Barisoff chuckled. "He always unhappy. But not all bad. He look after poor Miss Stella downhill there. She not, as you say, all there." He tapped his finger against his temple gently. "She never go out anywhere."

Mr. Simpson turned to Darling. "So, Inspector, I reckon

it'll take me four days to get back. I'll show the photo to people and talk to my grandmother. I could call you in under a week."

Wondering if sending the photo in the mail to Mr. Simpson's grandmother might be faster, Darling nodded. "I appreciate it. We, I think I mentioned, thought the body might be that of a man missing since the early twenties, but at this moment we have nothing to support that. We are looking for dental records from back east where he came from. He's certainly not going anywhere!"

Mr. Simpson nodded. "You know, Inspector, the more I think about that frog, the more I think that person is an Indian."

"Is the frog significant?"

"Like I said, we don't usually make amulets like this, but as it happens, frogs play an important part in the story of my tribe. My grandmother told me of a time when there was an extended drought and our people were starving, and the frog saved us. I couldn't do justice to the way she told it. You can see the mountain that is sacred to the Lakes People—Frog Peak. It's just west of here. I know people down south make these little animal figures, so he could be from Arizona, say, or New Mexico, or it could be one of our people who was given the frog by someone from there."

Darling nodded. "Whoever he turns out to be, he was murdered. And depending how long ago it happened, that murderer could still be alive. I look forward to hearing from you, Mr. Simpson. I envy you the ride back. Four days alone? It sounds idyllic just about now."

CHAPTER NINETEEN

TINA VAN EYCK, WHO HAD elected to drive herself today, pulled up in front of the station just as Ames and Terrell were coming out. She saw the two men standing in front of a late 1930s Triumph motorcycle, deep blue and silver, and her heart leaped at the momentary idea that Ames owned this beauty.

"What a creature!" she said. She walked around it, inspecting it closely. "Whose is it?"

Terrell took his hand out of his pocket and held it up. "Guilty," he said sheepishly.

"You never bought it here? It's been beautifully refurbished. I used to work on bikes in England during the war."

"No, I had it shipped out from home. I got it after the war. I wasn't sure I'd be staying around for any length of time, so I waited before I sent for it."

She leaned down and exclaimed, "Look at these rocker box inspection caps! They still look brand new. Have you had them off to adjust the tappet clearances?"

What Terrell said to this, as he leaned forward to point something out to Tina, was lost on Ames, who was feeling, he thought ironically, like a third wheel. He watched Tina with growing misgivings. This is the sort of thing she really likes, he thought. An angry young man on a motorbike, leather jacket, hair blowing in the wind. He stopped himself. Terrell was hardly angry. Still, he couldn't remember when he'd seen Tina more animated. He tried to pull himself together, but he could not follow a single word Terrell and Tina were saying. Technical mumbo-jumbo, he thought crossly. Turning on his heel, he went back into the station, quite convinced they wouldn't even notice he'd gone.

Sitting at his desk, he moved his writing pad into the wooden inbox, and lined his pencils up on the desk in an unconscious imitation of his boss when he was troubled. He tried to focus on what he would do the next day on the stalled Turner case, but a sudden peal of laughter from Tina, audible even through the closed station door, put paid to that. He looked at his watch. If they were to get dinner before the film, they'd have to get a move on. He got his hat and slammed it onto his head and then put on his coat and went outside. Tina was sitting on the damn thing.

"If we're going to make the movie, we ought to go," he said to Tina.

"Oh, right!" Tina jumped off the bike, adjusted her skirt, and smiled at Terrell. "You ever need anyone to work on it, you know where to find me!"

"I do, indeed," said Terrell, taking his leather helmet off the handlebar.

Tina linked arms with Ames, and they started up the

street toward the New Star Café. "That bike is a sight for sore eyes," she declared.

"He'll kill himself on it," he answered shortly.

"He won't. He's army trained. They're the best in the world. Now, if you tried to ride it, you probably would get killed."

"I wouldn't think of it."

He was very nearly silent while they waited for their dinner. He toyed with the chopsticks he would not be using and looked out the window moodily.

"You're not saying much. Feeling poorly?"

"Not particularly. What's there to say?"

"Is this about the bike? Is that what's got into you?"

"Well, it's obviously the sort of thing you like. I don't know why you'd waste your time with a boring guy like me."

It was Tina's turn to fall silent. Their dishes of chicken chow mein arrived and she took up her fork and looked fiercely at her plate.

There was something about her energy that ought to make Ames nervous, and it did. He took a forkful of chow mein and looked at Tina. Here we go, he thought, his appetite fading in spite of how delicious the food was.

Tina put down her fork and looked up at him. "I don't like jealousy. It's not attractive. It's dangerous. It doesn't make me feel special, it makes me feel ill. I thought you were bigger than that, Daniel Ames, but I find out now you're no different from other men. I liked you because you're decent and kind and straightforward. I have fun when I'm with you. I liked you because I thought you liked me and understood what kind of person I am."

"But I do like you," he protested.

"No, you don't. Not really. If you did, you'd never behave like this."

She stood up, dinner barely touched, pinned on her hat, and buttoned up her coat resolutely. "It's disappointing. You see me talking to another man and you suspect the worst. That means only one thing. You just have no idea what a real relationship can be. Enjoy the film."

Ames had stood up when Tina had, but she shook her head decisively and he'd sat down again. He sat on for some minutes, thinking of the golden curls of Tina's hair framed by her hat, and surveying the wreckage of yet another romance.

The waiter came by and looked at the abandoned plate. "She doesn't like Chinese?" he queried.

Ames shook his head. "She doesn't like me, apparently."

DARLING PULLED ONTO the grassy driveway of the house and turned out the headlights. He sat looking through the glass-panelled front door and could see the lights from the kitchen and sitting room reflected down the length of the hall. Home. It had become his daily beacon and refuge, the place where he could truly be himself, but this evening he was filled with a nameless dread. Well, that wasn't entirely true; he could name it. Guilt. He took a deep breath and got out of the car.

The air was fresh and cold and lifted in a slight breeze that rustled the massive blue spruce by the door. It made a little movement against the dark sky above it. He took courage and went in.

"I was in town this afternoon and bought some nice T-bone steaks for us. It's very simple tonight. Steak, salad, some of Mabel's buns," Lane called into the hall.

He stood in the doorway leaning one hand on the frame, watching her mournfully. "Hello, darling."

She looked up and put the spatula down and embraced him. "My poor darling. You mustn't look like that. It's too tragic for words." She pushed him into a chair and sat opposite him, taking his hands. "I know what's wrong, and furthermore, I think I know a little about why. Part of it, anyway."

Flabbergasted, he said, "I—"

"No, we'll have none of that. Dinner is ready. When we've had a bite and a glass of wine, I'll tell you all about it."

Darling ate, unsure whether to be elated or alarmed, but feeling just about able to enjoy a medium-rare T-bone steak and an excellent glass of wine without their turning to ash in his mouth.

"I found out from Angela, you see, who'd heard it from David, who heard it from the supermarket man," she began. "Of course, I was beside myself with fury, absolutely livid, you can imagine! I was powerless to even think of how I could help, and then I got a telephone call from Mrs. Vitali, also quite beside herself about I had no idea what, but she begged me to come into town, and so I did." She smiled. "It's a good steak."

Darling, slightly overwhelmed, nodded. "It is. You did well by it. You've been into town?"

"I know, you are *also* wondering what she wanted! She made me come around the back of the restaurant, which was closed because her husband, she said, was sick. Having the vapours, more like. The point is, Lorenzo has been behaving very peculiarly, and she noticed, on top of everything else, that he'd suddenly gone all cold toward you. So, we went to see Mr. Smith, who runs the electrical shop on Baker."

"Mr. Smith?" Darling managed, struggling to follow. "Doesn't he live next door? Didn't he put up the security lights?"

"Exactly. He has some very nice new shiny automatic electric toasters, by the way. You see, Lorenzo went to see him the other night, and he came back in a very peculiar frame of mind. Went straight to bed, which apparently is most unlike him."

Lane chewed another morsel of steak and then sat with her wrists perched on the edge of the table, her knife and fork in hand. "What we learned is that Mr. Smith—who, unlike some other people, is very positively disposed toward the Vitalis—heard some tosh that Lorenzo had been bribing you to look the other way. He'd heard it at the Chamber of Commerce meeting, and he wanted to give Lorenzo a little warning."

Darling frowned. "This is what I don't understand. Bribing me to look the other way about what? I couldn't get any sense out of the mayor, either."

"So that's what the mayor wanted to see you about. That was the funny thing, you see; Smith wasn't completely clear on that. But here's at least one concrete possibility: someone saw us in the restaurant at lunch once with a glass of wine. He, Smith, thought that whoever had reported it was originally going after Lorenzo, but because you are the inspector, someone got the idea that if you could look away from that, Lorenzo must be slipping you money, and if you're capable of taking cash, who knows what else you are overlooking. Thin edge of the wedge sort of idea. Mrs. Lorenzo thinks that her husband gave you short shrift because he doesn't want to bring you down with him. The liquor laws in this province are arcane beyond belief! Imagine it being illegal to get a glass of wine in a restaurant!"

WHEN APRIL LEFT the café, she made straight for the police station. She didn't know if it amounted to anything, but someone needed to know what she had heard. Terrell was just about to leave for the day when she came in. He was sitting on O'Brien's vacated stool thinking about the motorbike and whether his landlady would allow him to keep it in the garage.

He jumped off the stool in some discomfiture. "April. Good evening."

"Constable. Is that yours?" She pointed outside.

"Yes, it just came today. I had it shipped out from home."

"I don't know that much about them, but it looks powerful. Are you sure you want to take it on these winding roads?"

He smiled. "I'll be okay. Is there something I can do for you? I'm just waiting for the night man to come in."

She nodded. "There is, actually, I think."

He led her to his desk and pulled out his notebook. "A crime of some sort, I assume?" he asked, smiling.

"That's a good question. I don't actually know that

this is a crime, but I think it may have something to do with why that big galoot of an RCMP man is suddenly hanging around."

AMES HAD SLEPT very little, so, as was his custom when things came unravelled, he took himself down to the edge of the lake to spend a few moments alone as the dawn took hold. It was cold, and he perched on a picnic table, his hands shoved into his pockets and his hat pulled low, watching the lake ripple along the sand. He could scarcely name what he was feeling. An aching heart was the closest. Longing. If this was love, it was miserable. It was not enough, he thought, to just feel sorry for himself as he usually did. Something had to change. Why kid himself? He had to change. Tina's words had rattled around in his head most of the night, forming and re-forming, but though he understood them as words, he feared he did not understand them in his heart. He shifted, feeling the early morning chill climb up under his trouser legs. Was he being fanciful? What did he know about the heart? What did he really think of Tina? She'd accused him of not understanding her at all. Or how relationships are "supposed to be." He was a little overwhelmed by her, true, but he liked her strength, the way she was herself, the way she never diminished herself, but with sinking heart he realized he had not lived up to her, or really earned her. Until last night he'd not even known why she liked him. Because he was decent and kind. Could it really be as simple as that? But of course he wasn't. He was petty and ordinary. He'd been overcome with jealousy like a teenager. That wasn't decent. What would decent be like? Real decency? Real decency was Inspector Darling. With a heavy sigh he got up and climbed the hill up to the station. Today he was going to be occupied trying to find Turner's daughter.

TERRELL WAS JUST coming in to work as Ames arrived.

"No motorbike today?" Ames asked. In truth he was glad. Its presence would provide an embarrassing reminder of his own pettiness all the livelong day.

"No. I'll only be using it for longer trips. Coffee and breakfast?" Terrell indicated the direction of the café with his head.

Ames shook his head. "No. I don't think so. Not today."

O'Brien, who was just nestling his behind onto his stool, looked up at Ames and raised his eyebrows—a look Ames did not miss.

"I'll bring you a cup of coffee, laden with sugar?" Terrell suggested.

"Sure. Thanks," Ames said wearily.

"Someone missed his beauty sleep," remarked O'Brien.

"Yes, thank you, Sergeant. If you don't mind, I have work to do."

"Actually, I think I learned something important from April last evening," Terrell said, putting on his hat. "I'm hoping we can meet with Inspector Darling when he comes in, only maybe not with our mounted police friend."

"Well, run and get our coffee. Don't keep us waiting. Mine's cream and one sugar," O'Brien said, plunking some coins on the counter for Terrell. "No, that's all right, I'll get this, Sergeant," he added, waving away Ames's attempt to find coins in his pocket. "You look in no state."

DARLING WAS AT loose ends. He was waiting for dental records from Ontario; he'd had a call from a counterpart in Kingston who told him that the Turner wife had died, and the child had returned to Nelson when she was in her twenties. That meant she was here. Ames would be on to City Hall to look over marriage records. Good thing—Darling just couldn't bear to be in City Hall just now. Turning his mind to the John Doe case, he thought about Simpson riding home and wondered that the border was so easy to cross. He supposed it was, anywhere along the wilderness. He could hope for a call from Simpson sometime after that. And now, putting together what Lane had told him about her visit with Mrs. Vitali and Smith with April's judicious eavesdropping, which Terrell had relayed to him and Ames, it appeared the whole bribery nonsense had begun with a rumour. It might well have started at a coffee klatch with a group of merchants' wives, with Mrs. Tilbury at the centre. Why?

Of course, he had to look at his own ridiculous carelessness. It was against the law to sell wine with a meal in a restaurant, an absurd law left over from the days of Prohibition. Yes, he did look the other way, but Lorenzo wasn't selling his wine; he was bringing it out for rare special occasions and providing it free. He himself had seen others benefit as he and Lane had—for example, when they had told Lorenzo they were engaged. It was certainly not worth policing this sort of thing. But, he realized, by having benefited from Lorenzo's generosity, he was now suspect. He was, after all, the law, though the technicality of Lorenzo giving wine away as opposed to selling it meant any charges would never stick. Unless someone wanted them to. Other restaurateurs? People who wanted the Vitalis out of business? And why now, suddenly? Lorenzo had been running a restaurant there since well before the war. The other business owners had contented themselves over the years with keeping Lorenzo—and no doubt the other "foreign" business owners, like the Chinese, who had considerable business enterprises in Nelson—out of membership in the Chamber of Commerce.

And most importantly, was all of this connected in any way with the arson and notes directed at the Vitalis? With what he had learned from Lane after her visit with Mrs. Vitali, it seemed to him that there was something much more sinister at work than just gossip.

CHAPTER TWENTY

BARISOFF TURNED OVER AND PEERED toward the window. It was barely dawn. There it was again—a noise of some sort in the yard. With a groan he rose slowly and pushed the covers off and then lowered his feet to the floor. Having accomplished this he stopped, his hands resting on the bed beside him. Someone was talking. A woman. Frowning now, he shuffled into his slippers and went to the small window by his back door. There, in the middle of his garden, stood Stella Bisset from down the hill, barefoot and in a grimy and worn padded housecoat.

Alarmed, he hurried outside to where she stood. "Miss Stella! What you are doing? Come in, is too cold. Please, no shoes!"

Stella turned slowly toward him and said, "So kind. Who are you? Do you know where he is?"

Barisoff took her gently by the arm, "Please, Miss Stella. Come inside. I make coffee. You warm up. You know me, Barisoff. Who are you look for?"

Stella went compliantly, climbing the three stairs up to the house ahead of him. "Do you know where he went?"

Barisoff managed to get her to sit down, and then fetched a pair of thick wool socks for her. He was going to ask her to put them on, but she seemed incapable, so he knelt painfully on one knee and slipped them on her small and icy feet. Who was she looking for? Berenson? He usually looked after her. He saw that she had begun to shiver, and he took the grey wool blanket from his bed and wrapped it around her, and then busied himself with lighting the stove. Luckily the banked-up embers from the night before meant it would not take long.

"You are looking for Mr. Berenson, from store?"

At that, Stella seemed to come to herself a little. She looked around as if she'd just seen where she was and couldn't quite think how she'd got there. "Oh. Yes. That's right. He's not there."

"Is very early. He not open store yet. We have nice cup of coffee, some bread and jam, and then I take you to him."

Stella relaxed back into the chair. "So kind," she said.

LANE SAT AT the kitchen table thinking about what Mrs. Vitali had told her, and pieced it together with Darling's hurried phone call in which he'd told her Guilfoil, the RCMP man, was spending the morning with the files. Then she added in Terrell's information gained from April's eavesdropping the day before, which suggested that the bribery rumour seemed to have started with Mrs. Tilbury. Fair enough, but where had *she* come up with that notion?

Someone had set fire to Lorenzo's house, slipped warning or threatening notes into the café, and now accused him of bribing Darling. It seemed clearer, as she wrote these facts in little boxes and drew arrows, that someone was after Lorenzo Vitali. Professional jealousy? But, like Darling, she wondered why that would come up after all this time. She wrote "Mrs. Tilbury?" in the middle of the page, and added "Is whoever it is after Darling as well?" When the phone rang, she muttered, "Damn!" because she felt herself on the cusp of understanding something. She felt it slip away as she got up to answer.

"KC 431, Lane Winslow speaking." It took her a second to adjust to the barrage of Russian.

"I'm not really sure what to do, Miss Winslow. There is a lady here who lives by herself near the water. Usually Mr. Berenson looks after her, I think. A little funny in the head. Anyway, she was up here in my garden wandering around and didn't seem, you know, in her right mind. She seemed to be looking for Mr. Berenson, so I went to the store to get him, only he's not there. Hiro was just opening up. He said Berenson wasn't feeling well and was staying home. I'm using his telephone right now, at the store. I'm not sure what to do with this lady. I can take her to her house, but I don't think she eats properly or really even gets dressed."

Oh, dear, Lane thought, poor Barisoff having to cope with an addled woman. "I'll come there, but you know it will take an hour and a half or so. Should I bring anything? Do you think she is ill?" Should Barisoff drive her into town to see a doctor?

"I don't think she is sick, really. Not physically, anyway. I don't know what she has to eat, or about her clothes. She needs something warm to wear. She was in bare feet. I'm sure Berenson does his best." Barisoff wasn't at all sure about this. The Berenson he knew was stingy and foul tempered.

"Will you take her back to her house? How will I get there?"

Barisoff explained to Lane how to find the house, and Lane hung up the phone.

She pulled open her drawers and looked for some clothes she'd be willing to volunteer. A good pair of wool trousers, several pairs of socks, a wool sweater. Barisoff had said she had bare feet. Shoes? She looked at her small collection of mostly sensible shoes and boots. She had, she knew, quite large feet for a woman, and it would be unlikely any of her shoes would really fit, but she took out a pair of rubber Wellingtons. The woman would flop around in them, most likely, but that's what one did in Wellingtons anyway, and she could use them to go outside in the event, however unlikely, that she really had no shoes to her name.

She packed these things into the car, and then realized that she ought to let Darling know where she was going. It was going to be a cold but lovely March day.

She reached O'Brien. "Good morning, Sergeant. Would the inspector be available for a quick word?"

"I'm afraid not, Mrs. Darling. Most of 'em are out and about. Inspector is in a meeting. I can give him a message."

"Oh. Nothing bad, I hope?"

"Interview with an RCMP officer. That's all I know."

Lane knew that was all he could say to a civilian. "I just wanted to tell him that I was going up to New Denver and would be back, I hope, by early afternoon."

"Right you are; I'll make sure he gets this." He paused, and then said, "You take care, now."

Lane hung up, slightly bemused by O'Brien's sudden solicitude. What had brought that on? Was he worried about the investigation?

Her mind was full of Miss Stella in the initial part of the journey. It was the same the world over, she thought grimly. An older person, usually a woman, becoming addled in old age and having to cope on her own. She thought about her grandmother and grandfather in Scotland; they had each other and good neighbours. But what would happen if her grandfather died, if the neighbours moved? Her grandmother would be some miles away from the nearest village, absolutely on her own. Of course, her grandmother was not gaga and showed no sign of losing her wits. But she would surely lose her ability to keep up her garden or hitch up the pony and drive herself into town.

It was only when she was past Adderly Hot Springs, the steam rising off the murky sulphurous pool high above the road as she drove past, that her mind switched abruptly to what O'Brien had said. She had no idea what an investigation would include, but certainly interviewing each of the men would be part of the process. She wondered if Darling would tell her about the interview or be obliged to keep it secret, and then she resolved not to try to get information from him. What he could tell her, he would—at least she hoped so.

Lane pulled abreast of the cottage Barisoff had described to her as the home of Stella Bisset. A more neglected house she could not imagine. What once had been a tidy picket fence was now just a set of broken slats, with the frame of the fence listing so far forward it was practically lying on the ground. There had once been a garden, she could tell by the ancient evidence of some beds, now collapsing and overgrown. She could see some sort of outbuilding kitty-corner to the house in the backyard. It too seemed to be listing. Still, there was smoke drifting out of the cottage chimney, so Barisoff must have lit the fire.

With her arms full of the things she brought, including eggs, butter, and most of the loaf of brown bread she'd got from Mabel Hughes, Lane knocked at the door and went in. Barisoff was indeed by the stove; the kettle was boiling, and the inside of the cottage was almost too warm, which seemed to amplify the stale smell of garbage and unwashed body. Stella Bisset sat slumped at the table, looking blankly at the stove.

"Ah! Miss Winslow!" Barisoff said with palpable relief. "Is Miss Stella Bisset. Look, Miss Stella, is a friend, Miss Winslow. She can help, yes?" He turned away from the unmoving woman and said in a low voice in Russian, "She's really in a bad way. You can see for yourself. She certainly doesn't look after herself. I don't even know if she has enough wood. There are a few tins of food here, but I don't see that she opens them. Someone, Berenson I suppose, brought her a tin of cookies, and that's about all that seems to be touched. I don't think she ever dresses or bathes."

"I brought eggs and bread and butter. Can you start a

little scrambled egg for her? I saw a building out back. I'll go look for firewood."

"I should—"

"No, no, you stay. I should think she'd be more comfortable with you at this point." With this, Lane handed Barisoff the bag with the food, and then saw the little bedroom and went to put down her bundle of clothes on the bed. "We'll have to see about helping with the cleaning and dressing later."

Outside, Lane made her way along an overgrown path to the outbuilding and pulled open the door. The top hinge was loose, so the bottom of the door was scraping the ground and had got wedged in the tangled mass of grass, and she had to give it a good pull. She was surprised that the initial smell was of stale motor oil, and then realized that most of the space was taken up with an old car. Something from the early 1920s, she was sure. She'd have said a Model T Ford, but any insignia had long since disappeared. It certainly looked as though it hadn't been driven since then. Dust covered it and cobwebs hung down from the low ceiling of the garage. A beat-up licence plate hung by a screw. She shook her head. Poor Miss Bisset would certainly never be using this car again.

Her main objective was to find split wood for the stove, and indeed, around the front of the car, there were some untidy piles of damp wood. At the realization that the wood wasn't dry, she looked up and saw that the roof of the building was missing shingles.

Frustrated, she picked up an armful of wood. At least some of it could dry by the stove, but Barisoff would have to get some of his own. Berenson had been "looking after her"? In the most nominal way possible, she thought angrily. She would certainly have a word with him when he turned up again. As she approached the door, she tempered her thoughts. Berenson, really, did not have to take any responsibility for this woman, and in fact, as paltry as his attention was, he was doing her a kindness.

Inside she found Barisoff holding a forkful of egg to Stella's lips, as if he were feeding a suspicious child. Stella was frowning, looking anxiously at the fork.

"Go on. Is good. You must eat," Barisoff said soothingly. Finally, his patient opened her mouth tentatively and took the food. "Yes. That's it. Is so good, no?"

"Who are you?" the woman asked, when she had been persuaded to eat her scrambled egg and a bite of bread. She was holding a cup of black tea and seemed to be coming into herself. Her voice was soft, with a slight accent, Lane thought.

"I'm Lane Winslow. I thought I'd come along and see if I could help. How are you feeling?"

The woman did not answer this, but instead said, "Where is he?"

Lane glanced at Barisoff, who made the slightest shrug. "Mr. Berenson? He's not at the shop right now, but as soon as he returns, I can get him to come see you. In the meantime, I've found wood in the garage, but it's quite damp, so I'm going to ask Mr. Barisoff to go get some dry wood. Let me help you. You can have a bit of a wash-up and we can get you into some warmer clothes. Would that be all right?"

She looked up at Barisoff, who nodded, and seemed, she thought, relieved at being excused from the bathing and dressing part. "Yes, I go, and I find Berenson too."

It was as he was leaving that Stella Bisset looked up at Lane and said, "He was standing in the door, and then fell down. He was gone, just like that." She snapped her finger with a sharp vigour that surprised Lane. These non sequiturs were going to be difficult to follow.

Once Stella was somewhat washed and dressed in warm clothes, Lane put her in front of the fire with a cup of tea and busied herself with cleaning up the cottage. She boiled another kettle of water and used it to warm up the water for dishes, gathered the garbage in a pail and put it outside, wondering where someone in a place like this would normally dump garbage. In King's Cove you had to run your garbage up the road to the new dump.

It was when she was changing the bedsheets—luckily there was a second set that smelled musty but was clean compared with what was on the bed—that she found a case sitting on top of a little pile of records. Curious, she opened it and found that it was a wind-up record player.

She selected a record, "After You've Gone," and pulled it out of its brown paper sleeve. It looked to be in good shape. She considered for only a moment, and then she took the player and the record out to the little sitting room.

"I've found your record player, Miss Bisset," she said, trying to infuse some jollity into her voice. "I remember hearing this song a long time ago. Shall we have a go?"

Stella Bisset did not look up from where her gaze had settled on the front of the stove. Lane wondered if she had gone into some sort of stupor. Still, nothing daunted, she wound the player, suddenly remembering there was one of these in her father's library. She smiled. He'd not have been impressed with her selection for today; he was a Beethoven man. And if truth be told, so was she. She took the record out of its sleeve, wiped it on her shirt, then put it on the turntable, and carefully placed the needle on it.

The scratchy beginning of the orchestra playing filled the room, pushing the silence back, as if drawing a curtain. At first Stella did not respond, and then she looked up and saw the player. It looked as though she was going to speak, but then Marion Harris began to sing, and Stella was transfixed. She moved her head slowly from side to side and then, in a weak voice, began to sing, "After you've gone, and left me crying . . ."

She sang along with the record all the way through, and then, when the needle was oscillating back and forth over the end of the record, Lane lifted the arm off. "That's a lovely song," she said.

Stella looked transformed. She was smiling at the machine. "He brought me that, even before we left. I did love that song. I told him, 'After you've gone, there's no denying you'll feel blue.' But he told me he was taking me with him. But I couldn't, of course, you understand?" She finally looked at Lane. "Can you put it on again?"

"Yes, of course," Lane said, suiting the action to the word.

Stella swayed in her seat, smiling, Lane thought, over some sweet memories she must have nearly lost. She began herself to feel weighed down with a sense of inchoate nostalgia and was hoping that there would not be a request for a third playing, when Stella's face changed. She cried out suddenly and waved her hands in front of her as if she was trying to stop something.

Assuming it was the music, Lane snatched the needle off the record, wincing at the scratching sound, and turned to ask Stella what the matter was.

"That was why we had to go. He said the man was trying to get in!" She sounded frightened, and she looked at Lane as if seeing her for the first time.

July 1920

"**ARE YOU SURE?**" Estelle stood in front of the cottage with its front garden in full bloom. Sweet peas climbed the wall, and chamomile was interspersed with thyme and phlox in a wide border around a tiny lawn. He had picked the perfect time to show her. The morning light was still golden, and the three fruit trees at the front cast a gentle shadow that crossed the grass and climbed along the wall of the cottage. There was a smell of fresh paint. The picket fence was listing slightly, but someone had painted it.

"Do you like it? I bought it when the owner moved into town. She was a grand old gardener. She kept house for her son, who worked in the mines."

"And then?"

"And then what?" He pushed the gate open and waited for her to walk along the flagged stone path.

"The son. Why does he no longer need his house kept?" Estelle waited, poised between longing to go down the walk and make this place her own, and a dark premonition. She

241

tried to shake it off. Dark premonitions had accompanied her all her life.

He shrugged and shook his head. "He died. You remember that fire in the mine a couple of months ago."

The premonition gained ascendency. "Only one man died, and it was this one?" She turned and opened her hand to take in the cottage. She had known him. He had been one of the men, kind and gentle. She wondered now if it had been because of the proximity of his mother, lovingly keeping house for him in this little cottage just ten miles away in this village. Or maybe that's just how he was. When it was all over, some of the men had said he had saved the five others in the mine by pushing them out ahead of him. He'd not left himself enough time, and a beam had fallen.

"Come on. You're not going to go all superstitious on me, are you? The old woman was happy to get the money. She didn't want to stay, and she loved this cottage. She wanted someone to be happy in it as she had been, you know, before. Now you can be happy in it."

As much as I can be happy, she thought. She turned and walked slowly along the path, toward the door, pulling a handful of chamomile up and crumpling it in her hand. She held it to her nose, and she was flooded with some memory of being young, under a distant sun, in a distant life. And then she hoped that the man's mother had taken everything of hers away. She could not walk in and be confronted with a photo of him.

She pushed the front door open hesitantly and found herself in a tiny, enclosed space where he had installed a rack for coats and a bench under which muddy and wet boots and shoes could be left. The inner door, which he had painted yellow, was ajar; she opened it slowly and was relieved. Sun poured in the east window, and every stick of furniture was new. There was a tiny parlour with a fireplace, and beyond she could see the kitchen. On a table she could see the record player. She turned to him, one hand on her heart, and smiled. The green paint on the table seemed to cast its own light in the morning sun. To the right was a little bedroom. She went into it and was surprised by the size of the bed, and the dull shine of the brass bedstead. She exclaimed in delight. He had found a copper bath and installed it at the end of the room, and on a wooden rail he'd folded two large towels. They were new. When had she last had a new towel?

"What will I do here all day?" She was still smiling as she asked this.

"What you always said you wanted. Garden, read, listen to music. You see? You didn't see it yet." He pulled her into the parlour and pointed at the south wall beside the fireplace. "I bought all the books I could find."

Indeed he had. The bookshelf was four shelves high and full of books. She took in the loveseat in front of the fireplace, the lamp on the table, the little milk-glass pot of flowers on the windowsill.

She turned to look at him. Perhaps her premonition had been wrong.

"And you will have all the money you need. I will be here as often as I can. You know I have business to attend to in Nelson and Sandon. I have to go to the coast sometimes."

She tilted her head in acknowledgement. She was luckier

than the other girls, she knew. But she suddenly thought she would miss them and would likely never see them again. I cannot bring that life into this new one, she thought.

"I'm going to get your bags. We will spend a glorious all of today and tomorrow together. It will be just like a honeymoon."

"Where did you take your wife on her honeymoon?" She smiled and went through to the little kitchen. She did not want to hear the answer. In any case, she heard it, whispered into her hair when he came up behind her and put his arms around her.

"This will be my first real one. Listen." He held up his hand, and she turned to where he pointed. "After you've gone," sang a voice, the orchestra swelling in the little parlour. "Dance?" he asked.

CHAPTER TWENTY-ONE

AMES SAT BROODING AT HIS desk. He'd brooded away a good part of the day. He was being ridiculous. No, he *was* ridiculous. He was going to become, once again, the butt of Darling's jokes about his love life, and O'Brien had stared at him a bit too closely when he'd come in. He ran his hand through his hair, realizing he'd not combed it before he'd slammed his hat on his head when he'd left the house to sit by the beach. What exactly was wrong with him? He'd had a lovely woman, whom he admired and respected for her independence and talent—he'd learned that much from Darling, anyway—and then he'd become jealous when she exhibited those same traits he admired.

He knew perfectly well, when he examined himself in the light of day, that he didn't really suspect her of preferring Terrell. Though here he admitted his secret conviction that Terrell was the better man, so why not? In fact, she had said exactly why she'd liked him. Past tense. He nearly barked his scorn out loud. When had he ever understood a girl? And she was right. He wasn't being kind. He was being an ass.

"Sir? I was thinking of popping over to get lunch and some coffee."

Ames looked up at his imagined rival and knew what it was to be an ass, and what it would take not to be one. "Yeah, why not. I'm not making any progress. I could use a cup of coffee, to be sure. That one from this morning has worn right off."

April beamed when they walked in but then narrowed her eyes. "You okay, Sergeant Ames? You look a little worse for wear. A case keep you up all night?"

"I did not sleep well, it's true. I could use a full vat of that coffee I smell."

April poured the coffee and said confidentially, "It'll be that investigation. I don't blame you for being worried, but you have nothing to worry about. I'm sure the station will come through with flying colours. Mark my words, it's just gossip. You should hear my ladies here in the afternoons. They do nothing but tear down anyone who's not at the table with them. Well, that's not fair. Not all of them. Some of them try to temper it a little."

Ames hadn't even thought to be worried about the upcoming interview with the RCMP officer, so taken up had he been by his anger at Tina, and then himself, but he nodded. He watched Terrell smiling his thanks at April for the coffee, and her lingering smile for Terrell, and propped his elbows on the table and rested his head on his hands. How the hell was he going to make it up to Tina?

"Headache, sir? I have some Aspirin here." Terrell reached into his trouser pocket. "I thought you and Miss Van Eyck were going to the pictures; did you go for a booze-up instead?"

"No, Constable, we did not go for a booze-up. You were already interviewed, weren't you? What's it like?"

"Yesterday afternoon. I was so taken up with the arrival of my motorcycle I forgot about it. He's okay. Doesn't seem hell-bent on finding trouble. I haven't been here all that long, so I wasn't able to tell him much."

"I'm this afternoon. I'd like to get to the bottom of this. It's really not fair. I know the inspector is not perfect. He can be a bit rough on the help, but he doesn't have a dishonest bone in his body."

"The annoying thing is that if the rumour is not nipped in the bud, it will linger on, even if Guilfoil doesn't find anything."

"How are you getting on with the fire investigation?" Ames asked.

"Not very well. I'm kind of waiting for the next move on the arsonist's part. It's infuriating that we might not be able to stop it."

"THANK YOU FOR taking time this morning, Inspector Darling."

Unfailing courtesy, thought Darling. Well, that was a relief, whatever prejudices that courtesy might be hiding. "Certainly, anything I can do to help." They were in Ames's office, now the temporary quarters of the RCMP. Guilfoil's territory. Darling had not been on what he thought of as the

247

passenger side of a station desk since he'd been a sergeant himself, before the war.

"I will just want to have you walk me through your cases of, say, the last couple of years. Who was involved, the outcomes, and so on. And then we might run through some of your dealings with the locals, aside from any investigations."

"Who I shop with, where I have my lunch sort of thing?"

"Yes, that's right."

"I've brought all the files from the cases for the last two years. I can walk you through any you'd like to see, or would you prefer to go through them on your own?" Darling hoped he could go through them with him, but then worried that Guilfoil would suspect him of leading him, trying too hard to pad the results to make the station, or indeed himself, look good.

But Guilfoil evinced no particular suspicion. "No, no, I'd be delighted to have you walk me through. Much better than trying to piece together the reports. I'll make a few notes as we go, and then I might have you leave the files, and I'll have a quick look on my own. I think they'll make more sense after I've heard about them."

The afternoon passed with Guilfoil nodding, peering over his reading glasses and asking the odd question. Then came the case of the murder in King's Cove in the summer of '46. "You arrested this woman, Lane Winslow, I see."

"I did, yes, initially. It proved to be one of the longer-term residents of King's Cove who was guilty."

"And yet she turned out to have been in the same business as the victim. Both intelligence officers? A coincidence, certainly." Guilfoil watched Darling.

"Yes, certainly."

"You went on to marry Miss Winslow not a year and a half later."

"I did, yes." Something shifted in Darling. Guilfoil had done his research. And did he think Darling had let Lane off a murder charge because he was in love with her? Worry about how much Lane was going to be drawn into Guilfoil's suspicions began to take its place among his other anxieties. The conviction that Guilfoil knew a great deal more than he was saying hardened him toward his interlocutor. It annoyed him because it had the smell of an attempt to entrap him, to pounce if Darling said anything different from what he already knew.

"I'm just wondering, you see, because it's this sort of thing that might raise suspicion. Perhaps someone felt you were trying to protect someone with whom you had a relationship. You waited a year and a half to marry, but that someone hasn't stopped wondering. It becomes part of the gossip."

"Miss Winslow had only just come to the area from Great Britain. I had only just met her as part of that case. If you are asking if I had any doubt about her innocence, I had none. I arrested the guilty man just as he was in the act of trying to kill her. He later confessed, stood trial, and is serving time out on the coast. I sincerely doubt anyone gossips about that case. It was absolutely unequivocal." Darling leaned forward. "And further-more, no gossip is sustained for that length of time. It is a small town. There are always new avenues of gossip. No, I assure you, this suspicion about me arises from something recent."

Guilfoil leaned back in Ames's chair and dropped the 1946 file on the desk, adopting a thinking position. He rubbed his chin with his hand and then chewed his upper lip.

"Well, let's get on with these files."

They went through several case files, with Guilfoil nodding and prodding, and eventually putting each dossier in a kind of "out" pile.

"Now this one here. Tell me about it. It has political ramifications. The man you arrested in this case was a high-powered local businessman with political pretensions."

Darling explained that the businessman in question also ran a criminal enterprise and had ultimately been convicted of murder.

"So, no revenge factor here? No family member who can't forget?"

Darling looked at Guilfoil with slightly narrowed eyes. What was he up to? He seemed intent on looking for a reason for the rumour about his taking bribes as opposed to evidence of any wrongdoing. He felt again that momentary sense of suspicion that he was being manipulated, lulled into believing Guilfoil was on his side, perhaps causing him to reveal himself if he felt he had the man's support. Of course, finding the source of the rumour was like finding smoke. Could the fire be far behind?

"If I may say so, Inspector, you seem intent on finding out what caused the present gossip in the first place rather than looking for problems in our cases."

Guilfoil smiled and shrugged. "I am capable of holding two ideas in my head at once. Either there is just smoke, or there's a real fire. I have to look for both."

Now he's a mind reader, Darling thought glumly. "I see. Well, that's reassuring, I suppose. I can tell you absolutely that there is no fire, and that this is the result of, as you so quaintly put it, smoke. But, of course, you must conduct your investigation. So, shall we move on? This case was quite interesting because it did involve a crooked police officer. I have been much more careful in my vetting since then, I can tell you."

"I expect you're right about there being no fire. I'll be frank with you, Darling: I've never heard a whisper against the force until I was called in to do this. I've interviewed one of your men so far, gone through whatever he has. I suppose I shouldn't be revealing my hand. Let's say I suspect it has its roots in malicious gossip. If that's the case, any idea what could have set this off?"

"I've been racking my brains. According to April McAvity, the waitress at the café, it seems to have originated with a Mrs. Tilbury, who is passing it on from somewhere else, presumably. She and her husband have the hardware store. All this talk of smoke and fire reminds me: we have had a problem with arson, as it happens. Lorenzo Vitali, who runs a damn good Italian restaurant, has had an attempt on his house by someone with a gas can and matches in the middle of the night, and he's found a couple of warning notes shoved under the door of his restaurant. He has stopped talking to me for some reason, so now I am wondering if the matters are related."

Guilfoil shrugged and nodded, as if this could be a possibility. "Right. Well, I'll be talking to some members of the community later. The rest of these, then." He settled in and began to open the next file.

March 1921

THEY WERE SHOUTING now. It was worse than ever. Viola put her hands over her ears and hid under the covers. She never knew why they were fighting. She wanted, and didn't want, to know what they were fighting about. It scared her. She knew it was her mother's fault. She always sounded whining and desperate, like she was accusing him of something. If she was her father, she'd be angry too. Then the door slammed and there was quiet. She lay awake for a long time, fearful it would start up again. Fearful that her father had left for good this time.

In the morning, she brushed her hair carefully and put one side up with a barrette and pulled her linen dress down so that it was straight.

She hovered at the door of the dining room. Her mother was sitting with her chin resting on her hand, staring down at her cup of tea. A pile of letters and the silver letter opener were lying next to her. Sunlight streamed in the window. Viola wanted that shaft of sunlight to mean that everything was all right.

"Where is Father?" she asked tentatively. She could hear the maid in the kitchen and the sound of the kettle being clunked onto the stove.

"Gone to the mine. Where should he be? Sit down. I can't have you fluttering about like a wraith. Dina, could you hurry up with Vi's breakfast? She'll be late for school."

She called this at the door that led to the kitchen and was rewarded with the door swinging open and Dina, her cap slightly askew, hurrying in with a plate.

"Sorry, ma'am. Here you are, Miss Viola."

Sitting down at her place, Viola took her napkin out of its ring. She turned to her mother and, before she could stop herself, said tremulously, "Why do you always have to be so mean to him? I bet you're the reason he always goes away. When I get married, I will *never* make my husband want to go away!"

Her mother looked up, her face blanching. "How dare you? If you ever, *ever* address me in that tone again, I will send you away to school in Ontario so fast it will make your head spin."

Viola had never heard her mother speak in quite this tone of rage. She picked up her fork and tried to eat her scrambled egg, but she had lost her appetite. "I'm not hungry. May I be excused?"

"No, you may not. You will eat your breakfast. Cook has gone to the trouble of making it for you." Her mother turned away from her and began to go through the pile of mail but then pushed it away and turned back to her daughter. A growing pile of bills. Normally her husband would be dealing with them. Increasingly he'd been pushing them aside. "Listen to me. There are things you don't understand. Grown-up things. I know you're his little darling. The sun rises and sets on your father. But he's not all he seems to be."

Viola, sensing a relenting of her mother's initial fury, said, "But why does he go away all the time? Is it because of me?" She hadn't been doing well in school, and she had sensed that her father was exasperated with her.

"Oh my word, what a ninny! No, it is not because of you. He works, all right? He has big responsibilities. He has his office up at the mining camp." Her mother stopped abruptly.

Viola waited, but nothing more came. She bet he just liked to get away from her mother. She wanted to ask what they'd been arguing about, but her mother's mood was unnerving. She had threatened boarding school before, but that was usually because Viola was doing so poorly. After one school report, her mother had asked angrily why they had to be in this tiny, ridiculous town with its obviously inferior school when her father had a mansion they could all live in back home in Kingston. He had said there was nothing wrong with the damn school, and how the devil was he expected to run his western railway from Kingston?

August 1921

"BOSS, IT'S MRS. Turner." The door had a gold stencil announcing the head office of the South Eastern Mining Corp. It was closed.

"What does she want?"

"She is, er, demanding to see her husband."

James Rolland took his feet off the desk and peered past his secretary at the closed door. "Is she crazy?"

"I don't know. Doesn't seem crazy. Seems angry."

"That idiot has been gone for five months. You mean she

doesn't know? Go put her right." Rolland waved a hand to dismiss the secretary.

"Nope. She's not buying anything I have to say. You'd better see her."

Rolland scowled. "What the hell do I pay you for?"

Taking this as a roundabout agreement to see Mrs. Turner, the secretary turned and left the office. In the crowded and cramped outer office, Mrs. Turner was pacing, holding a fur-trimmed coat much too warm for the weather tightly across her chest. The secretary inwardly shook his head. Her face was jowly and plain ugly, he thought. He'd have left her behind too. "He'll see you. You won't learn anything more'n I told you."

The woman strode angrily into the inner office. "Who are you? Where is my husband? This is his office."

"Have a seat, ma'am."

"Don't 'ma'am' me! Where is he?"

Rolland sighed. "Ma'am . . . Mrs. Turner, he hasn't been in this office since I bought his railway concern. As to where he is, I couldn't tell you. Last I saw, he was living with that Estelle Bisset over in New Denver. You might go look for him there."

Mrs. Turner, her face white, collapsed into the chair she'd been offered. Her mouth opened and closed as she tried to settle on one question. "What do you mean you bought his railway concern?"

Rolland, worried about the shrill delivery of that last sentence, tried to pacify her. "I know men don't always discuss business with their wives. I paid him a fair price, considering he was broke. You should get on just fine."

"But I haven't seen him in months." Her voice had fallen, and she seemed almost to be talking to herself. "Broke? No. No, of course he's not broke. You must be mistaken."

"Ma'am, that information has been all over. He's been draining money like a water spigot. I heard about it and thought I could give him a hand. I'm sorry to have to say it, but he was spending it on cards, the woman, I don't know what all."

DAZED, MRS. TURNER sat in the back seat of the car. The chauffeur watched her through the rear-view mirror. He was impatient. He didn't like the roads he'd had to drive on, he didn't much like the look of the town of Sandon, and he hadn't been paid in some time.

"Madam?"

"You have to take me to a place called New Denver."

THERE WAS A small dry goods store on what passed for Main Street in what was barely a hamlet. Mrs. Turner stood rigidly by the door, waiting for the customer buying a bolt of sacking to finish up.

"Afternoon. Haven't seen you here before. Something I can get you? The young man behind the counter smiled, revealing crooked teeth and a receding jaw.

"I'm looking for an Estelle Bisset. She lives in a cottage somewhere." She spoke stiffly, as if shielding herself from further blows.

The young man waited a fraction of a moment, as if trying to think about how to word this. He wondered suddenly if this might be that man's wife. "She's away. In

256

Europe, I think. That's what I heard. With a, er, gentleman. As I heard it, ma'am."

"What gentleman?"

"Now there I can't tell you. I never did hear his name. I know he moved in with Miss Bisset a little while after he bought her that house. I know he was a railway gentleman."

Bought her a house? "Was it Turner?"

"Like I said, ma'am. I didn't ever hear what he was called."

When the woman had left, he wondered if he ought to get down the hill and warn Stella. He was minding the store today because she was feeling poorly. It was just lucky that the angry woman hadn't found her in the store.

CHAPTER TWENTY-TWO

Early March 1948

VIOLA FELT ONE OF HER headaches coming on. She had been working in the back of the shop while Gilbert went . . . where, again? To the post office to pick up a delivery? Relieved it was the day the hardware store was closed, she turned off the lights and left by the lane door. She thought of going home but decided to get something for her headache. She walked down the lane, crossed Baker Street, and then headed the one block to the Rexall on the corner. She was just about to step into the street to the drugstore when she saw a commotion in a doorway a little way down the street. Two people seemed to be struggling. Narrowing her eyes, she stopped and watched. There didn't seem to be anyone else around, just this jerky angry movement across the street.

With draining horror, she saw that it was Gilbert, pulling a woman toward him, reaching to kiss her, stroking her hair—no, he had pulled off the woman's silk scarf, exposing her dark lustrous hair. He was talking in a low voice, his mouth close to her ear.

The woman turned her face away, and then back, her red lipstick like a beacon, even in that recessed doorway. Another struggle. The woman pulled away, almost stumbled on the first step down to the sidewalk, and hurried down the slope. Viola could hear that the woman had said something, but she couldn't hear what.

Gilbert leaned back in the doorway, wiped his mouth with the back of his hand, watched the woman walking away, held that scarf to his nose. Viola could almost feel the longing in that deep inhale, and her heart began to pound loudly in her chest. She watched, almost choking, as her husband took the scarf away from his face, looked at it, bunched it with his two hands, and pushed it into his inside jacket pocket.

Viola had thought she would never move again, but found herself swinging away, almost unable to breathe, hurrying down the street away from the drugstore, away from Gilbert, away from what she could never unsee.

IT HAD BEEN days. She didn't even know how many. She turned the key in her father's empty house and stood on the threshold looking into the dead stillness of the long-empty place. The horror had been absolute. She could see over and over her husband holding that gold and black silk scarf to his nose. It had felt shockingly intimate.

She finally went inside, removed her gloves, and put them on the hallway table. There was more clearing up to be done. Especially, she thought with sudden bitterness, if she was going to have to live here. She shouldn't have left the house so long. She knew that's why she'd not sold it. Gilbert said he wanted the money. He could expand the business. She had once argued that it was hers and he'd become angry. Then she suggested they should live in the house. It was bigger than the house he had bought, and then he'd accused her of suggesting he couldn't make a decent living. "You never thought I was good enough. Not like your oh-so-perfect bloody father!" Now she didn't care what Gilbert wanted.

Standing in the close and deadened silence of the hallway, she felt her insides matching the darkness of the house, with its heavy drapes closed. She was dazed, as if she'd been ill and was waking up to find herself in a sickroom. She'd been dazed at dinner the night before, unable to talk. When he'd asked her what the devil was wrong with her, she'd said she had a headache. "No surprise, then," he'd said. He'd ignored her for the rest of the evening, and had left early in the morning, telling her to get a move on, they had deliveries to unpack. She'd told him she had a hair appointment and had come here instead.

She had an urge to go back to the box where she'd found the books. She remembered there were a few letters, some sort of housekeeping journal as well.

She pulled the kitchen curtains open just enough to let in the light, and it fell in a stream on the box on the table. Dust motes moved in the shaft of light, as if they'd been awakened from a deep sleep and were trying to find their bearings. She was overwhelmed with the feeling that it wasn't just her father's memory this house preserved—it was her mother's failure, and that she was failing, just as her mother had.

She pulled out the journal and leafed through it, saw that it was part daily observations, part to-do list, part shopping list. "Icy snow today. Viola home from school." "Get chimney man, new coat for Vi." The entries had stopped in 1921. That's when they'd learned there was no money. Dusty as it was, she held the book to her chest, remembering the last days of that spring, when her father had disappeared and they had shut the house. Her mother had never really been the same. They'd shut up the house and taken what little money there was and returned to Kingston—"tails between our legs," Mother had said. When her mother died eight years later, it had been almost a relief. Viola had returned to Nelson to live in this house, but when she married Gilbert she'd closed the house for good. Or she'd thought it was for good.

She reached back into the box and picked up the letters, surprised to see that most were returned letters, unopened. She recognized her mother's handwriting. Moving to the window she let out a gasp. They were addressed to her father. All of them, all sealed, all unopened.

SIMPSON WOKE, FEELING something digging into his back. It was still dark, but he could sense the grey edge of the dawn, even though it wasn't quite visible yet. It was the last night before he would be home again. He turned on his side and closed his eyes. His horse whinnied gently nearby. He was inundated with an image, and realized it was from a dream he must have been having just before he woke. It was a dream that had taken place entirely in the dark. Faces, one after the other in a steady stream, going so quickly he couldn't quite place them. They were in some sort of grid, like a box for pop bottles with dividers in it. He tried to release the residue of anxiety he'd felt in the dream, bring himself back to the edge of the forest where he lay. He listened to the beginnings of birdsong, inhaled the piney scent of the moist forest floor in the cold morning air. The darkness began to dissipate.

His grandmother set store by dreams. She'd ask him when he was a boy, sitting sleepily at the table, what kind of dreams he'd had. If he could remember, he would tell her; she would nod and drink her coffee as if nothing he said was a surprise to her. "That's your great-grandfather visiting. He just wants you to remember."

"Remember what?"

"What did he say to you?"

"He didn't say anything. He was building something. Then it turned into water and I woke up."

His grandmother had nodded again, pressing her lips together as if to say that pretty well confirmed it. "He wants you to remember we had to build things to live. He is worried all those memories will be washed away."

His mother had come in. "Don't fill his head with nonsense. He needs to get to school." He still remembered how tired she sounded. She was so young, but she looked like she'd been tired her whole life.

What would his grandmother make of this dream with the faces? He pulled the sleeping bag up to his ears against the chill and tried to capture even one of the faces. He must have seen thousands of faces in the war. Maybe his brain was just sorting through them. Or maybe they were the faces of the people who'd died. He opened his eyes. Why should he have dreamed this?

The dawn he'd sensed only a few minutes before showed now along the eastern horizon, and he breathed a grateful prayer. So often during battle, the light on the horizon had just been fire. He sat up. It was his last day. He would be home tonight, and even as he thought of the happiness of seeing his little brother and sister, his mother cooking up something good, his grandmother, still strong in her frailty, he felt a keen regret at the end of these solitary days. It was only when he had stood in the cool, looking out at the growing dawn, that he realized he was bringing something of the dead home with him, and he understood his dream.

GILBERT TILBURY HUNG up the phone. He'd had an uneasy morning. He'd moved the silk scarf into the pocket of a jacket at the back of the closet, and it wasn't there. He tried to remember if he'd moved it or put it in a different pocket. He had been watching Viola dusting the shelves, resentfully doing only a cursory job, and he sensed for the first time what it might be like to be afraid of her. She watched him like a hawk all the time now, lurking in the shadows at the back of the store, maybe even following him in the street. Oh, yes, she'd be quite capable of that. She hadn't said anything about the pretty woman who'd come into the store that day, but he was sure she'd store it up somewhere to hit him with later. It was ridiculous, as if it meant anything! She'd been one hell of a pretty woman, though.

"That was a guy from the RCMP. He wants to see us down at the police station. I don't know. Something to do with an investigation."

"What time do you have to be there?"

"Not just me. Both of us." He looked at the clock on the wall. "Half an hour."

"But we'd have to close." Viola could feel her anxiety rising.

"Can't be helped. Put that away and fix yourself up." This simple order suddenly felt risky, but she didn't respond. "I bet it's because I'm in the Chamber. I heard from a couple of others they've had to talk to them too." He kept his voice as carefree as he could manage, but he couldn't shake his anxiety. She'd been acting strangely. He could see it now.

Viola felt relief drain through her. She untied the turban that she used when she cleaned, and smoothed her hair. Would this be about what she said to the mayor's wife? She felt a surge of triumph.

THE TILBURYS SAT side by side in Inspector Guilfoil's temporary office at the police station, watching him shift papers, look through his glasses at a notebook, and then finally look up at them. "Thanks for coming in. Just trying to get a sense of the last Chamber of Commerce meeting. Do you recall that meeting?"

"Yes, sir. We mainly discussed how we could attract more tourists back to town. Summer's coming up and the war is good and behind us. We'd like to see it get back to how it was, with people coming to fish and camp."

Guilfoil nodded. "Good time to think about that. What was on your regular business docket?"

Tilbury frowned, trying to remember. In truth he just liked to go because there were drinks after and no women. A good night away from the house. He'd had quite a bit to drink that evening. "Um. There was a discussion about raising the fees. That was a bit of a discussion, I can tell you, and then there was a vote to admit a new fellow who's bought that motel on the way out of town there. Fellow called Denver. Harry Smith, he runs the electric store on Baker, brought up the subject of letting Vitali, that Eyetie restaurant guy, join."

Guilfoil looked interested and paused in his note taking. "He was in favour, was he?"

"Yeah. He raises it every couple of months. Most of the group's not too keen on foreigners. Lots of 'em fought against Italians, or their sons did. Janzon, he runs that little boating shop down near the water, he lost a son to them. Besides, we know he serves booze there. It's against the law. We got drinking places here. In fact, the biggest objection always comes from Albert Swindon, who runs the Metropol."

"That sounds like a matter for the police. I'm sure they have it well in hand." Guilfoil left this almost as a question.

Viola spoke up, her hands gripping her handbag. She would say it all again, to this man. Then it would be un-assailable. "They do not. In fact, I've heard that the inspector himself drinks there." She leaned toward Guilfoil. "It gives me no pleasure to say this, Inspector Guilfoil, but I was in there, Gilbert and I were, because we'd heard the food was so good. Nothing to write home about, I can tell you, and I saw that Vitali give the inspector an envelope. Right after, when he was paying the bill. And there was money in it." She sat back and stared at Guilfoil, challenging him. She could feel her husband's eyes boring into her, but she steadfastly ignored him. That would fix them, was all she thought. "They should shut that place down. I let Mrs. Dalton know," she added smugly.

Guilfoil had paused his note taking and now looked at Mrs. Tilbury. So perhaps the rumour had indeed started with her. "Are you sure this is what you saw?"

"Of course it is," she said. "Why would I lie?"

He hadn't accused her of lying. "And you are certain that there was money in it?"

"Obviously. The envelope wasn't sealed. You could see the bills." Viola could feel her husband staring at her, but she ignored him and kept her eyes on Guilfoil.

"Of course, we will follow up to confirm what you say." Guilfoil closed his notebook. It was a damning statement. Confirmation of what he had heard from the mayor.

"WHAT THE HELL was that about?" Tilbury demanded, yanking her arm to make her stop walking when they were on the street again. "We've never set foot in that restaurant."

"Let go of me!" She pulled her arm away and continued walking, her face set and looking straight ahead. "You've said it yourself, he should be out of business. Everybody knows something fishy is going on. I've just made sure."

Tilbury scrambled to catch up. "You're a complete moron. You can't lie to the Mounties! They'll find out. You heard him. They're going to 'follow up,' whatever that means. They'll find out you lied."

She stopped finally and turned to him. "It's my word against his. Who are they going to believe? A respectable Canadian business owner's wife or that foreigner with that trashy wife?" Viola resumed, turning her back to him. What if he was right?

She bustled forward and opened the shop when they arrived. Tilbury stood on the sidewalk, watching her push the door open, watching her briskly turn the Closed sign to Open. What did she mean about the wife? He had a sudden draining feeling that he didn't know her at all.

THE CHILDREN HAD gone to bed, and Simpson, his mother, and his grandmother sat at the kitchen table, mugs of coffee, mostly empty, in front of them.

"I hope you found what you were looking for," his mother said. There was a combination of weariness and anxiety in her tone.

His grandmother said nothing but only watched him, as if she was expecting something particular and had only to wait for it.

"It was nice up there. I met an English lady who was in the army in Europe. She was visiting a Russian guy who has a cabin right near one of the old pit houses. I feel like that is where we went when I was a boy."

"Yup," his mother said acidly. "An English lady and a Russian. Two for two."

"I also found these." He reached into his saddlebag, pulled out the envelope he'd been given by Inspector Darling, and took out the photos of the tiny swatch of weaving and the broken frog, and placed them in front of his grandmother.

She looked at them for a long moment, and then picked up the photo of the frog and rubbed her thumbnail along it, as if to feel the frog itself. She put it face down on the table and put her hand, fingers curled downward, on top of it. Almost a fist. "Where did you get this?"

Simpson told them about finding the body, and his visit to the police station, prompted by his finding of the broken frog. He pointed at the photo of the scrap of cloth as he spoke.

When he had finished there was another long silence. He could feel his mother shift in her chair, about to say something, but his grandmother put up her free hand to stop her. "No wonder he never did write to us," she said quietly.

"I GOT THE dental records," the dentist said. "I can double-check with your remains downstairs, but I had a look at them, and I don't think they are the same." He held up the envelope.

Darling nodded. They were standing at the top of the stairs down to the morgue. "All right. It was too much to hope, but let's go down and be sure." You could gather all kinds of necessary evidence, line it all up, and it still wouldn't do you any good, he was thinking. They would have to let go of the idea that they had Turner.

Downstairs he turned on the strong light over the workbench where their long-dead guest was reposing under a white sheet, and then stood aside to let the dentist through. He pulled the sheet off the grinning skull while the dentist opened his envelope and read through the sheets of paper.

"Turner had a chipped cuspid lower right and an infected molar when he was eighteen and had it removed. Lower left." He took his pen to move the lower jaw slightly so that he could look at the row of teeth at the back. "And this fellow has all his teeth in that lower quadrant, and no chip," he said, turning back to Darling. He wiped his pen and fingers on his handkerchief. "Had his wisdom tooth pulled on the upper right. As I thought. Not Turner."

Darling sighed and thanked him. He replaced the sheet, turned out the light, and ushered the dentist back up the stairs. That was that, then.

LORENZO VITALI SAT, unnerved by being at the police station. He'd been worried that he would meet the inspector there, but before that could happen he had been ushered into the upstairs office where Guilfoil was waiting for him.

Guilfoil gave him his hand and invited him to sit. "You've been having the devil of a time lately," he commented, watching his guest.

"Yes, sir."

"A fire at your home and—do I have this right—a couple of threatening notes?"

Lorenzo Vitali nodded. "Yes, sir. Two notes. I am afraid for my wife."

"I understand. I would be as well. Mr. Vitali, do you understand why you are here?"

Lorenzo looked down and then back at Guilfoil, his gaze direct and fierce. "I think so. I hear someone say I giving money to the inspector. Is not true. Even if I ever try to give him money, he never could take. He is not that kind of man."

"I see." Guilfoil looked through the leaves of his notepad. The story was well and truly out in the community. "I have testimony here that a witness saw you giving money to him in an envelope."

Lorenzo recoiled, frowning. "Is not possible. Who says such a thing? Is never happen. I thought was only what you call 'rumour,' but this! Someone say they saw something like this? Is impossible. That person is lying."

"I see. I do have it from several sources." In that same instant he realized that Mrs. Tilbury telling the mayor's wife might make it only one source. "You are certain there was never a time when a person might have seen something that looked like you giving the inspector an envelope? Passing him a letter, or perhaps you were paying him back for a loan he made you?"

"Inspector never lend me money." He looked down at the desk, thinking. "No. I never give him nothing. Only bill for meal. He give *me* money. How you can see from 'several sources' something that never happen?"

Guilfoil ignored this. "Now, is it true that sometimes you give alcohol to your guests? Have you given it to the inspector?"

Lorenzo was silent for a long while. "I no sell. Is crazy law. In Italy there is no law like this."

Guilfoil pursed his lips at this non-answer, and then nodded. "I won't disagree with you there, Mr. Vitali. But nevertheless, your guests sometimes end up with wine."

Shrugging, Lorenzo said, "Sometimes for special. Inspector and Miss Winslow get engaged, I have something for them, yes. Is not exactly against law."

"It's not exactly legal, either. Do you think this could be the source of your problem?"

Lorenzo looked outraged. "Someone want to kill me and wife because I give glass of wine? Is ridiculous!"

"It does seem far-fetched, to be sure. I understand you have tried to become a member of the Chamber of Commerce and you have been rejected."

"I try two times because I think is good idea for business. Is bad idea. I don't need for customers—they come for food. I do not go where I am not welcome."

Guilfoil heard the bitterness in Lorenzo's voice. "Do you think it's possible that they are upset about your liquor policy?"

"Is not 'liquor,' is wine! And no. I think because I am Italian. You also do not see Chinese restaurant man in Chamber of Commerce."

"If you feel so unwelcome, why do you not live in some place like Vancouver? I am sure conditions there are much more liberal."

"You make mistake. People here, most people here, very good. I have so many wonderful customers. Is such nice and beautiful place. Beautiful lake, beautiful mountains. I been here since 1934, never have this before. Okay, maybe not Chamber of Commerce, but everyone else so nice.

271

Inspector, especially. I am very angry someone think he take money. We was good friends, now is ruined!"

"Do you ever recall a Mr. and Mrs. Tilbury eating there?"

Vitali turned his mouth down and shook his head. "I don't think so, but I don't always know names of people who come."

Guilfoil sat chewing the end of his pencil thoughtfully after this interview. He was inclined to believe Lorenzo Vitali, but he couldn't prove what he was saying because he could not divulge who had accused Vitali of handing an envelope full of cash to the inspector. The fire had given him doubts as well. He had a momentary flash of wondering if Vitali set it himself, but quickly dismissed it. A man might burn his business down to collect insurance, but he'd be unlikely to burn himself out of house and home. He had asked if Lorenzo kept a record of his customers, but all he had was a book where those who called ahead for a reservation were recorded. Unfortunately, many people came in off the street and no record was made of them.

CHAPTER TWENTY-THREE

GUILFOIL STOOD WITH HIS HANDS in his pockets looking down on the street below. His interview with Lorenzo Vitali had only confused matters. In a lifetime of working with people breaking the law, the inspector had interviewed scores of people. He believed himself to be an astute reader of human nature. He believed he could distinguish someone telling the truth from someone lying. But if he examined his own conscience honestly, he knew that it wasn't always easy to tell, and he'd made mistakes in either direction over the course of his career. The ones that rankled him the most were those whom he'd imprisoned protesting their innocence, only to find later that they had indeed been innocent. Any unjust loss of freedom distressed him. Not that he believed in psychology—he considered it a lot of nonsense and a way to evade responsibility for one's actions—but he did allow that his particular anguish at having imprisoned the wrong man came from having spent most of the Great War in a German prison camp. He had felt the physical and mental diminishment of imprisonment, the slow erosion of any concern but that of the daily struggle to get enough food, to stay warm, the awareness of how quickly one could descend into utter selfishness in an attempt to survive.

He needed a break. The café with that pretty waitress who wanted to be a policewoman beckoned. Spatters of cold rain were beginning to hit the window. He put on his outer jacket and tucked his cap under his arm. At the door he paused and looked out. In moments the spatters had become a good solid rain.

"It's wet out there, sir. Can I offer you an umbrella?" said O'Brien.

"Thanks, Sergeant. I'm just going across to the café for a restorative cup of coffee. Can I get you something?"

"No, but thank you. I have my Thermos of tea."

Pulling up his collar and putting on his cap, Guilfoil went out and hurried to the café. He was surprised to find it nearly three-quarters occupied, in full hubbub, as if everyone on the street had rushed in to get away from the squall. Seeing no seats available by the window, he chose instead to go to the counter, where one seat was still vacant. It was an ideal spot. Because it was the single seat around the end of the long counter, he could see the whole café. A peal of laughter caught his ear, and he saw that a group of women had squeezed themselves into the booth he himself had occupied when he'd first come in and were fully focused on their conversation and plates of pie. Two pots of tea and all the cups and saucers and serving plates competed for space on the table. He recognized

Mrs. Tilbury. She sat against the window and was looking moodily out at the street.

Immediately the unbidden thought arrived: guilty conscience? Of course, you could not see that . . . but could you sense it intuitively? No. Not if you didn't want to commit an injustice. But of course the injustice in this case would be all one way. If Vitali were convicted of bribing officials, both he and the inspector would go down, losing business and position. If the good lady was found to be lying, nothing but a censure for wasting police time would be her fate. Unless one of the victims chose to sue her for libel. He shook his head. Neither man struck him as litigious.

"Already changed your mind about what you want?" April was before him holding a pot of coffee aloft. She looked unfazed by the number of people she was coping with.

He smiled. She was reacting to him shaking his head, he realized. "No, I wanted coffee, and I shall have coffee. And all those ladies seem to be enjoying the pie, so don't mind if I do."

April smiled and inclined her head, indicating the women in the window booth. "My usual klatch."

Guilfoil watched the women as April dished up his pie and pushed the sugar and cream in front of him. "Tell me, that lady looking out the window. What can you say about her?"

April looked up at where he was pointing. "Mrs. Tilbury? She's unhappy, and she can be a little mean. And she was one of them enjoying the gossip about Inspector Darling. And she doesn't like foreigners." She turned to him. "In fact, I wouldn't be surprised if that rumour started with her. Something is going on with her. She was walking along the street crying the other morning. I tried to help but she brushed me off. Still managed to make it in that afternoon, though."

Guilfoil nodded thoughtfully.

MRS. TILBURY FINALLY turned back to her friends. She leaned in, causing them to imitate her and move a few inches forward. "You mark my words: that Eyetie restaurant will be closed inside a week." She nodded with satisfaction.

Mrs. Smith frowned and said, "You can't know that! Why should it be?"

"Because I told that RCMP man about you know what." She leaned in farther and whispered, "The bribe." Then she sat back with a satisfied air. "We'll finally be rid of him."

"The inspector?"

"No, that restaurant."

"You've never eaten there," said Mrs. Smith. "You told me that yourself. I don't know why you have a bee in your bonnet about that restaurant. And I don't believe you about the inspector! What's going on with you?"

Another woman leaned over and put her hand on Mrs. Smith's arm.

"No. I mean it." She turned back to Mrs. Tilbury. "What are you up to, Viola?"

April, who had been cleaning up the next booth after the two men from a nearby construction site had left, heard most of the conversation. She had to stand aside as Mrs. Tilbury pushed her way out of the booth, abandoning her pie and forcing the two women next to her to stand up.

She stormed past April and out the door.

April wished Guilfoil was still at the counter, but he'd left quickly after he'd finished his coffee and pie. She did a quick scan of the café, saw that everyone was served, and went to Al in the kitchen. "Keep an eye on things. I'll be right back."

Holding a small umbrella, she splashed over to the police station and stood before a bemused Sergeant O'Brien.

"Miss McAvity? Where's the fire?"

"Very funny, Sergeant. That RCMP guy. Is he here? I have to see him."

"I'll just give him a call."

"Hurry. I haven't got all day."

LOOKING AT HIS notes later, Guilfoil was aware of a shift in his thinking. He began to allow the possibility that the target was Lorenzo Vitali, and the ruination of Darling's reputation was incidental. This threw new light on the question of the fire at Vitali's house. "Something's going on with that woman, you mark my words," April had said angrily. "If you'd been there a bit longer you'd have heard. She's been saying horrible things about that restaurant, and she's never even been in there!"

"Did you hear her say that?" Guilfoil had asked.

"Well, no, not exactly, but Mrs. Smith, she said that Mrs. Tilbury had told her before that she'd never even been in there."

This left the issue up in the air. She could have been in after she'd told Mrs. Smith she hadn't. Or she didn't want to admit she'd been into the restaurant. She'd stormed out of the café before April could learn any more. He straightened up his notes and decided to call it a day. He'd stop by the detachment and see how things were getting on, and then go home. Tomorrow might bring some clarity. He paused at the door of Darling's office, and then knocked.

"Come."

"Ah, Inspector," he said, putting his head in the door. "I'm just knocking off. See you in the morning." Best to keep things on a polite footing.

Darling nodded. "Good night, Inspector." He wondered how the inquiry was going, but certainly wasn't going to ask. Regardless of how it was going, he was innocent, and he just had to hope it would all come out right in the end.

VIOLA SAT STUNNED. The letter she'd been reading slid off her lap and fell to the floor. The others still waited to be opened on the table beside her.

> *Dear Sam,*
> *I know all about her, and I don't care. I just want you to come home. It doesn't matter about the money, or that woman. Your daughter is growing up without you.*
>
> *They told me you had left and taken that woman with you. I'm sending this to your office so that they can forward it to you. They pretend they don't know where you are, but they do, I'm certain of it. They told me you have gone broke spending money on booze and*

that woman. You're just like every other man,
it seems. My father warned me about you. He
said you looked smart, but you had a reputation
around town. I thought after we married and
moved away from all that, you'd change. But
now you have a daughter, and nothing more
matters. I forgive you.

Viola looked at the date: August 1921. The tone was so like her mother. Badgering and "forgiving." Then again, she said to herself, look at your own husband—maybe that's how you got to be like your mother. Pulling herself together, she picked up the other letters and began to frantically look through them. She found what she was looking for. It had been opened and was addressed to her mother.

May 1922
Edith,
Please do not look for me. I love Estelle and
I am going away with her. I have lost most of
what I had. I sold what I could and have left
you a small amount of money in the bank, and
I transferred the house into your name. You will
not hear from me again. Please tell Viola . . .
I don't know. Tell her what you want.
    ST

She pushed the letter back into the box and stood up. With something black and unfamiliar rising in her she swept the box off the table with a cry of rage. Dust, long lying dormant on the table, rose in a choking cloud. The one thing now seared into her raging mind was that she had been nothing to him. The father she adored. Nothing to him at all.

LORENZO LET HIMSELF in through the back door of the restaurant and stood in the kitchen in the dark. It was after midnight, but he could see well enough with the light from the security lamp over the back porch shining through the window. He was beginning to feel foolish. No one was going to come here in the middle of the night. It was just that same person trying to frighten him. He didn't like to admit to himself that it was working. He was frightened. Someone was after him. At least if he was at the restaurant, he could make sure nothing happened.

He walked to the door into the dining area and was about to push it open when he heard the back door kicked open so hard that it banged against the wall. He turned. A hissing figure dressed in black rushed at him, pushed him hard. He heard the crack as the back of his head hit the counter, felt himself sliding onto the floor. He was losing consciousness, he knew. He tried to lift his hand, to say something, to force his eyes to stay open. The sound of splashing assailed him, and he tried to understand what it was. The smell . . . the last thing he saw were flames, sudden devouring flames, then he felt himself slipping into hell itself.

THE BELL ON the fire truck clanged into people's dreams at 12:32 AM. Those people still awake up the hill from the train station rushed to their windows. Something was on fire. The smoke and increasingly visible flames came from partway up the street from the station. Some came out in dressing gowns, women with pin-curled hair, men with their hats hastily donned, to watch.

One of the people awakened was Terrell. He sat up at the loud clanging of the bell. Arson again? He listened for just a moment. The truck seemed to be going down toward the bottom of town, and not, as he feared, up the hill to where the Vitalis lived. He threw on his clothes and, careful not to wake his landlady, tiptoed down the hall to put his shoes on by the door. He needn't have bothered. She was at the top of the stairs, clutching her dressing gown at her neck.

"What's going on?"

"A fire, Mrs. Rollins. I'm just going to have a look. It's down near the station, so there's no danger."

Once on the street, Terrell ran down toward Baker Street and then along the slope toward the train station. The bank of shops and restaurants looked untouched, but he could see that black smoke was coiling into the darkness from somewhere in the alley and flames were beginning to lick above the roofline. Bolting to the lane, he found the fire truck squeezed into the tiny passage, attempting to battle the flames that were devouring the back of one of the businesses and beginning to jump to adjacent shops. The hose snaked down the alley to a hydrant on the street below and was stretched as far as it could go. It was Lorenzo Vitali's restaurant.

Immobilized by the flames and destruction, Terrell stood for a moment, and then caught sight of McAvity in helmet and firefighter's jacket.

"Is anyone inside?" he shouted, coming closer to him.

"I don't know," McAvity shouted back. "I wouldn't think so, at this time of night."

Seeing the men tied up fighting the blaze at the back, Terrell shouted, "I'm going in to check." He ran down the lane and around to the front of the restaurant and peered into the darkened dining room through the glass in the door. It took a moment to see the flickering yellow light under the kitchen door, and the smoke beginning to leak through the crack. Would anyone be there at that hour? Surely not. But he would never forgive himself if he were wrong. Even knowing that smashing the window of the door would supply more oxygen to the fire, he took off his jacket and folded it over his hand to break the window, only to find it had already been smashed. He tried the door and it opened readily. He flicked the light switch by the door, but it had been disabled by the fire.

The noise outside dimmed slightly, and he paused a moment to listen. Was that a human sound? "Hello? Hello? Is someone here?" he called, sprinting toward the kitchen door. He found it blocked by two tables pushed against it. He frantically pulled the tables away, dismayed by how heavy they were. Someone had pushed them there deliberately. More desperate now, he shoved at the door. Something solid had fallen behind it. With a final heave, Terrell managed to squeeze open a gap just wide enough to see a man's body, slumped against the door.

DR. PHILIPSON WAS undecided. The shock of it had almost caused him to shut his office for the day. Somehow he'd got through his last two patients, including a little boy whose mother held his hand the whole time he was getting his filling, so that she was underfoot, making everything take longer. There had been a fire overnight, he'd heard. That had helped keep his mind off things. Now he sat at his desk, knowing he should go home. His wife would be waiting, furious if he came home late for dinner. Her brother was visiting from Alberta. He knew what he had to do. And he didn't have to do it right now. Tomorrow would be plenty of time. But in the next instant that clarity was gone. He should tell Viola first. She had a right to know. She had every right to know first—to hear it from him, not from the damn police.

CHAPTER TWENTY-FOUR

"I REMEMBER WHEN HE GOT THIS," Simpson's grandmother said. "He was restless, like you. Remember, Mary? You used to get mad at him for always wanting to be outside, always going somewhere. He reached that age where he didn't listen to his older sister. He'd put his hand on your head and say you were too little to tell him what to do now." She stopped and looked at the photo again, drawing her hand across its image. "He'd been at a powwow down south, and he met someone from New Mexico, a girl, who gave him this. They make this sort of thing down there. He loved the story about the frogs, so he used to wear it around his neck." She shook her head. "He loved that girl, too. I just always thought when he drove away in that jalopy of his, he might not even go to the ancestors. He'd go straight to her. I told him to write to me, not that I thought he ever would, and he never did. I just thought, well, that's the way of children. They move away to their own lives."

Simpson's mother took her own mother's hand and held it in both of hers. "Mom, it doesn't mean that's him up there. Anyone could have one of those."

His grandmother shook her head. "This here, this is the proof." She pointed at the image of the scrap of cloth. "I know that weaving. I gave him that little bag for the frog. It's a special kind of weave. I'd know it anywhere." She looked up at Simpson, her face etched with a new sadness. "Are you going to telephone that policeman? Tell him who he's got there? You didn't tell me how that man died."

Simpson found himself almost unable to talk for a moment. He remembered his uncle as laughter and energy. He imagined him as an impetuous eighteen-year-old, always wanting to be away. It was hard to believe that man he'd seen laid out, covered by a sheet under the overhead light, the only smile left the leer of a skull, was his uncle Pete. "They told me he was shot, Grandma. Someone shot him."

His grandmother took a deep breath. "He must have gone up there to say goodbye to his ancestors like I told him to, before he drove off to find his girl. To tell them he was never coming back."

His mother began to cry.

"I'm going to telephone that police inspector in the morning. I'm not sure he'll be satisfied with just this as proof of his identity. They may want to know if he ever got his teeth fixed or broke an arm or leg or something like that, because they can see that stuff on the remains."

His grandmother sat quietly, holding the photo, but not looking at it. She seemed to be looking at something no one else would ever be able to see. Finally, she put the photo down. "He had a wisdom tooth on one side pulled out when he was maybe seventeen."

"Do you remember which one?" asked Simpson.

"Upper part of his mouth, I think on the right side. It was a real hack job, too. Said he'd never go to the dentist again. He broke his wrist climbing trees when he was ten." She shook her head. "I wonder why someone would shoot him. He never carried a gun. People always liked him. He had a way about him that drew people to him. He almost never got mad about anything." She put her hands on the table and heaved herself up, as if she had aged another decade in the hour they had sat in the kitchen with the photograph. "One thing is for sure: those people will never find who did it. I'm going to bed now."

LORENZO VITALI LAY in his bed at the hospital, his head and one hand bandaged. His eyes were closed against the morning light and his breath was laboured. His wife sat watching him, her hands folded together on her lap as if she were praying or holding herself together. She looked up at Inspector Darling's quiet knock, and then began to stand, but he motioned her down.

"How is he doing?" he asked quietly, pulling a second chair near her.

"They say he is lucky. Such luck!" She shook her head bitterly. "I didn't want him to go down to the restaurant last night, but he say it will help him think, and he will prepare for today's customers. I tell him we already do everything before we leave, but he is restless, so, here we are. His hair burn and one hand, and too much smoke in *polmoni*." She patted her chest.

"His lungs," Darling supplied. He turned to look at the patient and could feel renewed anger rising. "But he will be all right?"

"*Sì*. All right because he was on floor below smoke. He hit his head when he fall." She turned to look at him and reached out and took his hand. "How we can thank the man who save him? How did he even know anyone there?"

Darling held her hand. "He just wanted to make sure there was no one in the restaurant. He is a very good policeman." Darling didn't tell her about the tables being jammed against the door. He glanced at Lorenzo, who had opened his eyes and was watching him from under brows furrowed by pain. He must have been given morphine, but perhaps it was wearing off.

"We are finished. *Finiti*," Mrs. Vitali said quietly. Then, seeing her husband watching her, she jumped up and pulled her chair right beside him, taking the glass of water next to the bed. "*Acqua, caro mio*."

Lorenzo nodded and took the straw she offered. Only then did he realize the inspector was in the room.

"Ispettore," he croaked.

As if she had been waiting in the hall to stop people from taxing her patient, a nursing sister appeared and said quietly but sternly, "He is absolutely not to talk." She pulled his covers up and took his wrist, checking his pulse. "He has to sleep. It is the only thing."

At a little noise from Vitali, the nurse nodded at the

glass of water in Mrs. Vitali's hand. "He may have a little bit to drink. And then you must go."

Darling nodded. He watched as Vitali's wife gently put the straw into her husband's mouth and let him drink. She spoke quietly to him in Italian. When it seemed Lorenzo had drifted off to sleep, she put the water down and indicated to Darling that they should step outside.

"Thank you, Ispettore. Maybe later he can say something." She leaned against the wall with her arms folded and her head down. "It is *finito*. The restaurant." She shrugged.

When Terrell had called in first thing to talk to Darling, he had said that the dining room had been spared, and he thought it was only the kitchen that sustained the real damage.

"My constable said the dining room is still all right," he ventured.

"Thank you, Inspector, but I don't think so. I am here. I will call you if he can talk."

Darling left, thinking about the pile of ashes that was the life the Vitalis had built in Nelson in the last decade and a half. He wondered, if Lorenzo improved enough and wanted to restart his business, if there would be the means. It would cost a good deal to rebuild the kitchen, maybe refurbish the dining room. He thought about how hard immigrants work, and how often they zealously saved money. Maybe the Vitalis had done the same.

Back at the station he threw his hat onto the hat stand and sat brooding at his desk. "Ames!" he shouted, before he remembered that Ames had been relegated to a downstairs desk, and he picked up his phone and asked for him to be sent up instanter. Terrell had been kept at the hospital until late, both waiting for word on Lorenzo and having his own lungs checked, so he'd been instructed, by means of a quick early call to his landlady, to stay home and only to come in after noon if he felt up to it.

"Sir? How is Mr. Vitali?"

"Not very how, Ames. The arsonist is now an attempted murderer." He looked up as Inspector Guilfoil came in and stood by the door.

"Beastly business. I heard the racket last night. I understand it is the restaurant belonging to that Mr. Vitali. I think this changes the complexion of things, Inspector." He took the seat Darling indicated and turned to Ames. "Can you get the chair out of your office? You might as well hear this."

When they were settled, he began. "I didn't tell you, Darling, who said they saw you accepting an envelope of cash from Vitali." He paused a moment because Ames had uttered an exclamation of outrage. "As I said, I didn't tell you, but I learned something that casts some doubt on that claim, and in the course of this, I began to believe it wasn't you the person is after, but rather Mr. Vitali. I don't say I know who your arsonist is, but the rumours have been sustained and perhaps even started by Mrs. Viola Tilbury. She's the wife of the man who runs the hardware store." Guilfoil proceeded to explain what April had heard.

Darling rubbed his chin. "It's not going to be appropriate for me to talk to Mrs. Tilbury at this juncture, but it is possible she is lying about ever having been in the restaurant. It would be good to know why. I can't quite imagine that she's gone around setting fires, but we can't rule it out. I suggest we send Ames to see her. I believe I've seen her working in the hardware store. Perhaps we can bring her in."

Guilfoil nodded. "I think that's a good idea. Do you mind if I sit in when you talk to her? Not really my investigation, but I feel the overlap may be relevant."

Darling nodded and waved a shooing hand at Ames.

"Righty-ho, sir!" Ames said.

THE FIRE WAS all the talk that morning. There was a kind of shock that someone had been hurt. Some had even heard the person had been killed. The flavour of the conversations was evident in the café: voices were subdued, and there was a great deal of head shaking. April was shocked by the news, which she had heard from her dad, who'd been covered in soot and exhaustedly nursing a cup of coffee when she got up. She knew it was Lorenzo Vitali who had been injured, and listening to locals gossiping over their breakfasts, it interested her that his name had not come up, considering it was his restaurant. And she knew it had been Constable Terrell who saved him. Her heart had still not settled.

Much to her surprise, three of her usual afternoon ladies came early as well, apparently bound for a drive to Castlegar to see a friend. April noted that Mrs. Smith, Mrs. Renfrew, and the usually timid Mrs. Heatley sat looking dumbly at the menus, their normal chattiness markedly absent.

"Terrible about the fire," April said by way of opening when she arrived at the table.

Mrs. Smith nodded. "Poor Mrs. Vitali. Her husband is in the hospital. She came over when she got a call from the hospital and asked me to drive her there, and she hasn't come home. She couldn't talk much. I managed to get that there was a fire and he was hurt. Gosh, I hope he hasn't died or anything."

"It is a shame," Mrs. Heatley said. "I guess the other stores were damaged nearby, as well."

Mrs. Renfrew set her mouth in a disapproving line and then said, "We'll no doubt find he did it himself. You can't expect foreigners to practise all the safety they need to in a restaurant. Or they did it for the insurance. You always read about that happening in the papers. So now they've managed to burn themselves out and damage their neighbours. I hope they get charged. I mean, I'm sorry if Mr. Vitali was injured and all, but they have to be held to account like everyone else."

April, outraged, could barely talk. Finally, she said, "What'll it be?"

Their appetites were not dimmed by the tragedy at the restaurant evidently, and ham and cheese omelettes were ordered all round with extra toast, including for Mrs. Heatley, who, free from the disapproval of Mrs. Tilbury, was determined to have what the others did, and then some.

When April brought their omelettes, she was still finding it hard to keep her temper in check. She begged a cigarette from Al and went out to the back door. She found that it was once again raining, and she stood in the open doorway, shivering.

"I thought you said they were bad for you," Al said. "Shut the door, I'm freezing."

"Put a jacket on. I need this." She could not believe that Lorenzo Vitali had accidentally or deliberately set the fire. It was arson, no doubt about it. She knew from her father that they'd already been attacked once, but she didn't know what she was allowed to say. It infuriated her that she couldn't tell that self-satisfied, oblivious woman what was what. She wondered where Mrs. Tilbury was because if ever there was a time April would expect her to be gloating and serves-them-righting, it would be right now.

The cook ringing the bell brought her to. She tossed her cigarette out into the alley, deciding it did absolutely nothing to make her feel better and in fact went some way to making her feel light-headed, and went back through to the dining room. There was a new customer at the counter, and she gave him coffee and ordered him some toast.

The women were at least talking now, but quietly. April suddenly wondered if they felt guilt. They ought to. Had they almost finished? April moved near them and saw that they were not lingering over their breakfasts. In fact, Mrs. Smith, who seemed to have eaten only her toast, put her hand up when she saw April.

"Could I have my bill, lovey? We'd best be off."

"Certainly. I'll bring them all." April wrote out the bills, stilling a desire to charge Mrs. Renfrew a good deal more.

"You know what I'm going to do?" April said impulsively, while the women were fishing for change. "I'm going to start a fund to help the Vitalis get back on their feet. I'll put a jar on the counter."

Mrs. Renfrew humphed, but Mrs. Smith took a two-dollar bill out of her billfold. "That's a lovely idea. Here, this can start you off."

DARLING'S HAND HOVERED over the telephone. Guilfoil had gone back to his temporary office, and Ames had been dispatched to find Mrs. Tilbury, and he thought that in the momentary lull he ought to tell Lane what had happened. He knew already that she would be distraught and would, no doubt, come rushing into town, but he also knew that if he waited until he got home, she would be more upset that she could not have been of immediate use to Olivia Vitali.

That decided, he asked to be put through to KC 431 and waited, drumming his fingers on his desk.

"Ah, Lane," Darling said, when she answered.

Surprised by his use of her name, she said anxiously, "Is anything the matter?"

"Yes, I'm afraid so." He told her about the fire and Lorenzo's injuries and Terrell's rescue.

"Oh my God! And poor Mrs. Vitali! I must come at once. She can't be allowed to face this all by herself. I shall go straight to the hospital."

"I thought you'd say that. Stop by here if you get a chance afterward. You can let me know how they're doing. I shall go by on my way home as well."

"And you can get on with letting me know how your search for the rat that did this is coming!" Lane said.

Darling had no sooner hung up his receiver than the phone jangled again, startling him.

"It's that Indian fellow from across the line," O'Brien said.

"Well, put him through," Darling said, irritated by what he considered to be O'Brien's priggish tone.

"Inspector Darling. Tom Simpson here. I think that skeleton you have there might be my uncle, Pete Cooper. My grandmother recognized the frog and the weaving. It's called . . ." Darling could hear a piece of paper being consulted. "It's called Wasco weaving. She recognized it because she made him a little bag to keep his frog in. It's usually for baskets, but some weavers use the same pattern for cloth. She said he had a wisdom tooth pulled on his upper right jaw, and he'd broken a wrist as a child. His right, I think, if that helps to confirm it."

"We can verify the location of the wisdom teeth being pulled, and the coroner did mention a wrist." Darling paused. It was the confirmation he needed. It must be appalling for his family to discover this so many years later. "I am so sorry to hear this. Your grandmother must be distraught."

Tom Simpson sighed. "I'm sure she is, though she would never show it. My mother is pretty upset. He was her little brother. I am too. I was pretty close to him as a little boy."

"But how long had he been gone?"

"My mother says he took off in his Model T Ford in the spring of 1921. He said he was going to New Mexico to marry a girl he'd met at a powwow—that's a big gathering of all the tribes for games and ceremony and feasting and so on. My grandmother thought that's where he'd gone. It bothered her that he never wrote, when he said he would, but she just put it down to him being young and wanting to lead his own life. He was a bit of a rebel, my uncle Pete."

"You remember him well?"

"I do. I was pretty young, maybe four or so, but he taught me how to ride." There was a longish silence. "Inspector, I guess we're going to want to claim his body so he can be properly buried. I think my grandma in particular would like to see him buried up there, near our ancestors, but I guess that's not too likely anymore. Maybe if there's a church there. I think he was a Catholic. My mother is. If not, I guess we'll bring him down here."

"Yes, of course. You'll be coming back then, soon."

"I guess we will. We'll drive up, probably tomorrow."

"I'll look forward to seeing you again. I'll get started on writing this up. What was his surname again?"

"Cooper. My grandmother doesn't have any faith you're going to be able to find out who shot him. It's possible she even thinks you don't care all that much." He left this as a challenge.

"Your grandmother might be right about it being hard to do after all these years, but it doesn't mean we won't try. I don't like to see murder go unanswered."

"She'll be glad to hear that, Inspector. Of course, a lot of people wouldn't have thought that killing one of us would count as murder."

Glumly, Darling hung up. "Happen you're right," he muttered in imitation of the front gunner on his bomber crew during the war. Staring at the phone, he wished he'd asked if Uncle Pete had been armed. That would be all the excuse anyone would need.

CHAPTER TWENTY-FIVE

March 1921

ELAINE COOPER STOOD JUST INSIDE the kitchen door, holding a pail of water, watching her son. Her daughter had taken Tom shopping with her, so it was just the two of them.

"You'd best say goodbye. You won't ever be coming back. Say goodbye to me, to your sister, to your nephew. Say goodbye to your life here, to your ancestors up north. It is what you have to do."

He was leaning against the door to the bedroom, his arms hanging down, looking sheepish. "Come on, Mother. It's not like that. Of course I'll come back. We'll drive up, take a vacation."

"You'll tell yourself every year that you'll drive up, and every year you will be more a part of that family; every year you will belong more to that place and less to this one. And that is the right thing, to become part of your wife's family. You will have little ones, and you will be bound there." She put the bucket of water on the table and shut the door against the chill.

He tried to laugh, came forward, and put his arm around her. "You're a real gloomy person, you know that?"

"I'm a realistic person. Here, I made this for you. You can put that little frog that girl Judy gave you in it." She held out a perfect small bag, blue and white and red, intricately woven, with a little drawstring to close it. It was on a long cord that she reached up to put around his neck. He stooped over so she could reach. "You are leaving us now to start your new life, and we will not see you again, but this will remind you where you came from."

"I tell you what. I'll go and marry her, and then I'll bring her back here, and we'll all go together to see the ancestors. That way no goodbyes."

"No, my son. You must go say goodbye. That is the right way."

Pete Cooper laughed fondly and kissed his mother on the head. "You always gotta have the last word, you know that?"

LANE WAS DIRECTED to the room where Mr. Vitali lay, sleeping now. Olivia Vitali looked up when Lane paused at the door and knocked lightly. She rose and put her finger to her lips, indicating they should step into the hall.

Lane spoke first. "You poor thing! I can't believe it! How is Signor Lorenzo?"

Mrs. Vitali nodded, tears springing to her eyes. "He could have been dead," and then she seemed unable to go on. Lane enfolded her in an embrace. Finally, Mrs. Vitali continued. "It was that policeman, the one with a 'T' in

297

his name. He find him. If he did not find him, it would be too late. I give thanks to God for his life." Mrs. Vitali crossed herself. They sat down on chairs that stood against the wall. "All evening he worry, walking up and down, up and down. Refuse to go to bed. Then suddenly at almost midnight he put on his coat and go." She looked unseeing toward the nurse's desk. "I almost think he get call, he go so suddenly, but I did not hear the phone ring."

"You think he was meeting someone, maybe?"

Tears sprang into her eyes again and she shook her head. "I don't know. I don't know!"

"Could he have had a note? Was there another note delivered at the restaurant?"

Olivia Vitali put her hand to her mouth and frowned. "Oh. I don't know. I don't think so." She got up and walked back into the room, to the small bureau against the wall where her husband's clothes were folded, and took up the jacket. Part of the back had been burned, and the smell caused her to wrinkle her nose. She reached into the right-hand pocket and took out a folded piece of paper. Without opening it she brought it back and sat down, holding it in her hand as if it too were burning. Finally, she unfolded it. "You were warned. By morning your stupid restaurant will be gone," it said.

With a choking gasp, Mrs. Vitali exclaimed, "*Dio mio, Dio mio!* He try to protect the restaurant! For what? To die?"

Lane took her hand, alarmed at the desperation in her voice. "Have you been here all night? You must be exhausted. Will you let me take you home? Signor Lorenzo is in good hands here, I am sure, and you will be of no use to him if you are too tired." Lane reached over and took the note.

Mrs. Vitali did not answer this directly. She had pulled a handkerchief out of the sleeve of her cardigan, and now wound it around her long slender fingers distractedly. "I tell him he should not go to restaurant, but he insist. Now I understand why. He say he want to prepare but we already prepare everything." She shook her head. "Is no matter anyway. Restaurant is finished."

"But my husband said the dining room is not damaged. Surely it can be fixed."

"Why? So people can hate us some more? I don't think so. Maybe, when Lorenzo is better, we leave. We go to Vancouver, or America, or maybe even back to Italy."

Dismayed at the thought of Nelson without the Vitalis, Lane said soothingly, "Well, no need to make any big decisions now. All in good time. Right now, he is asleep, and you need sleep yourself. I'll take you home, and I can make you a nice cup of tea and tuck you in for a nap. Then I'll go see my husband at the station, and give him this note, and see how they are getting on with finding out who is behind this."

The resistance seemed to have left Mrs. Vitali, so looking into the room one more time to see that her husband was indeed in a deep sleep, she told the nurse at the desk that she would be back later on, toward dinnertime.

Leaning away in the passenger seat, looking at the streets as they climbed up toward her house, Olivia Vitali was silent. Suddenly she turned to Lane and spoke. "It is my fault. Everything is my fault. If I only say something to him."

"What do you mean?" asked Lane, puzzled. How could anything Olivia had done result in two attempts at murder, one nearly successful?

They had pulled up in front of the house, small, modest, like all the houses down this road. Lane could tell they would have a view of the lake below and the mountain opposite. In the silence she waited.

"This man, he start to bother me. He talk to me when I walk by in the street. One time he pull me in to door, try to kiss me, say disgusting things to me." She began to cry. "I was so scared of him, I can't even walk down the street."

Horrified, Lane said, "Who was doing this? It's dreadful!"

"Man from hardware store. I had to go get lights for Mr. Smith to put on porch, and I was so scared he will be there, but his wife was there. She was so nice to me. I don't think she know anything. I feel bad for her."

"Tilbury!" Lane said. "He's revolting. He tried to make a pass at me and all!"

Mrs. Vitali turned and stared at Lane. "You also? Maybe he just go around doing this to all the women."

"I wouldn't doubt it one bit," Lane said. "But you've come in for much the worst of it! You poor thing!" Still struggling with how the man's behaviour might have anything to do with the fires, she asked, "You think what he did to you and the fire might be connected?"

"He so angry, says such ugly words. Then he tell me he put a good word in for my husband. I don't even know what this means, but now I wonder: Is for Chamber of Commerce? Now I think because I say no, maybe he take . . . *vendetta*. I didn't say nothing to Lorenzo. Now this!"

LATER, LANE FUMED in Darling's office. She hadn't told him of her own brush with Tilbury because his behaviour toward Olivia Vitali had been so outrageous. "It's absolutely beyond the pale, this sort of thing! Are we living in the Wild West where men can behave that way toward women right out in the street, where anyone can burn someone out of town? Lorenzo was very nearly killed! What would that poor woman have done then? I wonder if it is Tilbury lighting those fires, and if she's right, that he escalated his anger at being rejected. Lane leaned forward. "One thing she said was interesting. She said—"

"Oh, excuse me," said a voice behind her. Lane whirled around and saw a tall, strongly built man of middle years in a smart uniform nearly filling the doorway.

Darling stood up and, indicating his wife, said, "Inspector Guilfoil, may I present my wife, Lane Winslow? Lane, Inspector Guilfoil of the Royal Canadian Mounted Police."

"How do you do? I think I expect you to be done up in red serge!" Lane offered her hand.

"Those are our party outfits," he said genially. "Horrible business. Have you sent Sergeant Ames to bring that Tilbury woman in?"

Lane looked puzzled. The Tilbury woman?

Darling furrowed his brow and looked at his watch. "He should have been here by now. I hope she hasn't kicked up a fuss."

"Maybe she wasn't at the hardware store, and he had to go find her at home. Well, let me know when he gets back."

He nodded at Lane, and then looked at Darling with one slightly raised eyebrow indicating, Darling was sure, that he would have married her too, given half a chance. He gave the door jamb a little pat and left.

Stifling a surge of irritation, Darling sat down and indicated Lane should as well. "You were saying."

"Only that looking in her husband's badly charred jacket, Mrs. Vitali found this." Lane produced the note with a flourish. "She couldn't make out why he needed so desperately to hurry off to the restaurant in the middle of the night. Apparently, he paced up and down and then bolted out just before midnight. It's clear he thought he could protect the place by being there."

"Same printing as in the last two. It certainly suggests murderous intent, though perhaps the writer did not anticipate he'd actually go there. Once there, however, the arsonist made damn sure he couldn't get out."

"It could have been from Tilbury, though why he'd be contacting the husband of the woman he was persecuting is a question."

"Wouldn't she have seen a note?"

Lane shrugged. "He got to it first, and he was trying to protect her. And that's another thing. Apparently while he was assaulting her, Tilbury intimated he'd put in a good word for her husband. She is wondering if this was about the Chamber of Commerce."

"Lorenzo has been rejected a couple of times. If that's what he meant, it's a filthy bit of blackmail to try on her."

"She had no idea what he meant and was certainly not having it. She was worried that her outright rejection of him would lead him to carry out a vendetta. This would certainly qualify. But why is Ames going to see *Mrs.* Tilbury?"

"I'll catch you up, shall I? This fire seems to have turned Guilfoil's mind away from suspecting me. It turns out that the woman who claims she saw Lorenzo giving me an envelope stuffed with cash is in fact Mrs. Tilbury, whose husband you now tell me was pursuing Mrs. Vitali. She is, according to my informant in the café, the one who is the most vitriolic toward the Vitalis and has possibly been the source of the gossip. The inspector is now inclined to think that Vitali is the intended victim here, and the effect on me is just a by-product of her anger at the Vitalis."

"But that suggests to me she knew about her husband's behaviour. Could she be the one responsible for the fires? A 'vendetta,' as Mrs. Vitali thinks, only not the husband, the wife? Is that why you are having her brought in? It makes a jagged kind of sense, I suppose, that she would make up a story about seeing Lorenzo giving you money."

"Yes, that's why we're bringing her in. I don't think we'd got as far as thinking she might be behind the fires." Darling looked again at his watch. "Where the devil is he? He should have been back ages ago."

"When Mrs. Vitali went to get the lights, she said Mrs. Tilbury was very sweet, and she assumed she didn't know about her husband. If she did, and she's covering it up like that, she could be quite mad, and not at all safe. What if she's resisting being brought in?" Lane asked. "How long has he been gone?"

"I sent him off twenty-five minutes ago," Darling said. "He's probably swilling tea and admiring the woman's china poodle collection." He picked up the phone and said to O'Brien, "Get me the Tilburys' number."

He phoned through and after six rings he gave up. "I'd better go see what's up."

Lane and Darling were standing at the counter while O'Brien wrote out the address. "I'll check the hardware store first," Darling was saying, when the door to the station opened, issuing in the fire chief.

"Ah, Chief McAvity," Darling said. "You've been at the scene."

"I have." McAvity paused, looking at Lane.

"Sorry. My wife. Lane Winslow. Chief McAvity from the fire department. He's April's father—you know, at the café? Lane has just been to the hospital and was telling me that Mrs. Vitali was surprised that her husband went out near midnight, but they found this note in his jacket." Darling, who'd pocketed the paper, handed it over.

"How do you do?" McAvity said to Lane. He read over the note. "Well. Here it is in black and white. How's that young constable?"

"He'll be all right. Some minor burns on his hands, and a bit of smoke, but he was sent home last night and I'm having him stay there and come in a bit late."

He had no sooner spoken than the man himself came in. "Hello, sir, Mr. McAvity. I feel fine, and I'm needed here. I don't think I can lounge around, under the circumstances."

McAvity reached out for his hand. "Good man. Without your quick work, that Vitali would be a dead man, for sure."

Terrell looked embarrassed by the praise, and McAvity turned back to Darling to give him his report. "Fire started just inside the kitchen door, I'd say. Gas again, only a whole lot more. When we got the alert, the fire had just started, and it already had consumed much of the kitchen by the time we got there. Constable Terrell heard the bell on the truck and was down there just after us. He was getting Vitali out and we were busy at the back. I don't know how you knew anyone was there," he said to Terrell, but did not wait for an answer. "I confess, I even wondered if Vitali started it himself. Some sort of insurance scam."

"It wouldn't be like him, for a start. And now we have this. He was in the kitchen lying on the floor, and the door into the dining room had been blocked so he couldn't get out. I don't know yet if he was knocked out, or was overcome with smoke and just fell, but he got quite a clonk on the head. It seems like our arsonist at work again, only with something more murderous in mind."

Lane, rapt though she was by this description of the horrors of the night before, touched Darling on the arm and said, "I just have to pop out to get something for Lorenzo. It won't take a moment."

Darling turned away from McAvity to say something, but she was out the door. She passed Hudson's Bay on the corner and was just drawing abreast of the hardware store near the end of the block when she stopped. There were two men in front of the store, one of them saying, "The place is closed? It's not like Tilbury to knock off in the middle of the day. He was open earlier; I saw him go in this morning."

Lane could see the Closed sign on the door.

"He's left his lights on—maybe he's just gone out to pick something up," suggested the second man.

"I haven't got all day. I'll get those bolts later."

She took only a second to consider trying the door. Locked. Darling had said Ames was here getting Mrs. Tilbury. The sense that something wasn't quite right caused her to turn back to the police station. McAvity was just leaving as she arrived.

"Ma'am," he nodded.

"I know you said Ames was going to the hardware store, and I just saw that it's closed and no one's about," Lane said to Darling when she'd made her way back up to the office. "Which, according to the men standing outside wanting to buy bolts, was unusual. One of them saw him go in in the morning. The lights are on, Closed sign on the door. I don't know why, but I feel a little uneasy about Ames. If he's had to go to their house, he might possibly be having to confront them both."

"I'm quite sure he can handle himself," Darling said. "Terrell and I will run up there if we have to."

"Well, I'm driving Mrs. Vitali back to the hospital in an hour or so, so I've got a bit of time to kill," Lane said.

"How will you occupy yourself?"

"Anything I could do here?" Lane looked around Darling's office.

Darling allowed himself the smallest smile. "I think we'll manage, thank you."

"Of course. I might pop down to the library, then I'll go have a cup of something at the café."

MRS. KILLEEN, THE librarian, was busy loading books onto a cart with her back to the desk when Lane came in. She was so intent on putting the books in order for shelving that Lane didn't like to disturb her. She finally must have sensed Lane because she turned around and hastily put the volume she was holding back onto its pile and smiled.

"I'm sorry. Good grief, it's been so quiet in here today, I was beginning to assume no one was coming in! Everyone off looking at that fire, maybe. How can I help?"

"I was hoping you would have some books about the local Indian populations."

"Hmm," Mrs. Killeen considered. "We could have some government publication on the Indian problem. I'd have to go look. It's not popular with the readers!" she chuckled.

"Indian problem? Is there an Indian problem?" Lane asked.

"Well, you know. What to do with them and all that. You know, all across the country."

Lane thought for a moment. "I was wondering about the local people."

"The local Indians? Goodness, there really aren't any."

"Books, or Indians?" Lane asked.

"Well, either, really. I mean, we did learn there used to be people who lived somewhere here originally, but of course they've disappeared."

"Disappeared?" Lane asked in surprise. "In what way?"

The librarian gave a little laugh. "Oh, I don't mean they've been killed off or anything like that! But you know, their way of life could never compete with the modern world. There are schools where the children go to learn our ways, so they can be completely integrated. That's more what I mean. But as tribes they've disappeared in any meaningful way."

"How odd. I've met a member of the Lakes tribe. He hasn't disappeared in any meaningful way."

"Goodness. That is interesting. Lake tribe. I've never heard of them. He'll be a renegade or some sort of hold-over, living in the bush on his own, I expect."

Lane shook her head. "He doesn't appear to be. He's a war vet, an expert in radio communications, and lives just across the border."

"Oh, well, of course." The librarian's puzzled look cleared. "He'll be an American Indian, won't he? That's different."

"He definitely said his people lived all along these lakes. He showed me a village where his people once lived."

"Oh, I don't doubt that. There are fascinating sites where Indians used to live. Goodness me, that is interesting about the fellow you met. You do sometimes see a Native person, but it's so rare around here. That there should be anyone left after all this time!"

"I got the impression there are quite a few left, his own family and many other people. They seem to have 'disappeared' up north and west and over the border when the miners and people building dams made their life here impossible. In fact, he told me that the place he lives now used to be the lower part of their territory."

"Well, that is interesting. I tell you what, I'll see what I can dig up from our own catalogue, and I'll see if I can get some more books in on the subject. Can I call you?"

"Thank you, yes. My name is Lane and I'm at KC 431."

"Oh, all the way out in King's Cove, eh? So pretty out there. So picturesque. Are you new here?"

"I've been here since the spring of '46. I'm married to the police inspector here."

"Oh, wait, I heard about that, that he'd married an English girl, and here you are! I have that nice Sergeant Ames in quite often looking up this or that."

"Yes, he is very nice, indeed. Well, thanks for your help. If you do run across something, let me know."

"There are lots of Indians north and west of here. They have reserves where they live. I can probably find you something about those, if you want; I just don't think there's anything really local."

Lane smiled. "Perhaps next time. Cheerio!" She waved and left the library in a pensive mood.

THE CAFÉ WAS almost empty, and April was busying herself wiping the long counter, lifting and putting down sugar dispensers and salt and pepper shakers. She turned when she heard the door and smiled broadly at seeing Inspector Darling's beautiful wife. "Hello, Mrs. Darling! How nice to see you. Where would you like to sit?"

"How about here by the window? If the sun shows its face, I can bask in it for a bit." Lane sat down and slid along the seat until she was by the window. "How are you, April? I just learned now that you are the fire chief's daughter. I met your father as I was leaving. He'd come to report to my husband on the night's doings."

April leaned against the opposite seat. "Isn't it awful? Everyone's been blabbing on about it all day, and of course no one knows what they're talking about. That poor man, Mr. Vitali! It kills me to listen to people being rude about him when he's in hospital with bad burns!"

"What have they been saying?"

"The usual sort of garbage, that he set it himself, either accidentally or on purpose. What I don't understand is why he was even there at that time of night. My dad couldn't tell me much except that Constable Terrell found him passed out on the floor of the kitchen."

Lane, realizing that she knew more, said, "He was very brave, Constable Terrell. He got a bit burned and inhaled some smoke. Apparently, the hospital let him go home last night. Of course, he was told to take a few hours off, but he's gone in to work."

She was taken aback to see April flush and look quickly at the door and then back, as if he might come in there.

"Oh," April said. "Is he all right?"

Aha, thought Lane, so that's where the dog lies buried. "I am absolutely sure the hospital would not have let him go home if he was in any danger," she said reassuringly.

"Where are my manners?" April cried, covering her relief. "What can I get you?" She stood up and pulled her notebook out of her pocket.

Lane gazed toward the counter. "I think I'm just ready for a nice cup of tea—and have you got a scone and some jam? I rather rushed away from my breakfast when my husband called this morning about Mr. Vitali and have had no time to think about getting any lunch. I'm actually just killing a bit of time until I pick up his wife and take her back to the hospital."

"Yes, I'll get that right away," April said.

Lane gazed out the window feeling the whirl of the morning was momentarily stilled and she could rest in its centre. She wondered if she was right, that April had a crush on Constable Terrell, and thought how lovely it was that in the midst of all the turmoil and danger, and madmen setting fires, the quiet call of love could still go on. But even love now struck her as of doubtful comfort. Could what Tilbury felt for poor Mrs. Vitali, pursuing her, threatening her, grabbing at her, be called love of some kind? And look at Mrs. Vitali, faced with the possibility of losing her husband, the man she loved. That was the trouble with loving: one day you would lose whomever it was, one way or another.

April arrived just in time to keep Lane from plunging further down that comfortless road, bringing a brown pot of tea, a mug, some cream, and a lovely tall scone with some butter and a little dish of jam. Lane realized she was famished.

"That looks wonderful. I might even eat two."

"As many as you like," said April. She gazed out the window in the direction of the police station. At that moment the sun did find a tiny break in the clouds. She turned back to Lane. "Don't you think it's wonderful what the police do?"

"It is, yes. I suppose I think it more worrisome than wonderful at times, but I'm married to a policeman. I tell you what is wonderful: the fire department. Your father must be unbelievably brave." She'd been near conflagrations: bomb sites in London, burned-out Resistance safe houses in France. She'd always been horrified by the idea of dying in a fire.

"He's okay, I guess. But I want to join the police. I told the inspector that."

Lane looked up from buttering her scone with interest. "Did you? What did he say?"

"He wasn't outright discouraging, but he said they didn't need anyone right away. Have you met that big lug of an RCMP man? I forgot his name—Inspector something. I told him, and his response was that 'there's always work a girl can do around a station.' Sounds like desk work, or worse, fetching coffee for the men!"

Lane smiled. "I take it fetching coffee wasn't what you had in mind."

"It sure is not. I heard there were women in the war over there doing all kinds of things, flying planes, being spies, and I don't know what all. That's what I admire!"

"You stick to your guns," Lane said. "In fact, I happened to be there when the big lug and my husband were talking. Apparently, you have already been helpful, picking up local gossip. They've taken what you've said seriously, you know."

"Oh!" April said, looking pleased. She'd heard rumours about the inspector's wife helping the police as well, over a couple of cases. "Well, I'm glad. I couldn't take that beastly Mrs. Tilbury bragging about how Mr. Vitali was finished!"

Lane sat on when April had left. Mrs. Tilbury again. And then she wondered if Guilfoil thought of April's contribution as gossip or information. After everything they'd done in the war, she thought, women seemed to be in about the same place they'd been before the war. She would talk to Darling about April. He, at least, had called her "an informant." Joking or not, it was a notch above "gossip." No need for the police to remain hidebound. Now she would go back to Mrs. Vitali and make sure she ate before returning to her vigil at the hospital.

CHAPTER TWENTY-SIX

VIOLA PACED AGITATEDLY. SHE'D FEIGNED a headache from lack of sleep when Gilbert had wanted her to get up and make him some breakfast; now she was dressed in her housedress with an old thick grey pullover. She couldn't seem to control her thoughts. Her head felt as if it was boiling inside. She tried to pursue the thought about her father. He was broke when he disappeared and there was a woman up at the mine, but that only led to a choking rage and, behind that, pressing terrifyingly, a deep black well of abandonment. And now this new, unbelievable information. She couldn't even think what to do about that. But the rivulet that opened and became a stream, and then a river, was her husband and that bitch of a woman. Well, she'd taken care of that. She knew someone was inside, but they'd get out. She frowned. They would. Through the kitchen door at the back. The fire hadn't been that bad. Anyone could push through a small fire like that and get out. That would take care of them. No one would stay here where they weren't wanted after that. She suddenly saw herself shoving the tables against the door and felt a wave of black panic. But no. That was only to keep him from chasing her. She obviously hadn't meant to hurt him. The relief was almost buoying. He'd have gotten out the back.

She wanted Gilbert back here. Why had she let him go to work? He needed to be here, to listen to her, to understand that she knew. She needed him here. She'd fix him, stop him for good. She stopped pacing and put her hand on the table, as if to steady herself. He would be angry. With her other hand she touched her face. A month ago he'd hit her, leaving only a small bruise, but now her whole cheek suddenly felt inflamed. What would he do if she confronted him with this? She pulled the silk scarf out of her pocket and sniffed it. It smelled of that woman. Her perfume. Her hair. Her skin. She imagined him pulling it out of his pocket to smell when she couldn't see him, to think of her in the night, pretending to be asleep next to her.

She turned and made for the closet in the spare room. The room that had been meant for their child, who never came. The rifle was there, and the bullets. She pulled open the cardboard box and loaded the gun, but she'd left the box too close to the edge of the table, and it fell, and the bullets cascaded across the floor. The noise added to the tumult in her head, but she focused, her hand on the rifle, on the central thought. This would deter him if he tried anything. She propped the rifle in the corner by the door into the sitting room and then reached for the phone.

TILBURY HAD BEEN surprised to see Sergeant Ames standing at the counter when he'd come out from the back at the sound of the bell alerting him to a customer. The only time he'd seen him in the shop was a few months before when he'd come in for some screws that were entirely unsuitable for the shelf he was apparently trying to fix in his mother's kitchen. He wouldn't call him handy.

"Morning, Sergeant. More screws?"

"Nope. Not today. I just need to have a quick word with Mrs. Tilbury. Is she around?"

Tilbury felt a flush of anxiety. Why would the police want to talk to his wife? Her peculiar behaviour came back to him. "No, she stayed home today. Bad headache." A headache from being up half the night. He'd heard her in the kitchen, heating milk, pacing. "What's this about?" He tried to still the anxiety in his voice, but he could feel it cracking.

"Just a follow-up on something she mentioned to the RCMP officer. Nothing concerning. He forgot to make a note of something, and he wanted me to check it out," Ames said, marvelling at his facility in half-truths, but of course his visit was in part as a result of what she'd told the RCMP. He could tell Tilbury was shaken, and he didn't want him alerted to what they suspected.

Tilbury spoke. "I see. I'm not sure she will want to talk to anyone right now. She had a late night. Had trouble sleeping. She gets migraines."

"Oh, I'm sorry to hear that. I promise I'll be quick. What's the address again?"

Tilbury stood watching Ames as he left, followed him

with his eyes as he turned back down the street. His heart was pounding painfully, and the idea came to Tilbury that he could have a heart attack. His dad had been only a little older than him, fifty-two, when he'd had his. He turned back to the storage room to continue the work he'd been doing: opening boxes to refill the trays in the shop with nails and screws, hoping the mundane work would calm him down. Instead, he sat down on a crate and closed his eyes, and his next thought scared him half to death: What if Viola had seen him? What if she knew? He reached into the inside pocket of his jacket instinctively, almost for comfort. It was gone. When had he last seen it? How long he sat, feeling his body almost swelling with his fear, he could not have said. The ringing of the telephone out on the counter shocked him.

"Tilbury's Hardware," he said into the receiver. His voice was shaking now.

"You have to come. I feel really awful. I think you need to take me to the hospital."

"Viola?"

"Who do you think it is? Please, I'm really scared. My headache is almost blinding me. I've taken Aspirin. A lot of Aspirin."

What was she saying? He held the receiver in a hand that was now sweating. "What do you mean? How much Aspirin?"

The only answer he received was the buzzing of a disconnected phone.

AMES FOUND THE house and considered parking the car half a block away so as not to alert her, but then realized that if she was reluctant to accompany him to the station, having to walk a struggling woman half a block might be a problem. Leaving the car doors unlocked and the keys in the ignition to be at the ready, he mounted the steps and knocked on the door. He noticed that all the windows he could see from there were curtained. With a migraine headache, she must want darkness. Maybe she really did suffer from them. He'd heard they were awful. No answer. He knocked again and was about to call out, but at that moment he heard movement inside, and he waited for her to open the door, enjoying the little shot of sunlight that promised spring. Not before there would be several more snowy days, he reminded himself. There was that year it snowed in late April. The minutes ticked by. Finally, he turned the handle and found the door unlocked. Pushing it open, he called out softly, "Hello?" The sitting room was empty and very dark. A quick scan revealed a large pre-war wireless in the corner, an upright piano, a couch and two chairs, a coffee table. And then suddenly she was standing in the doorway into the kitchen. What did she have? An explosion of sound deafened him, and he felt himself struck, going down, still conscious for a moment, the image of the book on the coffee table large in his mind. *Grand Opera*. He felt his head ricochet off the ground and then he knew no more.

THE HOSPITAL SEEMED quiet when Lane and Mrs. Vitali arrived. An ambulance was parked in front of the double doors. Someone came out of the hospital and lit a cigarette and went around to the driver's seat. Whatever urgency had brought him there had dissipated.

Lane said, "May I come up with you and just see how he is doing? I know my husband would want to know."

"Yes, of course," Olivia Vitali said with a nod. She had napped and eaten and taken a good deal of trouble with her hair and clothes. She didn't want him to worry about her, she'd told Lane. She wanted him to see that she was strong.

"You are strong," Lane had said. "And beautiful and elegant. You will cheer him up no end."

They stood now at the desk, waiting. Whatever emergency had come through the door must have taken the receptionist away, but she came from the office behind the desk holding a cup of coffee, looking perfectly relaxed. She sat down, arranged a few things on the counter in front of her, and then looked up frowning at Mrs. Vitali. She turned her gaze, and a smile, in Lane's direction.

"Yes?"

"We're here to see Mr. Vitali."

The girl looked at her watch and then said officiously, "Visiting hours are not for another twenty-five minutes."

"This is his wife. He was very badly hurt in a fire. She was allowed to sit up with him all night. We informed the desk in his ward we'd be coming back at this time."

The girl looked daggers at Mrs. Vitali again, and then picked up the phone and said quietly, but not quietly enough, "The wife of that Eyetie is here." She listened for a moment and put the receiver down. "You may go up,"

319

she said stiffly, and then turned away from them to attend to her coffee and arranging.

Lane stifled a desire to have a word. She might have that word when she got back down after checking on Lorenzo and leaving his wife there.

Mrs. Vitali either did not hear the slight or was too worried to care.

In the ward, the nursing sister at the desk was much kinder and said, "Oh, good. He's been waiting. He's had a good long rest and could use a little company. I don't know about two of you . . ."

"Oh, that's all right," said Lane. "I'm not stopping. I just want to see how he's doing."

"All right, then. Only a moment. Mrs. Vitali can stay as long as she'd like."

Inside his room, Lorenzo lay back against some stacked pillows, looking, Lane was alarmed to see, not much better than earlier in the day, but he smiled weakly and reached out his good hand to his wife, who moved forward and took it, pulling up a chair to be near him. She said something to him softly in Italian and he nodded, still smiling. Then he turned to Lane. "Miss Winslow, thank—" but he began to cough.

"No, no, no. Don't trouble yourself, Signor Lorenzo. I'm just popping in to see how you are getting on. I know the inspector is most anxious for good news."

He nodded and took his hand momentarily from his wife's and made a thumbs-up gesture. "I am okay," he managed.

"You'll be all right?" Lane said to Mrs. Vitali.

"I will take taxi if is okay to leave. Thank you so much."

She seemed to want to say more, but Lane gave a little wave and slipped out the door. Once at the desk she asked the nurse, "Is he progressing?"

"He's doing well enough, considering the circumstances. I can't tell you much as you are not family, but if you have anyone waiting to hear, you can tell them we are satisfied with his progress. His lungs, mostly. We are keeping him propped up to help his breathing." She stopped there.

"Thank you," Lane said. "My husband will be relieved to hear it."

In the elevator, Lane felt relieved. Deciding not to have a word with the receptionist, who in any case was dealing with an orderly, she made her way to the police station.

SHE PUSHED OPEN the door of the station just as Darling was tearing down the stairs, shouting something.

"Good God, what's the matter?" she asked. He looked frantic. Darling pulled on his hat and clutched her arm. "Something has happened to Ames. Possibly shot. Sorry, darling." He turned to O'Brien. "Terrell and I are going to the neighbour who phoned in. Guilfoil is alerting the RCMP. You don't move from those bloody phones in case there's any kind of call, ransom or otherwise!" And with that, he and Terrell rushed out of the station, Terrell pocketing a revolver.

"Damn! Ames took the car," Darling said furiously.

"I'll take you," Lane said.

They could see Ames's car, still on the street, and the neighbour who'd made the call standing on her front porch, looking anxious, her jacket pulled tight around her. But no sign of Ames. The house with the door hanging open must be Tilbury's, Darling thought. He jumped out of the car, followed by Terrell, and looked into the police car. The keys were in it.

Darling bent over and said to Lane, "We'll take it from here. Ames left the keys in the car. It might not be safe. Please."

Lane nodded. She could see he was beside himself. And he had a vehicle. She nodded and said, "Be careful." As she pulled forward, past the house with the open door, she could see the blood on the landing, and began her own version of a prayer for whomever it had belonged to.

THE NEIGHBOUR WHO'D called rushed forward now, holding a damp handkerchief in one hand. She wasn't crying now—thank God, Terrell thought—but was being lucid. Darling, he could see, was distressed.

"Okay, tell me again exactly what you saw. It's critical if we are to find them in time," Darling said, his voice preternaturally calm, as if to ease himself and steady the woman.

"Just what I said. I was in the garden, and I saw that man, I think he must be your policeman, open the door. Oh, wait. I think Mr. Tilbury was there. Or he just got there. It's so confusing. Then I went in the house. I didn't want the Tilburys to think I was watching them while they were getting a visit from the police. It might be embarrassing. Then I heard a shot, and I went to the window in time to see the policeman fall, sort of backwards with . . . blood . . ." She put her handkerchief to her mouth. "I was so shocked

I couldn't move for a minute. The way he fell, I knew he was probably dead."

Darling could feel his impatience and now despair pulling at him. "What then?"

"I don't know. I saw them both leaning over the body, and then I saw that Mrs. Tilbury was holding a rifle. I got scared and ran into the kitchen to call someone. I called the ambulance first, just in case. It always takes so long to explain where the address is. Then I called you, but you know that. When I'd finished, I ran to the window and I saw the car leaving, going that way. They were both in it, and I didn't see your officer, but he wasn't on the porch anymore." She pointed south.

"South. Not down toward Baker?"

"No, south. See, I thought that was funny because I was sure they would take him to the hospital, but they were driving in the opposite direction. I mean, it must have been an accident. I don't think poor Viola has been very well lately. Maybe she thought . . ."

Not wanting to hear what anyone thought, Darling turned to Terrell. "South. Away from the hospital. Going to meet the Slocan road? Run into the house and make sure they didn't leave him there."

"Ma'am, can I use your telephone?" Darling said urgently, already pushing past her into the house. As he feared, no one wounded had been brought to the hospital. What the devil were they up to? He put in a call to O'Brien, asking him to let Guilfoil know that he suspected they had gone out toward Slocan. Then he dashed outside. Terrell was just hurrying out of the Tilburys' house, shaking his head. Darling ordered him into Ames's abandoned car. "Let's see if we can make out where they've gone. Probably fruitless at this point." Darling slumped into the passenger seat, feeling only the terrible fear that Ames might indeed be dead.

TERRELL DROVE AS fast as he dared until they got to the turnoff that would take them either to the coastal road or to the gravel road up toward New Denver.

"What do you think, sir?" He had paused at the intersection.

"I have no bloody idea," Darling said, looking at each road. "If they really wanted to get away, they'd head out toward Castlegar and then the coast. But they've got Ames with them. If he's dead, they'd need to get rid of him." It was madness. Either direction would provide enough wild country to get rid of scores of bodies. And if he was alive? Every moment would mean more loss of blood or who knew what all.

The sound of a siren grew from behind them. Darling leaped out of the car and waved his arms. It was an RCMP vehicle. Darling leaned down to talk to the driver. "How many of you are there?"

"One car has gone north, and I'm here going south. Been given make of car and waiting for number to be radioed."

"At least we can split up now. I'll head up toward Slocan if you take the Castlegar road."

"Right you are, sir," said the Mountie, touching his cap. If he was concerned about being given orders by someone in the local police force, he did not show it. "I'll radio you if I find anything."

Darling shook his head grimly. "Don't have the equipment. Radio the station." That would have to change, he thought.

He got back into the police vehicle and ordered Terrell to take the turnoff on the dirt road.

"I just can't understand why they are driving around with him. Alive or dead, it makes no sense."

"People will do crazy things when they are in a panic," Terrell said.

They drove for twenty minutes, passing nothing on the road until they met a logging truck going so fast that Terrell had to drive into the ditch to avoid it. Darling glowered as it hurtled past them, then shouted, "Tilbury is in the passenger seat! I'm certain of it!"

CHAPTER TWENTY-SEVEN

MUCH LATER, THE ONLY LIGHT in the sitting room coming from the incongruously cheerful dancing of the flames in the Franklin, Lane and Darling sat, nursing scotches. Exhausted as they were, and as late the hour, there was an unspoken reluctance on both their parts to go to bed.

"It was a miracle we found him so quickly. Thank God that logging truck saw Tilbury at the side of the road waving like a madman. He thought Ames was dead. It must have been quite a sight, that massive truck racing along Baker Street honking his horn for all he was worth to get him to hospital. And Tilbury is sitting in a cell, not saying a thing."

"He'll make it," Lane said quietly. She could see that he was nearly inconsolable. "He's as strong as an ox."

Darling shook his head, not in negation but in vexation. "It keeps coming back to me that you were right, that it wasn't safe. I shouldn't have let him go alone. And now she's done a bunk. This whole thing has spiraled out of control. How did we get from a little attempt to damage Vitali's porch to two people in hospital and an armed woman on the lam? If he had died . . ." He couldn't finish the sentence.

Lane stood up. "Right. Enough. You cannot possibly be logical when you are exhausted and have had a day like this one. To bed. I'm going to make you a cup of cocoa and provide a hot water bottle for your feet. My gran used to do that when I was having a dark night of the soul, and it worked a charm. Up you get!"

"I'm not the one having the dark night," he said, reluctantly getting to his feet. "It's poor Ames."

"Well, I'm sure those nice nursing sisters have provided him with a hot water bottle for his feet as well." She kissed him gently and turned him in the direction of the bedroom and gave him a little push. "Off you go."

He trundled off compliantly enough, and Lane went to the kitchen, opened the fridge, and pulled out the bottle of milk. But then she put it down and rested her hands on the table, her head bent over them, her heart aching. It all was too much. Lorenzo burned and his business destroyed, Ames in hospital with his shoulder shot up. By the time he'd got to the hospital, he'd lost a lot of blood and suffered some sort of concussion from falling onto the sidewalk. Only another inch or two and he would have died right there, on Tilbury's threshold. Cheerful, ebullient Ames. It was unthinkable. And she'd never seen Darling in a slump like this. But of course, she thought, standing up straight and reaching for the saucepan to warm the milk, it was bound to happen. She had thought being a policeman's wife would involve being constantly worried, but now she saw how it might also involve bucking up, and tucking up, the actual policeman from time to time.

She boiled water in the kettle for the hot water bottle and put the little saucepan of milk on the burner. When everything was ready, she went to the bedroom, where Darling lay fast asleep with the light on. Uttering a nearly silent "humph," she decided these comforts would do just as well for her, so she turned out his light, turned on hers, and prepared for a soothing read and a nice cup of warm cocoa.

LANE, WATCHING DARLING drive off very early the next morning, his spirits back in the grimly determined range, thought about yesterday's events in the light of day. Darling had said that he'd met with Guilfoil before he'd come home, and the RCMP in the area had been radioed to keep an eye out for the fleeing Viola Tilbury. What he couldn't understand, and struggled with all through his cup of coffee, the only breakfast he wanted, was why Ames had been shot, and by which of the Tilburys. By the time he'd left, he had expressed the grim hope that Ames would be conscious enough to say who had shot him.

He also said he had got Terrell to go to Mrs. Ames and get her to the hospital. He had promised to let Lane know how he was doing the minute he found out. She was thinking now that if she heard, and if he seemed able to see anyone besides his mother and Darling, she would dispatch Tina Van Eyck to his bedside. That ought to cheer him up.

The dawn was lifting from grey to a gold that promised at least a partly sunny day. "I should bloody well hope so!" Lane said out loud to the horizon. Would it be too early to seek comfort from the Armstrongs? She'd never attempted it at this time of day, but if anyone was in the early-to-rise brigade, it would be them.

She went into the hall and put on her warm wool Mac jacket and her boots, and made her way across her yard, over the little bridge through the stand of still-bare birch trees, and walked along the road toward the post office. She found Kenny peering under the hood of his truck.

"Good morning," she called. "Everything all right in there?"

"Goodness, you're about early. I heard the inspector going off at the crack of dawn." He closed the hood. "Just checking the oil," he said, wiping his hands on a cloth. "In fact, you were off somewhere most of the day as well. Something happen?"

"Yes. Several somethings," Lane said ruefully.

The door opened, followed by the screen door and an eruption of barking and wiggling Westie. Alexandra seemed confused about whether she should be defending or welcoming. She settled on welcoming, and licked Lane's face happily when she was picked up.

"Are you sure it's not too early?" Lane asked as she was ushered into the kitchen. The stove was already warming the tiny space, the kettle burbling, and a frying pan heating up.

"Bacon and eggs," said Eleanor. It was not an invitation really, more of an order. It was all just what Lane had been hoping for. A mere cup of coffee was no breakfast at all in her opinion.

They were as rapt an audience as she could have asked for. They were horrified by Lorenzo's being hurt, and his restaurant, to which Lane had taken them once, burned out, but at the news of Ames, Eleanor's hand flew to her mouth.

"Never that lovely young man! It's wicked! Oh, that poor dear. He's such a good young policeman. Do you know how he is?"

"Frederick is going straight to the hospital. He said he'd telephone with that news first. I was thinking, if it looked like he might be able to stand a visitor, of letting Tina Van Eyck know—you know, the mechanic? I'm never really sure what stage things are at with them. Do you think that would be too interfering?"

"Certainly, it is the right thing to do. A pretty girl is just the thing. This is all just too dreadful. The inspector must be beside himself with worry about Sergeant Ames," said Eleanor.

"He is, actually. Poor Constable Terrell was supposed to be recovering from smoke inhalation after his heroic rescue of Lorenzo, but he's been called up as well. It's funny, I was just talking to that nice young woman who works in the café where they're always going. I had some time before I took Lorenzo's wife back to the hospital, and she told me rather wistfully that she'd like to join the police force."

Kenny frowned, wiping up the last of the bacon and egg on his plate with a slab of bread. "I don't think you can have women doing police work."

"Why ever not?" asked Eleanor, her eyebrows raised.

Looking as though he wished he'd not woken a sleeping dragon, Kenny said hesitantly, "Well, I mean, it's a very physical job, and . . . and people get shot!" he finished with a feeble flourish.

"You can sit here and look at me, and at our braver-than-brave neighbour who did . . . I'm not sure what, but I'm dashed sure it was more than she's ever let on, in that ridiculous war we just had—that was started, I should add, by men—and spout that sort of nonsense?" She turned back to Lane. "I don't know the young lady very well—I've only had several cups of tea in that little café when I've gone into town—but if she wants to be a policewoman, I think it's a splendid idea."

Lane smiled and nodded. The war was still near, at only two and a half years in the rear-view mirror, but she'd already picked up the trend of women having to content themselves with being homemakers now that the men were back and in their jobs. True, many jobs now were beginning to seem like women's jobs—teachers, waitresses, nurses, clerks, increasingly—but if women didn't remind the world what they did in the war and demand a wider range of jobs, they might lose the impetus altogether. She was about to say something about this when the telephone bell sounded from the Armstrongs' little parlour. Two longs and a short.

"Oh, that's mine, do you mind? This might be our inspector with news!"

It was indeed. A very relieved Darling was calling quickly, just to say that Ames had come to and was heavily sedated, that his shoulder injury was dire but not fatal. The only trouble was that he seemed a little delirious. Kept thinking he'd been on a camping trip with the Boy Scouts.

"If he actually was a Boy Scout," he added, "that would explain an awful lot."

"I'm so relieved, thank you, darling. I'm sure he'll come out of it. I think I'll call Tina Van Eyck. She'll want to know, I suspect."

"Oh my God," Darling said in a way that Lane could almost hear the disapproving shake of the head. "Look, I've got to go. See you tonight."

LANE BUMPED INTO the grassy parking area in front of the Van Eyck garage. It was just quarter past nine in the morning. The garage doors were already swung open, and she could hear metallic banging sounds coming from within.

"Hello?" she called, looking into the garage, which was murky in contrast to the sun beaming outside.

Mr. Van Eyck came around from behind a roadster. "Ah, good morning, Mrs. Darling. Car trouble on this fine morning?" He peered past her to where she'd parked.

"Good morning. No. All shipshape in that department. It's Tina I need to see, if she has a minute."

"Tina! Mrs. Darling here to see you!" Van Eyck called into the garage.

"Coming!" Lane could hear the clatter of a tool, and Tina came out of the shadows pushing a blond curl into her turban. "This bent tire rim is really giving me trouble," she said. "Hi, Miss Winslow."

Mr. Van Eyck looked for a moment as if he wanted to stay around to hear what was up, but he receded into the garage, leaving them alone.

"Tina, I feel horrible being the one to bring you this, and I can tell you he is going to be all right, but Sergeant Ames was shot yesterday and is in hospital."

Tina's hand flew to her mouth, and she blanched. A sound escaped her, but she said nothing.

"My husband has been to see him this morning. He's sedated—Ames, I mean—and has suffered quite a bad wound in the shoulder. Luckily the bullet missed—"

At this moment Tina found words. "Oh my God! Oh my God! This is what it's going to be like, isn't it?" Tears began to fall, but she wiped them away hastily. "I must go see him. Do you think . . ."

"Absolutely," said Lane. "I'm sure you are just what he needs. I can drive you in, if you like." She'd been planning to spend the day washing Stella Bisset's bedding and clothing, but delivering an emergency Tina to Ames would take very little time out of her day.

Tina considered for only a moment. "No. I have to change. I'll drive myself in. Thank you." She reached out and put her hand on Lane's arm. "Thank you for thinking to come for me. I mean it." She turned and hurried into the garage. "Daddy! Daniel has been shot. He's going to be okay, but I'm going into town to be with him."

"I should warn you," Lane said, "he's a little delirious just now, apparently. Thinks he's been camping with the Boy Scouts."

"Boy Scouts? Oh my word, wouldn't you know it!"

Lane smiled slightly as she drove up toward the main road. It amused her that both Darling and Tina had the same response to the idea of Ames being a Boy Scout.

Daniel. Of course, she'd known that was his name, but said like that, by the woman who most obviously loved him . . . that was a wonderful thing.

AMES STRUGGLED TO open his eyes, but his eyelids felt as though they were weighted down. There was a ringing in his ears. As if from a distance, he heard a voice. "Sister," it seemed to be saying.

He felt his wrist taken, held aloft by cool fingers, and then put down.

"Sergeant Ames! Are you awake?"

Of course he was awake, he wanted to say, but he could not properly move his mouth. He had a vague memory of having seen Darling at some point but could not quite remember why. It was odd to see him out in the bush like this. Should he even know him? No. Of course. He wasn't Darling. He was Spratley, the scoutmaster. He must have fallen off that boulder they were standing on. Hit his head. With a gigantic effort he managed to budge his eyelids and admitted a murky but overbright light. He closed them again quickly. He wanted to say it was too bright, but he could feel his mouth clamped shut, struggling with the "b."

"That's right. You really do have to wake up. Miss Van Eyck, could you pull the drapes shut? I'll give the sergeant a drink of water."

Ames could feel the straw going into his mouth and he realized he was desperately thirsty and began to suck on it. He tried again with his eyes, and this time he made better progress. It was light, but not blindingly so, and he could see two figures. One looming over him and another behind. He thought he recognized one of them, but in the next moment was completely mystified by his own condition. Where was he? No, wait, he knew. Spratley had said something. What had happened? He tried to move and felt a searing pain, though he couldn't immediately recognize its location. This time his mouth worked well enough to emit a groan.

The figure looming over him now touched him gently on a shoulder that didn't hurt. "Now then. No moving about. It'll hurt less if you lie still. I'll leave you with your visitor for a few minutes."

The strange woman retreated, and Ames heard a chair scraping and then a blond head swam into his vision. "Dad . . . upset," he tried.

"Not just your dad," Tina said briskly. She was glad Lane had warned her he was a bit delirious. "Your mom, your boss, and me."

"You're very pretty," Ames said, his voice a bit scratchy.

"Thank you. Do you know who I am?"

"No, but I like you." Ames had turned his head slightly in her direction.

Tina smiled and shook her head. "It's what you say to all the girls, alas."

"Am I in hospital?" Ames now frowned and tried to look around without moving his head.

"Yes. You were shot. And you banged your head."

"Spratley shot me? No. That can't be right." He closed his eyes and groaned once and then was silent.

Tina sat with him, watching him sleep, wondering if

he would wake up next time and know who she was. The nursing sister popped in once to check his pulse.

"He's been sedated. He might sleep for a long time, which would be good for him," she said quietly to Tina.

"Is that why he has no idea what's happened or who I am? He thinks he's a Boy Scout."

"That's funny. I actually knew him in school. I was the school nurse my first couple of years of practice. He was definitely a bit of a Boy Scout then. Always trying to be the best boy in class. My goodness, he tried hard. He'd be just the guy to try to help old ladies cross the street. I'm not surprised he ended up as a policeman. We can hope he remembers you." She smiled and shook her head. "He'd be a fool not to."

Tina had gone to the reading room and found a magazine and had brought it back to continue her vigil. She'd just turned to the first article when Ames made a sound. She looked up and saw him looking at her, his face a mask of puzzlement.

"Tina?"

"Yup. I'm pleased to see you recognize me. You didn't before. Water?" She moved to the water glass and held the straw for him. He sipped at it, not taking his eyes off her.

"But why are you here?" He stopped drinking and looked around, groaning at the pain of moving his head. "Hospital?"

"Right again. How are you feeling?" She put the water glass on the side table and looked at him with concern.

"Like absolute hell." He moved his good hand up to his head. "What happened?"

"You got shot in the shoulder and banged your head."

"And you're here?"

"You *are* swift today. Yes, I am. Well, I was hardly going to leave you in the lurch after you got yourself shot, was I? More water?" Her voice was puzzlingly soft.

"Shot?" he scraped out. Had he really been shot? Yes, that was what he remembered someone saying. By whom? Nothing seemed to come except that he appeared to be alive.

"Oh, dear. You don't remember at all, do you? That'll be the shock and delirium." Tina reached out and stroked his hair gently away from his face. "Your face is all scratched," she said.

Ames felt her hand and was amazed by it. He suddenly remembered just fine that the last time he saw her she'd walked out and left him at the New Star Café with a plate of chicken chow mein and a pretty clear indication she'd had it with him.

"Tina," he said finally.

"Yes, we've established that. You're an idiot, you know that? I've never been so scared in my life. Anyway, I'm glad to see you making an effort." She held the straw and cup of water for him, and he drank more. He wished he could sit up.

"How did I . . ."

"Well, I don't actually know much. Miss Winslow came by this morning to tell me. I don't know anything except that you got shot."

He drew his eyebrows together. He remembered a flash of light, or was it an explosion? Was that why his ears were ringing?

"Don't worry about not remembering. I'm sure you will."
She stopped and looked at him, her hands now folded on
her lap. "I hope there isn't going to be a lot of this sort of
thing," she said, touching his forehead again. She stood
up. "Look, I'm getting the evil eye from the nursing sister,
so I have to go. But I'll be back later." She leaned over
and kissed him with infinite gentleness on the cheek, and
whispered, "Now do what you're told."

He wanted to say something, anything, but instead could
only watch her out the door, his heart full.

CHAPTER TWENTY-EIGHT

"**INSPECTOR, AMES HAD ME LOOKING** into the daughter of your cold case, Turner, before he got himself shot up, and my chum at City Hall licensing just gave me a call. You'll never guess who she is," said Sergeant O'Brien, holding up a bit of paper.

"No, Sergeant, I won't," said Darling dangerously. He didn't care for guessing games at the best of times. This was not the best of times.

"Keep your hair on. Viola Turner married Gilbert Tilbury. In short—"

"In short, she is Viola Tilbury, currently on the run," said Darling, much surprised. "Are you going up to see Ames?"

"Yes, sir, if I can have leave to get away a little early today."

"You can go up as soon as Terrell gets back. He's doing the visitors' rounds just now. I understand Ames might be able to tell us what happened, so Terrell is going to collect what he can. I'll leave it to you to tell him about Viola Tilbury, née Turner."

"YOU LOT OUGHT to pitch some tents outside, seeing as you spend all this time here," the receptionist commented. She had begun to make her peace with the existence of Constable Terrell.

Terrell for his part had long ago accepted her. The world was full of people like her, and there didn't seem to be a whole lot that could be done about them. He followed his regular procedure when he had to visit anyone at the hospital. He touched the rim of his hat and said, "Miss," before he got into the elevator.

He was happy to find Ames fully conscious, with the paltry remains of his lunch pushed to one side. Healthy appetite, anyway.

"Constable Terrell, a sight for sore eyes. You couldn't bring me a ham and cheese from your pal April next time you come?"

"I could, sir. How long do you have to stay in?"

"A week? A couple of days? I don't know. Trade secret. It can't come soon enough. Some of these nursing sisters are terrifying. And then I'm supposed to hang around at home for a spell. I don't see me doing that. You've come to depose me? I can't promise much. Even with the drugs my shoulder hurts like the devil. And I've only just started to remember bits and pieces. I might not be a reliable witness."

"We'll walk through it slowly, sir. You may remember more than you think." Terrell settled in the bedside chair and took out his notebook.

Ames made a move to compose himself but ended up wincing instead.

"This is a darn nuisance," he complained. "All right. Shoot."

"Very funny, sir. Can you perhaps tell me everything you remember from the time you left the station? You were in search of Mrs. Tilbury, I believe."

"Okay, yes. I remember that. I went to the hardware store because she usually works there alongside her husband for part of the day, but he told me she'd stayed home not feeling well. I remember asking him to give me his address; he was a little reluctant and pretty suspicious, with a 'Why do you need to see my wife?' sort of attitude. I went back to the station to get the car, and drove up the hill to their address, parked, and went to the front door." He stopped here and closed his eyes for a moment. "I knocked . . . I don't know, twice? I heard someone inside, and it's possible I knocked again and then just turned the handle and found the door open and called out her name. Then a blinding light. Except the oddest thing is that the one thing I noticed just before the shot was a large opera book on the coffee table because I must have been giving the room the once-over."

Terrell wrote diligently in his little notebook. "Any chance you saw the shooter, Sergeant?"

Ames shook his head, perplexed. "It was so damn dark in there. I think all the curtains were closed. But we are going on the assumption it was Mrs. Tilbury, aren't we?"

"Well, yes, for the time being. You didn't see Tilbury himself there?"

"No, absolutely not. I'd left him down the hill."

"According to the neighbour, he was there as well, and

apparently the two of them must have carried you to the car and driven off."

"He definitely wasn't there when I was knocking on the door. Well, I don't think so. When did he turn up?" Ames asked.

"We don't really know. We brought him to the shop after he and that truck driver brought you in, and he's sitting in the cell refusing to talk. We're going on the theory that perhaps she expected him to come through the door."

"So, she wanted to shoot *him*? Bad luck for me! But it makes a little more sense. I couldn't imagine why someone I barely know wanted to shoot me." Ames tried again to twist into a more comfortable position.

"Here's something that will surprise you: Viola Tilbury is, in fact, the daughter of your missing person, Samuel Turner. Small world."

"Well, I'll be! Very small world. Does it have any bearing on this? Could she have shot me to cover up her relationship to him? No. It makes no sense. No one knew I was looking into her father's disappearance, and anyway, I bet no one knew she had a famous father. Unless they knew her when she was young. I sure didn't. But it is quite the coincidence." He took in a deep breath and winced. "I really shouldn't do that. Darling says sometimes coincidences are just coincidences, but they shouldn't be ignored." He closed his eyes and said, "It's very hard to understand how the Turner case has anything to do with this, but I suppose . . ." He opened his eyes and then closed them again.

"You look a little all in, sir. I think we were hoping you might positively identify who took a shot at you, and it does sound like it must have been Mrs. Tilbury. You don't remember anything else?"

"I'm sorry, Constable, I think it's the best I can do."

"Hello, you two."

The two men looked toward the door to see Tina Van Eyck hesitating on the threshold. "Am I interrupting?"

Terrell jumped up, pocketing his notebook. "Not at all, Miss Van Eyck. He's all yours. Is there something for him to eat in that bag? I don't think the hospital food is up to much."

"You're back," Ames said, recovering some of his earlier energy.

Tina came in, beaming and holding up a paper bag. "I've brought you some proper food." She put the bag on the chair and took off her jacket and unpinned her green hat and placed them on the end of the bed. "And I've brought something improving for you to read."

"I'll leave you to it then, sir. Call if you want anything."

Even with the threat of an improving read, Ames looked quite happy to be left in Tina's care. "Righty-ho! I'll see you back at the ranch in a day or two," Ames said, waving his good hand.

Terrell could just hear Tina saying, "Oh, no, you won't," as he went into the elevator.

LANE SPENT HER afternoon washing Miss Bisset's clothes and bedding, and because the weather looked uncertain, she had hung them on the rack above the stove, reflecting that the rack made more sense when the stove was a great iron behemoth of a wood stove that never went out, like the Hugheses' or the Armstrongs'. This done, she made a cup of tea and stretched out on the window bench, gazing at the lake beyond the trees. The steamboat from Kaslo and Lardeau was just making its way toward Nelson, emphasizing the quiet of the lake by its steady movement. The late afternoon light made her feel slightly melancholic. Hoping that the day had provided no more earth- or people-shattering events for her husband, she settled in to think about Stella Bisset. The state of her was enough fodder for melancholy, she thought. Even with the cleanup and the laundry Lane had done, Miss Bisset would deteriorate again quickly without proper care. The pathos of "After You've Gone" coming from the record player intensified in her mind. A tune suddenly manifesting from the distant past, like a musical ghost. What was interesting, she thought, was how it had seemed to bring Stella Bisset around. She'd been suddenly present, as if she was home again in some time she recognized and felt comfortable in. The present was nothing but mental fog and bewilderment, but the past was clarity and happiness. But then that frightened outburst on the second playing of the tune. "That was why we had to go. He said the man was trying to get in," she had said.

Lane sat up. She had tried to calm the distraught woman, to ask her who was trying to get in, but had received only a frightened shake of the head, and then Stella had seemed to sink into confusion again. Did the music release a memory from long ago or was it some more recent memory? Had something happened in the last little while? She wasn't sure how much danger a lone, not very *compos mentis* woman would face living on her own in a cottage so far out of range of any neighbours. She hadn't heard that New Denver was a particularly dangerous community, and she apparently did have that vile shopkeeper Berenson looking in on her.

Now in the afternoon, with Stella's sheets and her few garments drying, and the clouds moving in, promising rain, nothing about the Stella Bisset situation seemed really as it ought to be. And who was Stella Bisset, anyway?

Had she been there for many years? Judging by the cottage and the old record player, she'd have said yes. According to Berenson, he'd taken the shop over from her because she was already struggling to remember things. How long ago? Had she stayed on after being married to a miner who had died, living first off the store and then some sort of pension?

Heaving herself off the window seat and wanting fresh air to dissipate the ache in her heart over Stella's reduced and diminishing life, Lane put on her boots and jacket and went outside to survey the garden. She mused idly about turning it over only to find someone had been buried in her vegetable beds as well. As always, she was distracted by the lake, lying placidly under the shifting clouds. It had the most extraordinary ability to soothe, that great heavy space of water, and she gave herself up to it for a moment. Unbidden, the listing garage behind Stella Bisset's house came into her mind. She looked down at the damp and overlong grass, and back up at the lake. She ought to have a look to see if the roof could be fixed, then at least wood could be stored there without getting damp. A slow cascade of heavy raindrops began and drove her to her own garage, where she would spend a happy half-hour splitting wood, an activity she knew would make her feel virtuous and provide an invigorating spot of exercise.

The place she thought of as a garage was actually more of a barn. It had been used as a garage once, she knew. Kenny Armstrong's father had kept his car there, but after his death his mother had never driven it and had just left it parked there. She wondered now what Kenny had done with the car. The shelves with wooden boxes of mysterious bolts and widgets remained, as did an old round gas can, empty now for many years, and a couple of tires. Farther in the back, where on a cloudy day like this, light barely penetrated, even with both garage doors wide open, a door led into the other part of the barn, which comprised workshop and storage space. Her wood-chopping operations occupied the centre of the space now. What did linger was the smell of old garage, which she loved because it reminded her so much of the garage in her childhood home, where she used to play and explore when she could evade her nanny.

She took off her jacket and hung it on a nail, and got down to the business of splitting wood, which she threw into the wheelbarrow they kept handy for the purpose.

By the time she'd finished, the rain was pelting down in earnest, and she trotted the wheelbarrow to the house, trying to dodge the raindrops, and scooped up armloads of wood to pile next to the Franklin. Resisting the temptation to light the stove and settle in with a book and a cup of tea, she turned instead to the business of supper. She had been given firm instructions on the need to start stew early enough to make sure the beef was tender. She washed her hands and took the piece of paper she'd been given by Mabel Hughes with the instructions written out with a thoroughness and detail a child of five could have followed. Mabel had clearly been in some doubt about Lane's ability to do even this.

Much to her surprise, she had begun to find that cooking was . . . well, she wasn't so sure she'd extend to the word "fun," but something like it. And, she thought wryly, cutting the meat into little cubes as directed by the officious instructions, it kept her from feeling guilty about not tackling some sort of writing job. Having stowed the cast-iron soup pot in the oven, she reached up and felt the progress of the clothes she'd hung on the drying rack. They would be ready by the next day.

In the lull that followed, she wondered how Ames and Mr. Vitali were doing and decided to put a call through to Darling at the station.

"Hello, Miss Winslow. How are you doing?" Lucy the telephonist, situated in a little exchange at the Balfour store, asked. Lane could hear her putting jacks into the mysterious wall of connections.

"I'm perfectly splendid. Can you put me through to the station? Busy today?"

"Yes. There was some sort of problem with—oops. Here's your connection."

Smiling at Lucy's unabashed enthusiasm for listening in on calls she was placing, and realizing she was probably being overheard even now, Lane responded to Sergeant O'Brien's "Nelson Police Station, Sergeant O'Brien speaking."

"Good afternoon, Sergeant," she began.

"Mrs. Darling. Afternoon to you. I'll just put you through to the inspector."

Assuming this meant the inspector was not in the midst of some serious meeting, Lane felt a measure of relief about calling him at work. "Hello, darling, it's me. I've really only called to see how the two patients are."

"Good timing. Terrell has just come back and given me a full report. Lorenzo is making good progress; he seems to be breathing better. He was allowed to wander about a bit, though for obvious reasons, not to the smoking room. And Ames was visited by Miss Van Eyck not once but twice, and it seems to have done him a world of good."

"Twice!" Lane said, much cheered by this news.

"I did not, of course, ask for details, but I imagine there was something of the downed lover that brought out her true feelings. My understanding is that prior to making himself interesting by getting shot, they'd had quite a serious falling-out, brought on no doubt by his own failings."

"That's not a kind thing to say about a man when he's down. I'm glad there is someone in his life making a fuss of him," Lane said, knowing full well Darling had been beside himself with fury and anxiety over the shooting.

"You mean besides his mother? Quite. You're not proposing to come up to town to rally around as well?"

"Of course not. I have responsibilities here. Wood. Stew. That sort of thing."

"You are a ray of sunshine. You will be interested in this, I think. Before making a nuisance of himself, Ames had asked the clerk to search out information about the Turner

348

case, and they just called us with a doozy: Viola Tilbury, our gossip and suspected shooter, is née Viola Turner."

"No!"

"I knew you'd be impressed. And not only that, Terrell just reminded me that while Ames did not see who was handling the shotgun, the one thing he did see was a large volume about opera on the coffee table in the Tilburys' living room. It may be that his bookstore break-in is solved, at least. Of course, Mrs. T. is on the run and mister is sitting in our cells refusing to talk. We've notified the RCMP—well, Inspector Guilfoil did it for us, since he's on hand, as it were. What we don't know is if she is dangerous to anyone else because she is evidently armed. She certainly is bound to be dangerous to any law enforcement that catches up with her."

Lane heard him say something muffled to someone else. "Look, I'll leave you to it. You can fill me in later over supper," she said.

Hanging up the receiver on her ancient wall phone, Lane leaned against the wall and folded her arms. Now, that was interesting. Viola Tilbury, the daughter of Samuel Turner. What, if anything, did that mean? With some determination, Lane set about further preparations for dinner salad, in this case a salad of jarred string beans and thinly sliced onion, all the while her mind pulling to her neglected writing desk. Dinner sorted, she pulled out some sheets of paper, collected her atlas off the shelf, as a suitable lap desk, and sat down again on the window seat, where now the rain pattered against the glass. With some effort she resisted the temptation to look at maps, another childhood passion, and placed her pencil at the ready.

At last, she took up the pencil and wrote "Viola Tilbury" in the middle of the page, and with a dash separating them wrote "Tilbury," for the husband. Then she wrote "gossip" and "bookstore robber"—though she thought "gossip" hardly covered Mrs. Tilbury's lies about Lorenzo passing Darling an envelope of cash—above Viola's name. The new information was interesting, but was it relevant? Hard to see how, but she wrote "Turner" in a spot of his own to one side, and above it wrote "missing 1921." With that done, she drew a line between Viola Tilbury and Turner and wrote under her name "née Turner." Musing then on Tilbury, the husband, she wrote underneath his name "hardware store" and then slammed her forehead with the heel of her hand. Of course—what Olivia Vitali had confided in her! Under Tilbury she wrote "harasses and assaults OV." That elicited her next name on the page, which she put in the lower right. "O. Vitali," and then "L. Vitali." Under both she put "arson at house and restaurant." She contemplated this arrangement, which looked less like a map, because she didn't follow her usual procedure of laying the names out on an actual map location, and more like an addled family tree. Somewhere in that mess, there was certainly a motivation for Viola Tilbury, née Turner, to commit arson and shoot her own husband. When she heard Darling's car arrive, she jumped and looked at her watch. The whole process must have taken longer than she thought. One question loomed large, as she stacked the papers on the coffee table: Was Mr. Tilbury the arsonist, and was that why he wasn't talking?

CHAPTER TWENTY-NINE

Washington State, April 1921

"**H**EY, NONE OF THAT. YOU always wanted me to settle down, remember?" Pete Cooper cupped his hand around his mother's cheek and leaned over to kiss the top of her head. "How'd you get that short?" he asked.

"Giving birth to you," Elaine Cooper said. She turned and began to pack the food she'd prepared into his canvas rucksack. Four sandwiches with canned meat wrapped in a napkin she'd wrung out in cold water. She added four Hershey bars and two apples, and turned to look at him, more composed now. "You got your canteen?"

"Got my canteen. I'm not going to battle, you know. They have water where I'm going. And I bet they've got food too."

"You'll thank me," she said. She buckled the rucksack and then stood and looked at him. She was making too much fuss, she knew. She couldn't make out why she was so afraid. He was taking the same trip they'd made together many times. And no one should start out on a new life without saying goodbye properly to the ancestors. Once he moved south with that woman, he'd never be back. She just wished she didn't have to say goodbye to him too. "You got that damn frog?"

He reached under his collar and pulled out the string with the woven bag she'd made him. He dangled the little bundle to show her. "Right here."

"I blame the frog," she sniffed.

"If you could see how pretty she is, and what a great gal, you wouldn't blame this poor frog. He's just an innocent bystander."

His sister, who'd been leaning against the wall watching the packing of food, said, "Even if she was as ugly as that mutt outside, you'd still be going off. You just can't help yourself."

Her son, Tom, was perched on the table with his feet on the chair. "Will you bring me something? I want a frog too."

"I'll bring you a frog. You can get Mama to make you a little bag too."

They stood later for a long time under the porch roof after the last dust of his departure had settled. Finally, Elaine Cooper got up and dusted off her behind. Turning to go into the house, she said, "You watch. We're never gonna hear a thing from him."

Tom stayed on, leaning against the porch railing thinking of a road that just went on and on till it disappeared over a hill at the horizon. His heart swelled at the thought. He couldn't remember their last trip north as well as he'd like to. He remembered watching the road ahead from the back seat, thinking at every turn, and every rise, What's around that corner? What's over that hill? Then he'd go to sleep until they woke him up for a rest stop or a picnic by the side of the road. He remembered now, as he thought about Uncle Pete going to the ancestors, that when he'd been told they were going to see the ancestors, he'd expected real people, only there had just been the silence and the woods and the lake.

"I TOLD YOU he wasn't going to write to us," Tom's grandmother said. It was August, and the heat hung like a carpet over them, not a breath of air stirring. They sat outside under a canopy made of a sheet attached to their apple tree, drinking pop they kept in a bucket with ice they got from the iceman. She held the bottle of Coke to her neck.

"What do you think he's doing now?" Tom asked. He'd built a little tiny road in the dirt just past the patch of grass they were on and was running two toy cars on it. One was a little black iron Ford, and the second was a wooden car Uncle Pete had made for him.

"He must be in New Mexico by now. Maybe he's taking a honeymoon, driving around the country in that car," Grandma said.

"Whatever he's doing, he's busy not writing letters to us," Tom's mother said.

"I wish I could go there," Tom said, crashing the black car and rolling it over.

"You aren't going anywhere except to kindergarten. Only another week and a half."

"Do you think he'll remember to bring me a frog?"

His grandmother nodded. "If he said he will, then he will. You'll get your frog. One thing about your uncle Pete, he never breaks a promise."

TOM SIMPSON THOUGHT about his uncle's leaving now, as they were packing the car for the ride up to Canada. He'd driven away to see the ancestors, to talk to them about his new life, to say goodbye to them forever, and instead he'd stayed on with them, joined them. The whole time, his mother and sister had imagined he was living somewhere, married, having children, doing who knew what.

Now they were going to bury him. His grandmother had a vigorous spirit, but she wasn't so good physically. He packed a couple of pillows and a blanket in the back seat so she could lie back and sleep on the way up. If he were going on his own, he'd be camping, but now he was hoping they could find a place to stay nearby. He would drive straight to New Denver because his grandmother wanted to see where her son was found, then they would find a motel. He tried not to think too much about the part where they would drive all the way to Nelson so that his grandmother could see the remains of her lost son. Maybe they'd see if the Catholic Church in New Denver would accommodate him. Or they could bring him back to Colville. He wasn't sure about driving over the border with someone's remains. Would that even be possible? Bodies were shipped home for burial during the war. He would wait and see what his grandmother wanted.

DARLING PUT HIS fork down and slipped his napkin into its ring. "That was very impressive. Perfectly not-burned potatoes as well!"

"You make me blush," Lane said. "Leave the dishes tonight. You look exhausted. I'll do them in the morning."

"I shouldn't," he said.

"You should. Let's sit by the fire and do nothing for a while."

Once by the fire Darling shook his head. "It's really beastly about Ames. I don't know, the doctors don't know how long-term the shoulder damage will be, and I can't afford to lose him. He's being a bloody nuisance as usual," he added, attempting a smile.

"Why should you lose him? It's not the army, so he doesn't have to be fit enough to tackle the Somme, and it was his left shoulder. Isn't he right-handed?"

"Of course, you're right. I think I'm imagining he'll go off police work and choose to become a librarian or something. He was telling me just the other day how much he's actually been enjoying his research there. He didn't use to like it much. Not enough action. Now there is clearly too much action. Thank God Terrell is in good nick, though I don't think much of him tooling around on our roads on that damn motorcycle."

"You can put him to work as your driver till Ames is back on the job. That should distract him. Is there any chance of you getting anyone else on? I happen to know April at the café is dying to join the police force. I think she's taking a leaf out of her father's book. Aren't you already using her as a kind of informant?"

"Not in any official sense. More an interfering outside party, not unlike yourself. This police force must be the most incompetent in the province, since we cannot seem to budge without our canny informants like you and April McAvity."

"I'm sure she must have mentioned her aspirations to you?"

"She did."

"I hope you don't object."

"I don't object. I just don't really have a spot, especially as you are reassuring me Ames will be back," Darling said.

"She is very observant."

Darling shook his head. "She'll have to be more than that. She'll have to take some training. You can't just stroll into a police station and say, 'I'd like to be a policeman, or woman, please.'" He turned to her, looking at her face in the flickering firelight and reaching for her hand. "I'm extremely worried you're going to do that one morning."

"Certainly not. I was in uniform before. I've had enough of obeying a commanding officer, as good as the discipline no doubt would be for me. Could April not volunteer with you as part of her training?"

"I expect O'Brien would absolutely love that, having her underfoot, eagerly trying to be helpful."

But later, as Darling drifted off to sleep, he could quite well imagine O'Brien loving it. Less climbing stairs and going through files. He might never have to leave that stool of his.

LANE FOLDED AND piled Stella Bisset's laundry in a basket and then looked around to see what else she could bring her. It was still early. Darling had left before seven, filled with anxiety. He had issued cautions to her about the drive, and very strict injunctions against any impulse to bring Stella Bisset home with her, and then driven off into the morning mist.

Glancing at her watch, she closed the boot of the car and walked along the path to the post office. Eleanor might have something sweet on hand she could take for poor Stella.

As she crossed her little bridge to the adjoining road, she sniffed the moist morning air and felt a lift of her heart. The air was full of green, damp smells, a sign to her of the warming and the coming of spring. She smiled at herself. For someone who professed to love winter so much, she certainly was not above making a fuss about spring. Or summer for that matter—or, she was conceding when she saw Alexandra burst out the door of the Armstrong house, the autumn.

"Good morning, you," she said, hunching down to receive a few excited face licks.

"You're early," said Kenny, waving a spade in her direction. He had a metal bucket in his other hand from which wisps of smoke curled up.

"So are you for that matter. I'm on my way back up the lake to see that poor old lady in New Denver. I came to see if Eleanor has a bit of spare cake or a couple of biscuits on hand."

"I'm sure she's got something stowed somewhere. Go in and have a cuppa before you go. I've got to dump the ashes."

Eleanor tut-tutted. They were sitting before cups of tea and, though Lane protested that she'd had a good breakfast, pieces of buttered raisin toast. "It's not right for that poor woman to be on her own. There's an old people's home in town. She really ought to be there."

"I'm sure that's the sensible thing, but I think she has lived there for decades. I can't see how she'd cope being taken from her familiar setting. You should have seen the transformation that came over her when we wound up her gramophone and put an old record on. It was as if the light had come back into her eyes."

"Isn't that funny. I suppose music does that. Every now and then I hear an old song from the Great War on the wireless, and I must say it really takes one back. It makes me feel very nostalgic for the old days. Now it's all big band and swing music. It's all a bit too jiggety for me. I prefer the nice old music. And, of course, the gardening show." Eleanor got up and took a tin from the shelf next to the sink. "I do have some biscuits you can take, as a matter of fact. Vanilla. That shouldn't cause too much digestive excitement."

"Oh, thank you. I'm sure she'll be delighted," Lane said gratefully.

"As much as she can be delighted," Eleanor observed. "I suppose something sweet will lift any spirit. Perhaps you're right about removing her from a familiar place. But could come a time . . ."

"I know. Funnily, that old coot Berenson, who runs that little store—I've told you about him—he seems to have taken a proprietary interest in her. I don't really know whose place it is to remove an addled old lady from an increasingly dangerous situation, but maybe I should talk with him."

Biscuits and laundry in hand, Lane set off for New

Denver, worried about what condition she would find Stella in, and not looking forward to talking to Berenson. She cheered herself up by deciding she would stop by and say hello to Barisoff before she came back. As she drove north, the mist lifted and golden sunlight seemed to rise out of the landscape, setting the lake to sparkling. She opened the window and let the forest smells whirl around her, and she drove like that, her arm resting on the window until she turned toward New Denver and met her first logging truck, spewing gravel off its back wheels.

It was with relief that she bumped along the little-used driveway in front of Stella Bisset's home. She turned off the engine and sat in the silence for a moment, looking at the cottage. Thick moss grew on the wooden roof shingles, making the whole cottage look as though it was trying to nestle itself into the forest and disappear. With a jolt of relief, she saw that there was smoke coiling out of the chimney.

She collected the laundry basket and went along to knock on the door. She didn't expect it to be opened for her if Stella was alone, and it wasn't. She pushed it open and called out, "Hello? Miss Bisset? It's Lane Winslow. I was here a couple of days ago."

There was silence for a moment and then a sort of shuffling sound, and Stella came out of the little bedroom. She stood in the doorway and stared at Lane. She was wearing the trousers and sweater Lane had brought on her last visit, and over that her stained pink padded bathrobe. "Hello, dear," she said.

Lane smiled. "I've brought your laundry. How are you?"

"That was good of you. How did you get ahead of the guests?"

Lane put the basket on the table. Two things, she thought: One was, she noticed again a touch of some accent. And two was that she had no idea what Stella Bisset could mean. She would have asked, but she heard a hissing sound in the kitchen. She hurried to the stove and found a kettle boiling away its last drop of water.

"You were making some tea," Lane said. "You've got a nice fire going here. Let's try again." She refilled the kettle from the tap on the low sink, put it on the stove, and checked the fire. Stella must have been feeding the fire with every stick of wood she had. On the table was a teapot, the lid open, as if waiting to have water poured into it, but an inspection showed that no tea had yet been put into it.

"Have you had breakfast?" she asked pleasantly. Or supper last night? she wondered. She did a quick scan to see if there was any sign of food preparation or dishes used. With relief she saw a round breadboard, deeply scored, with a half loaf of bread turned over on its cut side.

Turning to look at Stella, Lane saw with anxiety that she had developed a fixed look on her face, as if she suddenly couldn't make out what was happening. "Right. Is your tea in here?" She looked at the shelf above the sink, and shifted some very ancient tins of baking soda, pepper, treacle. No tea. She turned back to look at Stella again and found her watching. She was about to try again when she saw a tin of tea on the windowsill.

Relieved that the tin had not been put to collecting buttons or coins but had actual tea in it, Lane put two spoons into the pot. "I'll just go out and get some wood," she said. "The kettle should be nicely boiled by then." She paused, waiting to see if Stella would respond, but she merely continued to watch the space where Lane had been standing near the window.

The morning had warmed up considerably, and even the dreary post-winter array of brown and flagging plants and grass looked encouraged by the sun. Lane stopped at the side of the house and surveyed the garden and the cottage. It must have been really lovely at one time, when Stella had been able to care for it. She wondered again what this woman's story was. She must have been in Canada for a long enough time to rid herself of her accent. When had she come to Canada, and for what? And she must have been beautiful as a young woman. She had a slender frame and long delicate fingers, and an oval face with eyes that would have been a clear blue at one time.

She was about to take up an armload of wood in the garage when she was taken with curiosity about the car. She circled it, squeezing through the tiny space between the back of the garage and the licence plate. The rumble seat was half open and she scooted to the side to pull it the rest of the way. Dust flew up and she waved her arm in a futile effort to dispel it. She could just see in the near darkness that something had been tossed there. Reaching in, she felt around, finding some sort of rough fabric in a bundle. A rucksack? She pulled at it, and there was a clattering, as if it had been caught on something. She pushed the rucksack to one side, reached for whatever it was, and found her hand clutching the business end of a rifle.

CHAPTER THIRTY

April 1921

THEY STOOD AT THE STATION in Jasper, suitcases at their feet, an icy wind whipping at them. From the distance they could hear the train approaching, a curl of smoke rising above the trees beyond the bend. Estelle felt her chest tightening as if the train were some terrible fate, one she'd been waiting for all her life. She'd been grateful when he'd sold the car to get more money for this trip. She had been willing to go along at the beginning, but as the endless miles fell away under the wheels of the car, as they moved farther east, she began to realize.

It had frightened her at first, but then the conviction grew in her that this was the moment, that at last she would decide for herself. She had had no idea how, until she watched him sell his car to a garage in Jasper. The man who bought it was wanting to build a fleet of taxis. She stood in the cramped office of the gas station, watched the men shake hands, and then the sudden realization of how it could be done made her move her head convulsively and look out the window, as if she feared her plans were visible on her face. The red metal sign outside advertising Mobil Oil was rocking in its frame in a sudden gust of wind.

In the smoky whirl of the train's arrival, passengers got off, tourists anticipating their glamorous holiday in the Rockies, and passengers waited to get on, resigned to going home to their normal lives. He took their two bags and pushed them down the aisle, stowed them under a seat near the middle of the car, then went back for her. She was standing on the platform, looking in the direction the train had come from.

"C'mon." His voice was kind, as if he were talking to a child, and had a kind of suppressed excitement, as if he were taking that child on an adventure that he had planned more to recoup some distant pleasure of his own childhood. He held out his hand and she took it, mounting the stairs and then following him to the seats he had chosen. They sat silently together, with him leaning on the armrest looking out the window, his leg bouncing up and down the only sign of some inner agitation. He watched the last few passengers coming and going through the door into the station. She sat very still, with her handbag on her lap, both gloved hands resting on it. She did not look out the window, but rather down the passage between the seats.

He turned to her, as the doors up and down the train began to close. "I'm glad you picked that hat. You look wonderful in it. Just like my girl should. Here, let me get that coat." He reached over to help her, but she shook her head.

"I'm still so cold from the outside. I'll keep it on for a while, no?"

She wanted to say something more, make conversation, but she was afraid the wrong words would come out if she opened her mouth. Instead of "Thank you," she might say "I don't want to run away," or "Why do I have to be punished for something you did?"

"Hey, don't you worry, my girl. We're going to have a grand time."

She nodded. Why was he treating it as if they were off on a little holiday? Can a man's life mean so little? The train lurched with a clang and then stopped and lurched again. "I will find the toilet," she said, getting up.

Still clutching her purse, she got up and walked back down the aisle, stepping over the leg of a portly man who was stretched out three seats behind them and already appeared to be asleep. The train now was moving slowly, but it would begin to pick up speed. She had only a few moments.

Afterward, with an almost giddy elation, she waited at the end of the platform until the train pulled away and there was no danger he would see her. She watched the last of it disappearing before she finally stirred, and then she walked quickly toward the station exit. He would not come after her.

"IF YOU'RE SURE, ma'am." Mr. Seymour looked at her askance. "There's a lot to running a place like this. Getting stuff in and the like. It's hard in the winter."

"I am quite familiar with the winters here, Mr. Seymour.

All the customers already exist. I do not have to find more. Am I not right?" She looked around the shop, at its bins of grain and shelves of cans and bags of flour, and smiled, unable to fully take in that it would be hers.

"That's true enough. Well, if I'm honest, I don't have much choice. They need me back home now my dad's poorly. I just don't want you to bite off more than you can chew." Mr. Seymour scratched the black beard that belied his youth and looked around the shop. "You see you don't get taken advantage of."

She'd already been taken advantage of. All her life. Even by the man who loved her. How he loved her! She had scarcely believed it in the beginning. He loved her in spite of everything. She unconsciously felt the side of her arm and made as if to tuck a stray hair under her hat. She still felt the place he'd held her arm until it bruised, though it had been months. Maybe that was love. It was certainly the version of love she experienced as a child. But perhaps that was the moment she began to feel something inside her that resisted, finally, finally, him, her father, all of them. That, and the money she had saved. Money that she was now handing over to Mr. Seymour to purchase his little store. Money that, if *he* had known, he would have taken because he had lost all his own.

She walked down the steps and looked along the downward slope of the road, at the bottom of which her own little cottage sat. The cottage he had given her. She had a notebook in which she had diligently written all the instructions, how to work with the farmers, how to get goods in from town. She felt free. She could scarcely recognize this feeling of elation. And in the next moment her heart began to ache for the man who died so that she could finally have this freedom.

PERHAPS IT WAS the grandmother in the group that spurred Sergeant O'Brien to stand up when Tom Simpson came through the station door with two women, one of a venerable age, and two children.

"Afternoon. Is the inspector here?" Tom Simpson asked.

He was, and he was expecting them. Terrell and the children were dispatched to the café, where he knew April would fuss over them and make them milkshakes. Darling invited Tom and the two women to his office.

"You've had a long drive," Darling said when he had been introduced to Tom's mother and grandmother. "Let me get some tea sent up." When he picked up the phone, he found O'Brien was already ahead of the game.

They sat in silence for a few moments and then Mrs. Cooper spoke. "I'd like to see my son, please."

TERRELL IGNORED THE heads turning as he and the children went into the café, and said, "Would you rather sit in a booth or at the counter?"

"The counter has turny stools. Can we sit there?" Angie asked. Her hair had been tightly plaited, and she wore a pink dress. Her little brother wore a white shirt that had come partially untucked, and his hair was escaping its earlier energetic combing.

"I like those too. This all right for you?" Terrell bent down to address Bobby, who was clinging to his sister's hand.

April, who had been running some pie to a booth, came back around the counter and beamed at them. "Who do we have here?"

Terrell settled little Bobby on a stool and said, "This is Angie, and this is Bobby, and I think all three of us are interested in your milkshake menu. Their mother and grandma and brother are just doing some business over the way."

April nodded and glanced in the direction of the police station. "We have vanilla, chocolate, and strawberry. They're pretty big. How would you two like to share one?"

"Do we have to?" Angie asked, looking anxiously at Terrell.

"I tell you what," he said. "We'll start with you sharing one, because I've had one of these, and believe me, they are very filling, and then if you still have room, you can share a second one."

Angie considered this and then turned to her little brother. "Okay, Bobby, we're going to share one. What one do you want?"

"Strawberry!"

"Okay. We will have a strawberry milkshake, please," she said with aplomb. It was clear she was quite used to commanding proceedings where her little brother was concerned. Terrell smiled. He bet it was a benevolent dictatorship.

"You, Constable?"

"I think I'll have the vanilla."

DOWNSTAIRS, SIMPSON'S GRANDMOTHER asked to be alone with the remains, and Darling, Tom Simpson, and his mother waited across the hall in the interview room.

"If that's him, I wonder what happened to his car? He used to be so proud of that damn thing. Model T. He got it second-hand and kept it in mint condition," Simpson's mother said.

"Rotting somewhere, no doubt. Whoever did this must have taken it. They'd have gotten a nice car out of the deal," Simpson said.

"I think now that we are pretty sure it is your brother, Mrs. Simpson, we can certainly keep our eye out for the car, but I agree with your son. It's probably sitting in a field somewhere rusting," Darling added.

"I just can't figure out how he'd get in a place where someone would kill him like that. He was so good-natured. I can't believe he'd start a fight with anyone. I mean, I bet no one would think twice about shooting one of us, but still."

"Can you tell me a little bit about why he might have come here?" Darling asked. If he'd come to reclaim some property, or pursue a prospecting venture, he could have run afoul of someone.

Mrs. Simpson shook her head. "He was supposed to be going to New Mexico to get married. Before he went there, he came here to say goodbye to the ancestors. He met a girl earlier in the year. I don't know why he had to go that far away to find a girl, but that's love, I guess. He said he was going to bring her back, but I didn't think we'd ever hear from him again." She shook her head sadly. "I never thought it would be for this reason. Poor girl, too.

She must have been there waiting for him."

"You never heard from her?" Darling asked.

Mrs. Simpson shook her head. "We never even knew anything but her first name. He was a bit goofy. He was younger than me, a bit like a kid, full of high spirits. I think he wanted it all to be a surprise."

They all turned. Tom Simpson's grandmother was standing in the doorway. "When can I take my son from here?" she asked.

WHEN THEY HAD left to collect the children, Darling went back upstairs, and he saw Guilfoil in Ames's office standing at the desk, decisively closing a file. He looked up at Darling.

"I'll be making my report to the mayor. Given that Mrs. Tilbury, the only person who claimed to have seen you take money, is now on the run somewhere after possibly shooting a police officer, I think we can safely close the file. And if I'm honest, I'd like to get back to work at the detachment. We still have to find the damn woman, after all."

Relieved, Darling shook hands with him. "I won't say I'm sorry to see you go, but I look forward to continuing to work with you when I have witnesses or criminals on the lam. Thank you for your work. I think I worried you would hamper what we do here, but you were an unobtrusive presence, when all is said and done."

"You're to be congratulated. Everything at the station seems shipshape and Bristol fashion. Your men are very loyal to you, by the way."

Darling smiled. "I'm loyal to them, though perhaps that

oughtn't to get out. I'll walk you out."

"I presume the inspector has upped stakes," O'Brien observed, watching out the window as Guilfoil climbed into his RCMP vehicle. "I imagine we got a clean bill of health—though I guess you couldn't say that about poor Sergeant Ames. He looked a bit peaky yesterday. Have you been today?"

"Do I look like I've had time to linger at the bedside of a sick sergeant? Finally!" he added, as Terrell came through the door.

"Sir," said Terrell. As he walked to his desk, he added, "They are going up the lake to New Denver. Mrs. Cooper wants to be near where he was found, and Mr. Barisoff has offered them accommodation."

LANE STACKED AS much wood as she could by the stove with what was available in the garage, then put Stella's clothes away and the washed linen into the cupboard. She shook her head at the beautiful copper bath in the bedroom. It surely had not seen use for some time. It was thickly layered with dust and seemed to be full of socks and at least one ancient red leather high-heeled pump with a button strap. It must have been a lot of work to use this tub even when its owner was healthy and in her right mind. Water heated on the stove, buckets of cold water from the kitchen to bring it to the right temperature. Whoever installed it had at least equipped it with a drain that piped the water through the floor to drain away under the cottage.

She stood now, undecided, looking at Stella, who was slumped in front of the stove, one hand on the table crumbling a piece of bread. How could she leave her here? She would have to talk to Berenson, ask him if he knew anything about her people, if she even had people, suggest he go see her every day. Maybe Barisoff would be willing to go from time to time to make sure she had food and clean clothes, because something told her Berenson was the type of man to dig in his heels if he thought he was being ordered about.

She hunched down in front of Stella to be on an even level with her and took her hand. She was about to speak when the old woman pressed her hand with a slight spasm and said, "Tu pars alors?"

"Vous êtes française, madame?"

Stella now looked up into Lane's eyes and nodded.

"But I wish I had known!" Lane said in French. She straightened up and pulled the second chair to be near Stella. Would speaking French allow Miss Bisset to be more present? "That is lovely. We can sit and have a little chat together. How long have you lived in this beautiful cottage?"

Stella looked slowly around the little space that comprised kitchen, dining room, and sitting room and shrugged. "I have been here a long time. So long. He found me."

"Found you where, madame?"

"Up there." Stella lifted her hand and turned her palm as if she were throwing petals.

"He was your husband, madame?" Perhaps she had people after all. If her husband was dead, she might have a child, or his relatives.

But Stella frowned and shook her head, and Lane

couldn't tell if she meant she had no husband or she could not remember a husband. One thing that was clear was that she was struggling with memory in both languages. After a moment she said, "Tell him . . ." and then she trailed off, and she turned again to the stove.

Berenson must know something about this, Lane thought. She stood up and with as bright a voice as she could muster said, "I'll leave you now and I will tell him to come and make sure you are all right, yes?" "He" might as well be Berenson as anyone else, at this point.

Stella did not look up and seemed now lost in some vast emptiness of her own.

When Lane was outside again, she experienced a surge of liberty from the closeness of the cottage and from what the inside of Stella Bisset's mind must be like. She bumped slowly along the grassy drive to the main road, chiding herself for her lack of charity.

Before she had gone twenty feet she stopped. How had she not seen it before? But of course, without being taught what to look for by Mr. Simpson, she would not have noticed at all. There, in the little stand of trees that marked the beginning of the surrounding forest, she saw a small but clearly round depression. The remains of a pit house, slender trees growing out of it, as the forest worked the slow process of retaking its land.

Driving slowly forward again, she was considering how the forest one day would take over the little cottage Miss Bisset lived in. There was a log cabin a short hike away from King's Cove that had collapsed and sunk into the earth and been so overgrown with bush and trees that it was scarcely visible from the road anymore.

Nature reclaiming her own. Such reflections were not going to feed the baby, she realized. As she bumped up toward the village, she again began girding up for a conversation with the repellent Berenson. She pulled in front of the store, grateful at least that an afternoon sun was beginning to creep through the clouds that had made the day seem grey and shapeless. She pushed the door open, heard the bell above the door, and called out, "Mr. Berenson?" There was no answer. She tried again, louder, calling out toward the door that must go into the back storage area. Muttering a frustrated "Damn," she went back out to the car. He can't have gone far, she thought, leaving the place open like that.

She might as well go visit Mr. Barisoff for a bit and then try again later. He could be picking up supplies somewhere. Did he drive a truck or some sort of van? Of course, he must drive something, and no vehicle was parked here. Relieved about putting off her interview with him, she made her way to Barisoff's cottage.

It was alive with activity. There was a car parked behind his little white van, and she could hear children's voices coming from somewhere. The car, she saw, bore a Washington licence plate. Before she had made half the distance to Barisoff's steps, the door opened and the man himself was waving at her.

"You are just on time. We are about to have tea. You must come in and meet Mr. Simpson's family!" he called out in Russian.

"MY PROFOUND CONDOLENCES for your loss, Mrs. Cooper. It was a terrible shock finding him. I am so glad to meet the family that loved him." Lane sat opposite the old lady. The loss of a son was beyond imagination.

"I understand from my grandson that you, and this man here, treated him with dignity. I thank you for that," the old lady said. "I'm not surprised Pete came up here in that precious Model T of his, I guess. He came to say goodbye to our people, our ancestors, before he took off all the hell-and-gone away to New Mexico, where his girl was from."

Tom Simpson was standing at the small window with a cup of coffee in his hand, watching the children play outside. It would be raining soon, and they would have that energy inside this small cabin. The policeman had said they could take the body in the next day or two, after the reports were finished. In any case, the family had to sort out what was to be done with him. It would be largely up to his grandmother, and she was clearly still mulling it over.

He had tried and tried to imagine how his uncle had come to die and be buried like that. Shot at close range. He looked down and shook his head slightly. Whoever did it might still be alive. Might still be around here somewhere. What would he say if he were ever caught and brought to trial? He could say anything: that Pete Cooper had tried to rob him or pointed a gun first. It wouldn't matter to any court or judge that Uncle Pete didn't have a gun and would never try to rob anyone. Still, something happened. Pete could be precipitous. He was full of laughter and playfulness, but he could get mad, too. Maybe there was an argument. But how? Under what circumstances? He heard his mother's chair scrape and turned to see her go out to the yard. She would be worried because the rain had started. He looked over at the table then, surprised to hear his grandmother chuckle.

"He loved that damn car. I didn't think it would make it all the way to wherever he was going. It used to have an insignia on it that said 'Ford' but that got stolen one night when he was in town. He just laughed it off. He said it looked better without it. That was the kind of person he was. Nothing too much bothered him."

Lane frowned, her memory triggered by this. "What do the letters 'Wn' on a licence plate mean? Is that 'Washington'?"

"That's what used to be on our plates, maybe ten, twenty years ago. Why?" Tom had sat down and was watching Lane intently. Darisoff was busying himself at the stove. He had said he would make them all a good cabbage soup for supper.

"I think it's possible that I might have seen that car," she said.

———————

CHAPTER THIRTY-ONE

"I **'VE GOT NOTHING TO SAY,"** an exhausted and bleary-eyed Gilbert Tilbury protested. "My crazy wife is out there driving around the countryside with a loaded rifle for all I know, and you've got me locked up so you can ask me stupid questions."

It was clear to Darling that Tilbury was in a slightly different mood than when they'd first locked him up. Now he seemed more prepared to talk, or at least be outraged.

"The RCMP are on the lookout for your wife, Mr. Tilbury. If there is anything at all you can tell me, it might help. Where might she go? Was there some place you holidayed together? Some place that might have meant something to her?"

Shaking his head, Tilbury threw up his hands. "Nothing ever meant anything to her but the glory days of her rich father. I was certainly never going to measure up to dear old dad. She's been scrounging around in that old house of his digging up old memories, and she's been getting weirder and weirder." He said nothing about the missing scarf. "In fact, she even said, when we were careening across the country with that man she shot, 'I'm going to find Daddy.' Or something like that."

"That man she shot was my sergeant. Can you tell me why she shot him? You were there." Darling still wasn't entirely sure Tilbury hadn't been the one doing the shooting.

But this line of questioning caused Tilbury to go mum again.

Darling placed Tilbury back in his cell and was starting up the stairs when O'Brien hailed him from the landing.

"What is it, Sergeant?" At seeing O'Brien gesturing, Darling said, "All right. I'll be up in minute."

The last thing he heard as he started up the stairs was Tilbury plaintively crying out, "Are you just going to leave me here?"

Terrell was just coming into the station when Darling made it up to the front desk. "Constable. How's the patient?"

"Miss Van Eyck was there again with food, sir. Oh, and another improving book."

"Do him good," Darling said with satisfaction. "Now, O' Brien, what's so urgent?"

"The mayor, sir. He wants you over there double-quick."

"Now? What the blazes is the rush?"

"Search me, sir. But his secretary seemed pretty insistent. Maybe he likes people coming double-quick because it makes him feel important?"

Darling took the stairs two at a time to get his hat and coat because the weather was exhibiting sure signs of delivering cold rain. With a muttered imprecation at "bloody March," he was about to go out the door when O'Brien spoke again.

"Oh, and I nearly forgot, sir. Your missus. She called from the store up in New Denver, saying she thought she'd found something important and was going to have a look at it and call you again later."

IN THE END it was just Lane and Mr. Simpson. She had worried that Stella would become anxious with a lot of people. Lane was surprised to hear strains of music at the cottage. She opened the door, saying in French, "Madame? May we come in?" She could see Stella, standing in front of the Victrola, swaying slightly, watching the record turn. She had not wound it sufficiently and the music wavered in and out of pitch. Stella turned finally and looked at her visitors, her expression going from blank to wide-eyed alarm. She put her hand to her mouth and uttered a little cry. "He is back!" And then she crumpled to the ground, knocking the needle off the record with a loud scratch.

"Oh my word!" Lane exclaimed, rushing forward. She knelt over Stella and lifted her head, calling out her name. "Get me some water," she said to Simpson. "Madame, please!" She fanned her with her hand and wondered if there were smelling salts in the cottage. "Mr. Simpson, there is a little cabinet in that room with some medications. Can you see if there are smelling salts?"

Simpson hurried into the next room, and Lane could hear him opening the cupboard and moving the few bottles. Then he was back, holding out a vial. "This might be them," he said, unscrewing the cap, which resisted at first. It had not been opened for a long time, he could see. There was rust in the threads.

Lane seized it, took a whiff herself, and then gasped, rearing her head back as the ammonia tore into her nasal passages. "That's the one," she breathed, and held the bottle under Stella's nose. It did the trick. Her eyes fluttered open, and she turned her head violently away from the vial. She was so slight that Lane could lift her to her feet on her own, but Simpson helped her take Stella into the bedroom, where Lane propped pillows behind her and put the shredded quilt over her. Tom brought a glass of water and then stood in the doorway, turning his hat anxiously in his hands as he watched Lane try to administer it.

Lane looked up at him. "I think she just fainted and needs a bit of recovery time. Why don't you pop out and have a look at that car? If you go around the right of the house, you'll see the garage. I'll look after Miss Bisset."

Simpson nodded, looking concerned, and then went around the side of the house and found the garage. It was a much older structure than the cottage. It appeared to be giving up the ghost, collapsing in on itself. But one of the two doors, falling off its top hinge, was permanently open, and he could see the car. It had Washington plates, all right. With some effort he pushed open the second door, shoving it across the raised tufts of grass. His heart gave an anxious beat. It was an old Ford, and the Ford insignia was gone.

He walked forward slowly and reached out to touch the black curve of the wheelhouse, encrusted with the greasy dust of years, and moved forward, his hand running along the body. Squeezing around the back, he looked into the rumble seat and saw what Lane had seen. A canvas rucksack and a rifle. He touched the rucksack. It must have kept relatively dry over the years enclosed in the rumble seat. His grandmother had said he had a canvas bag. She had made food for the first part of his trip, and he carried it in the bag. He picked it up and pulled at the buckle and looked inside. There was only a little pile of shredded paper. He pulled this out and held it in his hand. It looked as though an animal had been at it to get at whatever had been inside. Walking closer to the door to get more light, he could see at once that it had belonged to a Hershey chocolate bar. He would take the bag to his grandmother. She would know it for sure. Why was his uncle Pete's car in this old garage? He looked back at the cottage. Had he come to this house? He frowned. Had Stella Bisset been the girl he had been going to marry? Or was that woman responsible for his death?

DARLING MADE HIS way to the mayor's office pondering Lane's message and wondering how worried he ought to be. It wasn't until he was seated in front of the mayor that one of the almost unconscious list of dangers running through his mind reared up. Why hadn't she said what it was she was looking into? Of course. That beastly shop-keeper would be listening in.

"Are you listening to me, Inspector?"

"Yes, sir. I'm sorry. Something has come to me about one of our investigations." He could feel his anxiety beginning to rise.

"Well, I hope it's who the devil set the fires. I don't care for that Vitali business. I may not eat there myself, but I can't preside over a town that takes prejudice to that sort of extent."

"No. But I think we may have a strong lead on that; we are down to one or two individuals." What had she found out? And where was the armed and mad Viola Tilbury? With an effort he calmed himself. Viola could be halfway to the coast by now. Lane was safely in New Denver helping the old lady. There were enough unknowns in this case without inventing any more.

"I'm glad to hear it. How's your sergeant? Was that related to your investigation of the arson?"

"Not at the time, but it may turn out to be." But Darling could not stop the whirring of his mind. What the bloody hell was she up to? And why was he having to sit here answering Mayor Dalton's quite patently unurgent questions?

"I just wanted to let you know, Darling, that I got the report on the investigation, and it seems to exonerate you and your station completely."

There's that qualifier *seems* again, Darling thought. "Yes, thank you, sir. I'm relieved. Unfortunately, in the interim, the gossip and suspicion are all over town. That will take longer to die down." He didn't add that he held the mayor responsible for a good chunk of the gossip by starting up this investigation.

The mayor tossed the report to one side and sat back in his chair, sucking on his pipe. "Yes, I see your point. Believe me, as a politician I've been subject to that sort of thing myself. Very hard to beat back. We'll have to counter it. Maybe through the *Nelson Daily News*. I've got a tame reporter there. I'll get my secretary to put something together and get it to him. Front-page stuff. That should put the damper on that sort of talk."

"Yes, thank you, sir. That should be very helpful." He could feel he was about to be dismissed. Should he take advantage of this moment of goodwill? "Sir, I wonder if the funds could be found to equip the police vehicle with a radio transmitter? It's pretty standard equipment in most police vehicles nowadays."

Dalton frowned. He didn't like losing control of this moment of mayoral magnanimity. "You've done all right without one, haven't you?"

"Yes, sir, after a fashion. But in a situation involving the pursuit of a dangerous individual, as we were recently, we were very much hampered by not being able to communicate with our partners at the RCMP." Was he overplaying the fact that they were not as well equipped as the Mounties?

But Dalton waved his hand toward the office door. "I suppose. Get me the figures and let my secretary know. We can take it from there."

"Very good, sir. Thank you."

The mayor shook his head and stood up. "Listen, about the investigation. It had to be done, Darling. Couldn't have that sort of talk going around the place, undermining the work of the police." He held out his hand. "No hard feelings, eh? Never thought for a moment that there was anything in it."

Darling shook the offered hand. "No, sir, of course not, sir. Thank you."

With an exhalation of relief, Darling was back out on the street. Why any of that had been urgent, he couldn't imagine. Muttering "politicians" under his breath, he hurried back across the street and barrelled into the station. At least they might get a police radio out of the deal.

"Any calls?" he asked.

"No, sir. Not of any importance. A woman called from across the lake because she thought she saw a prowler last night. I've sent Terrell out to interview her. He was happy to take that bike out for a spin to look into it. The mayor well?"

"Tip-top." Nothing from Lane then. He was momentarily relieved, and then found that her silence only increased his misgivings. Terrell was busy, Ames still lying about in the hospital, no doubt having his brow mopped by Miss Van Eyck, and his lot would be to sit here to await Lane's call. He sat at his desk and actually twiddled his thumbs, and finding it did nothing for him, picked up the telephone receiver and put a call in to the hospital. Once put through to the ward, he said, "This is Inspector Darling, Nelson Police, inquiring about Mr. Lorenzo Vitali."

"His wife is with him now, sir. He is doing quite well. I expect we'll be able to send him home to convalesce very soon. I can't say more than that."

Relieved by this, he leaned back in his chair. What would happen to him? According to Terrell the restaurant kitchen was badly damaged, but the dining area was completely salvageable. Would Lorenzo have enough money to do the repairs?

He stared moodily at the telephone. Nothing from

Lane. His train of thought returned to the Tilburys. If Viola had started the rumours about Lorenzo and himself to get at Lorenzo, perhaps she was behind the fires. But why? What could she possibly have against Lorenzo, or the restaurant? Would prejudice drive her to this? And what did her husband know? He pulled his foolscap pad forward and began to make some notes with his perfectly sharpened pencil, and then threw the pencil down, his hand shooting out to prevent it from rolling off the desk.

Then he remembered what Lane had told him about Tilbury harassing and following Olivia Vitali. Did Viola Tilbury know? Would that be enough to send a woman on this murderous rampage? Possibly, if she were unstable, and Viola most certainly was. He had picked up his pencil again when the phone rang.

"Finally!" he muttered, seizing the receiver.

"This is the third time this individual has telephoned. It's not an emergency; I checked on that before I said you were in an important meeting, but now that you're back: it's that dentist. He's pretty impatient."

"Put him through, O'Brien. An angry dentist is in no one's interests." Darling tried to still his disappointment. Not Lane.

"Inspector Darling? Dr. Philipson here. I think there's something you ought to know."

When the call was over, Darling rubbed the heels of his hands into his eyes, as if that would somehow clear his brain. He wanted to shout "Ames!" and have him pop up in his doorway. Instead, he took the stairs two at a time and shouted "Terrell!" only to be reminded he'd already gone off on his bike. Was this what Lane had found out?

"I want Terrell the minute he gets back," he said gruffly, but O'Brien was attending to the telephone.

"For you, sir."

"Thank God! Put it through to Terrell's desk." Darling darted to the desk and seized the handset when it rang. "Darling."

It was not Lane.

"Hello? Am I speaking with the inspector—Darling, is it? I didn't quite catch who the man said he was putting me through to."

"Yes, Darling here."

"Oh, good. I don't know if I should have bothered. My boss didn't think so, but I was uneasy about the way she was behaving."

Alert now, Darling stood up straighter, glancing at O'Brien. He heard the front door and saw Terrell coming in. "Who?" Could Viola have touched down somewhere? "Where are you calling from?"

"Oh, sorry, yes. My name is Brian Eddy. I work up at the offices of the Sandon Mine. This kind of crazy-acting woman came in this morning demanding to see someone called Turner. I'm the secretary, so anyone coming in starts with me. I told her I'd never heard of him, and she began shouting that I was a liar and the like. That's when my boss came out, and she started in on him. She didn't look at all well. Hair all over the place, and I was sure I saw blood on the hem of her dress.

"The boss tried to calm her down and sent me for a glass of water. He talked to her for a while, offered to call someone for her, and then managed to get rid of her when she refused any help. I told him we should call the police, but he said she was all right now. But like I said, I don't feel all that easy."

"Was she armed?"

"Armed? Good God, no, sir. But if she had been there's no doubt she'd have taken pot shots at us. My boss told me after she left that the Turner she was looking for used to run the place back in the day. He told her the last he heard of him he'd gone off with some woman in New Denver. But that would have been over twenty years ago. He said that woman used to run the store there, but he didn't think she was still there. That seemed to be enough for her, but like I say, she didn't seem all there."

CHAPTER THIRTY-TWO

THE AMORPHOUS MISGIVINGS DARLING HAD been having now coalesced into full-blown fear. Lane had absolutely no idea what she was walking into. No, that was wrong. She must have some idea. If this is what she'd found out, on its own it would not pose a risk, but with Viola Tilbury, armed and crazy, saying, "I'm going to find my Daddy," it had all the risk in the world. The Tilbury woman seemed to have no hesitation about shooting people. No, wait. He stopped pacing. According to what Dr. Philipson had said, Viola wouldn't know where he was. But now she'd gone to Sandon, and they'd sent her to New Denver. He had to reach Lane, to warn her.

He cursed Barisoff for a troglodyte fool. Who lives in the modern world without a telephone? He'd better warn Berenson, but a call put through to the store got no answer.

Terrell had returned and was standing respectfully, watching Darling pace by his desk.

Darling waved at him. "We need to go up the lake,

pronto. O'Brien, don't be away from that telephone for one second. If my wife calls, you are to tell her . . ." Tell her what? He himself was uncertain about the nature of the danger. A man uncloaked? A trigger-happy lunatic? "Tell her she is to stay away from everything."

"Right you are, sir," said O'Brien. "That does seem a bit vague, as instructions go, though."

"Just use your bloody head," Darling said fiercely. He turned to Terrell. "Bring a weapon."

O'Brien, too, was beginning to have misgivings. This whole carry-on could extend well past his quitting time. Watching his colleagues jumping into the car, Darling waving his arm as if he was shouting "They went thataway," O'Brien shook his head and reached under the desk for his tin lunch box. The Thermos of tea remained almost untouched, and the buttered scone awaited him, wrapped in its greaseproof paper, and had he seen the wife put some raspberry jam in it? They would provide temporary comfort.

STELLA BISSET WAS sitting up in bed, a cup of tea by her side. Lane had asked Simpson to wind up the gramophone and put the record back on, though she herself was beginning to feel haunted by the song. Because the shock had somehow been connected to him, Lane asked him to wait in the living room, go through the pile of records, and find another record to play.

Simpson called her quietly from the kitchen. He didn't want to cause Miss Bisset any renewed alarm. "I'm going back out to that car," he said quietly. "I don't think there is any doubt it was my uncle Pete's. You all right here?"

"I'm fine. Thank you. I don't think, in the long run, she can stay here. She'll have to get some medical attention."

Lane watched for a moment as Simpson passed the window on his way back to the garage. So, it was his uncle's car. Her brain scrambled about, trying to put the pieces together. The body in Barisoff's garden, the car here. And that strange exclamation from Stella Bisset, "He is back." A vision leaped into her mind of Stella—younger, angry? Frightened? Aiming her rifle and firing on Uncle Pete at close range?

A little uneven gasp from the bedroom reminded her that first and foremost she had to deal with the now elderly and ailing Miss Bisset. When the patient had had her tea, she would drop Simpson off at Barisoff's and proceed to the store to discuss the whole business of Stella's care with Berenson.

For now, anyway, Stella Bisset was calm, composed even. Lane spoke with her in French. "Are you feeling better, madame?"

Stella nodded. "But that man?" she said, her brow knitting. "I was so certain . . ."

There was no doubt in Lane's mind that the music had been a good idea. It made her lucid, if only temporarily.

"Yes, tell me about that. You thought you had seen him before?"

"But I have. He was dark, just like that, and stood in the doorway." She shook her head, as if clearing dust from inside it. "He was so angry. I had never seen him like this before. It frightened me. Everything changed after that.

I was a young woman then." She nodded with something that looked confusingly like satisfaction. "Young. I knew what to do."

Mr. Simpson would not have been alive, or at least he would have been a tiny child, when Stella Bisset was young. Did he look like his uncle? Is that what she was seeing?

The door banged, causing them both to jump. Someone was shouting. The needle was ripped off the record. In the next moment, Berenson was looming in the door of the bedroom, his dishevelled beard working, his eyes blazing with what, Lane wondered. Fury? Fear? With a start she realized he was holding a rifle.

"What the hell is going on?" He advanced two big steps, his boots hitting the floor with menacing strength. "What have you been saying?"

Stella Bisset recoiled and shook her head with little frightened movements. She looked, Lane thought with alarm, like a tiny child, fearful of an enraged adult. She stood up, trying to place herself firmly between Berenson and the bed.

"I was going to come and see you, Mr. Berenson. I feel we ought to talk a bit more about Miss Bisset and how she can be helped. You've been so wonderful, but I'm beginning to worry it is not enough." Lane was thinking fast, trying to distract him from whatever had infuriated him. "Let's sit in the other room and let Miss Bisset rest. She fainted. She seems to have had a shock. I was just going to give her a cup of tea."

Then it occurred to her. Where was Simpson?

Berenson's angry energy seemed to stall.

"Why should she faint?" He looked past Lane. "What's the matter with you?" he asked Stella, suspicious again.

Nerving herself, Lane put her hand on Berenson's shoulder. "Let's let her rest." He made a movement as if to shake off her hand, and acquiesced reluctantly, turning and going into the little kitchen.

"Not in her right mind. She's crazy as a coot. You don't want to believe anything she tells you." He pulled out a chair and sat down heavily. He didn't let go of his rifle.

Her heart pounding, Lane poured some water from the jug into the kettle and stoked the fire. Tea for every bloody emergency, she thought, though what it might accomplish here eluded her. Perhaps it was just the inherently calming effect of the ordinary little movements of preparation. What had become of Simpson?

The kettle on, Lane took up the teapot, still full of the earlier tea. "I'll just go throw these tea leaves on the flower bed. They love it."

Berenson made no response as Lane walked past him, quaking inwardly, to the door. When she opened it, she nearly jumped out of her skin, but managed to stifle the exclamation that threatened to give her away. Simpson was crouched on one side of the stair, armed with the rifle from the rumble seat of the car. It surely wouldn't work after all this time, she thought. Simpson had his finger to his lips. She looked a question at him.

"He's armed. Give me a signal if he escalates," he whispered.

"There you go!" Lane said brightly. "Enjoy your tea leaves. The garden is already sprouting," she called into the house. "Spring already!"

Why was Simpson unwilling to come in? She could find out later. "Don't stay here," she whispered. "He'll see you."

Hoping Simpson had heeded her advice to hide, Lane finished making the tea, her mind desperately trying to put all the pieces together with Berenson glowering at her. Stella saying "He is back" at seeing Simpson. Berenson shouting "What have you been saying?" Simpson suddenly reluctant to be seen. He must have found something in the car, besides the rifle. How the bloody hell long could she drag out this tea business? She would have to get Berenson to leave, to go back to his shop.

"Mr. Berenson, I'm really worried. She's barely coping. She could burn herself or set the place on fire. It's only thanks to you, I'm sure, that she is still in one piece. You've been so kind. Do you know if she has any relations? A grown-up child, a sister? Anything?" Would he see through her attempts to play him up?

"She's got no one," he said gruffly, and then looked around. "I got her some sugar. Where's it gone?"

"I didn't find any," Lane said. "I thought it would help her with the shock."

He shook his head, his hand on the rifle slackening a little. "She's like a little kid. She just puts a spoon in and eats it straight out of the bag."

"How long has she been like this?"

"Been getting worse. Started to get forgetful eight years ago when she had the store. Then she started repeating stuff. Been getting a lot worse lately in a big hurry. Seems to be in another world."

Lane nodded. She imagined it was something that could get a lot worse without one really being aware until one suddenly realized the person couldn't cope at all and had stopped making real sense. "Have you been friends a long time?"

He nodded, as if to himself, but said nothing for some time. "She was a fine woman, one time," he said finally. He picked up his teacup and drank back what was in it.

Lane moved to refill his cup. She had to keep him talking, find out what she could, and somehow get him to leave. "That is very sad, to see someone deteriorate like that. Is she a widow?"

"I got her away from that place. I didn't care about those other men. Then when I came back, I found her running the store." He waved his hand vaguely toward the town. "I took it over then."

"Mr. Berenson. She can't live here on her own. She could deteriorate quickly. She needs constant care. I understand they have places in town that would care for her."

Berenson shook his head slightly. "Can't take that risk."

STELLA FELT HERSELF elated, almost floating. She was on a green meadow, and she knew something wonderful was near. She felt herself rise, hovering in the soft air, her happiness one with the light and air. She could see the cottage just below, the green shoots in the garden growing. Fascinated because she could see them actually rising out of the ground, she stayed. There was a man at the door. Dread began to pull her down. She felt herself falling. The shoots had stopped growing. They began to wither, and she wanted to reach out and stop them, but she could not move any limb. She was frozen. She could only see the door open and the man standing there. She was reaching for something. She wanted to stop, but her arm moved of its own accord. She could feel the cold of the steel barrel in her closed fingers. There was someone else there. Was it Papa? It felt like him, spreading anger like a fearsome black fog, pushing light away. Dread consumed her, choked her. She had to turn away now, now, before it was too late. She tried to turn her head, to leave, to fly back up into the sunlight, but she was like lead, the weight of terror bearing down on every limb. She saw the man's face, anger turning to surprise, then fear. He was backing away.

The blast was deafening. She could hear herself screaming, over and over, "He's dead! He's dead!"

LANE JUMPED UP and rushed to Stella's bedside at the sound of the scream. Stella was sitting bolt upright, her tattered coverlet pulled to her neck with both hands, staring with wide eyes straight ahead. "Madame, you are all right. We are here," she said in French. She reached for Stella's hands.

Her eyes wide with fear, Stella turned to Lane and said softly, "Il l'a tué."

"Qui, madame?"

"He, who is behind you," she said, still looking at Lane.

"What's going on? What's she saying?" Berenson stood menacingly over them, the gun firmly back in hand. "Talk English!" he shouted at her.

Stella was still talking in French. "He made me help him, to take him to bury him in the woods up the hill, and pile rocks on top. There was no priest, nothing. Sometimes I see him walking in my dreams. Now he is back. I saw him. Did you not see him?"

Lane patted Stella on the shoulder. "There, it's all right. You rest, madame." She stood up, wanting to get him out of the room and away from Stella, in case she reverted to English. "She's just had a bad dream. I dare say she could be a bit calmer if you'd just put down that gun." She spoke firmly now, as if she were talking to a recalcitrant eleven-year-old boy. She began to whoosh him back out of the room and to her enormous relief, casting a dark suspicious glance back at Stella, he obeyed her, and grudgingly turned.

Lane's mind was flying. She must get Stella out. At any moment she could go back to English, or he would guess what she'd been saying. And then she remembered Simpson, still hovering outside.

"Look, Mr. Berenson. She's in a dreadful state. I think I ought to take her to town with me. She's badly under nourished, so I could get her into hospital for a few days, and in the interim I can find a place for her." A plan had begun to form. "I'm just going out to the car to get the rug." Then what? "Could I leave you here to shut everything down, get rid of the perishables and so on? And maybe you could pack a little bag for her, and I'll come back and get it from you at the store tomorrow."

Was it a risk leaving him there with her? It would only be a moment. She had to get Simpson out of the way, back to Barisoff's. Without waiting to hear what Berenson thought of the plan, she rushed outside, looking for Simpson. He was at the side of the house, still at the ready.

"What's going on?" he whispered.

"I'll explain later. Get back to Barisoff. Don't let Berenson see you. I'm going to get her out of there."

"You're sure?" Receiving a quick nod, he turned to go around the back of the cottage.

She raced to her car and pulled the rug off the back seat. She always kept it there for winter emergencies, and for the picnics she fondly imagined she and Darling would enjoy on summer days by the lake.

She found Berenson milling around in the kitchen, opening and closing cupboards. His rifle lay on the table. She momentarily thought of seizing it, but everything depended on absolute calm. He hadn't threatened either of them, really, and while Miss Bisset had seemingly accused him of killing someone, it could be a product of her unsound mind.

"She's got garbage in here rotting. Rats or something have been under the sink," Berenson complained.

"It's so good of you to take this on." Lane, wondering how clean his own digs were, tried to sound bright and held up the woollen rug from the car. "Got it."

In the bedroom Stella now lay back on her cushion, her eyes closed, but they flew open at Lane's soft "Madame?" Lane felt her heart sinking. There was no recognition at all in that look. "Madame, I am going to take you to a safe place. You remember nice Mr. Barisoff? We will go there first. Come. Let me help you get up." She spoke very quietly, in soothing French, praying that Stella Bisset would be present enough to allow Lane to remove her without protest.

To her immense relief, Stella pushed herself upright, and

then moved the quilt off her body and swung her legs to the floor. "We are going to visit?" Her voice was childlike, her tone pleased. An outing.

Lane beamed. "Oui, madame! Exactly that. We will have a lovely visit. Let me get your shoes." Lane looked wildly around and saw only the threadbare slippers. They would have to do. Thank God Stella was wearing the trousers she'd brought her. Stella had one sock on; Lane pulled the covers farther down to find the other and slid it quickly onto her bare foot. She wrapped the rug around Stella's shoulders and slid the slippers on her feet. "Voila! You are all ready."

Stella stood on her own and shuffled forward, clutching the blanket at her breast. In the little kitchen she stopped, frowning at the sight of Berenson emptying things into the garbage bucket.

"Is he not amiable?" Lane said. "He is going to tidy everything, and it will be all ready when we get back."

Berenson stopped, scowling. "Talk English. Looks like this is it, eh, Stella?" His voice rose angrily, as if she were deaf.

Stella recoiled and then saw the rifle on the table, and she shrank further back against Lane, and then raised her own hand and stared at it. Alarmed, Lane put her arm around Stella, who had begun to whimper.

"That's it, madame, we are going for our visit now." She used the pressure of her arm to move her gently toward the door. "Thank you for this, Mr. Berenson!" she called out, infusing as much friendliness into the sentence as possible. Really, she thought, I should take to the stage. Pretending to the poor addled woman we are going on an outing and pretending to a possibly murderous man that he's just a helpful neighbour. Well, no different really to what she did during the war. Intelligence work often involved plenty of acting. Stella sat compliantly in the car next to her. Her heart pounding with fear, Lane tried not to drive too fast onto the main road, both for Stella's sake and not to arouse suspicion in Berenson. Once on the road, however, she drove as fast as she dared, and made for Barisoff's.

How much time did she have for what she had to do? Berenson might just chuck the whole cleaning thing and head back to his store, thinking of the business he'd be losing. She pulled the car as close to Barisoff's cabin as she could and then raced inside, to find only Barisoff in possession.

"They are settling into the other house. Why should they not stay here while their business is sorted?" he asked. He was sitting before a pile of peeled potatoes. "I will make a nice supper. Perhaps you can stay?"

"No time just now. I have Stella Bisset in the car. I will bring her in, and I want you to keep her here. Under no circumstances must you let Berenson in. I must go and telephone the police. I will explain later!" She turned and went to fetch Stella, whom she found already out of the car and looking bemused by her sudden change of location.

"Look, madame, here is Mr. Barisoff. He will give you something to eat and you can have a nice visit." She tried to keep the anxious hurry she felt out of her voice. Stella seemed particularly sensitive to tone, if not always to words. Behind her, Barisoff had come out and was standing beside Stella, speaking quietly.

"You come for visit. I very happy to see you."

Stella smiled and put out a hand and said in French, "How do you do? I am Estelle Bisset."

He put his arm around Stella and then turned back to Lane and made a "Go, now!" motion with his head.

Without a second thought, Lane was back in the car and driving to Berenson's store, praying he'd left the door unlocked and that he was still at Stella's cottage. He'd obviously been divided between fear of what Stella would say and the fear of having to stay and tend to her when she was in a very unstable state. That couldn't last if he came to suspect, even for a moment, that she had told Lane that truth.

CHAPTER THIRTY-THREE

APRIL SHOOK OUT HER APRON and hung it on the hook in the tiny hall at the back of the café. It would be fine to use again another day. "See ya," she called into the kitchen, and receiving a cigarette-muffled reply from Al, she pulled on her gloves, buttoned her jacket, cast a look down the back of her stockings, and stepped into the alley.

The afternoon, what remained of it, could almost be called sunny, after an overcast and drizzly morning. She was aware, as she came out the alley and stood indecisively, of feeling both the fizziness of spring coming and a kind of restlessness that leaned toward wanting something, though she didn't know what.

Liar! she told herself. She knew what she wanted but knew she must ignore it, so she turned down the street and then onto Baker and down toward Lorenzo's burned-out restaurant.

It was extraordinary, she thought, that it hardly looked damaged at all from the front. The only indication something was amiss was the broken window and the Closed sign hanging in the door, just when people might be stopping by for an early dinner. A couple who was clearly headed down to the train station paused in front of the restaurant.

"That's a nuisance," the woman said. "I've been telling Emily how lovely the food is. We'll have to take her somewhere else. What's the matter with people? Why would anyone burn a restaurant?"

"Maybe it was one of these so-called accidents for the insurance money," answered the man. "I thought I heard a rumour about him. Still, good food, I've got nothing against him."

April couldn't stop herself. "It was in the paper. The poor owner was trapped in there and nearly died. He's in hospital now. And they don't have any insurance. They may not be able to get back on their feet again."

"Oh, that *is* a shame!" the woman exclaimed. "Can't someone do something?" She looked again at the front door of the restaurant, shaking her head, and then said, "I hear it, darling. We'd better get down there, or poor Emily will think we've abandoned her."

April stood watching the couple moving down the street. So not everyone was against the Vitalis. She might very well have a jaundiced view of people because of the little klatch of women who came into the café, and not even all of them were against the Italians. After all, her jar was beginning to fill up nicely. "Can't someone do something?" It was the sort of thing people said every day, heaving the responsibility for doing something out into the ether, where exactly no one would do anything.

With her chin set in a determined line, April turned back up the street and made for City Hall. The mayor was her father's oldest friend. She'd give him a piece of her mind, and she could get him to cough up some money for her fund, while she was at it.

LORENZO VITALI WAS settled in his favourite armchair with his feet on the ottoman. Mrs. Vitali had set it so that it looked out the window, with its view across the lake, the late afternoon sun casting golden shadows across the sliver of water below.

"Don't make so much fuss," he said, catching his wife's hand as she tucked the blanket around him. "I'm all right."

She could tell he was trying to sound all right, but she felt the burden of his underlying sadness and anger. "I made you veal parmigiana. You know how you love it. We don't need to think about anything now, just you getting better."

"You are an angel. There was nothing decent to eat in the hospital, but they were kind, very kind. I was surprised at such kindness. I will have to find a way to thank them."

"You are not finding a way to do anything just now. You heard the doctor. Rest, rest, and more rest. I am in charge now. You will do what I say, eh, *carissimo*?"

Lorenzo gazed out the window. He didn't look down toward the town and the water or the mountains beyond, but up at the sky. He had loved looking at the sky since he was a child. It always gave hope, filled as it was with the aura of a faraway promise. It was the promise of the sky, he often thought, that got him to Canada. He wanted to shake his head at the sky now. Why did you bring me here for this? He closed his eyes, listened to his wife in the kitchen, and struggled to hold on to the comfort of that to the exclusion of the despair that had gradually taken hold of him. The realization of what they faced now had become clear.

It would be up to him, and he did not think he had anything left. He had seen the doctor talking quietly to his wife as he sat on his bed, dressed, the little suitcase next to him, waiting for them to get him to the car. He had been dazed by the effort of getting ready to leave the hospital, but now he wondered what they had been saying.

He opened his eyes. She was there with a cup of tea. "What is this?" he asked, smiling. "No coffee?"

"No coffee. The doctor wants you resting. Coffee is too exciting."

He took her hand. "What else did he say?"

The worry in his voice caused her to stoop down next to him. "That is what he said. No coffee. You are going to be fine. He said with rest, your lungs will fully recover. No, it was me he was warning. I will have to give up my occasional cigarette. The smoke will be bad for you." She smiled at him, and then stood up and kissed him on the forehead. "Really, that is all."

"But I will have my coffee in the morning!" he called into the kitchen after her.

It was later, in the evening, while Lorenzo was dozing and listening to the radio, that there was a quiet knock on the door. Olivia looked anxiously at her husband, but he raised his hand and nodded.

"Mr. Smith, Mrs. Smith. How nice for you to come. Thank you, he is going to like this very much. Please, is okay for a few moments." Olivia came in from the vestibule followed by the Smiths. She was carrying a cake.

"I knew I shouldn't make any kind of casserole," Mrs. Smith said. "I could never touch the wonderful things you make. But I thought a nice chocolate cake would cheer things up. Hello, Mr. Vitali. We're sorry to barge over like this. We just wanted to see how you are doing."

Lorenzo smiled, feeling almost happy. Happier than he had been for some time, he realized. The Smiths were good people. "You are very nice to come. I love chocolate cake very much. Now we see if the missus will let me have any. She is very . . . how you say?"

"Strict?" offered Mr. Smith, pulling up a chair next to Lorenzo. "I have one like that, too!"

"That is it. Strict."

Mrs. Smith watched for a moment, and then said briskly, "Mrs. Vitali and I will just go and cut the cake and, ah, I see you are drinking tea; we will go and get some more ready." She looked significantly at Mrs. Vitali, implying with a look in the direction of the men that they ought to be left to it.

"Yes," Olivia said. "You must come and help me. We will all have cake. Just this once, I let him!"

"Well, old chap," Smith said, when the women had disappeared into the kitchen. "It is a dreadful business."

Lorenzo nodded and then shrugged. "Truth is, is no business now. We have saying in Italian, *Quel che sarà sarà.* It is like, 'What happens will happen.' Nothing you can do."

"Well, that's why we've come over, old fellow. I had a

chat with a couple of the fellows, and if it's all right with you, we'd like to go down and just have a look around inside, see how bad things are. It might not be as bad as you think."

"You are so kind, Mr. Smith. Even if not so bad—" Lorenzo coughed suddenly and held his handkerchief to his mouth. "I have no money to fix," he managed to sputter between coughs. "Anyway, maybe is a sign. I don't think so I can go back inside."

"There. Don't you fret about it. Step at a time, what? First thing, you get better, okay?"

VIOLA WOKE WITH a start and found herself looking out her car window. It took her a moment to orient herself. Her arm was numb where she had lain on it uncomfortably. She sat up abruptly and wiped her mouth, peering over the steering wheel at the store. She'd gone to sleep. Had she missed her? The place still looked quiet through the trees, but the woman could have come back from wherever she'd been and could be inside now. She pushed open the car door and swung her feet out. Her legs were stiff from inactivity, and she felt her exhaustion when she stood up. She had not slept properly for two days, but it didn't matter. She was so close.

The sound of a car made her duck, but of course where she was hidden in the trees no one would see her. This must be her. She would watch, make sure first. The car pulled up by the gas pump and a woman got out and made her way hurriedly to the door. The shock made Viola feel momentarily faint. Her! She looked swiftly around her, as if the forest would provide some answer. Why was *she* here? Feeling almost sick at the memory of Gilbert and this smirking woman, she reached into the car and pulled out her rifle. She felt the power of the rage at everything she'd lost because of her father and that woman. She shook her head as if to straighten its contents. No, this was not his woman; this was one of Gilbert's.

THE FRONT DOOR was locked, and Lane let out an exclamation of frustration. There must be a back door. The ground behind the building was lower than the front. Two rickety wooden steps had been built to bring the walker down to the path across the back. Somewhere up the road she heard a car approaching. If they were going to stop for gas they'd be out of luck, she thought, hurrying down the two steps. Her real anxiety was whether she would be able to catch someone, anyone, at the Nelson Police Station. Somewhere, prowling in the back of her mind, was the uneasy thought that she didn't really know that what Stella told her was true, but she couldn't take the risk.

The resounding "crack" when it came was shocking. Lane stopped, looked up where the bullet had seared through the corner of the building just above her, splintering the wood, and then dived onto her stomach, her hands going instinctively over her head. In the next instant she was crawling desperately along the uneven path to get right behind the building. The shot had come from the road. She hoped. Slumped against the back of the building, she wondered with sudden horror if it had come from the woods behind the store, and she was sitting now directly in the shooter's line of vision.

Her heart pounding, she waited for another shot. Had she heard stealthy footsteps? One thing was certain: her hope that she had somehow fooled Berenson into agreeably staying behind to clean up Stella's cottage was dashed. Her mind flew to Stella, now being cared for by Barisoff. Her attacker would know she wasn't driving Stella to Nelson. Would he guess where Lane had deposited her?

Moments ticked by. There was no renewal of the attack. For one wild moment Lane wondered if it was simply a hunter in the nearby woods. She had to get to the phone. Praying she wasn't making too much noise, and that Berenson was not behind the building instead of in front of it, she made a crouching dash to the door. With a gush of relief, she found it was open.

It was dark inside compared to the outside, and before her eyes had adjusted, she tripped loudly against a wooden crate, and hissed her anguish at a sharp pain in her knee. She froze, listening. Still silent. Her eyes adjusted to the murky interior of what was obviously a storage room. She could see the outline of the door a little above her, the light from the shop itself showing through the gaps. With one last listen, she started forward, using her hands to feel for any more impediments, and made her way up the three steps to the door. She pushed it a foot and a half, stopping again to listen, cringing at the squeak in the hinges. Her own heart seemed to be making most of the racket. Right behind the door she found herself in front of the shelf where Berenson stashed the telephone.

With shaking hands, she grabbed and clicked it. Her relief at hearing an answer, "How can I connect you?" almost rendered her mute.

"Nelson Police Station, please. Emergency." She was sitting on the floor, one ear on any sound coming from outside.

"I'm sorry, madam, you will have to speak up," said the voice with a slightly impatient tone.

Lane cupped her hand over the receiver and said, in as loud a whisper as she dared, "Nelson Police, emergency!"

"One moment please, madam," said the maddeningly imperturbable voice.

The silence was so absolute that Lane feared the line had gone dead. It was at that moment that she was sure she heard some movement outside the front of the store. With infinite caution, still clutching the receiver, Lane rose above the counter so that she could just see the grubby front window. A shot blew the window out and she dropped like a stone.

O'Brien's voice came down the line. "Nelson Police Station, Sergeant O'Brien speaking."

Someone was violently trying to wrench the handle of the outer door. Lane said, "Sergeant, is my husband there? Is anyone there?"

"Ah. Mrs. Darling. Expecting your call. I'm here, as it happens. But you will want to know, Inspector Darling and Constable Terrell are on their way to New Denver. Is that where you are?"

"For now," Lane said acidly, hearing the renewed assault on the door handle. At the back of her mind a question was forming. Why was Berenson struggling to get into his own shop? He had a bloody key, surely? But front of mind was that Darling was on his way. "How long ago did they leave?"

Before he could answer a blast was aimed at the door. The bullet lodged somewhere in the floor right next to the counter she was crouched behind.

"Was that gunfire? Are you safe?" O'Brien asked, gratifying urgency in his voice.

"Not much," Lane said. The shot must have been badly aimed. The door was still not yielding. "How long ago?"

"A good hour and a bit. They should be there soon. Can you get to safety?"

Several tart answers crossed her mind, to the effect that if she could get to safety, she'd be there now. Instead, she said, "Thanks, Sergeant."

Just as she was about to put the receiver down, she heard him shouting, "Don't hang up! Leave the receiver—"

The smashing of the barrel of the rifle against the door, for what else could it be, spurred her into action. First, she looked at the receiver she had just dropped on the floor. It was good sturdy Bakelite. You could bean someone with it, if they were unsuspecting. Smash. The door was giving way.

"I know you're in there!"

Shocked, Lane stopped her scuttle back down the steps into the storage area. A woman's voice! Another shot, this one whistling past her head where she was momentarily congealed and smashing into the wall beside her.

"Berenson's not here!" she shouted.

"It's not him I want, you whore!"

God almighty! Whoever it was wanted *her*? Spurred by sheer survival, she was down into the storage area and out the door, where she paused in the blinding sunlight, leaning against the wall, her breath coming in heaving gasps, and considered her escape options.

CHAPTER THIRTY-FOUR

TERRELL, DARLING WAS GLAD TO note, drove with less of the cautious desire to baby the car than Ames. Indeed, there were moments when he squeezed his fist beside him, to resist the impulse to grab at the door on some of the turns. Suffice it to say, they were making good time.

"I expect Miss Winslow—sorry, I should say Mrs. Darling; Sergeant Ames always calls her Miss Winslow. Anyway, she is quite resourceful, sir, should she find herself in any danger," Terrell offered, glancing at Darling.

"I'm quite sure you're right. The problem is Berenson does not know what is on its way. According to the people at Sandon, Viola Tilbury thinks her father's lover owns that shop. My wife likes 'Miss Winslow,' by the way."

"He is going to get a shock, for sure. But it's unlikely Mrs. Tilbury would shoot him, don't you think?"

"I don't know," Darling answered, exasperated. He wanted to say that he just hoped Lane was well out of the way, perhaps even now driving back, planning to park an addled old woman in their spare room. How desirable that seemed just at this moment! He watched the road ahead of them, hoping to see her car coming the other way.

DECIDING AGAINST THE indignity of scrambling about in the bush, trying to avoid getting shot, Lane fixed on a more direct plan. There was a tidy pile of firewood stacked at one side of the door under a sloping shelter. She grabbed a sturdy specimen and made her way back along the path and up the side of the building. She could hear from the sound of the woman's voice shouting that she knew someone was in there, that she was still on the threshold. Lane paused at the edge of the building. That sound was the breaking of the rifle. She was reloading. Her heart beating anxiously, she peeked around and saw that the woman was looking down, pushing a bullet into the chamber. Lunging forward, Lane reached her and brought the wood down hard on her arms, sending the gun flying. The woman screamed her frustration and pain and turned on Lane.

In this moment of a pause in the action, Lane had time to look at her, trying to place her. Someone in a shop, in Nelson. She held the piece of wood down by her side now, trying to reduce the threat, but didn't let it go.

"Look, can we talk? I don't know who you think I am—"

"I know exactly who you are! I saw you with him. You and that Italian whore! He has them all over town, it seems."

It clicked. Olivia Vitali had told her about Tilbury. But how had she herself come into this woman's line of fire all the way out here? "Mrs. Tilbury, look. I'm going to go pick up that rifle so no one gets hurt. You look exhausted and hungry. I'm sure there's some food and something to drink in Mr. Berenson's shop." Lane had put down the piece of wood and now held her hands up, a gentle gesture of calm.

Lane could hear the sound of a truck behind her. She dared not turn to look. It stopped, revved its engine, and was quiet. She could see the dust it raised out of the corner of her eye. She could only think of keeping Mrs. Tilbury in her sight and trying to get the rifle.

But Mrs. Tilbury had lost interest in Lane altogether. She was watching the truck, wide-eyed. Lane wanted to turn to see who was getting out, slamming the door of the truck, but she couldn't take her eyes off the woman, for Mrs. Tilbury had gone white, and her mouth had fallen open, slack with shock.

"Daddy . . ." she whispered, and then she fell into a faint.

SIMPSON, WHO HAD been making his way back to Barisoll's cabin through the woods, had just arrived at the road. The shot galvanized him. It was coming from a little farther up the road. How could it be Berenson? He hadn't heard the man's truck leaving the cottage. He knew Lane was going to use the phone in the little gas station, and he broke into a run. He heard a second shot, then a third, then a woman shouting. Had Miss Winslow foolishly decided to confront Berenson? No, that didn't sound like her at all.

He ducked into the trees and bush so that he could come level with the store without being seen. What he saw was Lane Winslow striking the rifle out of the hands of a woman. He just had time to register where the weapon had fallen and was preparing to run out to retrieve it, when suddenly the little space in front of the store felt like the parking lot of a busy train station. First a truck pulled up next to the two cars that were already parked willy-nilly, and Berenson jumped out, that damn rifle still glued to his hand. Then the woman fainted, and Lane was down trying to help her, then another car rolled up, and Darling and that constable were jumping out.

Berenson hadn't seen the police car; he was intent on the two women.

"What happened?" he asked, his voice shaking. He frowned at the woman on the ground. Who was she?

"It's all right, she just fainted," Lane responded, wondering why the devil everyone had to go about the place fainting. "I need to get her some water. Do you have smelling salts in there?"

Berenson was about to respond when he wheeled around. Someone had shouted, "Turner! Put your weapon down and step forward."

Lane stood up, looking in shock at the speaker. Darling! But why—

Suddenly she felt herself seized. Berenson had slipped behind her and had his arm across her neck, pulling her backward. She heard the rifle clatter to the ground, could feel his body twisting momentarily and then saw the flash of a massive hunting blade right in front of her face. It glittered menacingly in the late afternoon sun. They were moving steadily backward, and she felt her feet scrambling, unable to get a footing, unable to stop him from dragging her.

Terrell darted forward to attend to Mrs. Tilbury, but Berenson shouted, "Leave her!"

The sound reverberated in Lane's head because he was shouting right into her ear. There was a movement on the right, in the trees. Lane looked sharply sideways, trying not to move her head or alert her captor. It was Simpson, holding one finger to his lips and pointing toward the back of the building. Lane registered this, blinked twice, tried to focus on what was happening in front of her. She could see Terrell and Darling inching forward. Darling had a revolver. She hoped he was a good shot, but then she knew he would never make the attempt as long as she was in the deadly embrace of . . . Turner?

"Are you—" she started.

"Shut up!" he snarled, holding the knife close to her face.

Lane shut up. Why was Berenson behaving in this desperate manner? Nobody else knew what she knew. But of course. He knew she knew, and he would have to get rid of her to keep it that way. How would his mind be working right now? Get rid of the police somehow, drive away with her in tow, kill her and dump her somewhere, and go on the run?

"Turner, there's nothing against you right now. Just let her go, we can talk about this." Darling again, calling from where he stood.

Why did he keep calling him Turner? As if on cue, Viola Tilbury came to and sat up slowly, brushing her cheek where it had lain against the dirt in the drive. Terrell tried again to make a forward move.

"Back!" ordered Lane's captor, flashing the knife, jerking it upward.

It took only a moment, and then the pain in Lane's

cheek flared up like a blade of fire. She could feel blood moving wetly down her face and onto her neck. She saw Darling start forward, and then heard the loud clear voice, right behind her.

"Now!"

She raised her arm and drove her elbow backward as hard as she could into whatever part of Berenson's body she could find. She was rewarded with an "Oof!" The arm Berenson had around her neck slackened, and she bent forward, trying to wriggle free, just as there was the crack of wood on skull. Berenson crumbled behind her, his arm dragging at her so that she was forced to pull forward a few steps to keep herself from falling.

She turned and saw Simpson holding a piece of Berenson's firewood, looking quite satisfied over her unconscious assailant. She was about to say, "Thank you," when alarm registered in his face.

"Ma'am! You're hurt!" He dropped the wood and dashed into the shop.

Darling was beside her, his handkerchief out, and he pressed it against her cheek. "Just a flesh wound, with quite a lot of blood," he said, but his voice was shaking.

Terrell had finally succeeded in his task of collecting the still-dazed Mrs. Tilbury, who had now come to enough to demand to be unhanded, and then to see Berenson in a heap on the ground. She pulled with unexpected strength and almost succeeded in freeing herself. "Daddy! Let me go! What have you done to him?"

"He's all right, ma'am. We'll just put you in the car, and then we can attend to him." He handcuffed her and walked

416

with her struggling and protesting to the car. He put her into the back seat, and then leaned against the door to watch the proceedings.

Simpson came out of the shop with a clean cloth, a box of Band-Aids, and a bottle of mercurochrome from the small stock of basic medical supplies Berenson kept on hand. Darling moved to take over, but Simpson politely waved him off. "You may want to bind him up, Inspector. I didn't hit him that hard."

There was a bench under the window, and Simpson led Lane there, brushing enough of the shattered window glass away with his elbow to allow Lane to perch on it while he attended to her cut.

"You might have a bit of a scar here," Simpson said, some regret in his voice.

Lane smiled and then winced. "Will I? I've always wanted one, like a pirate." She felt the sting of the mercurochrome and winced. "Ow! Besides, it will match the one on my chin." She pointed at the bony edge of her chin where a knife attack in Germany was recorded with a very fine, slightly raised line.

"You'll be a funny colour for a while," Simpson said, pulling open a bandage. "A couple of these should hold the cut together. Hold this against your cheek to keep it from bleeding anymore."

Darling was standing over Berenson, who had just begun to stir, handcuffs at the ready.

"You know," Lane said, directing her voice toward Darling, "it's not true there is nothing against him. I believe he shot Mr. Simpson's uncle."

"COULD YOU LOCK up here? Are you sure you're going to be all right?"

Darling was standing by the passenger door of the police car where Viola Tilbury and Berenson sat in the back, cuffed and surly.

"I'm fine. Are you going to tell me what's going on? Is this man the missing Turner?"

"Long story involving a dentist, but yes."

"He and Mrs. T. will have plenty of time to catch up on the ride back," Lane said. "Blimey!" she exclaimed suddenly, taking the handkerchief Darling had given her away from her cheek. "I've left O'Brien hanging on the line. He must be beside himself if he stayed on. Look, I'm going to get Miss Bisset to the hospital, and I'll be along home after that."

"It's stopped bleeding," Darling observed. "Your cheek is a lovely shade of sickly yellow. If I get home first, I'll be ready with omelettes and scotch."

She kissed him quickly and ran back to the shop. Really, she thought, as she heard the car drive away, it was a miracle the gas pump hadn't been hit in all that gunfire.

The phone was still on the floor, the receiver beside it. She picked it up. "Sergeant O'Brien? Are you still there?"

A raspy sound of electricity followed and then, "Mrs. Darling? About time. You all right?"

"Everyone is all right, Sergeant. The inspector and constable are on the way back with a couple of miscreants for the cells."

"Right you are. Well, the night man's come in. I'll leave him to it." He paused, covering his alarm with his usual nonchalance. "I'm very relieved, Mrs. Darling. There was an awful lot of shooting."

Smiling, Lane thanked him for being there, if only in spirit, and hung up the receiver. She put the telephone back on its shelf, the first act in tidying up the shop. The lovely, understated sergeant. She should bring him some of Eleanor Armstrong's lemon biscuits one day soon.

"The constable gave me these," Simpson said, holding up a couple of skeleton keys on a rusty ring, which Terrell had located in Turner's jacket pocket. "Not that they'll do much good. Anybody wanting to rob the place could come in through any of these shot-up windows."

"It's so tempting to want to sweep up, but that can be for later. I'm sure the gunshots were heard all over the place. Barisoff and your family will be worried. And I have to get that poor old lady to town."

They closed the shop up as well as they could and made for her car.

"How did you know it was him?" Simpson asked her.

"Because she told me it was him. She thought, when she first saw you, that you were your uncle, miraculously come back. So, your uncle must have come there all those years ago. I don't suppose we'll ever know why, but I have a sort of idea. There are the remains of a pit house just on the forest side of the cottage. I wonder if he came to visit, just as you did, and found the cottage and was upset it had been built there."

"Ah. You saw that. I always knew there was another one nearby. The cottage is close to the water. It turns out my ancestors like a good view just as much as these people." He waved his arm vaguely to encompass the little village nearby.

"You taught me to see them," she said. "I wondered if he went to the door for something as innocent as asking them if he could come onto their land and got shot for his trouble."

"I remember my uncle Pete. He was very sociable and very direct. He could just as easily have knocked on the door and said, 'Hey, buddy, you know this isn't your land?'"

"A beastly end. He was going off to be married, to start his life. It's so unjust. There is still a lot to understand. It turns out that man is not Berenson at all, but a former railway baron called Samuel Turner who disappeared back in 1921. He apparently lost most of his money and left his wife and daughter. I wonder if he left to be with Stella Bisset. I also wonder who will run the store. The village will need the petrol station and the store."

Simpson nodded, saying only, "Hmm."

"I'm sure my husband will be back tomorrow with his crime scene people. I'd best get that poor woman back to town. What is the next step for you?"

"To get back my uncle Pete and give him a good burial."

"I'll see if my husband can authorize him to be brought back in the van. Do you have a plan?"

"I must discuss it with my grandmother. It will be as she wants it."

Lane reached out and touched Simpson's arm. "Listen, I want to thank you. I might have had my throat cut before anyone else could move."

"Group effort, don't you think? You were ready with that elbow right on cue."

"For a moment I felt like I was right back on the front." Of course, she knew she wasn't supposed to say that, what with the Official Secrets Act, but just at the moment she couldn't see the harm in it.

"For a moment we were," Simpson said with a sad smile.

SIMPSON AND BARISOFF helped Miss Bisset to the car. "I tried to give her a little soup that I made for dinner. She didn't seem to want any," Barisoff said. "I wish you could stay. Maybe you will come back?"

"I fully intend to. I'll need to get her little cottage sorted, if nothing else, and maybe try to clean up the shop. Mr. Simpson tells me they will want to have the remains returned for a proper burial. In the meantime, it's beginning to get dark, so I'd best be on my way. It's a good one and a half hours back."

CHAPTER THIRTY-FIVE

BERENSON—TURNER—HAD NOT PACKED anything for Stella Bisset, so Lane, not wanting any further delay, established her in the back of the car with the blanket. Her passenger seemed uninterested in anything and collapsed against the door when it was closed, looking blankly ahead. Lane kept up a cheerful chatter in French for the first forty minutes of the trip and then lapsed into silence. It was dark now, and Lane wanted to concentrate on the road, and hoped that the good people who lived between Kaslo and Nelson would be decently in their homes, having dinner and relaxing by their hearths listening to the wireless, rather than cluttering up these winding and difficult gravel roads.

By the time she arrived at the hospital, Stella had fallen asleep. Lane got out of the car, leaving her there, and, wondering at the sheer amount of time she appeared to be spending at the Nelson hospital, went in to seek help. Explaining to the man at the desk that she had an elderly patient who was malnourished and not in her right mind, Lane was beginning to feel the approaching end of her mission, and exhaustion was setting in.

The receptionist dispatched an orderly with a wheelchair to collect Lane's passenger and then remarked, "You might need a bit of help with that cut." As the doors opened and Stella Bisset, awake now, but still unnervingly oblivious to everything, was wheeled in, he nodded in her direction. "Did she do that to you?"

Lane shook her head and put her hand up to her cheek. She hadn't realized the dressing had come off somehow. Probably when she'd been hoisting Miss Bisset into the car. In truth, she'd quite forgotten her cheek altogether, and as if it had been waiting in the wings for a bit of attention, it began to throb. "I was hoping to just push off home," she said. "It's a long drive."

The man raised his eyebrows and peered again at her cheek. "Could need stitches, could get infected. Let's get it attended to."

Accepting the inevitable, Lane said, "Could I make a quick phone call?"

"Certainly. Help yourself. I'll get someone for you in the meantime."

Lane put in a call to the police station and found that Darling was still there.

"I've got Miss Bisset to the hospital, and they're insisting on attending to my cheek. When I'm done, I'll head home, and I'll be the one waiting with the omelette and whisky. I'm dying to ask how the ride back with those two was, but I will save it for when we are safely in front of our own fire."

Lane was led into a little treatment room, where a very cheerful doctor, for whom business had quite evidently been slow, surveyed her, put out his cigarette, and got to work, pulling sinister-looking objects out of a glass-faced cupboard.

"I'm Dr. Walden. Been in a knife fight?" he asked, carefully removing the Band-Aids. Lane could feel blood welling up.

She tried to stop herself from smiling. "A very unequal one, as you can see. The other party hasn't a scratch on him."

"Whoever did this temporary repair did a good job. You still will need a couple of stitches, and if you are very, very good and don't do anything foolish like dance the Charleston or gallop around on a horse until it's healed, it should leave only a very faint scar."

"I'm sorry to hear that. I was hoping for something more dramatic. What's the point of a knife fight if you've nothing to show for it?"

EXHAUSTION FOUGHT WITH residual adrenalin in Lane as she drove back to King's Cove. The winding road felt longer in the dark, interminable, she thought at times, but at last she was coming down the hill from Bales's store and gas station, past the road to the little school where she'd enjoyed a brief career as a teacher just before Christmas. There below was the still water of the cove, somehow luminous even in the dark, as if lit by stars.

Once safely inside her house, she started the fire in the Franklin to take off the chill and considered her next step. A bath. And then she'd prepare the omelette makings in anticipation of Darling's return. In the bathroom she looked at herself in the little mirror as the bath filled. There was still a lurid streak of yellow from the mercurochrome, and the doctor had placed a bandage neatly over the stitching, so she was not able to admire it. She smiled at her reflection, thinking that she really didn't mind about the scar, but stopped when it caused her cheek to ache.

In her dressing gown, cheese grated and eggs in a blue bowl ready in the kitchen, Lane stretched out in her chair in the sitting room and put her slippered feet on the grate. She decided languidly that she would devote her time waiting for Darling to trying to piece together the sequence of events that led to the shambolic day. The fire was warm, and the flames had a comforting and mesmerizing effect that made her smile slightly. She woke with a start to find Darling giving her a gentle shake.

"Shall we skip the omelettes and just go straight to bed?" he asked softly. He leaned over and kissed her on the forehead as a replacement for kissing her mangled cheek.

Lane sat up. "Not on your life! I'm absolutely famished. And no one is sleeping around here until I know everything."

"Everything?" he asked. "Before the omelette? You can't mean that." He took her hand to pull her out of the chair. "I could very well ask you the same question. How did a mercy trip to an addled old lady turn into the mad Viola Tilbury taking pot shots at you?"

"You might well ask," she said, leading the way into the kitchen and turning on the stove. "I'm guessing she assumed Stella would be there but saw me instead. I understand why she was trying to shoot me: she thought I made a pass at her husband."

"Did you, indeed?" Darling said, holding the loaf of bread over the breadboard. "One piece of toast or two?"

"It depends—lightly toasted or something more robust?"

"I shall stand over the toaster like a cat at a mouse hole. How did you come to be making a pass at Tilbury? He hardly seems your type."

"In the usual sort of way, I'm afraid. I had gone into his shop to look into buying something, and apparently he misunderstood my intentions. I had been on the point of setting him straight in no uncertain terms when I realized that his missus had been standing by the storeroom door, and I really wanted to spare her an ugly scene, so I left in a hurry. I see now she might have interpreted that and my silence as collusion." She whipped the eggs and dropped the grated cheddar into them. "Anyway," she said, pouring the eggs onto the sizzling butter. "How do you know what my type is? I might quite like a smooth, oily man who gives offence with every word he utters."

Darling nodded and shrugged thoughtfully. "It's true. We haven't been married long. There is still so much to learn about you. Ha!" he cried, pouncing on the toaster and dropping the wings open. "Perfect. Now the other side."

"Never mind about that. What I want to learn about is the conversation in the car on the way back to town. Did Mrs. Tilbury say what she was doing there? Did she know Berenson, Turner rather, was her father and had come there to find him?"

"No. She learned it from Philipson. She'd been a patient

of his and knew him when they were both young. He remembered the scandal of it all when her father left. When Berenson was sitting in his chair with his abscessed tooth, Philipson recognized him from those dental records he'd got from Kingston. Of course, he should have come directly to us with that, but he felt some misplaced obligation—perhaps because she was Turner's daughter—to let Viola know first that her father was alive and well. Of course, he had no idea of how fragile her mental state was becoming, any more than her husband did, till it was too late. This must have put her right over the edge. Once she saw Turner, she recognized him at once, in spite of his hairy outer appearance. It shocked her that he had been hiding out all these years, running that shop, making no attempt to find her. She had learned from some retired colleague of her father's up at the mine in Sandon that his paramour had run that shop, and she went there on the off chance the hussy, as she put it, was still there, and would know where her father was. Oops! It takes less time for the second side. We should take notes about this; we might never burn toast again."

The second side of the toast was indeed slightly darker, but still well within the meaning of the act. Darling pulled them off and proudly held them up for her to see.

"Yes, very clever, darling. Bring me the plates."

When the plates were bare of omelette, Darling said, "I'm surprised you haven't mentioned noticing something new about me."

Lane gazed at him. She did know, but she preferred this. "New tie? No, no, wait. That shirt I got you."

"Neither. What is new is that I am not making a fuss about the fact that someone tried to cut your throat. I want to. It is all I can do not to. I'm very, very cross about it. If I could have stopped on the way back and thrown him over the cliff on that bit of road you hate so much, without arousing any more suspicion about my ethics, I would have done it without hesitation. I'm glad you had that cut attended to when you were at the hospital. What did they say?"

"I appreciate your self-control. I was told that if I behave and don't dance or run about and let it heal properly, I will have barely a scar. I am, as you can imagine, disappointed."

"You want a scar to show that you don't take nonsense from people?"

"No. I want one because they are romantic and impart an air of mystery. When I was very small there was a Russian soldier on the run from someone. The army, I suppose. I found him up in this little copse of trees I used to sit in above my house. Anyway, he frightened me, but then it turned out he was just starving and asked me to bring him food. He had a great scar just under his cheekbone that I thought was quite wonderful. I promised I would. The next morning, early, I stole some food from the larder, just like little Pip, and ran back up the hill, but he wasn't there. I waited until afternoon. It was very snowy, and when I couldn't stand the cold anymore, I left the bag of food and went home. That evening someone came to tell my father a soldier had been captured. I don't know what happened to him. Executed, I shouldn't wonder." Lane shook her head sadly. She'd put that story so far inside her that she was surprised to find herself face to face with it again. "I think ever since then I've always thought a scar would be a fine thing."

"Anything of the kind would be fine on you," he said tenderly "Come, a dram of scotch? There are still things to be told."

"So, it wasn't a happy reunion between father and daughter?" Lane asked, now settled into the armchair.

"I imagine for Viola Tilbury it was most unsatisfactory," Darling said. "Here she'd been waiting all these years to be reunited with her father, and she got very short shrift from him. She asked him, calling him 'Daddy,' why he'd left her. First, he tried to say it was all water under the bridge, and then, pressed by the now-crying Viola, he said he hadn't got along with her mother, that he couldn't have stayed another day with her, to which of course she asked, 'What about me?' and he answered, 'What about you? You're all right, aren't you?' It must have been the final crushing blow for her; he had never really considered her at all in his decision to leave."

SIMPSON'S MOTHER HAD taken the two children to bed in the second cabin, and Simpson and his grandmother now sat at Barisoff's table in the light of a kerosene lantern. Barisoff had been invited to sit with them. Coffee cups and a can of condensed milk sat on the table. The murmur of the logs burning in the stove marked a moment of quiet.

"I have decided," said Elaine Cooper. "We will bury him with his own people. He came here to say goodbye to our ancestors, but he did not leave. He should be with them now."

"Not in the church here?" Simpson asked. "There's a Catholic church."

She shook her head. "The government gave us a small reserve. I have a second cousin who still lives there, though most of our people have long since left. Annie Joseph. She will help. It is near a place called Oatscott. That is where he wants to be. You will go and see her tomorrow and ask her if we may bring Pete to be among his ancestors."

"Will there be any trouble with the authorities?" Simpson asked his grandmother.

"There is always trouble with the authorities. You can call that inspector tomorrow before you leave and tell him. He will have to help us with the transport." She took a sip of her coffee. "We will need some sort of coffin. It won't have to be as big as a regular coffin."

At this Barisoff nodded. "I can help with this. I have boards I was maybe going to use for shed. But I don't need shed so much. I can make tomorrow."

"Thank you," said Simpson's grandmother. "When it is the right thing, it will go well."

DARLING STOOD BESIDE O'Brien's desk in a state of momentary thoughtfulness.

"Good morning, sir," his desk man said. "What are you proposing to do with all our guests?"

"For a start, I think we'll let Tilbury go. He's an ass, but I don't believe there's a statute that allows me to hold him just for that. His wife is dangerous because she's unbalanced.

We'll have to charge her with attempting to kill my wife, and attempted murder of a police officer for shooting Ames. I'd be quite happy to lock Turner up for good and throw away the key, but I suppose that's out of the question. I hope to be charging him for the murder of Peter Cooper. He too was intent on killing my wife, so we'll throw that in as well," Darling said. "What's happened with Ames? Is he out of the hospital yet? He might be pleased to learn his missing industrialist is not only found but is a murderer."

"He's—" began O'Brien, when the telephone bell rang. "Nelson Police Station. Yes. He's right here. Let's give him a moment to get up to his office and I'll put you through." O'Brien put his hand over the mouthpiece and nodded at Darling. He gave his boss enough time to doff his hat and coat in his office and then put the call through. It was Tom Simpson.

"Good morning, Inspector. Can I ask how Miss Winslow is? Did she get that cheek looked at?"

"She did indeed, Mr. Simpson. The attending doctor was full of your praises for the patch job you did." Darling paused. "And I was not able to thank you for knocking that knife-wielding idiot over the head and getting her away from him."

"Well, there's one use for the recent war, I suppose. Patchy medical knowledge and the ability to get out of scrapes. What worked was that she understood my intention and acted on it. She is a strong woman. My grandmother would call her a warrior."

"You're right about that," Darling said.

"I'm telephoning because we have discussed the burial of

my uncle Pete. We'd like to bury him on reserve land, near a place called Oatscott. It is not that near and apparently hardly anyone lives there, though my grandmother says we have a relation there. I'm driving there today to discuss it with her."

Darling made notes. "I confess, I've not heard of this place. I'm guessing it is not an official burial ground as I would know it, at a church."

"I guess not, but there are people buried there. My grandmother thinks there might have to be authorities involved."

Darling drummed his fingers on the desk in a quiet roll. "I'll contact someone in Victoria. This is a new thing for me."

"That's more or less what I expected. Can I phone back this afternoon to see what's what?"

"Yes. Can you give me until, say, four?"

"My grandmother says the ancestors want him there, and they will make it possible."

"Let's hope your ancestors are on the job today, then. I've never known bureaucrats to be swift or helpful."

When he had hung up the receiver, Darling turned his seat and looked at Elephant Mountain, whose main contribution was to display a sliding golden light as the promising sunny morning took hold.

CHAPTER THIRTY-SIX

I **'VE BEEN PASSED UP THE** line several times," Darling said into the receiver. "Could we skip any further intervening steps and connect me directly to whoever has the ultimate responsibility? Or are you he?"

"I am Conrad Grimes, head of Provincial Indian Affairs. How can I help?" If he'd been offended by Darling's little rant, he did not show it. The perfect bureaucrat, Darling thought.

"This is Inspector Frederick Darling, of the Nelson Police. I have a request from the family of a deceased member of the Lakes tribe, who would like to bury him on reserve land at a place called Oatscott. I just want to check on procedure to be followed, if any."

There was a long silence.

"Lakes? I'll have to look them up. We don't have many dealings with them."

Darling could hear a rustle of paper and a hastily muttered order to someone to get information from files. He waited.

"I've just asked my secretary to get me the relevant file.

In any case, we will need to place one of our officials at the scene. The Indian Act has recently changed to allow for religious practice, but we'll have to make sure they are on reserve land. This will take anywhere from two to four weeks."

"Four weeks? Why can't it be sooner than that?"

"I don't have the personnel to just send people willy-nilly around the province at a moment's notice."

Darling took a breath and reminded himself to be patient. "But—"

"Look, Inspector, you can't have these people just burying people wherever they want. If we didn't monitor what goes on with those Indians, they'd be planting bodies all over the place, and then no doubt claiming it as Indian land. Ah. Here we are. Lakes, Arrow."

Darling could hear the rustling of paper and waited. One thing was certain: he was going to do his damnedest to keep the Simpsons from having to wait.

"You know—Darling, is it? They effectively have no presence in the province. They just upped stakes and left more than forty-five years ago. Some of 'em moved south into Washington State or joined up with other tribes north and west of there in the Okanagan. They were given a reserve in 1902, at their request, I might add, but didn't bother sticking around. Claimed the land they'd been given was not right. There is, practically speaking, no one there now. Why do they need to bury someone here anyway?"

Darling explained the circumstances of Peter Cooper's murder.

The agent listened and said, "Well, that's as may be.

I'm still going to have to send someone out there. That's going to take time."

"Look," said Darling, "this family has been through enough. They would like to bury their family member and get back to their lives in Washington. In any case, I can't keep the body here indefinitely, and I doubt the Americans would be happy about the remains being dragged back across the border in the family car." He paused. "What if I can be the official eyes and ears you seem to need? I'm in charge of the Nelson Police Station, so I have legal standing. If the problem is that you are worried that they stick to reserve land, I can be there to attest to whatever you need me to. Give me the coordinates, and I'll submit a report, in triplicate if you'd like." He did not add, "You sound like the kind of man who likes things in triplicate," which hovered dangerously on his lips.

"I HAVE TO get back to work," Ames was saying. "The station is running short-handed, they have two prisoners on hand who have to be processed, and there's all that business of the fire to be sorted, and the inspector is tied up with this body that was found up in New Denver." He was sitting lengthwise on the couch in his living room at home with a pink, blue, and yellow crocheted blanket over his knees, and was obliged just at that moment to lean forward to have a pillow tucked behind his back by Tina Van Eyck.

"Lunch is just coming!" his mother called from the kitchen.

"I'll stay for lunch. Your mother's gone to a lot of trouble, especially with her wrist still bandaged. But then

I must actually go to work. Poor Dad is on his own with a radiator and an axle. You, of course, will do what you're told." Tina did not wait for a reply but went into the kitchen to help with lunch.

Ames, in the sitting room, could hear the quiet soothing sound of their conversation from the kitchen, and had to confess that as ambitious as he was, he was feeling pleasantly drowsy after the exertion of leaving the hospital with instructions and painkillers. He had an elaborate bandage over the wound and his arm in a sling to keep his shoulder immobile for the next couple of weeks. The sun was pouring in the window, making the outdoors look warmer than it was. He woke from his doze to see Tina standing over him with her jacket and hat on.

"And you wanted to dash off to work. I think your mom has kept your lunch warm." She leaned over and kissed him on the cheek and made for the door, where Mrs. Ames was waiting. "Are you sure you'll be okay?" Tina asked her. "He's an awful handful. You're very brave to tackle him on your own."

Mrs. Ames laughed. "What can I do? I'm his mother. I'm used to it. And I should say, as a testimonial, he's not that bad most days. I should think anyone could get used to it."

"I'm right over here!" Ames said.

Tina looked at him and shook her head. "Good luck. Call me if you need reinforcements." She gave Mrs. Ames a quick hug and was away.

Ames slurped his tomato soup and ate his grilled cheese, feeling slightly mutinous.

"It's no good taking on like that. She's a lovely girl. I'm

only sorry that you are bound to mess this one up as well." His mother was sitting in the armchair opposite him with a cup of tea. "As you know, I never did care for Violet. She was bossy and hell-bent on changing you to fit her idea of what a husband ought to be. An iron and disapproving will, and not that bright."

"You haven't noticed, I suppose, that Tina can be quite bossy?"

"Well, yes. But she doesn't want to change you. To hear her tell it, she quite likes you just the way you are. She thinks you're kind and sensitive. I tried to disabuse her, of course, but you know what girls in love are." She sighed and sipped her tea.

Ames put his empty soup bowl onto the coffee table. "Now you're being ridiculous. She dropped me like a hot potato just before this all happened. Abandoned me at the New Star Café to finish my dinner on my own. No. Take it from me, she's just feeling sorry for me."

"I never said she thought you were particularly bright about women, but she does love you. All you really have to try to do is not ruin everything. Do you think you can manage that, at least? As to going to work, we'll see how you are tomorrow. Darling has called several times to check on you. I can't imagine *he* loves you that much, so he must need you back at work."

"I don't see where you're building up my confidence," Ames complained, popping the last of his sandwich into his mouth.

SMITH AND MR. Collins, who ran the fishing tackle outfit, Mr. Clear, the pharmacist from the Rexall, Mr. Douglas, the carpenter, and even Carruthers from the service station stood in the dining room of Lorenzo's restaurant. They had asked Iverson from the equipment supply store to come along. The smell of smoke still hung in the air.

"It's not too bad in here," Carruthers commented. "Still smells. Might need a good scrubbing and a coat of paint."

"It's the kitchen that took the brunt," Smith said, pocketing the keys he had picked up from Mrs. Vitali and pushing his way into the kitchen area through the charred, damp, smoke-stained door. The four men stood in the blackened wreckage of the narrow kitchen shaking their heads.

"It's a real shame," the pharmacist said. "This is what comes of letting things get out of hand. I didn't see it at first. I was hearing the rumours about the police, and all that really unnerved me. Always thought Inspector Darling was the real thing, and I let myself get doubtful because of the rumours. We should never have let Tilbury take control of the goings-on at the Chamber. I blame myself. When he got on his hind legs objecting to letting 'foreigners' into the organization, I just thought it was easiest to let it go. He can be nasty if he puts his mind to it. My own grandparents came here from Ireland not that long ago. This is the result of letting that kind of talk go unchallenged."

"You can hardly blame yourself for what that crazy wife of his did. I hear she's as mad as a hatter. But I do think we ought to get behind fixing things up in the future. Now then, Douglas, Iverson, what do you think needs doing here? It doesn't look to me like any of this is salvageable.

What's it going to cost to put it back together?" He watched while Iverson and Douglas walked around peering at the charred remains of the equipment and cupboards. "The fire chief's daughter has apparently been collecting money in the café, and it's adding up to quite a healthy sum."

DARLING HAD JUST listened with satisfaction to Terrell explaining that Smith and some other businessmen were going to take the repair of the restaurant in hand, when a call was put through from Tom Simpson.

"I have good news for you," Darling said. "The Indian agent is going to let me stand in for the government. It's not a position I relish, I must say, but it means we can go ahead without delay."

"Thank you, Inspector. I really appreciate the trouble you've gone to. I have been to see the Elder at the reserve in Oatscott, to ask if Uncle Pete can be buried there, among our people. We would like to proceed tomorrow, if that can be arranged?"

"I will make sure of it. We'll get the van to bring his remains to New Denver, and we can follow you to the reserve."

"Can you ask Miss Winslow if she would like to come? I was telling Mrs. Joseph, the Elder who lives there, about her and her interest in our people, and she would like to meet her. I know my grandmother would be pleased, too. I warn you, it is a long trip. It is more than two hours from here, and that is if the weather holds. My grandmother says it is traditional to conduct a funeral in the morning, but I think under the circumstances . . ."

"We'll leave early and try to get you there as soon as possible. Do you have a coffin?"

"Mr. Barisoff made a small coffin for him." He chuckled. "My grandmother really likes him, which is unusual, because our people didn't always get along with the Russian settlers."

"HELLO, DARLING. ARE you calling to tell me you will be home late? I have a nice pork chop from a nearby farm for you."

"No, I am calling to tell you that you have been invited to the funeral of Pete Cooper, which we have arranged for tomorrow. There is an elderly woman who seems to be almost the only one living on the reserve, and she has expressed an interest in meeting you. I've looked for the place on a map, and it is quite out of the way, on the other side of the Columbia. Will I be eating that pork chop on my own like a grandee, or have you got one for yourself?"

"Never mind that. We can't go empty-handed. If she is an old lady living so far out of the way, there must be things she could use. And the children—I should get something for the children. All right. Thanks for telling me. I'll rush off to Bales before he closes and pick up some things."

CHAPTER THIRTY-SEVEN

THE DAY DAWNED FOR THE funeral of Pete Cooper, the sky a mix of grey and streaks of pale blue and gold. Darling hoped they would balance out on the blue side as the day progressed. It would not be particularly warm, and rain would make the day difficult. The driver of the van carrying the remains had left Nelson before dawn, and he now sat at the turnoff at King's Cove as instructed, and waited, yawning and smoking, the window open a crack for some fresh morning air.

Lane, wearing her only suit, a dark green tweed, and a black hat, had opted for sensible lace-up shoes. Darling wore the dark suit he'd worn for their wedding.

"And there he is," Lane said, pointing as they came down the curve of the turnoff. The van was across the road. Flicking the cigarette onto the road, the driver put his vehicle in gear and waited for Darling to drive ahead of him.

"According to Simpson, his grandmother would call you a warrior," Darling remarked, checking the rear-view mirror to make sure he wasn't getting too far ahead of the van.

"That sounds like something good."

"It sounds like something not conducive to domestic bliss. Or leaving my cases alone. Because here we are again."

"You can hardly blame me for this. As you pointed out yourself, I was just trying to help an old lady. It's not my fault her so-called carer turned out to be a murderous ex-lover. Nor can you strictly blame me, come to that, for Mr. Barisoff's finding poor Pete Cooper buried in his garden."

"You say that," he said good-naturedly, "but I remain suspicious. How's the cheek?"

"Slightly achy. What will you have to do today?"

"You mean as a government envoy? They want me to verify that the burial takes place on reserve land and send a report. I would rather just be the respectful mourner."

At Barisoff's, the remains, wrapped in the sheet from the morgue, were carefully transferred into the coffin. Mrs. Cooper, Mrs. Simpson, and the children stood by as the coffin was moved into the van. Lane was next to the old lady, who stood very still.

In spite of the passage of twenty-five years, Lane thought, to have lost a child to a senseless murder must be almost insupportable. She reached out and touched Mrs. Cooper's arm.

"Come, Miss Winslow. Help me collect what we have to take," Mrs. Cooper said to her.

Lane followed the old lady into the cabin. Mrs. Cooper was moving slowly, as if today her age told on her even more. Laid out on the table were two wooden apple boxes with a number of paper-wrapped parcels and some canning jars that contained canned berries, and others with dried berries, and another jar with something else Lane could not identify.

Mrs. Cooper saw Lane's puzzled look. "That is dried camas root. It's delicious. I bet you never ate anything like it." She waved her hand over the boxes. "When I knew we would have to bury him, I brought what he would want for the meal. I have smoked salmon and smoked deer meat as well. We're going a long way, but no one will go hungry!" She nodded as Lane picked up one of the boxes.

Mrs. Cooper stopped her with a look. She nodded her head in the direction of the activity outside. "You know, he's a lot like his uncle Pete. Easygoing like him. He always took things as he found them. But since he's been back from the war he just can't sit still. I think it was his uncle Pete calling him. I hope that when this is over, he's going to be a little more like his old self."

"You know," said Lane with a smile, "that's exactly what my grandmother would say. I'll be right back for the second one."

BARISOFF WATCHED THE preparations, his expression sombre. When the Simpsons were getting into their car, he went and held the passenger door open for Mrs. Cooper. "God go with you," he said, taking her hand for a moment.

She nodded. "Thank you, Mr. Barisoff."

The drive was long. It was thirty miles north to Nakusp on a winding road made muddy by recent rain and snowmelt. They turned and drove for more than two hours south before Simpson, in the lead car, began to slow and finally stop. They were at a small landing with a cable ferry that would take them over this narrow stretch of the Columbia River.

On the ferry, Lane leaned out of the passenger window and watched the river flowing south, sparkling in the sunlight. She could feel the thrum of the engine underneath the car. We are crossing the river Styx, the boundary between the earth and the underworld, she thought.

Once across, the cortège made its way very slowly and carefully, climbing for some distance on a narrow, rutted dirt road. They could hear the engine of the van struggling with the climb. At first, when the procession finally stopped, Lane thought it looked like just more of the same scrappy forest they'd been going through, but then she saw that a path wound into the wood. Simpson and his family alighted from their car, and Lane and Darling joined them, staying a little behind.

"We'll go down here," Simpson said to Darling. "We should get the coffin out and put it here. The burial ground is up that way." He pointed up toward a rising hill. "That way the man who drove the van can get off home."

Darling nodded and went to talk to the driver, who got out and helped Darling move the coffin onto the ground away from the road.

Even as they began their walk along the path, they could hear the van revving and the gears grinding as the driver attempted to turn it and head back to Nelson. The children, after their long confinement in the car, chased each other around their mother and older brother, squealing and laughing.

They arrived at a slightly sloped clearing, surrounded by tall evergreens. At the top of the slope there was a cabin, and further toward the middle a fire crackled near a long table that had been made by putting boards on supporting sawhorses. Coming toward them was a short elderly woman with deep weathered lines in her face. The woman approached Mrs. Cooper and spoke to her in their language, her eyes crinkling in a smile.

I would like to be so warm and self-contained when I am her age, Lane thought. It was impossible to tell her age, but Lane had the sudden fancy that she had lived forever. Two older men joined them from where they had been tending the fire. There seemed to be no one else there, and she wondered if these three were the last people living on this reserve.

Simpson cleared his throat and spoke in a formal voice. "This is Annie Joseph, who is an Elder who lives here, and she helped me to find the right place. Thank you for making us welcome here. And this is Mr. Al Benjamin, and this is Mr. John Seward." Simpson introduced each one of the visitors. When he got to Darling, Annie Joseph smiled and took his hand in both of hers. "Inspector Darling. The government man. You must be the first one to ever make it this far!" There followed a formal shaking of hands, led by Mrs. Cooper and Mrs. Simpson, and then Darling and Lane, with the children bringing up the rear.

"You are all welcome here," Mrs. Joseph said. "I have made some tea that I got right from these woods here.

We call it Hudson's Bay tea. We will drink that and get to know each other. I know you had a heck of a long drive to get here." She led them to a little table in front of the cabin where enamelled and porcelain cups were set out next to a kettle.

Tom had brought Barisoff's shovel from the car and put it against the cabin. "I'll be going up in a minute to dig the grave."

As they sat, Annie Joseph pointed to the long table. "I had the boys make that so that we could have our meal there."

Until that moment the two children had been standing shyly by their mother. Angie pulled her mother's hand. "Can we go play?"

Mrs. Cooper said something to her daughter, who turned to the children. "Don't go far. We have to collect some cedar boughs in a minute here."

"You better take a cookie with you," Annie Joseph said, holding a plate out to the children.

Cookies in hand, the children ran off to explore while the adults sat with their cups of tea.

The sun filtered through the stands of trees that surrounded the clearing, and Lane took a deep draught of the pine-scented air. "This is very good," she said. "It reminds me a little of teas at my grandmother's house. They collected flowers and things from the woods near where we lived. I wish I'd paid attention to what they were!"

"It's good for you, too. I drink it all the time, and look at me!" She smiled and patted her heart. "Maybe later I can show you some of the plants you can gather for tea."

When Simpson had had his tea, he took up his shovel. "I'm going up to the burial ground now. Would you like to come and see it? It's very beautiful up there," he said to Lane and Darling.

"Yes, indeed, thank you," Lane said, standing. They excused themselves and followed Simpson and the two older men along a path that disappeared into the trees.

His mother got up too. "Thank you for the tea, Grandmother. I'll take the kids and go collect those cedar boughs. If they haven't fallen down a cliff yet!" She moved away from the house and called out, "Hey, you kids, let's go. We have a job to do!"

As they wound through the woods, Darling and Lane could hear the high-pitched calls of the children. The path began to climb steeply. Lane was grateful for the shoes she'd chosen. She thought about the two old ladies, alone now together, talking, free of the constraints of the formality that accompanied the tea drinking. What would they talk about? She knew that Annie Joseph must be asking Elaine Cooper about her son and commiserating with her at his terrible lonely fate. Annie Joseph, she thought, would be a very comforting presence for the dead man's mother.

They cleared the trees finally and found themselves, panting a bit from the climb, on a bluff with a magnificent view of the valley and the river below, and the mountains extending away beyond.

"Here. I'll show you," Simpson said, beckoning Lane and Darling. The two older men had rolled up their sleeves and were beginning to mark out the place where they would dig the grave.

Leading them toward a line of trees, Simpson pointed. "See here? These are the old graves, from the old days. They used to bury people sitting up, so the graves are round like that."

Lane and Darling saw a number of circular depressions, most of them overcome with moss and small plants, but in several four stones were just visible placed in a circle in the middle of the depressions.

"Those four stones are typical. Over here, there are graves more like what you might be used to." They walked a little way back toward where the two men had begun digging, and he pointed to several rectangular graves with mounds of dirt on them. "Now people leave something that mattered to the person. A toy, a hat, even a pair of boots, like over there."

"Would anything be buried with the body?" Lane asked.

Simpson shook his head. "No. It's not really the way. Just a little something from their life. That's it. I'd better get over there and help those two old fellows! You two feel free to explore and enjoy the view. I'll give a shout when we're done."

LANE AND DARLING stood at the edge of the bluff looking out. "For a final resting place, it's hard to beat," Darling commented. He put his arm around her shoulder.

"Those two old ladies are lovely. I'd like to be like Mrs. Joseph if I make it to such a venerable old age. It would be wonderful to be wise and have some perspective about life."

"I've always wondered if old people are really wise, or they just seem that way because they've seen it all before," Darling commented, taking her hand. "Let's have a stroll about."

"Maybe that's what wisdom is," Lane said. They heard a sudden shriek of laughter from the children, somewhere in the woods. "Or maybe *that* is," she added.

THE CHILDREN AND their mother were back, each carrying an armful of cedar boughs, five-year-old Bobby dragging his with some effort, the fronds trailing on the ground. Lane and Darling had followed them down to the cabin, and Lane offered to help Mrs. Joseph with clearing up the tea things but was waved away with a smile.

"Is this enough, Grandma?" Angie asked. "We picked a whole bunch!"

"That sure is. There comes Tom, so they must be ready for us."

The procession made its way up the hill until they arrived at the road. Simpson, Benjamin, and Seward collected the coffin and led the way to the gravesite. Elaine Cooper and Annie Joseph were directly behind them, followed by Mrs. Simpson and the children, Lane and Darling at the rear.

At the graveside, Elaine Cooper instructed Tom to line the small grave with the boughs while she prayed quietly. Tom waved Darling over, and the two of them adjusted ropes under the coffin and lowered it into the grave.

Elaine Cooper had carried a cloth bundle with her and opened it now and took out a leather rattle. She marked a steady beat and then began to sing. The chant of the song and the gentle, rhythmic beat of the rattle was suddenly joined by the call of a crow, high in one of the trees.

"That is the song of our family," Elaine Cooper said after her chant died away. She handed the instrument to her daughter. "Please sing your brother's song. He has not heard it for so many years."

Mrs. Simpson looked reluctant for a moment, but then took up a song, shaking the rattle more tentatively than her mother had. In the silence that followed, Tom lifted a shovelful of earth, and his grandmother took a handful and threw it into the grave, followed by each of the others in turn. When that was done, Tom and the two helpers filled the grave.

"He is home now, and I bet he'd like something to eat," Elaine Cooper said.

LANE HELPED AS Mrs. Cooper and Tom's mother unloaded the boxes of food and spread the contents onto the plank table. A blue enamelled coffee pot was on a grill over the fire, already sending up steam and the heady smell of coffee. It seemed to Lane to be a lot of food for such a small group, but then she remembered her own grandmother. Always better to have too much than too little.

Elaine Cooper walked along the row of food with a small plate, taking food from each dish, and speaking. "These roots are the first food, and these berries are the sweet of the land. Of the meats, fish is honoured first, and then deer." When she was finished, she said, "This is the spirit plate." She began a prayer, offered the plate to the four directions, and then called the children over. "Bobby and Angie, you take that out and put it under those trees over there so they can enjoy too."

Angie and Bobby, pleased to be given an important job, walked carefully toward the edge of the wood, each holding one side of the plate unsteadily.

"Please, eat and drink," Elaine Cooper said, indicating the gallon jug of water. "Could you fill those cups?" she said to Lane. As guests, Lane and Darling were given plates first, and then Mr. Benjamin and Mr. Seward followed up, heaping their plates with smoked fish. Annie Joseph, who felt herself the hostess, demurred until Lane and Darling had helped themselves, and only then did Mrs. Simpson begin to fill plates for Bobby and Angie.

"Take as much as you like," Elaine Cooper said. "When you eat lots, he gets to eat too."

The coffee had begun to bubble, and the steam coiled upward into the trees around the clearing. "Miss Winslow, give that dried root a try," Mrs. Cooper said.

Lane took the root on her plate and gave it a nibble. "That's delicious," she said after a few moments. "Sweet and crunchy. I must learn how to prepare it."

"She could tell you that. She's been doing it her whole life," Mrs. Cooper said, nodding toward the cabin.

Lane watched Darling with Seward and Benjamin standing near the cabin, plates in hand, talking together. She had moved on to the smoked salmon, so like smoked fish she had eaten as a child. Darling had his plate and was listening and nodding as Benjamin pointed outward in the direction of the river.

Lane turned back toward the fire and saw Mrs. Simpson about to lay cups out on the table. "Here, let me help. That coffee smells divine."

"There's nothing quite like coffee boiling on an open fire," agreed Mrs. Simpson. She had a can of condensed milk and pushed the triangular opener into the lid on two sides. She moved the coffee onto the table and pulled the lid open, splashing water from the glass jug into it to help sink the grounds.

"Actually," said Lane, after she'd poured a dollop of condensed milk into her mug and watched it swirl, delighting in the contrast of hot coffee and cool spring air, like this, under the sky, "I might have another piece of that camas root."

WHEN THEY HAD eaten, Elaine Cooper gathered up another plate of food and made a motion with her head, and Tom took his uncle Pete's rucksack. She turned to Lane and Darling. "Mr. and Mrs. Darling, I know Annie Joseph would like to talk to both of you for a while. We'll be back soon."

As Pete Cooper's family made their way back up the hill, a discussion broke out about what could be put on his grave.

"Can I put a marble on for him?" asked Bobby. "I brought this one. It's my best one!" He held a blue cat's eye in the palm of his hand.

"He's going to like that," his grandmother said, rubbing his head.

"I have my favourite ribbon," Angie said, holding up a green ribbon.

"That's good," Elaine Cooper said, nodding. "He's going to like all those things."

Plunking herself into the chair by her cabin, looking

happy to be sitting, Annie Joseph patted the empty chair beside her. "Here, you take a load off your feet, government man, and you too, Mrs. Darling." She beamed at them. "I heard you are interested in our people. It's a story I'm always happy to tell."

TOM, WHO HAD held the folded rucksack in his arms, placed it on the grave mound near the plate of food. All the hope, all the joy that had filled his young uncle when he had driven off with this bag, had come to this. He angrily wiped a tear away and stepped back. His mother rubbed his arm and put a rusted toy car beside the rucksack, and then nodded at the children, who had been watching their brother, looking anxious. They put their offerings on the mound, Tom put an arm around each of them, and they leaned against him.

"That inspector brought these back to me," Elaine Cooper said, holding out the remains of the woven bag and the little stone frog. She positioned the cloth on the grave and then turned to Tom. "Pete always said he was going to bring you back a frog. I bet he'd want you to have this one."

IT WAS NEARING evening. Tom Simpson had been instructed to go fetch a box to be left with Annie Joseph. It contained sugar and flour and cans of various kinds. Lane was reminded that they too had a box and went to collect it. Darling followed her. "I don't feel I've done much here today but eat and talk. The least I can do is carry the box."

"It's been beautiful, don't you think? I hope Mrs. Cooper

and the Simpsons have had some measure of comfort, coming to this lovely place. Here, let me get these bags of candy out." Lane took the bags and went to find Mrs. Simpson, who was washing cups and plates in a metal washtub.

"I bought the children a couple of bags of penny candy. Are they allowed to have it?" Lane asked her.

For perhaps the first time that day, she saw Simpson's mother smile. She moved a strand of hair off her forehead with the back of her wrist and said, "Sure. That's nice of you. Angie, Bobby! Come over here. This lady has something for you," she called out to where the children were standing, talking shyly to Annie Joseph.

Lane stooped down to be at their level and gave them each their little brown bag of candy. "It's been very nice to meet you, Angie and Bobby. Whenever you come up to Canada again, you must come and visit me. And I hope you like jawbreakers. I've never seen them before. They're just enormous!"

Angie, ever the eldest, gravely took both bags and handed one to her little brother. "Thank you, miss." She gave her brother a little bump with her shoulder.

"It was nice of you both to come." Mary Simpson nodded up toward the burial ground. "I never stopped missing him. I always wondered what his life was like when he left us." She smiled and shook her head. Her children had emptied their bags on the plank table and were going through the contents. "I used to boss him around just like she does. But then I had to go away to this boarding school in Spokane. Maybe if I didn't have to go, he never would have thought about leaving us like that. By the time he was old enough to go, they closed the school, so at least he didn't have to go through that."

Approaching Lane and Darling, Simpson said, "You have a long way to go tonight. We are going to stay on here for a few days. My grandmother and Mrs. Joseph have a lot of catching up to do." He shifted onto one leg and looked momentarily at the ground. "I want to thank you both. For coming, and for finding out who killed him. A lot of times that doesn't happen. It gives us all some peace. You would have liked him, Miss Winslow." He nodded at her. "I know you would have."

"I'm certain that is true," Lane said, offering her hand. "I have to thank you. If I hadn't met you, I would never have known the whole important history of this place. I will never see it the same way again. And thank you for saving my life."

Darling offered his hand. "Good luck with that job, and safe journey when you head home. And if you are ever back this way, you must come and see us. I can always be reached through the station."

DUSK WAS CASTING deep shadows across the clearing as they stood together at the moment of parting. Elaine Cooper said, "Now we are grateful that we had this day together, and we give thanks four times. *Lim limpt.*"

The others took up the thanks. "*Lim limpt, lim limpt, lim limpt.*"

Holding a bag, Elaine Cooper approached Lane as she was starting up the hill to where the car was parked. "You have a long way to get home. We always send someone away with food for the journey." She smiled. "You like that root so much, I gave you extra!"

"I will never forget this day, not if I live to be a hundred," Lane said, taking Darling's hand on the way back to the car.

CHAPTER THIRTY-EIGHT

I T WAS SATURDAY, AND LANE and Darling were on their way into town. It had been one of those days you get even in early April, when there was a sampling of all possible weathers. A massive hail had greeted them at breakfast, clattering against the windows, and now, several hours later, the sun had emerged, and the temperature outside was almost warm.

"It is a country," said Lane, watching the passing landscape, "that can, as my grandmother says, hide a multitude of sins. Some of them real actual sins. Look at those mountains across the lake there. They look wild and pristine and like someplace never trodden by anyone, but underneath could be the whole now-silent history of generations of people, like Mr. Simpson's people, who've just been unceremoniously moved along. Or it could be full of people hiding out, refugees from their own mismanaged lives. Didn't Ames work a case while we were in England with an old lady who ran away from a respectable English family and lived like a hermit in the woods across the lake? And now Turner, growing a beard and an uncouth manner and hiding out just over the next mountain, as it were, leaving his daughter to a life of uncertainty and eventual madness."

Darling nodded. "It does change one's view of things. It's so easy to sink into the idea that things are right as they are, and always have been. I am sure the Lakes People never imagined that their way of life would end, and we, who collectively caused it, imagine our lives are the right ones, the ones that will always be the way they are. I can't imagine, for example, that little gas station in New Denver not being manned by a grizzled old relic like Berenson. But it was all an illusion. Berenson was Turner, and all he thought he'd gained was draining away like Stella Bisset's senses." He looked at Lane. It would be nice to live in the illusion that this—Lane, the lake, his work, at least—was forever. "It's a good thing Hiro Wakada has agreed to run that little store until it's sold. Gas stations are few and far between. Mr. Simpson expressed some interest in it at one point, surprisingly. That and Miss Bisset's cottage."

"Why surprisingly? In a way it's his, that cottage," Lane said.

"Well, I mean, he'd got plans to take a job at a radio station where he lives in Washington. It would mean leaving his family."

"Or, if you look at it from the point of view of all his ancestors, coming home to his family. You know, my ancestors were largely from Scotland, even though none of us has lived there for a couple of generations, until my grandparents went 'back' there. But when I went to see them after they moved from Bilderlingshof, I felt the tug of it. Almost visceral, as if the ground itself was pulling me, saying, 'This is home.' Fantastical, I know, especially as I'd never been in Scotland in the whole course of my life before that, but I felt it."

"I spent the war in England, where my people presumably come from, and I can't say I had the same experience."

Lane smiled. "That's just because you are a block of wood, not a sensitive like I am."

"Substitute the word 'nuisance' for 'sensitive' and we are in agreement."

Darling parked the car near the police station, and they walked down to Lorenzo's restaurant, the main object of their afternoon trip into Nelson. The front door was open, and there was a tumult of construction sounds coming through it. Inside they found the curtains had been removed, and the tables were piled in the corner with the chairs. The kitchen door had been taken out, and from inside the noise of hammering and sawing had supremacy. The smell of ash was being replaced with the smell of fresh sawdust. Lorenzo and Olivia were standing in the doorway with Mr. McAvity and April looking on.

"This looks like progress!" Lane said enthusiastically.

Lorenzo turned and reached out and took her hand, and then Darling's. He was leaning on a cane and had to clear his throat before he spoke with his new, slightly raspy voice. His body showed all too clearly the ordeal he had undergone, but his face shone with its old light. "You have come to see what good people can do.

Miss April and Mr. Smith and everyone help so much to raise money. I get very good deal on things for kitchen. Stove, refrigerator, everything."

"And we will join Chamber of Commerce. Special invitation," said Olivia, rolling her eyes, but smiling.

Lorenzo gave a little shrug. "No more wine, is only thing. Is bad law, but what can you do?"

"It's what I believe is called 'cupboard love' on the part of the Chamber," Darling said. "They want you back open as quickly as possible so they can get a decent meal again." He turned to April. "Congratulations on your money-raising efforts. From my position, where I mostly see bad things going on, I realize that a few malcontents with loud voices can completely colour one's view of a place. It really turns out that Nelson is full of fair-minded people." He shook her hand warmly. "By the way, do you still want to join the police?"

April cast a warning look, but it was too late.

"What?" said her father. "Join what police? I hope you haven't been entertaining any of her mad ideas, Inspector."

"It's not a mad idea, really. I told her she'd have to go to the coast to the academy. It's all your fault, as I see it. You've taught her what it's like to be of service."

"Her mother would be turning over in her grave!" McAvity said with the grudging air of a man who knew he was going to lose.

April kissed her father on the cheek. "I knew you'd see reason!"

"I don't see reason at all. But I suppose if it's something you really want, there's not much more for me to say. Will they even accept women in the force, Darling?"

"There have been women in the police in Vancouver since before the Great War. They still have a somewhat limited role, but that will change. I think the war has considerably altered how women are seen."

"Ha!" said April.

"What I learn from my Olivia is women much stronger than men. You want something to happen? Ask a woman," said Lorenzo, smiling fondly at his wife.

"Now I am going to ask you to come home and rest, and then we plan menu for new restaurant. Doctor say he won't need cane for long, but for now, yes. Everything good take time," said his wife, indicating the door with a tilt of her head. "Thank you, Inspector, Signora, for coming to see. Is so wonderful, no?"

"It is wonderful, indeed," Lane said, kissing Olivia's cheek.

"Only one moment," Lorenzo said to his wife, and he moved to one side, gesturing for Darling to follow. When they were out of earshot, he shuffled a bit with embarrassment. "I only want to say so sorry for way I treat you. I was scared. I heard rumour that you take bribe money from me, and I want everyone to think we are not friends, so no one think you can do such a thing."

"My dear Lorenzo," Darling said, taking his hand. "You have nothing to apologize for. I completely understand. Now, let's hear no more about it, eh?"

"I HAVE TO stop in at the station for ten minutes. I need to make sure the transfer of the two prisoners pending their trials is in order," Darling said.

"Oh, good. There's something I'd like to pick up. I'll meet you back at the car. Should I pick up something for poor Ames, stuck at home as he is?"

"I suppose you want to mollycoddle him too, now? He's coming back to work soon. Does he need all this fuss made of him? Anyway, that's what the lady mechanic is for. You can telephone him when we get home and ask after him, if you insist."

Smiling at the return of her husband's normal demeanour, no doubt brought on by the immense relief of Ames being out of danger, Lane turned and made her way to the electronics store. Tilbury, she knew, was back at work in the hardware store and also had what she wanted, but it would be a frosty Friday before she darkened his door again.

Mr. Smith was all smiles when Lane mentioned what he had done for the Vitalis and the restaurant.

"It was nothing. A redress for what they've gone through. They should be open again in a couple of weeks," he said. "The wife and I will be first through the door. We're their neighbours. Lovely people. Shouldn't happen to a dog what happened to them. I blame myself for not standing up."

"But you did," said Lane. "That's the main thing."

"You are kind to say so. Now then, how can I help you?"

Lane said what she wanted and, the transaction complete, she took her purchase and stowed it in the back of the car and went into the station to pass the time with Sergeant O'Brien until her husband was at liberty.

"Good afternoon, Mrs. Darling," O'Brien said, his smile broader than usual. "Recovered from your misadventure?"

"That's a perfect name for it; it was indeed the furthest

thing from an adventure. I'm dandy, thanks. Better than poor Sergeant Ames, I'm sure."

"He's young. He'll mend. I believe he's going a little crazy under the constant care of his mother and is itching to get back to work."

"I must thank you for staying on the line the whole time. I think I felt a little stronger knowing you were there."

O'Brien coloured. "You were very brave, Mrs. Darling."

She smiled and shook her head. "I've just seen Mr. Smith at the electronics outfit. He and his business chums have really done a wonderful thing, helping out Mr. and Mrs. Vitali like that."

"Good civic spirit, that," agreed O'Brien. "I guess I'm going to have to break the habit of a lifetime and take the missus out to eat there. Don't normally go out for supper when there's always a good meal to be had at home. Here's the inspector." He gave them a wave as they left, and then added, "See that you keep out of trouble, Mrs. D."

"Out of the mouths of whatever the hell he is," remarked Darling, holding open the car door with a grim smile.

APRIL WAS SITTING with her father over a mug of tea in the office of the firehouse. They'd strolled back from seeing the progress at the restaurant and were feeling quite pleased. He was leaning back in his chair and regarding her over the steam from his cup. "I'm glad you have a few minutes before your shift. I wanted to have a word."

April's heart sank. "Look, if this is about me wanting to go into the police, I'm pretty determined. I mean, I don't have to go right away, but there's a summer course in Vancouver I can start with. It starts in May, and I'd be done by September. You'd hardly know I was gone."

He smiled fondly. "Hardly at all." He straightened up and moved about uncomfortably in his chair. "That's not what I wanted to talk about, actually. It was something else."

Unable to imagine what else could be on his mind, she sat, looking at him curiously.

"Now listen, I wouldn't normally interfere in your personal life; you're a grown woman now, after all. But . . ." He stopped and rubbed his hand across his mouth.

Colouring, April said, "But what?" She feared where this was going.

"Look, I've never met a nicer young man, and that's the truth. I took to him right away. We're both from the Maritimes, I guess, that's part of it. He's smart, honest, a hard worker, got a good education."

"Dad, what are you blathering on about? Who is?" But she knew, and her heart sank. She regretted her question immediately. She didn't think she could bear to have her closest feelings exposed suddenly, shattered by this parental scrutiny.

"Young Terrell. I'm not blind, Pumpkin." He stopped and looked distractedly out the door at his fire truck. "Under normal circumstances, I'd be thrilled."

She went from dismay to irritation. "Not that it's the way you say it is, or that it's any of your business, but what 'normal circumstances' would those be?"

"Well, after all this business with the Vitalis. Look how people have treated them, even after all these years. Some people can't seem to get past the fact that they are foreigners."

"First of all, Constable Terrell is not foreign, he's Canadian, probably for more generations than we are. And, by the way, the Vitalis are Canadian as well. And anyway, look how everyone came through, giving money to my fund and all."

"Yes, all right. Point taken. But it wouldn't be easy. The children might not be accepted. Would it be fair on them?"

"Children? I barely know this man and I'm already having children with him? Really, Dad, you should get a hobby. Anyway, you're barking up the wrong tree."

"I don't think I am. And if you want to know my real concern, it's that he's a policeman. It's a dangerous job. Look at poor Sergeant Ames. It was just nip and tuck that he didn't die. You could end up a widow, and I couldn't bear that for you."

"With my fatherless children," April retorted. "Really, Dad. The whole thing is moot. Even if I did care about him, which I don't," she said, crossing her fingers behind her back, "I wouldn't expose him to the scorn and disparagement of the people around here by dating him, so you can relax."

"Ah. There you are selling him short, my dear. I bet he'd cross any ocean for the girl he loved. And by the way, he's asked me if he could take you for a spin on his Triumph tomorrow. I've told him you'd be glad to."

April got up. "Oh, for Pete's sake, Dad. Make up your mind!" She kissed him and went off to the café.

TOM HAD RIDDEN for an hour, and now sat, his horse shifting under him as it pulled up mouthfuls of grass. He was looking north at the stretch of flatland that rose like a golden sea toward the foothills. He suddenly realized that he felt no pull to go there, that the dark urgency inside him was gone. He felt free for the first time in a long while. I could go back, he thought. I could live in that cabin and run that store. He put his hand on his chest, unconsciously feeling for the frog now in its new bag, around his neck. He remembered his grandmother's story of the frogs that saved their people. He wondered, though it had failed his uncle, if it had brought this new quiet to him now.

"C'mon, boy," he said to his horse, turning west. It would be dark in an hour, and he had promised he would be back. This same pressure had defied his desire to feel still inside his whole life. The war had made it stronger. The idea that you could get away, that you should get away, that there was a place out there somewhere that you could go where you could be quiet inside. And now the restlessness was gone. Did the frog have something to do with that?

The sun was going down and the air had chilled. Tomorrow he would start that job at the radio station. Had his uncle felt that same need to be always on the move? He tried to remember if his uncle had always lived in the house or had come and gone, but he could only remember the times he spent with him, learning to ride and . . . what else? It was funny how memory was cut away, leaving only a few moments of time. Pete Cooper had been cheerful, always joking around, but somehow his death cast a pall over this memory of him, as if, looking back, maybe Pete had been trying to cover up some sadness with all that joking.

But that was silly, he knew. You can't know when you

will die; it is not the future that casts shadows but the past. He would ask his grandmother. He knew his mother carried a kind of quiet anger that always seemed to be just under the surface. She had had to go to boarding school when she was very young. She never talked about it. It amazed him now, watching the orange glow stretching across the western sky, how little he knew, how little anyone said, or perhaps how deep he was in his own concerns that he had not paid attention.

Then the idea came to him that maybe he'd been called by Pete's spirit to come and find him. That's what his grandmother would say.

He smiled and turned homeward. Maybe Angie and Bobby could have better memories one day, of the older brother who was always there.

He smiled. He wasn't sure how, but he knew the darn frog had come through after all.

CHAPTER THIRTY-NINE

ERRELL PARKED HIS BIKE IN front of the Ameses' house and knocked on the door. It was answered by Mrs. Ames, who he noted still had a bandaged wrist.

"Constable Terrell," she said enthusiastically. "How lovely of you to drop by. Daniel will be pleased. I don't think he's happy having to sit around convalescing. Look, Daniel, Constable Terrell is here! Here, give us that hat."

Terrell smiled, relinquished his leather helmet, and asked after Mrs. Ames's wrist.

"It's getting better in its own good time," she said, holding it up for him to see. "Not as bad as the patient with his bullet hole. He always was one to try to one-up the other fellow."

Terrell saw Ames across the room on the sofa, struggling to adjust the cushion behind his back.

"So that was the racket outside! Thank heavens!" Ames exclaimed. "Human company. I'm going around the bend here."

"Very nice, I don't think," his mother scoffed. "I'll overlook that for your constable's sake. Tea, everyone?"

"Thank you, Mother. And did I smell some sort of cake baking?"

"Yes, you did. A nice big slice for the constable, and not a crumb for you." She disappeared into the kitchen.

"Please, Constable, sit down. Bring me news from the outside." Ames indicated an armchair and leaned forward eagerly, clearly still nursing his shoulder in its sling.

"Thank you, sir. You look in better shape than the last time I saw you."

"I am. That's the devil of it. I feel well enough to be back at work, but there's been a conspiracy between the mater and the doctors about the need for 'rest.' What's a sling for if not for rest? I could at least do files or something. Please, all the news from the station, sparing no horses. And you can start with why I got shot. Has there been any development on that front? Darling told me on the phone that the whole thing has been sorted, thanked me very much for my part, and rang off. Not a single detail. He's found a new way to torment me!"

"It's a remarkably complex and intertwined story. A bit like Mrs. Cooper's weaving."

"Mrs. Cooper? Who's she?" Ames asked.

"Maybe I should start at the beginning. That fire at the Vitalis' and your bookstore robbery? Turns out they are related, a father-and-daughter story. Mrs. Tilbury lit the fires, and her supposedly disappeared father wrote that book that all the copies of were stolen."

"What do you mean *supposedly* disappeared?"

"It turns out that your railroad baron, Turner, has been alive all along, unbeknownst to his bitter daughter, Mrs. Viola Tilbury."

"But where has he been?" Ames asked, astonished.

"I'll explain, but let's finish with the daughter first. She grew up and married a local businessman, as you know, all the while assuming, along with everyone else, that her father was dead. She got wind that her husband was flirting with women all over town and had set his sights on Mrs. Vitali—apparently, he's not very discreet. I think in the beginning she thought she could scare the Vitalis away, so she set the first fire and sent the notes to scare them. Meanwhile, she found the copies of her father's autobiography in her childhood home, which has been sitting empty for a couple of decades, and distributed them, no doubt feeling very proud of him. Her husband was already upset about how she carried on about her wonderful father, so she dropped them off anonymously. Then she found out her father had been a womanizer as well and she stole them all back and burned them. When the Vitalis did not respond to the first fire by leaving, she set about starting a rumour that he was bribing the police, thinking perhaps that that might cause him to be shut down."

"Which is why we had Guilfoil crawling all over us," Ames said, leaning back against his cushions.

"Yes, sir. In the meantime, Mr. Tilbury, for his own reasons, had been working against Vitali all along with a few like-minded merchants to keep him out of the Chamber of Commerce."

Ames waved his hand in an impatient gesture toward his shoulder, and then winced at the movement. "Are we getting to the part where she decides to shoot me?"

"Yes, sir, that's coming. I'm just trying to put the whole thing in order. Mrs. Tilbury was certain that the bribery story would get the restaurant closed down, but I don't think she really thought about the effect of her actions on the police department. So, when nothing happened to Mr. Vitali, she went back to her original tactic, fire, and things took a really dark turn. She lured Vitali to the restaurant and then set it on fire. It's not known if she meant to actually kill Lorenzo, but she'd pushed the tables against the kitchen door to keep him from escaping out the front, or maybe to keep him from giving chase. I don't think she was thinking very clearly at this point. She claims she thought he could get out the back door. If she had managed to kill him, it would have been murder, whether she intended it or not. What really seemed to be driving her is fury at her husband and her disillusionment over her father. So, while we were investigating the fire—"

Ames raised his hand. "You've modestly left out the part where you rescued Vitali," he said. "I'm not so far gone I don't remember that."

"Thank you, sir. Anyone would have done the same. So, while we were busy with the fire, Mrs. Tilbury, having set the fire, and in a more confused state, stayed home from the hardware store pretending to have a headache."

"Now we're coming to it. I'm sent off to find her to bring her in for a chat."

"That's right. Meanwhile, she calls her husband claiming she's taken too many Aspirin and needs to go to the hospital. He's pretty convinced at this point she's crazy enough to try to kill herself, so he closes up and hurries home, just in time to see you get shot."

"And why?" asked Ames.

"She meant to shoot him. She actually tried to set a trap for him. He'd come home, she'd shoot him."

Ames leaned back, frowning. "Just my bad luck."

"Yes, sir. Very bad luck. Now we get to the discovery that Turner is still alive. Dr. Philipson, the dentist, is involved with this part. Because of your requesting Turner's dental records, Philipson was able to get them sent out from Ontario. He'd given them to us, but he'd also had a look at them himself. With a real twist of fate, I'd call it, there's an old guy called Berenson who runs the little gas station and store in New Denver—you remember him?"

Ames nodded. His mother was hovering in the kitchen door, also listening.

"Anyway, he gets an abscessed tooth and has to come all the way to Nelson to get it pulled. That's when Philipson realizes he has the real Turner, alive and well, right in his chair.

"Unfortunately, I think at this point, he makes a decision that may have been the thing that sent Mrs. Tilbury over the edge. He decides she ought to know her father is alive, so he tells her first, unaware that she was already becoming unhinged. Only then does he tell us. He also tells us that Berenson, a.k.a. Turner, has of course not given his address, so after Mrs. Tilbury and her husband drive off to get rid of you, she dumps both of you by the side of the road and drives off. She seems to have gotten the idea she should try to find her father. She goes to Sandon and talks to someone there who knows very little, except that her father's old girlfriend, an Estelle Bisset, might know. All they knew about her was that she'd once run the store in New Denver. So that's where Mrs. Tilbury finally went. In the meantime, and very luckily, Tilbury, realizing you're not dead after all, flags down a logging truck, and gets you back to hospital."

"My word!" exclaimed Mrs. Ames from the door.

"I'll say!" Ames agreed. "Well. Thank you. I could use that cup of tea and piece of cake now. You surely think I've earned it by being shot," Ames said to his mother. He turned back to Terrell "So, while I've been relaxing in hospital, Mrs. Tilbury has been locked up. We have some dandy charges to throw at her. Arson, two counts of attempted murder." He shook his head. "I bet she gets off on a crazy ticket!"

Constable Terrell leaped up. "Please, let me help, Mrs. Ames."

"You can go bring the tray, Constable, if you will. I can manage the cake. Thank you so much."

"WELL, THAT'S THAT, then," Ames said, wiping cake crumbs off his lip some time later. "How did Turner react to being found out? Has anyone confronted him yet?"

"Oh, the story is not quite over, sir. It has to do with the body Miss Winslow found out in New Denver. As you know, I think, that body turns out to be an uncle of Simpson's, that Indian fellow who came up from Washington. The inspector's wife was the one who discovered he'd been shot by Turner back in '21. It's not really clear why yet; Turner isn't talking. In fact, he very nearly killed Miss Winslow when he was apprehended. Oh, that was after his daughter tracked him down, found Miss Winslow, and tried to shoot her as well. She thought she was another of her husband's paramours." Terrell told them about the arrests of Turner and Viola and finished with what he knew of the burial of Pete Cooper among his ancestors.

"Wow! Miss Winslow!"

"Daniel worships the ground the inspector's wife walks on," Mrs. Ames said. "I'm afraid this will only add to his adoration. And he's not wrong. She's pretty remarkable if half the things he tells me are true."

"I wouldn't say 'worship the ground,' but she does keep defying death," Ames protested.

"Oh, I would," said his mother. "So how did she discover that that Turner fellow shot Mr. Cooper?" she asked.

"As far as I know, it came from the old lady Stella Bisset, who must have been Estelle when she was Turner's girl-friend. She's pretty old and mixed up, and I don't know if it will hold up in court. Apparently when they were young, she was being kept by Turner. Then it's not really clear why, but he ran off for a number of years, perhaps to get away from the murder, or mounting debts. In any case, it looks like he ran out of what money he had and thought he could come back to Estelle's cottage. He found her running the store but already beginning to lose her grip. I don't think he bought the store, he just took it over, and she sat in her cottage continuing to deteriorate. It suited him to learn everyone thought he'd disappeared or might be dead, so he changed his name and started a new life.

"Miss Winslow had become concerned about the condition Miss Bisset was in and was trying to help her and discovered she was French. Miss Bisset seemed to have a slightly better grasp on reality when she spoke French. It turns out it was Turner who shot Pete Cooper and hid his car and the rifle in the garage at Stella Bisset's cottage. Poor thing has been quite traumatized. Evidently, he made her help him cart the body to the bush behind the cabin that belongs to Mr. Barisoff now and bury it. Miss Winslow found the car there and realized, I guess, that it had a Washington plate, and asked Mr. Simpson to come have a look at it. When he turned up at the cottage, Miss Bisset thought he was Mr. Cooper come back from the dead, and that's when it all came out. I confess," Terrell added, putting down his cake plate and leaning back in his chair, "that I will be very disappointed if Turner is not convicted. Unfortunately, it is my experience that some people's lives are more valuable than other people's lives in this country. Oh, and did you know that Miss McAvity wants to join the police?"

"Sheesh! I feel like I missed all the action!" Ames said.

"Hardly," Terrell said, nodding at the bandaged shoulder.

SATURDAY EVENING BROUGHT rain, and Lane and Darling, who had planned to walk to the Bertollis' for a drink, contemplated the deluge through the windows of their front door.

"We have umbrellas," suggested Lane.

"We also have cars. What's the point of the modern world if we can't make use of it?"

"You can't seriously be proposing we drive one tiny mile. Where is your plucky pioneering spirit?" Lane reached into the stand by the door and took out two umbrellas, handing one to Darling.

"Haven't we been intrepid enough?" he protested.

Lane and Darling stood now on the Bertollis' porch, shaking out the umbrellas and leaning them against the wall. The collies were shushed, and their host exclaimed, "You walked in this! Down, Lassie. I'm sure they're happy to see you too. Hot toddies all around? Angela is just reading to the boys. Thank God we've got March behind us. Here. Settle down on the couch and I'll be right back."

The large and flickering fire in the massive stone fireplace in the Bertollis' luxuriously refurbished log cabin provided almost the only light. Lane, her cheek still bandaged, sat next to Darling on the couch with her head on his shoulder, gazing at the play of light along the walls. They could hear Dave Bertolli in the kitchen clattering their toddies into being.

"Horrors! Lane! Your cheek!" Angela rushed into the room and sat down in the armchair by Lane, seizing her hand. "You're worse than the children having to be patched up every day. I want the full story."

Lane smiled, something that almost didn't hurt anymore. "It's absolutely dandy. A very minor mishap that looks much worse than it is."

"Ha!" Angela said. "Dave, those drinks, pronto!" She collapsed back in her chair. "Why do children insist on hearing the same story over and over?"

"On the way!" Dave brought the tray of steaming mugs that exuded the heady promise of heated whisky. "I've put a little extra honey in these. You look like you could use it." Having handed round the comforting drinks, he continued. "I'm very glad to hear, from the grocer no less, that you've been exonerated." He snorted in derision. "What a bunch of nonsense. That anyone could have believed for a second that you were on the take is ridiculous!"

"I must say, when everyone I am normally on good terms with began to give me the cold shoulder, I did wonder the same thing. I suspect people secretly want something scandalous to talk about. Anyway, the main thing is it's been put to bed, and Lorenzo will be staying on to dish up those lovely meals again, thanks to all those same people, who were quite relieved none of it was true." He shifted with a touch of embarrassment. "Listen, Dave, I have to thank you for not believing—"

"No, no, no," said Bertolli. "Completely unnecessary. No one in their right mind would have paid any mind to such utter bilge."

Angela turned to Lane. "Now, everything, and not a detail left out!"

DARLING STOPPED IN surprise, slices of bread in hand. "What's this?" He was looking at a gleaming new steel boxlike object where his winged toaster should have been.

Lane, leaning against the stove waiting for the bacon to

cook in the frying pan, said sweetly, "It's a toaster. You put the bread into those slots, and it is automatically toasted to perfection."

"You're trying to put me out of a job? How can I retain any sense of manhood if that thing does all the work?" He slid the bread into the slots and then out again in an exploratory way.

In its characteristic manner, Sunday breakfast was nosing into the lunchtime hour, and this Sunday in early April pulled the stunning trick of being warm enough to have the French doors open and the porch table pressed into service for the first outdoor breakfast of the year.

"Should it become necessary, I could provide testimonials as to your manhood," Lane said. "I'm sure it doesn't depend on toast."

Darling kissed her, his lips lingering hopefully on her mouth.

"Absolutely not. The bacon is too far gone. Put that bread in and give it a whirl."

Outside, the sun warming them into a state of bliss, Lane said, "Poor Amesy. How long will he be out of commission?"

"There's someone who's manhood you should worry about. He seems completely incapable of doing anything for himself, with his mother fussing around like that. And now Miss Van Eyck. He has the luck of the devil, that man. What did you think of the toast?"

"It was very good. I'll miss the other toaster. It was so aesthetically pleasing and kept you on your toes. And now all you have to do is sit around like a pasha, waiting for it to pop up." She turned to look at him. "I must say I had a conversation with Mrs. Simpson that has made me really think a bit. She adored her younger brother, and it sounds like she used to watch over him like a hawk; you know what elder sisters can be."

"I don't, actually. I never had one. I am an elder brother. I don't know if that comes to the same thing, but I think not. I believe I treated my younger brother with utmost disdain."

"I am sure you did not. He's completely devoted to you. But I am an elder sister, and I must say, I feel I've failed at the job. Mrs. Simpson said she was sent away to school, and I think she lost that strong connection with her brother. She was really sad about it, I can tell. Or about being sent away to school. It made me think about my sister, Diana. I mean, granted, I can never remember a time when we got along, but I do remember when she was a tiny baby I was quite taken with her. I wonder now, if we'd been brought up differently, if she and I would be close. I mean, it's this business of separating family members. The circumstances may be different, but once you sever the natural ties, like with poor Mrs. Simpson being sent off to boarding school, it's very hard to get back what you had."

"I'm pretty sure that people cannot take responsibility for what their siblings do. I hope that Mrs. Simpson does not truly feel she has any responsibility for her brother's death, any more than you should feel responsible for whatever it is your sister is doing. Life, I'm afraid, delivers these blows, and the absolute powerlessness we feel in the face of them is perhaps where this sense of guilt comes from—that no matter what we might do, or could ever have done, this terrible thing has happened and could not be changed."

Lane nodded and smiled affectionately at him. "For a stolid policeman you do have flashes of wisdom." Then she stretched out her legs, sinking deeply into her canvas chair, and folding her hands around her cup of coffee. "Well, at least neither of us has to worry about Ames. Tina will soon put him right."

ACKNOWLEDGEMENTS

WITHOUT THE HELP AND GUIDANCE of Marilyn James, (Smum iem Matriarch) of the Autonomous Sinixt, it would not have been possible to write this book. I am deeply indebted to her for the history, protocols, and ceremonial details in this story, and most especially for her kind and generous support for the project. *Lim limpt.* I'd like to give my thanks to K.L. Kivi of Maa Press and Lori Barkley (staff anthropologist for the Autonomous Sinixt) for their enormous help in reading and advising on historical and geographical details. Any errors are entirely my own.

When I was a child growing up in the Kootenays, I remember seeing very few Indigenous people along my little stretch of the lake. I was to learn only recently the amazing and, sadly, not entirely unexpected story of the "disappearance" of a people who had lived for many thousands of years in a considerable territory that included the Arrow Lakes and the Columbia Basin headwaters and extended right across the border into Washington State. As settlers, farmers, miners, loggers, dam builders, and the like pushed into the area in the eighteenth and nineteenth centuries, they not only disrupted the way of life of the Lakes People (a.k.a. Sinixt), but even flooded out their villages and gravesites with dams. Because of their being forced out of the area, heading north, east, west, and south, the provincial government declared the Arrow Lakes Band of the Sinixt People "extinct" in 1956. This was a detail I found particularly disturbing. Of course, the Sinixt are not extinct, and never have been. Because my books often address historical matter in the Kootenay area, I felt Lane and Darling ought to learn of the people whose territory they live on.

I was extremely lucky in meeting Dr. Paula Pryce, anthropologist, whose wonderful book *Keeping the Lakes' Way*, a study of the reburial project begun in Vallican, Slocan Valley, in the late 1980s, first inspired me to think about this story. I felt that it was a story worth telling and including in the Lane Winslow series, since no historical referencing of life in the Kootenays can be possible without including so important a nation. It was Dr. Pryce who introduced me to Marilyn James. And it was Marilyn James who, around a great fire at the camp at Vallican, listened to my proposal about how Lane Winslow and Inspector Darling might come to know about the Lakes People. Marilyn, Lori, and K.L. entered into the spirit of the book, and Marilyn spent many hours making sure I got the details and protocol of both the Sinixt culture and history, and in particular of the burial, right.

Special note: It was relatively common in the early part of the twentieth century for Lakes People to make the trek back to the northern reaches of their territory, fishing, hunting, and reconnecting with the land and the ancestors. Marilyn herself talked of her grandparents coming north in their Model T from Colville in the summer. Annie Joseph, who is depicted in this book, was a real person who was the last known resident of the reserve at Oatscott by the Columbia River. She died in 1953. There is a stunning archaeological site in nk̓ʕáwxtən (Vallican) that has the remains of a sizeable village of pit houses, the origins of which date back thousands of years, still there under the watchful eye of Frog Peak.

Thanks always to my wonderful husband for his undying support and tireless ear; to my readers, Sasha Bley-Vroman and Nickie Bertolotti, for being ever willing to be the first eyes on the viability of the latest Lane Winslow adventure. To the wonderful staff at TouchWood Editions, toiling away seemingly without missing a beat through a historic pandemic: Taryn Boyd and Tori Elliott, publishers, always so kind and generous with their time and support; Kate Kennedy, editor and absolute champion; along with consulting editors Claire Philipson, Renée Layberry, and Meg Yamamoto for their careful reading and editing of the text; Curtis Samuel, publicist, a delightful and untiring advocate for Lane Winslow; and deepest gratitude to Margaret Hanson for the beautiful cover of this and all the other books, covers that stop people in the street and cause them to rush into stores to buy them. And that brings me to my gratitude to the readers. You make it all possible.

IONA WHISHAW was born in British Columbia. After living her early years in the Kootenays, she spent her formative years living and learning in Mexico, Nicaragua, and the US. She travelled extensively for pleasure and education before settling in the Vancouver area. Throughout her roles as youth worker, social worker, teacher, and award-winning high school principal, her love of writing remained consistent, and compelled her to obtain her master's in creative writing from the University of British Columbia. Iona has published short fiction, poetry, poetry translation, and one children's book, *Henry and the Cow Problem*. *A Killer in King's Cove* was her first adult novel. Her heroine, Lane Winslow, was inspired by Iona's mother who, like her father before her, was a wartime spy. Book #7 in the series, *A Match Made for Murder*, won the Bony Blithe Light Mystery Award. Visit ionawhishaw.com to find out more.

THE LANE WINSLOW MYSTERY SERIES